Advance Praise for *Moses the Heretic*

"Like the Biblical Moses who led his people into the Promised Land, Daniel Spiro's Moses offers us a vision of a Promised Land. ... This land offers the world the "milk and honey" of respect, acceptance and peace. There will always be those who say that this is a dangerous journey ... that we are better off where we are, bound by history and ignorance. I hope and pray that this astonishing and deeply honest book will be the trumpet call to all who are caught up in the tragedy of the war between the children of Abraham, leading us, as sisters and brothers, to take the first bold steps that will lead this region to true peace."
> —Reverend Christine Brownlie, *Minister of the Unitarian Universalist Congregation of Blacksburg, Virginia*

"In *Moses the Heretic*, Daniel Spiro spins a story which draws us in while taking up the complexities of a world we often want to turn away from. By entering the heart both of the middle east conflict and of the Jewish community, Spiro humanizes those who are too often demonized and creates compelling arguments and understanding for a more hopeful future. He does what most clergy hope for – to write the sermons he believes need to be heard and to have the ideas within them repair the world."
> —Rabbi Patricia Karlin-Neumann, *Senior Associate Dean for Religious Life, Stanford University*

"A smart, audacious and entertaining book that re-imagines the biblical Moses in the modern world —- deeply rooted in scripture, full of compassion and insight, and yet hard-wired to today's headlines."
> —Jonathan Kirsch, author of *Moses, A Life* and *The Grand Inquisitor's Manual*

"Daniel Spiro has written a masterful novel that weaves powerful spiritual teachings of Judaism and Islam into a gripping and charged story of contemporary politics, passion and intrigue... Rabbi Moses Levine is an unabashed God-Wrestler, whose soaring rhetoric and political passion plows through the landscape of contemporary

American Jewish life like a spiritual tornado, upending conventional wisdom and complacency in his wake. The national conversation Rabbi Levine has started on how we learn to understand and coexist with "the other" is long overdue."
—Steve Masters, *President, Jewish Alliance for Justice and Peace*

"As lucid as it is thought-provoking, and as poignant as it is provocative, *Heretic* is a brilliant novel of ideas. This book entertains and enlightens from start to finish, and yet ultimately, it has but one message: that each of us must pursue peace with a passion. I can think of no better summary of Jewish philosophy than that."
—Douglas Stone, *co-author of Difficult Conversations and former Assoc. Director of the Harvard Negotiation Project*

"In the tradition of imaginative midrash [interpretation of Jewish texts], Daniel Spiro dares to tackle the big questions in his fascinating work."
—Rabbi David Greenstein, *Rabbinic Dean, Academy for Jewish Religion*

"I love this book! It brings together in a constructed reality all the tension between the practical existence of the Abrahamic family and the prophetic ideals according to which we are supposed to be living. It is a great story and thus fictionalizes and brings much closer to home the moral and political choices that we all have to face."
—Rabbi Marc Gopin, *Director of George Mason University's Center for World Religions, Diplomacy and Conflict Resolution, and author of Between Eden and Armageddon*

MOSES
the
HERETIC

A NOVEL

DANIEL SPIRO

AEGIS PRESS

Aegis Press

P.O. Box 3023
Del Mar, CA 92014

www.theaegispress.com

Copyright © 2008 by Daniel A Spiro

Design and layout
Jonathan Gullery / RJ Communications
51 East 42nd Street, Suite 1202, New York, NY 10017

Library of Congress Cataloging-in-Publication Data

Spiro, Daniel, 1960-
Moses the heretic : a novel / Daniel Spiro.
p. cm.
ISBN 978-0-9747645-3-5
1. Rabbis--Fiction. 2. Prophets--Fiction. 3. Nobel Prize winners-
-Fiction. 4. Psychological fiction. 5. Religious fiction. I. Title.

PS3619.P577M67 2008
813'.6--dc22
2008030268

ISBN: 978-0-9747645-3-5

Manufactured in the United States of America

First Aegis Press paperback edition published 2008

*To the Memory of
Julius Bertram Spiro (1912-2002) –
A free thinker.
And the most humble man I've ever known.*

"Rabbi Simeon said:

There are three crowns.
The crown of Torah,
the crown of priesthood and
the crown of kingship.
But the crown of a good name
excels them all."

Ethics of the Fathers: 4:17

PART I

CHAPTER I

"What does it mean to be a Jew? That you're good with books and bad with screwdrivers? Or that you're rarely lost for words and never at a loss for opinions? Does it mean that you love your spouse but revere your mother? Oh, I don't know—maybe that's not reverence, maybe it's a sense of guilt, but whatever it is, our mothers' power over us is almost infinite.

"All cultures have their own distinct personalities, and they also have their distinct biases. For centuries, Jews have had trouble appreciating Jesus because they were too hung up on 'the Christ.' Now, we face an even greater bias — we can't appreciate the unique beauty of Islam because we're so hung up on Muslim fanaticism. Well, let me tell you, I've seen both sides of Islamic culture — the best and the worst. And I have to say, if the Jewish people don't open their eyes to the majesty as well as the tragedy of Islam, we'll all be in for a rude awakening, and our beloved Land of Israel will never enjoy the peace she so desperately deserves."

Rabbi Moses Levine,
recipient of the Nobel Peace Prize,
addressing a biennial conference
of the Union for Reform Judaism, 2005

East Jerusalem—February 2002. The first thing I remember, waking up from the cab ride that resulted in our kidnapping, was Moses' face. He was staring right at me, expressionless. We both were lying on cots inside a cell, which in turn was inside what we then and always since have referred to as "the dungeon."

The dungeon was a single windowless room measuring roughly 25 by 30 feet. Our cell occupied one corner of the room. It had nine foot sides, an eight foot ceiling, and steel bars all around and above. It contained the two cots, two bedpans, and literally nothing else. On the far side of the dungeon was a stairwell leading upwards, and near the entrance to the stairwell sat our hosts, on either side of a desk.

Sick from the after-effects of the stun-gun and whatever other means they had employed to subdue us, we lay there, listless. Finally, I noticed my thirst and sat up, the better to see and communicate with the guards.

"Water," I said, in a hoarse, shaking voice. "Could I please have some water?" The guards barely registered that they had heard me, but one of them filled a cup from a pitcher of water on the desk and pushed it through the bars, setting it on the floor of our cell. I drank half, and gave the rest to Moses. Then I sat, staring through the bars at the stairwell beyond.

During our first few days in captivity, that stairwell and those steel bars held most of my attention. I was obsessed with the idea of escaping and could not stop fantasizing about pulling apart the bars and sprinting past our guards and up the stairs to my wife and children. But I must have known, subconsciously, that neither Moses nor I was about to overcome our captors with brute force. He was tall and lanky. And I was ... just the opposite. We exemplified both sides of the spectrum of Jewish manhood.

Even so, it was inevitable that I would make an attempt at escape, albeit a pathetic, ineffectual one. I can't be sure how long we'd been cooped up when I finally snapped, but it certainly wasn't more than two or three days. Moses had been virtually silent all that time — whether from shock or from intense concentration and prayer, I couldn't be sure. But the silence was unbearable, and it was compounded by the guards' brutality. Every day, morning and night, they would enter our cell, one standing guard while the other used a bullwhip to deliver a series of lashings to each of us in turn. After a few of these sessions, I simply couldn't take it anymore. And that morning, when the guard unlocked our cell door, I made a run for it.

Somehow I succeeded in pushing past the first guard and was on my way to the beckoning stairwell when the second guard stepped in front of me. I saw a massive gun staring me in the face.

"Come on," he spat, baiting me with his non-trigger hand. "You want out?"

"Richie!" It was Moses, breaking his self-imposed silent vigil. "Don't be stupid — get back in here!"

I turned back. Moses, of course, was right. No matter the cost, I needed to stay alive for my family back in America. The guard with the whip seized my shoulder, heaved me through the cell door and onto the floor, and slammed the door behind me. I may not have succeeded in escaping, but at least I had shocked Moses into speaking again. And it was talking to Moses that made what came after infinitely more bearable.

Our imprisonment has been the subject of books, documentaries, and even folk songs. At the time, though, we could only speculate from a few bare-bones facts about how we came to be in such a predicament.

I could surmise that while riding in our cab, Moses and I had been shot with stun guns and were probably given sedatives. But I couldn't have known then that our cab driver transferred us to a car driven by another terrorist who delivered us to East Jerusalem. Or that our dungeon sat a full 30 feet below a modest-sized bungalow that seemed perfectly innocuous to all who passed it on the street. I correctly assumed that troops would be sent in to find us, but they failed in doing so, thanks to the fact that we were kept in a well-hidden location. Finally, I had no idea that our Palestinian captors, in some sort of ultra-sick joke, placed the hidden stairwell that led to our dungeon behind a bookcase. What I did know was that at least one of our hosts had read the *Diary of Anne Frank*; he joked that our situation could be compared to Anne's, only our guards were playing the role of the Frank family, and the Israeli soldiers patrolling the streets of East Jerusalem played the role of the Nazis.

It would be hard to exaggerate the number of times in the dungeon that Israel was compared to the Third Reich. That number grew geometrically when our captors read bios that the American media published about Moses and me. Then, for the first time, they learned we were both rabbis and that I was the child of a Holocaust survivor.

Our jailors wanted us to know precisely how evil it was for a so-called "People of the Book" to come into their country, kick out hundreds of thousands of residents from their homes, and treat the ones who remained as if they weren't even human. Sharif, one of our hosts (and barely 20 years of age), showed us pictures of relatives who had been killed by the Israeli military. Nieces, cousins, uncles. The last picture was of his father.

"He was riding in a car with friends. They were going to watch me play football. One of his friends was called an enemy of the state. To me, he was just a man who came over to have tea with my father and talk about the town where they both grew up. My father had nothing to do with politics. Nothing! He sold fruit.

"Somehow, the Israeli army got a tip about how to find my

father's friend, so they followed him, and when they had their chance, they blew up everyone in the car.

"The Israelis can blow up my father, a fruit seller! Then they tell us that *we* are the terrorists. 'It was only a government protecting its citizens,' they like to say. Well, the Nazis were a government too. And I am sure they claimed to be protecting their citizens."

One of the things that kept me sane in East Jerusalem was Moses' language skills. He had been fluent in Arabic for years, but it wasn't until well into our stay that our captors learned that fact. At first, when they spoke Arabic, they'd glance over to us to see if we could understand them. With Moses playing dumb, they gradually spoke more and more freely about matters related to our captivity. Then, when they weren't paying attention, Moses would whisper to me what he had heard.

From his eavesdropping, Moses learned the purpose of our kidnapping: to gain the release of hundreds of Palestinians who were imprisoned in Israeli jails on terrorism charges. Several days after we were captured, Moses also learned that at the same time we were abducted by a phony cab driver, so were six others. All six, like us, had been staying in five-star Jerusalem hotels. Four were Americans, two were South Africans. They were taken in pairs to dungeons much like ours.

For weeks on end, coping had remained nearly impossible for me. I kept thinking about my wife and children in Maryland and how much they needed me. Or I would think about my dad and my sisters back in Jersey. But even if I had had no family at all in America, I still would have been frothing at the mouth for the chance to be free. Moses seemed to endure the lashings well enough, but I wasn't nearly as stoic. Nor was I especially pleased about having to smell the perpetual scent of our urine and feces. The bed pans were emptied frequently, but this was still a dungeon, 30 feet below ground, with little fresh air. Candidly, one of my greatest joys in captivity was to remind myself that our hosts had to suffer from the same stench we did.

Things seemed to get worse one day when Moses' information pipeline was broken. Blame the arrival of Hafeez Ali, our "protector," which is the meaning of his name in Arabic. When Moses pointed out that translation, I laughed at the irony, but only because I wasn't yet aware of all the ways Hafeez would change our lives.

For one thing, Hafeez put an end to the lashings. He also directed our guards to stop using nicknames for us. They had taken to calling Moses "Osama" and me "George," owing to our respective resemblance to Osama Bin Laden and the character that Jason Alexander played on Seinfeld. I'd heard before that I looked a fair amount like George, but the resemblance wasn't nearly as close as that of Moses to Osama. Other than the fact that my friend had a wider face and a trimmer beard, the two could well have been mistaken for one another. In any event, Hafeez recognized that our lives were humiliating enough in the cell. We should at least be called by our real names.

As it turned out, Hafeez and Moses had a mutual friend— a Palestinian doctor. Unaware of Hafeez's connection with the "struggle for Palestinian liberation," as my hosts liked to call their movement, the doctor ran his mouth regarding an American rabbi he knew who had been kidnapped (Moses). The doctor, we later learned, told Hafeez about how this rabbi was extremely sympathetic to the Palestinian cause and yet now, ironically, found himself as a hostage. Hafeez also learned during that conversation about Moses' command of Arabic.

When he walked into the dungeon for the first time, Hafeez interrogated his three colleagues about whether they had inadvertently revealed any information to Moses by speaking in that language. Upon learning the truth, Hafeez grabbed one of the men by his neck and threw him to the floor. Then, for the next several minutes, he angrily shouted at them. I couldn't make out many of the words, but the drift of his diatribe was unmistakable. From that point on, the only captor who told us anything of substance was Hafeez himself.

The following day, Hafeez walked in and approached our cell. He was the oldest of our captors—I took him to be around 50. While not as tall as Moses, Hafeez was easily over six feet and had a solid, athletic frame. I told Moses that if Hafeez had attended Columbia—the college where Moses and I met as undergraduates back in the 70s—he might well have been able to start at defensive end.

Unlike our other hosts, Hafeez was always clean-shaven. In fact, he could have passed for a Jewish-American corporate executive. I later learned that Hafeez was a practicing physician at an Israeli hospital in East Jerusalem that treated a high percentage of West Bank Palestinians. It was through one of his grateful patients that Hafeez became mixed up with, well, terror.

"Moses Levine," he said, his eyes focused exclusively on my cellmate. "I know who you are and what you stand for. I know you understand certain things that other Jews do not. I've heard your exact words: 'We took Palestinian land in the 40s and more of their land in the 60s, and now we've got the chutzpah to blame them for all the violence.'

"*You*, Moses, must deliver a message to your fellow Jews. We will ensure it is broadcast around the world."

"I don't have any special knowledge. I —" Moses began to respond, but it was pointless. Hafeez was not looking for dialogue.

"Silence!" he yelled. "Hear my words. They will be your destiny. Your sages have taught that to save one life is to save the whole world. Now, it is time for you to tell the Hebrew people that they have an opportunity to save not only one life, but thousands, even *millions*. To do this, they have but a single option: to leave Muslim land! I am talking about everything that you call the Middle East. It belonged to us until it was seized by the Crusaders. Then, after they stole our land, they put your people in concentration camps and slaughtered them like cattle. For that, the Crusaders owe you their own land. So leave us and go back to Europe—the home of your ancestors, the place where Jews developed a rich culture before it was destroyed through no fault of my people. What was that culture called? Oh yes: *yiddishkeit*.

"I know you recognize that the Jews deserve a piece of Europe for the way the Europeans have treated you over the centuries. The same United Nations that put the Jews here where you are not wanted can find you a place in Europe where your people will be embraced. Everyone there will understand the validity of your claim—especially if you act soon, while witnesses to the Holocaust remain alive. In Europe, you can build a secure state where you can live in peace with your neighbors. But here, you will live in a perpetual state of war."

Hafeez threw Moses a pen and a notebook full of blank paper, a momentous toss, as events have unfolded. "Write down your thoughts," he said. "When you are ready to speak these words from your heart, with all your *neshama* (soul), we will film what you have to say."

With that, Hafeez left the dungeon—no doubt looking forward to an escape from the smell.

Moses didn't write a thing. He knew Jews would never gain a European homeland … nor would they want one. He acknowledged, in fact, that such an opportunity, if ever it existed, was long gone. But what I found interesting was that Moses didn't argue with Hafeez, as I might have done. I might have explained the Jewish claim to Eretz Yisrael (the Land of Israel). I might even have lectured Hafeez about the way he reduced all Jews to Ashkenazim, to *yids*, when in fact Sephardic Jews developed a rich tradition of their own in Spain and then, later, in places like Istanbul, Sarajevo, and Amsterdam. I might have mentioned that the battles the Jews have won to secure the state of Israel were no less legitimate than the Muslim seizure of the same land centuries earlier. Fortunately, Moses knew better than to engage in such discussions. He simply took the pen and paper and sat quietly, apparently contemplating the option he had been given.

The truth is that Moses had no intention of doing Hafeez's bidding, but he wanted Hafeez to hope that he might be persuaded. That required drawing Hafeez into a dialogue. Moses had watched enough James Bond movies to know that he was no James Bond. He couldn't fight his way out of a cell, nor did he possess a laser-emitting wristwatch or an acid-filled fountain pen. He had only one weapon available: his tongue. Moses understood better than anyone the power of provocative dialogue. Whether speaking on behalf of the Palestinians at a pro-Israel march or on behalf of the Israelis in a Palestinian dungeon, Moses knew that, to be effective, he needed to reach deep into the subconscious of "the other" and insert alien and disturbing concepts. That was his scheme in dealing with Hafeez; he just hadn't figured out yet how to pull it off.

Moses had the first of his fateful dreams on or around the last day of February, 2002. He dreamt of a voice, Moses later told me, which offered a message that is familiar to any rabbi because it came from the Torah. And yet it wasn't directed to a character in a book, but personally to my friend.

"Go and assemble the elders of Israel and say to them: the Lord, the God of your fathers, the God of Abraham, Isaac, and Jacob, has appeared to me and said, 'I have taken note of you and of what is being done to you in Egypt, and I have declared: I will take you out of the misery of Egypt to the land of the Canaanites, the Hittites, the Amorites, the Perizzites, the Hivites, and Jebusites, to a land flowing with milk and honey."

On later nights when the dreams continued, the words Moses heard didn't flow precisely as they did in the Torah. But this dream was different. It was straight from Exodus, 3:16-3:17.

Indeed, these were the very words that God spoke to the Biblical Moses in the form of a burning bush. When *my* Moses woke up, he grabbed me and told me about the dream. And all I could do was make a lame joke.

"It's just like the charge you were given by Hafeez—except he wants you to go back to the land of the Germans, a land flowing with hops and barley."

Little did I know how sick that joke would become in my mind. The next day, another of our hosts, Abdul, showed up with pictures of the slaying of Paul Marcus, a senior vice president with Vantage Enterprises of Savannah, Georgia. Marcus, I'm told, was kidnapped only minutes after Moses and I were shot with the stun gun in the back of the cab. I understand the video of Marcus' death was widely available on the Internet before the FBI was able to remove it from circulation. We never saw that video, but we saw the still photos: first, Marcus looking directly at the camera; next, Marcus' torso with his head removed and blood splattered in all directions; next, Marcus' severed head, facing downwards; next, Marcus' severed head facing upwards; and finally, a hooded terrorist pouring a can of Budweiser beer into Marcus' slack mouth.

A few hours after we saw the photos, Hafeez returned to the dungeon. He pulled up a chair to within a few feet of the cell.

"Good morning," he said, in an uncharacteristically gentle voice.

"Good morning," I replied.

Hafeez's demeanor quickly changed. "Was I speaking to you?" he snarled, before turning again to face my friend. "Moses, I am here to address you and you alone. From this moment on, your friend shall not speak to me—not today, not tomorrow, not *ever*! And he shall not look at my face. If I see him gazing at me for any length of time, I shall have his face disfigured. Is that clear?"

"Very," Moses said.

"Good. You are probably wondering about the pictures that you were shown earlier in the day. I authorized you to see them. What did you think?"

"They're the product of deranged minds. Anyone who would cut off a person's head and then make a joke out of it is certifiably insane. It's really that simple."

"Is it, now? You are telling me there is no lesson to be learned here—you have merely written this off as the conduct of madmen?"

Moses thought for a moment. He wondered whether Hafeez was testing him. "There are always lessons in life," Moses replied. "Every morning in this cell I wake up with lessons. But I'm not a mind reader. Why don't you just get to your point?"

"You said it yourself in that book you wrote, *Exodus: Then and Now* — how, with the passage of time, weapons technology will advance further and further."

"You call your butchering an example of advanced technology?" Moses asked.

"First of all," thundered Hafeez, "I had *nothing* to do with the manner in which Paul Marcus met his end. Secondly, of course I was not referring to swords and knives as advanced technology. Are you that stupid that I have to spell out everything for you?"

"Apparently so," Moses replied.

"Very well. I will say it so plainly that even your pedestrian rabbi friend can understand. Your book was quite correct in what it said about technology. There was a time when my people could only use swords and knives to kill. Then, we learned to use pistols and rifles. Next, we developed more powerful guns that could fire many bullets very quickly and bombs that could blow up entire buses or cafes. Last year, the world watched as we took over planes and used their fuel to destroy thousands of people and tall skyscrapers. And it will not be long before we have nuclear weapons like you do, like the Pakistanis have, that we can use to wipe out whole cities. Someday, we will have weapons that the Americans do not have today, and we will be able to use them to destroy our enemies as easily as we can walk to the post office.

"Those photos you saw are a message from my comrades to the world — not just for you, but for *me* too. Carving up a human head is not my way. My comrades know that; they simply do not care. They had a point to make and they wanted to drive it home.

"You can find Arabs who will shake your hand and agree to concessions. Maybe they will even command armies who will try to enforce the compromises they have negotiated. But until all the land is returned to the People of the Prophet, you will not have peace. The genie is out of the bottle, and no peace treaty can put it back.

"Those pictures are a reminder that freedom fighters will use every weapon at their disposal to chase you away. Some soldiers might prefer an airplane with fuel that can kill thousands—a new, impersonal kind of weapon, and a very deadly one. Other soldiers might prefer an old-fashioned way of killing—something more intimate, something that plays on ancient nightmares. A severed skull works nicely on that level, yes?"

"It's pure barbarism, you know that," Moses replied.

"After what my comrades did," Hafeez continued, "what I know is that the Israelis will never agree to the prisoner exchange we have asked for. But they have had some time to consider it, and they have ignored us, so maybe now at least they will take us at our words. This is our message — *the war will not end until you end it*—either by killing us, or by leaving us. You cannot simply imprison us. As you can see for yourself, that is not a long-term solution."

During the weeks after we first saw the Paul Marcus photos, Hafeez Ali entered our "home" roughly every other day. In each case, he pulled a chair up to the cell and began a conversation with Moses that never lasted less than an hour. On none of these occasions did I even glance at Hafeez, let alone say a word in his presence. I determined that the easiest way to live by his rules was to lie on my cot, close my eyes and attempt to understand as much of the conversation as possible—or at least the parts that were in Hebrew instead of Arabic.

After the conversation about the Marcus photographs, Hafeez pinned them up on a wall of the dungeon opposite our cage. We knew what the photographs were, but they were far enough away that we could no longer see them in vivid detail. Several days later, he handed Moses new photographs. This time, we didn't see one dead hostage but two. In one photo, Barney Frederick, a banker from New York City, lay on his bed with a gunshot wound in place of his left eye. A second photo showed Clifford Dyson, another New York banker, with a face so riddled by bullets that it was no longer human.

This pattern of brutal murders continued until all six of the other captives had been killed and photos of the corpses graced the walls of our dungeon. I attributed my own survival solely to my friendship with Moses. Our hosts had no respect for me whatsoever, but Moses was different: they respected him *and* they wanted his help. Coming as they did from a culture of loyalty, they had to assume that since Moses and I were lifelong friends, if my life were threatened, Moses would never consider speaking out for their cause.

After the first conversation about Marcus, Hafeez refused to discuss either Marcus' murder or any of the others. "There is no need," he said. "These pictures are worth a thousand words." Instead of talking about blood and guts, Hafeez and Moses spoke at length about broad political issues. And just as often if not more so, they spoke about theology—Muslim theology, Jewish theology, even Buddhism. It was clear that Hafeez was extremely well-read.

"Other than in medicine, I am … how do you say it? … an *auto-didact*," Hafeez claimed one afternoon, well over a month after our abduction. "That is the best way to learn. Schools will warp all your motivations—they will make you learn for the sake of outside rewards. I want to learn for the sake of learning."

Moses could have made the same statement himself; it was right out of a sermon I had once seen him deliver in Memphis. I felt like jumping up and mentioning that sermon to Hafeez, but I didn't dare. My only movement was to open my eyes, which were facing the steel bars and the mildewing ceiling above our heads. I began to wonder if, somehow, excrement vapors were rising from the bedpans. That got my mind off whatever it was that Hafeez was talking about, and I went back to playing the fetus opposite Moses' role of playing, well, *Moses*. By then, you see, he had come to view himself as the incarnation of his namesake.

CHAPTER II

"Leviticus says at 19:17: 'You shall not hate your kinsfolk in your heart. Reprove your kinsman but incur no guilt because of him. You shall not take vengeance or bear a grudge against your countrymen. Love your neighbor as yourself: I am the Lord.'

"But what if your neighbor is not one of your kinsfolk? What if he's not one of your countrymen? What if his parents and their parents have been enemies of your people? What then? Do we say that passage doesn't apply? I say it applies even more so!"

Rabbi Moses Levine, speaking at a
Jerusalem conference entitled
Israel and the New Intifada, 2002

En Route to the Land of Israel—Earlier in February 2002. On February 5, 2002, Moses and I boarded a taxi from my home in Silver Spring, Maryland to Dulles Airport. Our ultimate destination was Tel Aviv. Moses and I planned to spend two weeks in Israel, mostly to sightsee. We had been invited to participate in a two-day conference in Jerusalem entitled *Israel and the New Intifada*. This was a reference to the Palestinian uprising that began in September 2000 and ultimately claimed many lives on both sides of the great divide.

The night before the conference began, Moses and I spent

the evening at a Tel Aviv party hosted by a classmate of mine
from rabbinical school who made aliyah not long after we grad-
uated. ("Aliyah" literally means "ascent," and "making aliyah"
is the term commonly used among Jews for moving to Israel.)
He invited the Israelis with whom Moses and I had stayed in
touch. It was hardly surprising that whereas all my friends at
the party were Jews, at least a quarter of Moses' were Arabs.

We spent the next morning and much of the afternoon at
Neot Kedumim, a biblical landscape reserve located halfway
between Tel Aviv and Jerusalem. At around three, we headed
back to our hotel in Jerusalem to clean up for the night's
festivities. Our ultimate destination was the Old City and, in
particular, the Western Wall.

"Isn't it incredible," I told Moses, when we finally arrived
at the blessed spot, "that the holiest place in the world to our
people is a *wall*?"

"It's so Jewish," he replied.

I was reminded of Rome and the majesty of St. Peters. You
could have been raised by wolves and yet you'd have to marvel
at its architecture, not to mention the masterpieces that adorn
it. And while neither of us had been to Mecca, we had both
seen pictures of the Kaaba in the evening when the lights are
on. Even if there weren't a soul in the plaza, and even if we had
known nothing about its history, the sight would still have been
awe-inspiring.

Of course, there are more than a billion Muslims in this
world and well over a billion Christians; by contrast, there
are fewer than 15 million Jews. So I suppose it shouldn't be
shocking that when you go to Jerusalem and look for the visual
center of Jewish spirituality, you don't see a colossal, exqui-
sitely designed architectural work. Instead, you see a simple
stone wall. A remnant of what was once much bigger and more
impressive. A reminder not of the gods, but of the human condition, which above all else is ephemeral.

Well, maybe the Western Wall isn't so simple. Certainly,

it's not just *any* wall. It's a structure that enables us to cele-brate history. That's what we Jews do — we elevate history to the stature of the holy, and few if any structures have more history, and therefore more holiness, than the Western Wall. It was erected 2,000 years ago as a retaining wall to surround the Temple that Herod rebuilt on the same spot as Solomon's Temple. According to Jewish tradition, this was the setting for a number of the most momentous events in the Torah.

Moses Levine knew full well the connection between the Jewish people and the Temple of Solomon. He also knew that this was just part of what fueled our people's hunger to build not merely a Jewish state, but one located in the Land of Milk and Honey. He could criticize the wisdom of that choice—he could call it impractical, reckless or self-indulgent. But the attitude that led to our return to Zion is deeply entrenched in our souls. Moses recognized that once the Jewish people had settled part of the land of Israel and successfully fought for the nation's survival against seemingly limitless enemies, we weren't going to give it up—at least not all of it. Not after everything we had endured over the centuries.

The next day was the day of the conference. Moses and I were members of a panel of rabbis who discussed the following topic: "What Would Moses Do?—Applying Jewish Ethics to the Israeli-Palestinian Divide." This was before my friend ever dreamt he was Moshe Rabbenu (literally, "Moses our Rabbi," it is one of the most popular Jewish ways of referring to the hero of the Exodus). Even before those dreams began, Moses was obsessed with his namesake. Many of us on the panel were generally superior Jewish scholars to Moses Levine, but on the topic of Moshe Rabbenu, his knowledge was pre-eminent. The obsession began at rabbinical school and continued while he plied his trade in Memphis. It was to spike during the time he worked on the publication of *Exodus: Then and Now*, the first part of which had focused on the conduct and values of the Biblical Moses.

Our panel spoke for two hours, the first of which went very slowly. We each said a few words about how Moshe Rabbenu has inspired us in our lives. Then, we paid the obligatory homage to all the Israelis who had to suffer through the Intifada in a land that was supposed to ensure Jewish security. None of the panelists was from Israel, and that fact was implicit in our charge: to explain how the rest of the Jewish world would apply Jewish ethics to stem the tide of violence in the land of Israel.

It hardly came as a surprise that Moses Levine was the one to turn up the heat in the room. Moses had no patience for the elevated, almost academic nature of the panel's discourse. He knew that the audience consisted primarily of lay people, and maintained that rabbis should never preach to a group of lay adults without addressing their viscera and their hearts every bit as much as their intellects.

"I want to discuss the frustration I've heard from the American Jewish community about 'moral equivalence,'" Moses said. "Jewish people feel the need to demonstrate to the world that we're not morally equivalent to the Palestinians. My old friend Rabbi Gold and I often talk about moral equivalence, don't we?"

"It sticks in my craw," I replied. "Like you said, I'm not alone."

"Rabbi Gold thinks it's important to convince the world community that our conduct is not morally *equivalent* to the Palestinians', it's morally *superior*." Moses continued. "He reminds me that Israel is a peace-loving democracy whose people would be happy to exchange land for peace. But according to my friend, the Palestinians are completely out of control. They have militias that have no accountability to the government. And they're unified only by the idea that if we Jews won't leave the Holy Land willingly, the Arabs are obliged to drive us into the ocean.

"Have I described your position fairly?" he asked me. "I don't want to distort it."

I had to think for a moment before responding. Obviously, he was poised to rip my argument apart. "Let me say this," I finally replied. "I'm sure that some Palestinians are truly willing to compromise. But they don't have any real power. First of all, they're a small minority. And even if somehow they could gain control over their government, they still couldn't control the militias.

"So how do we make peace with the Palestinians? How do we make concessions? Moses, I've heard you say it a dozen times — 'You don't pet a cur dog; he'll just bite you!' Maybe you should consider that here. The Peace-Now crowd would have us lower our shields and give up a large fraction of our land. They talk as if our Arab neighbors were really our friends. But they're not, at least not yet, and if we treat them as friends, we'll pay with Jewish blood."

"Richie," Moses began, seemingly forgetting that we were speaking to a group of several hundred people, "let's cut the crap. OK? No straw men with me.

"I've never said we should lower our shields. Who was the first Jew you know who proposed a wall between Israel and Palestine that we could use during times of Intifada?"

"You were, Moses," I said, like a boy being lectured by his parents. But his statement happened to be true.

"The issue isn't whether we should turn the other cheek," Moses continued. "It's whether this obsession with fighting the idea of 'moral equivalence' is helpful or harmful.

"Let's get back to Moshe Rabbenu. He told our people that the Promised Land will have to be taken by *force*! Remember the words from Deuteronomy 9:3: 'It is *He* [God] who will wipe them out. *He* will subdue them before you, that you may quickly dispossess and destroy them, as the Lord promised you. And when the Lord your God has thrust them from your path, *say not* to yourselves, 'The Lord has enabled us to possess this land because of our virtues.'

"Remember that? Moses said that God gave us the land because our enemies were wicked and because God promised the land to the Patriarchs. It wasn't because we were saints. We were stiff-necked and idolatrous then. And today? We're a lot like the Palestinians — consumed by self-interest. We happen to control the disputed land, so we can afford to be more magnanimous than they are, but not much more. You know what a hellhole the Gaza Strip is, and yet even there we cling to our settlements. Yes, I should say we're equivalent enough."

"You're forgetting one thing," I replied. "We don't kill innocent people. They do. And that's the real difference between us."

"It's nice to have a selective memory, isn't it?" Moses said. "How about we look at the whole picture? In the Torah, we killed all sorts of innocent people, especially when our holy land was at stake. Our God didn't just tell us to seize the land; he made sure we seized it ruthlessly. The Palestinians feel that they can resort to force against us because for them, it's a matter of defending *their* holy land.

"We've also got to remember why the Muslims resent us so much. They love this land just like we do. They're taught that their Prophet rose up to the heavens here. And for centuries, the land belonged to them. Then who should come along but the European Christians. You know damned well what the Christians told the Muslims, because they said the same thing to us: 'It doesn't matter if you're a People of the Book. Your soul can't be saved unless you become a Christian. In the meantime, we will take all the land because we have the power to do it.'"

"Moses," I said, "I don't need a history lesson."

"I think you do. Now fast-forward to the early part of the last century. More and more Jews were settling here and talking about building a Jewish state. But the Arabs still were the predominant residents. In fact, it wasn't even close — they were in the clear majority. Then, a few decades later, some of the Europeans go insane. They exterminate six million of us. They turn our skin into soap and lampshades. They perform experiments on us. They —"

"Yes, Moses, I'm aware of the Holocaust."

That comment actually slowed Moses down for a moment—I'm sure he didn't want to come across as patronizing—but he quickly regained himself, and made up for lost time. "So after it was all over and the camps were liberated, did we get a slice of the Bavarian pie? Or the Rhineland? Or some other part of the continent that insulted us, corralled us, abused us, tortured us, and finally slaughtered us like hogs? That would have been the fairest result, but that's not what happened. The Jews got together with the Americans and the Europeans, among others, and we decided to settle our score with Europe first by partitioning Palestine, and then by conquering *Muslim* land. And why not? The land didn't belong to the Muslims, right? It belonged to the colonizers from Europe, like just about everything else on this damned planet!"

Moses had reached the point where even he knew it was time to calm down. I probably could have taken some gratuitous shot at the lather he had worked up. In fact, I could see one of my fellow panelists getting ready to confront him. But I wasn't going to let that happen; I understood too well where he was coming from, and it was a perspective that needed to be voiced more often in Jewish circles, even though Moses tended to take it too far.

"Are you suggesting," I asked, "that we leave Israel and go back to Europe?"

"Too late now," he replied. "The Arabs have used so much violence over the years—military measures, terrorism, you name it—they've practically legitimized our right to keep the land as long as we can defend it."

"Then what are you suggesting?" I asked. "Should we hold

an open election and let everyone in Israel and the Territories vote, and let the majority form a single government over all the land? Because if we do that, the Arabs will take over very soon; they've got the numbers."

"No, I'm not advocating a one-state solution. You know I consider myself a Zionist. We deserve our own homeland like everyone else."

"I'm not following you, Moses," I said, getting exasperated. "You say you want a two-state solution—the Jews get part of the Holy Land, the Arabs the rest. That's what most of us think. Where's the disagreement then? Exactly how to divide up the land?"

"Look," Moses replied. "I've wished for a long time that we had never clamored for a chunk of the Middle East. I can't stand violence, I can't stand living in a neighborhood where my family isn't wanted, and I don't recognize the legitimacy of colonialism. That's why I believe that in 1947 the land belonged to the Arabs, not the British.

"But we're here now, and the question is, what would Moses do about it? I don't mean the man with the magical staff; I mean Moses our rabbi — the man who commanded us to stop mistreating slaves, be good to our neighbors, and share land with the poor.

"Here's what you're missing, Richie. You think this is all very simple. The Jews are being reasonable; the Arabs aren't. We Jews know there's a compromise solution out there, and if the Arabs weren't savages, all we'd have to do is engage in a little horse trading over land, and we'd get it done. Isn't that your point?"

"Forget my point," I said. "Make yours."

"Fine. This isn't about horse trading. It's about two peoples who don't like each other, don't respect each other, and don't *trust* each other. Before you can make peace, you've got to build up that trust.

"The first thing Moshe Rabbenu would do is address his

own people and tell them to stop demonizing the Arabs. He'd remind us of how we and the Arabs came from the same ancestors. He'd point out that we've done better over the centuries in dealing with Muslim rule than Christian rule. He'd talk about how, in the Middle Ages, when we came into contact with the Muslims, our two peoples enjoyed an incredible symbiosis and out sprang perhaps the greatest religious philosophy this world has ever seen. Look at Maimonides or the original Kabbalists. What would they have accomplished without exposure to Islam?

"I'm telling you, there's no closer religion to Judaism than Islam—not the perverted, violent Islam, but the *real* Islam — and there's certainly no God as close to the Jewish God as the God of the Muslims. Our peoples lived together in peace for a long, long time. If we could only open our minds to the beauty and uniqueness of Islamic teachings, I've no doubt we'd become more pious lovers of God. And I've no doubt we'd become better friends with the Muslim world if we publicly announced our friendship with Palestinians and recognized our own role in seizing what was then *their* land.

"How much of that land we give up is a secondary matter. We have to admit the truth about history and treat our so-called enemies with dignity. Then, we'd see what they have to say, and we could take the dialogue from there."

Our panel spoke on the first day of the conference. The next day, Moses and I came to breakfast with smiles on our faces because our business in Israel was finished. Yes, we were heading out to the conference, but we were dressed casually and looking forward to sitting back, relaxing, and listening to other Jews go at it. You know the old line: "two Jews, three opinions."

Moses and I had been staying at the Hotel Ezra, just off the Davidka Square in the heart of Jerusalem. The square is known for its monument to the Davidka mortar launcher that was featured prominently in Israel's War of Independence in 1948. When he first saw the monument, Moses pointed out that it was a reminder of how enthralled Israel is by its military prowess.

"I'm as much a fan as they are," I replied. And why shouldn't I be? To be fulfilled as a Jew, you had better remember the days of glory; how else do you cope with all the centuries of agony?

Hotel Ezra was less than a mile from the convention center, and the day before, we walked to the conference. But that day I felt lazy, so we hailed a cab. We rode in silence, which was unusual for a cab ride with Moses. When I take a cab with him in D.C. or New York, he typically uses the time to practice his conversational skills in whatever native language the driver speaks. In Israel, Moses generally takes the opportunity to question the driver about politics. But that morning, there was no banter at all. Moses must have decided the trip would be too short to glean any real information.

After we passed the Beit Strauss on our right, I could see the top of the convention center in the distance. I turned to Moses to ask him a question, and then I heard a loud crackling sound. That remains my last memory of the cab ride.

CHAPTER III

*"Do you know what's odd? When I became a scholar
after they threw me out of the temple in Memphis,
I chose to specialize in the Exodus and Moses. But
when I was a kid, I was more intrigued by the story of
Joseph and his dreams. Mine have always been very
vivid. Of course, I used to think everyone else's were
too. Then, when I was a bit older, I told my mother
about my dreams, and she convinced me that they
were a lot more elaborate than other people's. That
motivated me to figure out if they had some hidden
meaning—like Joseph's.*

*"What is it with me and dreams, I'd wonder. Why
do I experience them differently from everyone else?
I've never been able to answer that—until now."*

Rabbi Moses Levine, speaking to Rabbi
Richard Gold from inside a cell in East
Jerusalem, 2002

East Jerusalem—March 2002. I can go a month without
remembering anything that happens in my sleep, but for Moses,
during our captivity, it was completely different. Every morning
in the dungeon, for weeks on end, he'd report to me another of
his dreams. Invariably, he experienced it as Moshe Rabbenu.

I didn't place much importance on this at first. Then, one morning, as I lay awake, I watched as my friend appeared to be in a trance—a violent trance. He didn't move his arms at all, but his head shook from side to side, and on his face I saw a look of absolute rage. That wasn't at all the Moses I knew. He had me wishing we had an exorcist; it sure looked like he needed one.

I approached Moses to try to wake him, but Sharif yelled at me to leave him alone. Sheepishly, I obeyed. For the next ten or fifteen seconds, I sat and watched as the two bastards outside of the cage laughed at Moses' pain.

Finally, Moses came to his senses. He opened his eyes and sat up on the bed. Then he uttered the English words: "This is happening for a reason."

"What are you talking about?" I asked him.

"This. The kidnapping, this dungeon, my dreams. It's all happening for a reason."

"You mean like some transcendent, cosmic purpose?" I asked.

"Yes," he said. "I've never believed in such a thing. I've never believed in a God who tampers with the laws of nature. But something's happening to me. I can't deny what I'm experiencing."

"Tell me," I said.

"He was raping someone in his sleep!" said Sharif. "It got you all excited, didn't it, rabbi?" That stupid comment sent Sharif into hysterics. And I wanted to tear into him, but I kept my thoughts to myself. It would have been a waste of energy to argue with the fool.

Moses didn't say a word for the next hour. He knew we couldn't speak freely—our hosts were as fascinated by his behavior as I was. Finally, when they stopped paying attention to the goings-on inside the cage, Moses explained what had happened.

"Think back to the last dream I told you about. I was in ancient Egypt, the adopted grandson of the Egyptian Pharaoh, but I learned that I was really a Hebrew.

"I broke up a fight between two Hebrew slaves, and I told them that slaves shouldn't fight their own people, they should join together and fight their *bondage*. Remember that?"

"Yes, of course."

"Well, in my dream last night, I was the same person—Pharaoh's grandson. And I was walking near a construction site when I saw this huge Egyptian man whipping an elderly Hebrew slave—and I mean whipping him five, ten, fifteen times.

"The two of them were alone; the other slaves were working at the back of the building. And there I was, watching it all happen, with my blood boiling. 'Stop it!' I yelled. 'Stop it now, you son of a bitch! Can't you see you're killing this old man.'

"But he didn't stop; he just sneered at me.

"So I walked over to him and hit him in the face as hard as I possibly could. Then I shoved him to the ground.

"As he lay there, I beat him with my fists until they bled, and then I beat him some more. I didn't need to, but I couldn't stop myself. Richie, it was like all the stories we've heard about the Germans, the Russians, the Portuguese, the Spanish ... the memories of all the pogroms in history were welled up in my soul, and I let it all out on this one Egyptian bully until he lay motionless, his blood mixed with my own on my fists and his battered head.

"And when I finally got up, who was standing and staring but two Hebrews—two young, Hebrew men.

"'We get your point,' one of them said. 'It's what you said yesterday — we can't simply ask to be free, we need to fight for our freedom. Now go. Save yourself. And don't worry about us. We understand what to do.'"

After recounting the dream, Moses simply looked at me and shook his head. "Maybe it's the dungeon putting me over the edge, I don't know. But lately, I've been thinking that if I've been dreaming the dreams of Moshe Rabbenu, it could be because I *am* Moshe Rabbenu."

"That's funny, Moses," I said.

"No, I'm not joking. I'm really not."

"You think you're Moses."

"Let me say it this way. I'm beginning to think of myself as Moses' latest incarnation on Earth."

I could tell he was serious. It was one of the lowest moments of my captivity.

If you know your Torah, you should be able to tell by now that the situations that appeared in Moses' sleep didn't occur in the same order as they appeared in the Good Book. Moses had his first dream as Moshe Rabbenu—the one about the burning bush—*before* he dreamt about fleeing from Egypt because he killed the Egyptian. In the Torah, though, the burning bush appeared *after* Moshe Rabbenu fled from Egypt. With the passage of time, I became almost as fascinated by the dreams' order as by their content. In fact, this was a big reason why, one morning, thinking that I should take notes on Moses' dreams and record my own thoughts about our experience, I asked him to rip out a section from his notebook so that I could keep a journal. In hindsight, I wish he had just said no.

When Hafeez came to see us—that is, when he came to see Moses—my friend never referred to his dreams, not even once. Hafeez would ask Moses what was on his mind, and Moses might reply that he was thinking about the Torah and then discuss the very passage that he had dreamt about the previous night, but he always kept quiet about the dreams themselves. Moses' favorite discussion topic with Hafeez was, instead, Islamic violence. Moses was resolute in condemning it, whether it was aimed at Israel, the U.S., or any other country. He and Hafeez argued about the topic for weeks, seemingly to no avail. But then they had a breakthrough, and it was prompted by a concession from Moses.

The concession stemmed from a dream Moses had had the previous night. This is how he described it to me:

"I was walking up the steps of the palace. Scores, perhaps hundreds, of Hebrew slaves lined the steps. They were applauding me, and nobody was trying to stop them. As I walked up the steps, I recalled having killed an Egyptian man, inspiring two Hebrew disciples to begin an insurgency, and then escaping from the reach of the Pharaoh's army.

"The Pharaoh's men were right behind me as I entered the palace and headed straight for the throne room. Somehow, I knew the Pharaoh would be there waiting for me.

"He said to me, 'Moses, it has been a long time since we last saw each other. Much has happened since then. It appears your warnings have come to pass.'

"Then, more memories popped into my head, memories of my having told the Pharaoh back when I lived in his palace that the Hebrews are a freedom-loving people who won't continue to serve Egyptian masters in peace. I had warned him that terrible things would befall the Egyptians if the Hebrews weren't released from their bondage. I used the word 'karma'—as in the Egyptians were bringing bad karma down on themselves by basing their economy on Jewish slaves. I hadn't once mentioned God's retribution. I hadn't wanted to turn this into a battle of the gods; then he might have fought to the bitter end out of pride.

"I told the Pharaoh it was hardly surprising that Egypt was suffering. That's what happens when you treat human beings like cattle.

"Then he said to me, 'You speak of cattle? What of our cattle that have become sick and died? And the terrible storms, which devastated our crops? And the Hebrew violence has been the worst of all. At first, we would hear about a slave here and there striking out against his master. But recently, the Hebrews have set out to take the life of one child from every Egyptian family. Yesterday, they killed my own son, my own beloved son.'

"I told him I was sorry, but he didn't believe me.

"'Sorry?' he said, and then he paused and looked at me

searchingly. 'We have captured some of these murderers. And in each case they say that *you* have been their inspiration. You have told them to rise up against your own people, the same people that raised you to become a prince.'

"I replied that I had told the slaves to stand up for themselves and showed them the value of fighting back. But I never told them to murder a child in every Egyptian family, let alone the Pharaoh's child."

"You should have seen his look—a changing mixture of fury and sympathy. 'I gave you love, a home, a kingdom,' he said. 'And this is the way you repay me? I have considered crushing your skull and displaying it to all of your friends, those savage slaves who would not know how to survive a day out of captivity. But I have decided to give you a worse fate than that. I have decided to give you what you have asked for.

"'Take your Hebrews. Lead them into the wilderness. You will see what it is like out there away from the order we have wrenched from chaos. Out there, in the desert, you will finally enjoy the freedom you seek. Then, when you find yourselves dying from hunger or thirst, or torn apart by the swords of savage peoples, you will realize how lucky the Hebrews have been to live here under my rule.'"

That was as far as the dream went. And, in fact, Moses never did dream about the manner in which the Hebrews actually fled into the desert. He assumed it took place unceremoniously and without the help of any divine miracle.

"One of the things that struck me from the dream," Moses continued, "was how God never entered into the equation. Faith in God might have inspired the Hebrews to fight for their freedom, but there were no supernatural events. And the Moses I dreamt about? He was the Hebrews' John Brown, but he wasn't the Abe Lincoln. Basically, all he did was beat the daylights out of an Egyptian, talk to a couple of Hebrews, issue a warning to the Pharaoh, and leave town. Others did the real work."

"Do you still think everything that's happening to us is happening for a reason?" I asked.

"I don't know," he said. "That sounds so fundamentalist, doesn't it? But I keep having these dreams and remembering them—every morning, a new one. And I'm convinced there's a real opportunity here, Richie. It involves me, and it involves Hafeez. He's the conduit."

The day that Moses described that dream, Hafeez didn't show up in the dungeon. Strangely, Moses recalled no new dream when he awoke the next morning, and he was visibly more reflective when we spoke. By the time Hafeez arrived a few hours later, he couldn't help but notice the change.

"You look different," he said to Moses, as he pulled his chair toward our cage. "You seem more at peace."

"I've had an epiphany," Moses replied. "One that I think you'll like."

Without revealing how he had come to his insight, Moses went on to explain much of what he had learned from his reveries about Egypt. He told Hafeez that he had a greater appreciation for why he had been captured and why so many Israelis had been killed by Palestinian "freedom fighters." Those were his exact words; they were enough to make me even sicker than I already was.

Moses went on to say that given the time to reflect, his respect for terrorism as a strategy had grown, and so had his sympathy for those who feel that violence and terrorism is the only way to bring about justice. At times, he said, it may have been the best strategy available to an oppressed people. "Maybe it could have done some good in Nazi Germany; who knows what may have happened if we had assassinated Hitler in the 30s? Maybe our acts of violence were what freed our people from Egypt, not God's miracles."

Hafeez seized the opportunity to try to convince Moses to accept the justification for Palestinian terrorism in particular, but Moses wouldn't take the bait. The most he would concede was that he felt more strongly than ever that the Israelis shouldn't demonize their enemies by invariably labeling them as "terrorists."

"I suspect that if you took any oppressed people," Moses said, "most of them, deep down, would support terror if they thought it would be effective—if it would save enough lives or right enough wrongs. The U.S. Government certainly reasoned that way when we bombed Hiroshima and Nagasaki. But I don't think Palestinian terrorism is going to accomplish anything—except more killings. I say we've reached the stage in human development where just about any kind of terrorism is counter-productive. Someday, Hafeez, maybe I can convince you of that."

Hafeez simply scoffed at Moses and walked out of the dungeon.

Most evenings, Moses and I went to sleep at about the same time, but almost invariably, I was the first to wake up in the morning. That was actually one of my favorite times of the day. I would lie in bed, wondering what dream Moses would awake to tell me. It was the time when I got some of my best note-taking done, as well as some of my deepest thinking. As I reflected on what I had been hearing in the cage, I realized that, subconsciously, I had been soaking up more and more of Moses' philosophy of life.

Back then, early in the morning, I'd think a lot about Baruch Spinoza. Spinoza was one of Moses' favorite philosophers. Before I came to East Jerusalem I had little use for him, but Moses gave me a deeper appreciation for what he stood for and why he matters.

Spinoza was a heretic first and a Jew second. Unfortunately, he lived in a time and a place (17th century Amsterdam) when an outspoken philosopher couldn't afford to be both and remain within the Jewish community. Moses the Heretic, by contrast, was fully accepted as a Jew, even by those who disliked him. In fact, once he left the Red States and broke ground at a synagogue in Maryland, my friend could keep not only his Judaism but also his pulpit. He used that pulpit to preach a philosophy of God much like what Spinoza preached centuries before, a philosophy that I had always heard dismissed as pantheism—a trivial, almost childlike equation of "God" with "the world." Moses explained to me that he was no pantheist, and neither was Spinoza.

By "the world," Moses taught me, we all refer to a seemingly endless collection of finite beings (animals, vegetables, minerals, particles) that occupy specific places at specific times, and then disappear—as if to oblivion. Spinoza's God is nothing like such a collection. Spinoza may not have believed in the supernatural, but he did believe in transcendence.

God, Moses said, is *the ultimate*. And *the ultimate* is neither finite nor ephemeral. *The ultimate* encompasses all things—the finite and the infinite, the ephemeral and the permanent, the static and the dynamic, the unified and the multifarious, the living and the dead. *The ultimate* transcends all the dimensions that we can perceive—and that includes time as well as space.

The ultimate, Moses continued, mustn't be characterized in terms of human personality traits or approached in terms of biblical stories, which tell us more about ourselves than about God. We're no more "Godlike" than we are "ant-like," and we can't keep deluding ourselves to the contrary with myths about "miracles." If we wish to know God, we're best served by thinking rationally about the world as we know it; with the right vision, we can find divinity manifested wherever we look. As to such "ultimate" questions as what will become of human beings after our bodies die, in the end we're left with few answers and certainly none that is definitive. But that last teaching was Moses', and not necessarily Spinoza's.

"Spinoza was wrong when he taught that many of the

deepest philosophical questions are answerable by logic alone," Moses said. "But he was right in saying that our highest form of knowledge—higher even than reason—is *intuition*. And for the hardest questions, that's what we have to fall back on, our intuition, which if we're smart has been honed by hours upon hours of reasoning, soul-searching, and prayers for wisdom."

In our cage, Spinoza was practically a third resident. I would be asked to consider, for example, his teaching that the biblical Prophets weren't necessarily wiser than other human beings but were merely gifted with more vivid imaginations. Candidly, I couldn't help but wonder if the same could be said for Moses Levine. He would regale me with incredibly detailed stories about the Hebrew experiences in Egypt or in the wilderness, stories that couldn't be found either in the Torah or the Talmud. Moreover, he increasingly shared with me the perception of what I took to be the epitome of insanity: the idea that he was the incarnation of his biblical namesake. I thought such an idea to be sacrilegious nonsense, and I desperately hoped to dispel it from Moses' head.

With that goal in mind, I'd question my friend about whether his claim to be Moses' current incarnation was consistent with his Spinozistic view of the world. Spinoza, I pointed out, taught that "the free man thinks of nothing less than of death" and contended that mind and matter are but two parallel aspects of the same thing, which seems to suggest that when the body dies, so too does the soul. But Moses remained undaunted.

"I'm not a slave to Spinoza's teachings," he said. "Spinoza has given me a basic orientation towards God, and an impetus to use my brain and trust my intuition. He hasn't bound my mind.

"The truth is that none of us knows what happens after we die. We can neither prove the possibility of reincarnation nor disprove it. That's why the Jewish sages have been all over the map on the issue."

"Perhaps," I said, "but today, in our community, not many people admit to believing in reincarnation."

"Look," Moses replied, "my mind is conflicted on this issue, so I choose to follow the teachings of my gut—that I'm having these dreams as a reminder of a form that my soul embodied a long time ago. If I'm truly the incarnation of a great leader, we'll all see signs to that effect. I will, you will; so will the world. If I don't see them, I'll know I've been deluded. I wouldn't be the first.

"Anyway, you can be confident that I'll keep an open mind about all this. And I'll never forget that whoever we are, as long as we're human, we'll remain ignorant about the ultimate questions. That's one thing I know that Spinoza didn't."

During our stay in the dungeon, I spent a fair amount of time arguing with Moses about the significance of his dreams. Mostly, though, I simply listened, absorbed, and served as scrivener. I saw myself, above all else, as my friend's chronicler, not his critic.

As a scribe, I found myself repeatedly writing about two types of dreams. One took place on Mount Sinai; the other after Moses returned from Sinai the second time and found not a golden calf, but a group of Hebrews wanting to learn about the law.

Moses would relate detailed conversations he had had with other ancient Hebrews about the hundreds of do's and don'ts in the Mosaic Law. Sometimes, when a provision of law was stated, it was accompanied by a moral rationale. There were instances, however, when someone requested a justification, and none was given.

When Moses was recounting these dreams, I was absolutely entranced. One aspect of the dreams that especially fascinated me was the role of two brothers—and I don't mean Moses and Aaron. When Moses came down from the mountain the second time, he and Aaron were the primary spokesmen who explained the law to the people. But on Sinai, where the law was being conceived, Moses mostly played the role of a sponge, and Aaron was nowhere to be found. The law itself was being crafted not by a supernatural "God," but rather by another pair of brothers—Isaac and Asher. Moses had a say, to be sure, but for the most part he deferred to the more powerful minds of the brothers.

If you're thinking that you've never heard of Isaac or Asher, you're not alone. They can't be found either in the Torah or the Talmud. Call them mere figments of Moses Levine's prophetic imagination. But they were the main vehicles through which I heard my friend's interpretation of what Judaism stands for and why. And they were also crucial players in convincing Moses of his destiny.

Even in his dreams, you see, my friend never thought of himself as the ultimate Jew. Isaac and Asher did the heavy lifting. They were the young men who watched him kill the Egyptian slave driver and conceived the insurgency that was to follow. They—or Isaac, to be specific — physically sculpted the Ten Commandments. And they were the ones who instructed Moshe Rabbenu on the meaning of those commandments as well as the hundreds of other laws that would come to be associated with Moses' name.

The brothers understood that in order to create a new religious civilization, they needed a single human face to inspire loyalty and trust. They also appreciated how difficult it would have been for any flesh and blood human being to serve as titular leader, main strategist and primary tactician. So, my friend explained, they divided up the authority, and the result was an amazingly efficient system—one that has withstood more than 3,000 years and numerous pogroms.

Moses Levine was humbled by all the revelations he was experiencing. He was humbled by being "chosen" thousands of years ago to serve as the figurehead for the Jewish people … a role he viewed with the utmost of respect. And he was humbled by the idea that he was being chosen today to continue Moshe Rabbenu's legacy, albeit in ways that even he couldn't yet understand.

Thinking about Moses' dreams was one of the two high points of my days in East Jerusalem. The other, believe it or not, was listening to his dialogues with Hafeez. Obviously, they were painful at first—I essentially had to keep both my eyes and my mouth shut for an hour, and sometimes considerably longer. But I took to heart what Moses had said about the role of Moshe Rabbenu in ancient Israel: it was his job to inspire the loyalty and trust of the Hebrews. So why shouldn't I, a Hebrew, place some trust in my friend? It wasn't like we were in some sort of maximum security prison and had to outwit or outfight a whole regiment of evil soldiers in order to escape. Moses only had to reach the mind of a single Islamic intellectual, a single *rational* Islamic intellectual, who surely could free us if he wanted to. Moses had already persuaded me that just because a person is a "terrorist" doesn't make him insane—misguided, yes, but not insane.

The "sport" played between the two men was simple enough to describe. On the surface, the competitors were engaged in a primarily calm, reasoned search for political and theological truth. Both competitors spent a lot of time proving that they were not only able to argue, but also to listen. They would go out of their way to praise their opponent whenever a point was especially well presented—even to state the point back in their own terms, so as to demonstrate that they had fully absorbed it. But they would never allow an argument to be made without providing a counter—lest the opponent detect a sign of weakness.

Moses, for his part, never once raised his voice. Even when he expressed his passions, which he did frequently, he did so in a measured tone. Hafeez, by contrast, often yelled at Moses, but I'm convinced that the yelling was mostly a matter of show. Hafeez apparently felt the need to demonstrate to our other hosts that he was as much Moses' master as he was theirs.

Beneath the surface, the two competitors each had an agenda, and their job was to convince the other to adopt it. Moses' advantage—call it a *road*-court advantage—was that Hafeez revealed his agenda from the very outset of the relationship, whereas Moses wasn't nearly so open. With each passing week, though, my friend's agenda became clearer, at least to me. He wasn't trying to convince Hafeez about who should control Eretz Yisrael—Jews, Palestinians, or the international community. Moses could care less if Hafeez wanted all the Jews to return to Bavaria. "It's not going to happen," he told me, "but I can hardly blame an Arab for wishing it would." Instead, Moses' goal was simply to persuade Hafeez that terrorism, however justifiable in theory, could no longer be defended in practice — not given the world as it stands now, with all its ethnic loyalties, religious differences and increasingly devastating technologies. As a result, he argued, since Moses and I had been captured in a terrorist act, the only moral response on the part of the Palestinians would be to release us with no strings attached.

After a few weeks of their discussions, I became convinced that Moses was gaining the upper hand, yet he still didn't seem especially optimistic about our release. His assessment finally changed when he and Hafeez spent an afternoon talking about their childhoods. Moses' confidence level soared once Hafeez revealed a single fact: that he was raised without siblings in a Ramallah orphanage.

"We've got him," Moses told me. "Believe me, he's been listening. What I didn't know before was whether he could afford to release us against the orders of his superiors. Now I think he can. A man like Hafeez would be willing to sacrifice himself if he thought justice required it. What he might not risk is retribution to his family.

"We already knew he had neither a wife nor children," Moses continued, "but I just assumed he had brothers, sisters or parents who were still alive. Thank God I was wrong."

That night, Moses had another dream about his namesake. It was the last such dream he remembers having in East Jerusalem. Here's what he told me (and yes, by then I was used to his habit of referring to his namesake in the first person):

"Let me begin by dispelling this whole nonsense about my being prevented from entering the land of Canaan because God was punishing me. I've always hated that part of the Torah. What kind of God would make someone live out the rest of his life alone in the wilderness just because he struck a rock when he was supposed to wait for it to produce water?

"In my dream," Moses continued, "I made the decision to stay in the land of Moab, but Asher put the bug in my ear. He said that it was time for the people to grow up—to become a 'people of priests.' He'd talk about how the Israelites had become too dependent on a single leader, and how the rank and file needed to claim more responsibility. I wanted to argue with him, really I did, but he was a hundred percent right."

"What about the story of the rock?" I asked.

"Oh, Isaac came up with that one. He wanted everyone to think I was being punished by God to show that all human beings are flawed and should never be the objects of worship. That's a big part of what Judaism's about, isn't it?"

"Absolutely," I said.

"Anyway," Moses continued, "in the dream, I watched as the people left me to head for the Promised Land. And the next thing I knew, I was all alone. The brothers had picked out a perfect place for me to stay, an area with plenty of game and vegetables. Still, I was alone.

"Then a couple of deer approached me, and they were followed by an antelope. I thought for a moment about killing them for the food, but I just couldn't. They were the only living creatures I was likely to see. And that's when it dawned on me: my people were about to go into the Land of Canaan and butcher all sorts of innocent people in order to claim the land, just like it says in the Torah. And I decided right then that my vocation in life from that point forward would be to serve as a counterweight to that slaughter. I would never again kill another animal. Even if it meant that I would starve, I was determined never to kill. I could uproot a plant, but I wouldn't take another animal life, and I wouldn't eat the flesh of another animal. To me, that flesh would always represent the act of killing.

"I also decided that eventually, when my body died, I'd be reincarnated in another human form. That process would continue indefinitely, from one form to the next, and in each lifetime I'd somehow work to stop people from killing.

"There had already been too much killing in the world and there was about to be even more in the 'Promised Land.' I realized that being a Jew means to honor the sanctity of God, and that means to honor the sanctity of life. Every time I sit down to eat, I want to remember that. I want to remind myself that we don't need to kill in order to eat, certainly not in the 21st century. Needless killing has got to stop. To me, that's at the heart of what it means to be 'kosher.'"

When Moses finished telling his story, he looked down at his bed pan and then up at the mildewed ceiling. "I'm really ready to leave this place, Richie. I don't want to have another dream. I want to remember that one above all the others. I want my purpose here on earth to be about peace, first and foremost. That means living gently. No meat. No hatred. No violence. Just love for life in all its forms."

"Love for Hitler?" I asked.

"That would be quite a challenge," he shrugged. "But ideally, yes. We could have justified killing him if that would have saved lives, but we can't justify hating him. And I'm sure you'd agree that we can't justify eating him."

"Now *that* I will agree with," I replied, smiling.

"Loving and nurturing need to become habits. We have to reinforce them every way we can," Moses said. "That's really all I'm saying."

Two, maybe three hours later, Hafeez walked into the dungeon. My friend was waiting for him.

"Do you know what?" Moses said. "I was just daydreaming about coming back here someday at a time when this land is no longer controlled by the Jewish people."

"I like that dream," Hafeez said. "Jerusalem should be what it was before colonialism. There were a few Jews here then, but it wasn't called Israel. The land belonged to the People of the Prophet."

"I think it should belong to all the peoples of Abraham—a tribute to our ability to live together in peace," Moses replied. "If you're familiar with my writings, you know that I believe that. The Jews can have Tel Aviv, Haifa and Beersheba. The Arabs can have Mecca, Medina, and Damascus—plus the West Bank and the Gaza Strip. The Christians can have Rome, London and Athens. And Jerusalem can belong to us all as an international city. I only wish you'd let us go so I could make my dream come to life."

Hafeez was silent for a moment. Then he barked out my name. "Rabbi Gold. Do you agree with what your friend has said?"

I was shocked at the question. Surely, I thought, it was a trick. So I kept my silence.

"Moses," Hafeez said, "tell Rabbi Gold to turn to me, open his eyes, and answer my question. *Now!*"

Moses made the request, so I responded. "If you would let us out, yes, I swear to you that I'll do anything in my power to work for that goal."

Of course I realize how self-serving that sounds having come from my lips. But the truth is that with the passage of time, I had learned to appreciate Moses' vision of an international Jerusalem. It isn't antithetical to Zionism. In fact, it's the logical fulfillment of the Zionist dream—to create not just a state for Jews, but a truly *Jewish* state.

"Aha!" he bellowed, facing the other guards. "Did you hear that? The rabbi speaks. And he lies too." Hafeez then looked me in the eyes for the first time in weeks. "I know duplicity when I hear it. You would never turn over Jewish land to the United Nations. You would go straight to the police and tell them to bomb every man, woman and child in Gaza.

"Abdul!"

"Yes, sir?" Abdul replied.

"Fatten them up tonight. Bring out the choicest steaks. Spare no expense. This shall be their last meal. Let them enjoy it like men."

So that night we ate well, even the new vegetarian, and ignored the added pressure on the bed pans. Moses skipped the steak, but they also served us falafels, baba gahanoush, koshari, pita and fruit. It was indeed a meal fit for a free man.

Just before we went to sleep, Moses grabbed me by the arm and told me to listen carefully: "I can't explain why, but I have this feeling that tomorrow, we'll discover whether I've been deluding myself. We'll get the sign one way or another.

"Right now, Richie, neither of us can be sure what these dreams mean. All I really know is that we may not survive this hell hole, but if we do, this is one human life that's not going to be wasted. That much I can promise."

CHAPTER IV

*"I'm looking down the road 100 years, maybe less, and assuming that we keep going down the path we're headed. I'm thinking about a twisted 16-year-old prodigy, whose father beats him and whose girlfriend just told him she wants her freedom. He needs an outlet for his anger. So he spends a few days tinkering in his garage with the latest technology and then emerges with this little contraption he's rigged. He gets in his car, drives a hundred miles to the nation's capital, walks down Pennsylvania Avenue, and blows up both the White House **and** the Capitol Building in a single blast.*

"It would be a pretty remarkable feat in our day. But in 100 years, I could see people saying, 'Isn't it strange that doesn't happen more often?'"

Moses Levine, from his
National Book Award-winning work,
Exodus: Then and Now, 1998

Atlanta, Georgia—January 1996. Moses' first job as a congregational rabbi was at a Reform temple in Memphis. When my friend got the axe after a little over two years there, he left Memphis and moved back to Atlanta, where he had lived immediately after graduating from college. Moses even returned to his old employer at the Southern League Against Poverty, but this time, he negotiated a part-time position. He told his boss that he needed to spend a lot of time researching and writing. "I'm going to write a bestselling book about the Jewish people," he said. The response was laughter, but as we all know now, Moses' claim turned out to be prophetic.

Published in June of 1998, *Exodus: Then and Now* took twenty weeks to reach the New York Times Bestseller List and a lot longer than that to leave it. *Exodus* won the National Book Award and earned Moses his first trip to the White House, frequent invitations to television news shows, and the extreme wrath of my wife, Rachel, who considered the book (and its author) anti-Israeli. Personally, I loved *Exodus*. Even though I didn't agree with some of its conclusions, I had no doubt that Moses' perspective deserved to be taken seriously.

What amazed me about the book's success was that *Exodus* started so slowly. Moses thought he needed to establish himself as a scholar before his opinions about modern times could be respected. As a result, the first part of *Exodus* contained nothing that was especially provocative. My friend contented himself with providing meticulously researched commentary on the story of his namesake and the ancient Hebrews as they left Egypt, wandered in the wilderness, and ultimately conquered "the Promised Land."

For nearly two hundred pages, *Exodus* seemed to be but the latest in a long line of rabbinic treatises that sing the beauty of Jewish tradition to a world infatuated with modernity. But any such impression would have ended abruptly once you began the last chapter of Part I. This was no tribute at all. This was an attempt to chronicle the ancient Hebrews' brutality and inhumanity as they seized the land that has come to be known as "holy."

Exodus set forth one biblical passage after another, until the sheer quantity of the violence countenanced by the Jewish God almost swallowed up the impressions of love and charity that are imbedded in Jewish philosophy. Moses quoted, for example, the passage in Deuteronomy in which God led the Hebrews in capturing all the towns of Sihon, the Amorite king, leaving no survivor. Then he pointed out that later in Deuteronomy (20: 10-16), our Lord issued directives to His people for entering the Promised Land.

> When you approach a town to attack it, you shall offer it terms of peace. If it responds peaceably and lets you in, all the people present there shall serve you at forced labor. If it does not ... you shall put all its males to the sword. You may, however, take as your booty the women, the children, the livestock, and everything in the town—all its spoil — and enjoy the use of the spoil of your enemy, which the Lord your God gives you. Thus, you shall deal with all towns that lie very far from you, towns that do not belong to nations hereabout. In the towns of the latter peoples, however, which the Lord your God is giving you as a heritage, you shall not let a soul remain alive.

My friend's attempt at chronicling the dark side of the Bible hardly stopped with the Five Books of Moses. He included, for instance, the passage in Judges in which the Lord directed the Judites to defeat 10,000 Gentiles at the battle of Bezek, which inspired them to capture their enemies' leader and cut off his thumbs and his big toes. The Judites went on to attack Jerusalem—"they put it to the sword and set the city on fire." (Judges 1:8)

You get the idea. So did all of Moses' readers. What they didn't appreciate, until they read Part II of the book, was how the gruesome portions of the Torah related to the Jewish exoduses of the 20th century.

Part II of Moses' work dealt with the Jews repopulating the land of Israel, both during the initial half of the 20th century and then later, when immigrants came from places like Ethiopia and the former Soviet Union. In those chapters, he continued to include a plethora of interesting facts and figures, but the tone was different. This was no longer "Professor" Moses Levine; this was Moses Levine the prophet. And his primary point was unmistakable:

The land of Israel is, indeed, holy. Potentially, it is as close to a Garden of Eden as we will find on this planet. This is a place that drenches its inhabitants with a reverence for God and a transcendent sense of meaning. In such an environment, the spirit of brotherhood—the notion of loving thy neighbor as thyself—may someday become the governing principle. Still, every Eden has its serpent, and the land of Israel is no exception. In this case, the serpent doesn't offer fruits from the tree of knowledge, but rather, military power—*superior* military power.

Moses taught that those who seek authority over the land face a fateful choice: to base their authority on the weapons of military might or the spirit of his namesake's philosophy. If the concern about those weapons comes to dominate the impulse to love thy neighbor as thyself, the land of Israel would become a killing field and, ultimately, would devour all of its human inhabitants. The land would remain holy, fertile and available for resettlement, but the generation who turned it into a battle-field would die.

"According to Jewish tradition," Moses wrote, "the commandments number 613. But to those who dwell in the Holy Land, one commandment reigns supreme: 'You shall not take the name of Adonai, your God, in vain.' That doesn't refer to using swear words in connection with God's name. It prohibits you from claiming to honor God when in truth you are guided primarily by your lust for money, power, or some other selfish aim. In the land of Israel, because so many people call themselves servants of God, passions are inevitably incited. Hypocrisy will be spotted wherever it exists, and hypocrites will be punished severely. Such is the price of pretending to be holy.

"Woe unto he who becomes enamored of his own power, his

own perceived invincibility. Woe unto he who attempts to grab for his own tribe too much land that other tribes view as holy. Woe unto he who forgets that all land, and especially the Holy Land, belongs to God and God alone. Woe unto he who believes that peace comes more from defeating one's enemies than from loving them."

That last sentence generated some controversy within the Jewish community. Moses Levine was called a closet Christian, not a *real* Jew. He, of course, denied the charge, saying that to agree with Jesus about values is simply to practice Judaism as it ought to be practiced, for Jesus wasn't simply Jewish at birth, he was Jewish at death, and one of the purest examples of the Tzaddic (righteous man) who ever lived. It was Paul, Moses said—as Buber and others have argued before him — who invented Christianity as a truly non-Jewish religion.

In Part II of his book, Moses chronicled the Zionist impulse as it has been expressed throughout the 20th century. He discussed how it wasn't enough for Jews to have their own state; they wanted one built on the so-called Promised Land. The Zionists understood the power of that land to inspire the greatness of the Jewish people. They came to believe that their own hopes for a true homecoming could never be fulfilled anywhere else.

Moses Levine feared that the latter belief would prove to be the Jews' undoing. It was quite clear to anyone who read *Exodus* that (a) nobody venerated Eretz Yisrael more than the book's author, but (b) it was precisely because of that veneration that Moses wished the Jewish State had been placed in another part of the world, one where the land was just as arable but the neighbors not nearly so hostile. If Moses could rewrite history, a piece of Germany would have been given to the Jews back in the 1940s as an independent country. In addition, the United Nations would have carved out an "international territory," encompassing nothing more than Jerusalem and a region expanding perhaps a dozen kilometers from the city in every direction. The United Nations would control that territory, representatives of all three of the great Abrahamic faiths would populate it, and the city of Jerusalem would be consecrated as the holy city of God. Its model would not be a city at all, but rather a person: the biblical character of Hannah, who donated her only child to a priest so that this infant (Samuel) should grow up to be perpetually in God's service.

While Moses' vision for Jerusalem as the "holy city of God" may have been a novel one, his idea of internationalizing the city was anything but. The United Nations proposed doing so in 1947, and the Jews were amenable to the idea. The Arabs, ironically, were not.

"With all the secular places in the world," Moses wrote, "there deserves to be one small ecumenical space devoted to the love of God. In this place, peace must reign supreme, and justice must be equated with charity. What's mine is yours, what's yours is mine, what's ours is God's, and what's God's is ours … and that of our children.

"Such a state would be much more *Jewish* than any tribal homeland. For who are the Jews but some of the world's oldest and most devoted monotheists? Wherever the unity of God is beloved, and wherever God's people are honored—and I don't mean God's 'chosen' people, I mean *all* of God's people — there we shall call home."

Exodus' ecumenical and pacifistic vision moved many a reader. My wife, Rachel, was one of them. But she was moved to scream.

Even though we first read *Exodus* in its bulky manuscript form, Rachel immediately could see its marketing potential. "They couldn't have written it any better in Syria," she said. "Just how many Israelis would he like to see murdered? The anti-Semites are going to use this as grounds to stop supporting Israel. 'No more weapons! No more self-defense! Just peace, love and the U.N.!' It's nonsense, but it's just well written enough to do some serious damage. That's what worries me."

I couldn't totally disagree with her—and I'm not just talking about its being well written. Moses was correct in the way he characterized my position at the conference — Israel's enemies were real, and so were their weapons. If Israel were to disarm, the Arabs would blow all the Jews into the sea—and this time, nobody would be there to part it for us. Moses loved to cite the Noah story for the proposition that while God promised never to destroy the whole human race, He never said we wouldn't destroy ourselves. But that only played into Rachel's point. To guard against a destruction of biblical proportions, she argued, we Jews have to arm ourselves, and we can't rely on the impotent and largely anti-Semitic United Nations. There really is no alternative for Israel than to build up its military might and be very careful about negotiating away anything that could compromise its security.

I appreciated her perspective. And yet ... there was something about the spirit of Moses' words that resonated with me. We Jews talk incessantly about peace. In fact, when we're not discussing it, we're singing about it or praying for it. Wasn't Moses simply saying that in an effort to preserve peace, Jews have strayed too far in the direction of vigilance and paranoia? The Holocaust in particular has made us a people of war—one whose initial impulse is to defend against potential enemies, rather than to try to turn them into friends.

You walk down the street in Israel and you sense an aggressiveness that is probably not what the Jewish sages had in mind. I can't argue with Moses that we should be known above all else for our warmth and gentleness, not our toughness. And if our own homeland has turned into such a war zone where gentleness is a luxury we can't afford, how is that really our homeland? How isn't that just another ghetto—albeit one of our own construction? Moses' book led me to think about these and other related issues concerning war and peace. And any book that is inspired by love and that gets me to think is worthy of my support, whether or not I agree with its conclusions.

Exodus was published to rave reviews. Soon, Moses was invited to talk about the Middle East on several national talk shows. Those appearances turned out to be the break his book needed to hit the big time.

I've always believed that most great people would have forever toiled in obscurity had their genius arisen in a different time and place. Perhaps that's even true with my friend Moses. When he arrived in Washington, D.C. to do his first national cable talk show, Moses was walking into a climate that can only be described as polarized. His voice and his message came to be seen as the antidote to that polarization.

The TV networks, you may recall, felt compelled to demonstrate that they were fair and balanced. It hasn't always been that way, but it certainly was then. In order to pull off their cherished neutrality, the networks identified legions of talking heads whose views on just about every issue were completely predictable. "Hi, I'm ____, and I'm coming to you from the left." "Hi, I'm ____, and I'm coming to you from the right." "Hi, I'm ____, and I'm coming to you as an apologist for the government of Israel." "Hi, I'm ___, and I'm here to say that Zionism is racism and the Palestinians are always right." Of course they didn't always announce their bias so blatantly, but they might as well have.

I, for one, was sick of those people. I didn't want to listen to knee-jerk "conservatives" or "liberals;" I wanted to listen to visionaries who might happen to be passionately liberal on some issues and conservative on others. When it came to Israel, my center of gravity was foursquare in support of the Zionist cause, but I knew that neither side had a monopoly on truth, and I also knew that in order to be a true moderate, a Jew couldn't simply say "We don't like the Settlements" and then go back to the incessant bashing of Arab militants. The blame-the-other-guy routine was getting old. Instinctively, I understood that in their own way, most Zionists were every bit as biased as the Islamic terrorists.

Enter into the equation Moses Levine — tall, thin, bearded, and with just enough gray hair to give him credibility as a man of experience as well as fervor. He became, almost overnight, a news-talk sensation. Moses was different from the other talking heads because you couldn't predict what he was going to say on any issue unless he had addressed it in his book. When the topic was American politics, Moses was generally liberal, but he could often side with the conservatives, particularly when the topic involved the way religion was frozen out of the public schools. Even on the topic of Israel, Moses was difficult to characterize in terms of conventional ways of thinking.

One moment, you'd hear him talk about Israel like he worshipped the place. Listening to Moses, Americans who had never set foot on Israeli soil would comprehend for the first time how that small piece of land could transform so many agnostics into spiritual souls intoxicated by the thought of God. And Moses' message wasn't merely one of universal brother and sisterhood; he proudly identified himself as a Jew, a man whose religiosity is shaped by the particular texts, language and culture of the Hebrew people. Moses, in short, was an ambassador par excellence for Judaism and its connection to Eretz Yisrael. But as much as he could wax poetic about our people's love for Jerusalem, that's how passionately he spoke about the tragic conflict between the Israelis and the Arabs. His solution, given that the Jews were now fixtures in the Middle East and weren't about to leave, continued to involve internationalizing Jerusalem. That, he acknowledged, couldn't happen until the Arab world renounces violence. Still, it was hardly a proposal that you'd expect from a Jewish partisan.

The American public didn't know what to make of this guy. But whenever Moses appeared on television—regardless of the network or the program—the show's ratings tended to rise. Not coincidentally, the networks rapidly looked for other talking heads who weren't nearly as predictable or doctrinaire as the old guard and who viewed TV appearances as opportunities to think aloud with other intellectuals, rather than to score debating points and show off their IQs. It was a short-lived trend, unfortunately, for the networks couldn't find many speakers as charismatic as Moses, and they soon returned to the comforts of finding ideologues to predictably spout off their wisdom. But at least the trend lasted long enough to catapult Moses into the national limelight as the face of a new generation of deep-thinking, open-minded voices.

CHAPTER V

"It doesn't impress me much to see Jewish people take care of other Jews or black people take care of other blacks. Of course that's a good thing, but it's only the beginning of our responsibilities. You know what I enjoy seeing more? Black leaders who go out of their way to appreciate the great Jewish theologians, like Heschel and Buber. As for Jews, any of them who live in the United States and don't give a damn about black people, I ... I couldn't care less about all they do for their own kind. I'd just want them to go back and read their history books and remember that for a long time, black people were America's Jews. In fact, they probably still are."

Rabbi Moses Levine,
addressing the First Baptist Church of Harlem, 2002

New York City, September 1976: Say what you want about Moses' idealism, but there's no denying that he came by it honestly. I learned this soon after we first met, and the profound parallels in our lives became apparent. Both of us were raised by strong, passionate female figures whose Judaism shaped their outlooks on life. And both of our mothers died during the summer after our senior year in high school—in each case, after a long and excruciating bout with breast cancer.

My mother was a Holocaust survivor whose family was almost entirely decimated by the Nazis. Her only surviving relative was an uncle who had emigrated from Poland to the Lower East Side of Manhattan in 1918, before she was even born. Throughout her stay at Dachau, my mother remembered her uncle's address, knowing that if she were ever freed, she might have a place to live. Sure enough, she located him, and he took her into his home. That's where she met my father, whose family owned an antique furniture store in Greenwich Village. Shortly after I was born, we moved to Teaneck, New Jersey, just across the Hudson River. My father opened a second store there and a third uptown in Manhattan. Our family had clearly joined the upper middle class. To my mother, though, our material wealth meant nothing compared to our commitment to the Jewish people. She constantly preached to me that Hitler could kill our bodies, but we must never let him kill our Judaism.

Over and over again I heard my mother quote the words of the philosopher, Emil Fackenheim: "Jews are forbidden from giving Hitler posthumous victories." I wanted to honor the faith that martyred so many of my mother's relatives. And I wanted to honor my mother. That's probably why, from the day I learned her illness was terminal, I vowed to become a rabbi.

Moses, when he was an undergrad, could have imagined a hundred careers more to his liking. His perspective was shaped by the influence of his own mother, whose attitude toward Judaism was one of both love and frustration. Miriam Levine would never have survived the Holocaust. Inevitably, she would have stuck her neck out too far in confronting her oppressors and would have demanded that other prisoners do the same. Even growing up in Birmingham, Alabama, where Moses was raised, Miriam constantly felt let down — if not by Judaism as a faith, then at least by the Jewish people.

Miriam's message to Moses about our religion was altogether different from the one I heard from my mother. I was raised to think of Judaism as a religion of pragmatism, one that impels us above all else to take care of the health and well-being of ourselves and our families. I was told that Judaism was a way of life, more than a set of beliefs, and that that way of life is centered on the need to raise children so that they're educated, upstanding people who earn a respectable living. My mother also toasted the way Judaism takes activities that other religions treat as sinful—such as getting drunk or having non-procreative sex — and pragmatically turns them into acts of holiness, as long as they're properly controlled. Thus, Jewish adults are directed to get good and drunk on Purim or, if married, to have sex on Friday nights. Such is the pragmatism of Judaism—it allows us to appreciate ourselves as spiritual beings made in God's image but with very animalistic needs. And what kinds of animals, my mother would ask, aren't concerned first and foremost with themselves and their families?

Miriam Levine understood the Jewish obsession with pragmatism, but that didn't mean she accepted it. To her, the beauty of our religion was in its ideals. Moses was raised to believe that Rabbi Akiva correctly identified as Judaism's fundamental principle "love thy neighbor as thyself," and Miriam did her best to live according to this principle. She worked long hours as a teacher in a school for African Americans, while her husband toiled away as a low-paid salesperson in a clothing store. The family couldn't have afforded to send Moses to Columbia without a boatload of educational grants, but Miriam never cared about her family's paltry bankbook. As long as they had their education and their compassion, she said, she would consider the Levines rich.

The way Moses described it, Miriam put him through the most bizarre Jewish education imaginable. It was focused on the idea of courage—the courage to fracture, at times, the letter of the law in order to honor the spirit that makes Judaism majestic. That spirit, Miriam thought, was iconoclastic, intellectual and egalitarian.

Periodically, Moses' dad would have to bail Miriam out of the county jail. When she got bored, she liked to grab a sign protesting racial segregation and picket some government building without a license.

When Moses was 14, Miriam seized upon an idea to teach her son that it was Judaism's ethical teachings, not its rituals, which mattered most. She decided that the family would abstain for a full year from observing any religious ritual.

Miriam removed the mezuzahs from the door posts of their home and proclaimed that they would not set foot in their synagogue until the year came to an end. She also declared that during Jewish holidays, they would follow none of the prescribed rituals. Instead, they would gather together as a family and discuss books about the lives and teachings of the great Jewish leaders of the past. Miriam's favorites were Hillel, a figure who lived in the first century B.C.E. and preached much of the same philosophy that would soon be associated with Jesus of Nazareth, and the Baal Shem Tov, who was born around 1700 A.C.E. and became the inspiration for Hasidism. Both of these men stood, above all else, for warmth, empathy, humility, reverence (born of love, not fear), and the imperative of helping the needy. Yes, they respected the importance of Jewish rituals, but not at the expense of practicing an ethic of love.

One Shabbat evening, Miriam showed up outside her synagogue with a big sign. On the front, it read "How much have *you* done for the poor lately?" On the back, it read "Why so little?" Moses and his father were asked to carry signs of their own, but that's where they drew the line.

Miriam's Judaism was a lonely one. She knew a number of Jews in Birmingham who were deeply concerned about social justice, but none was as relentless in that pursuit as she was. Miriam was truly a Jeremiah, preaching to anyone who would listen that in surviving so well materially while forsaking the plight of the Negro, the American Jewish community had lost its spiritual soul. As a child, Moses knew that his mother was odd, yet he never doubted that she was also unusually inspired. His faith in his mother's critique of Judaism was, in fact, confirmed when he obtained a very special book at around the time of her death.

A Century of Jewish Life in Dixie: The Birmingham Experience, was published in 1974 by the University of Alabama Press. It chronicled the first hundred years of the Birmingham Jewish community. While the writer was obviously proud of the community's achievements, Moses took this work as proof that Judaism, in practice, had lost touch with its ideals. Page after page lauded the Birmingham Jews for their success in business and for the philanthropic generosity of the millionaires who became the cornerstones of the community. But for Moses, the book taught a different lesson: here was a community, coming together in the name of Akiva's faith, which refused to stick its neck out to help another people in their time of need.

One night in college, Moses read to me from the book's discussion of the Civil Rights movement. Moses explained that in 1963, when 19 rabbis came from New York to Birmingham to demonstrate against racial segregation, the local Hebrews couldn't do enough to stop them. The locals mocked the New York rabbis as "nineteen messiahs" who were threatening the survival of a community that had worked hard to get along with both Birmingham's black people and its Christian whites. "There's your Jewish pragmatism," Moses said. He was especially affected by the following words, which came from a memorandum that was widely circulated among the Birmingham Jews of 1963:

> "Although the Jewish community is relatively small, approximately one-half of one percent of the total county population, Jews normally play a prominent role in civic, cultural and business affairs.
>
> The Jewish community leadership generally believes

that Jews, as such, ought to stay out of the desegregation fight on the ground that it is a 'Christian problem' between whites and Negroes and not simply a racial problem."

"Those are the people you'll be preaching to if you become a rabbi," Moses told me. "They'll mouth Akiva's words while in synagogue, but they're just like other Americans. They're not willing to sacrifice or take any real risks.

"American Jews never learned the right lesson from the Holocaust," Moses added. "It should have taught us to fight evil like the *truly* good Germans, the ones who stood up to Hitler. But we don't seem to understand that. We only learned how to survive better as Jews."

CHAPTER VI

"The world's full of intelligent people, but heroes are in short supply. Oh, there are many who'd risk their lives for their principles, and yet what use is that unless their principles are chosen wisely? Some brave men are taught to hate and to give up their lives in order to kill their enemies. When they die, they are often called martyrs. I call them fools.

"Every now and then, though, you find a man or a woman whose courage serves at the feet of their wisdom. They're not merely willing to fight, even die, for their principles. They're willing to set aside their biases and follow the path of wisdom, as difficult as that sometimes can be. It's tough to admit you're wrong. It's tough to embrace what you've been fighting against. But a hero must open his mind to the voice of reason.

"When Richie Gold and I were in Israel, we were lucky enough to meet such a man. He made mistakes, but in the end, he showed me the meaning of virtue more clearly than anyone I'd met before or since.

"Rest in peace, my friend. You deserve it. When your world—your God—needed you, you were there."

Rabbi Moses Levine, giving a tribute
to a martyr at Temple Akiva, 2003

East Jerusalem—April 2002. When I woke up in the East Jerusalem dungeon the day after I dined on steak, my vegetarian friend was standing by the side of his bed. He had a look of anticipation, as if he could already feel under his feet the stairs that would lead us from our hell-hole. The date was April 9, 2002.

"Did you dream last night?" I asked.

"Not that I can recall," he replied. "Richie, this is going to be a wonderful day, I just know it."

I didn't answer. Hafeez had me convinced I was about to meet my maker.

Moses was up that morning by 6:00, and I arose at 6:30. For hours, we paced in our cage waiting for something to happen, but nothing did. At noon, Sharif and his cousin Mustafa brought us our lunch. No steak this time—just pita bread, hummus and water.

Fifteen minutes later, the door opened at the bottom of the stairs, and I assumed my customary position of lying on my bed, face up, with my eyes closed. Before anyone said a word, I heard a loud crackling noise, and a nanosecond later, another. I might have recognized the sounds had they not shocked me so. At first, I clenched my body tighter than a drum, taking some relief in the fact that I was conscious. *Cogito, ergo sum*, I reasoned. My next thought was nicer still: something had obviously happened, but whatever it was, it hadn't happened to me. After lying motionless for a few seconds, I couldn't restrain myself any more—my eyes needed to open. And when I looked around, I saw Hafeez bending over Sharif with a syringe in his hand.

"Forgive me, my friends," he said in Arabic—one of the few sentences in that language I could understand—before injecting both of our guards with sedatives.

Then Hafeez turned to us. "Now we must leave."

As we prepared to bid goodbye to our East Jerusalem home,

I was in a daze, but not Moses. It was as if he had known exactly what to expect. Moses later denied that, of course, and yet he couldn't deny that he had been waiting all day for Hafeez's arrival and believed that one way or another, Hafeez would be removing us from captivity, alive and in one piece.

As we pushed the bookcase aside to enter the main floor of the house, I started to ask what was happening when Hafeez cut me off. "Sheket bevakashah!" Hafeez barked. In other words, shut up and listen, please.

"It is now 12:20 p.m. in East Jerusalem, or 5:20 a.m. on the East Coast of the United States. In a little over three hours, unless you can get to the right people first, eight bombs will go off in the central train stations of Boston, New York, Philadelphia and Washington. We do not have time for conversation. You must do exactly as I tell you.

"The Israeli army has a small office building nearby. I will drop you off near the back. Ring the buzzer at the door, and when the guard answers, tell him right away it is important to let as few people as possible know you have been freed. If the word gets out, it might ruin everything.

"So, here is what I know about the plot. Unfortunately, it is not much. In each of the four cities, three men are involved in the mission. Two will detonate suicide bombs. They will be staying at a hotel not far from the train station. I have written down for you the names of the hotels, but I do not know the names of the bombers or their room numbers. The third man in each city is supposed to confirm to the bombers at 7:45 a.m. local time that the plan is a go. He will knock on their door, walk in, tell them to strap on their bombs, and then leave them to their work."

We had been walking to Hafeez's car while he was talking. As soon we got inside, he handed Moses a thick manila envelope. "You will find in here," he continued, "a set of computer disks with a large amount of information about the freedom fighting infrastructure in Palestine and in Lebanon. The sooner the Israeli army can use that information, the better. In six hours, two men are coming down to your dungeon to take over guard duty, and when they see their friends unconscious and the cage empty ... well, you understand. By then, I will have driven down to the Negev and put a bullet in my eye. Where my soul goes after that, I hesitate to guess." By the time Hafeez finished those words, we were heading west toward the Jewish part of town.

"Any questions?" he asked.

"Many," Moses said.

"You only have time for a few," Hafeez warned.

"How are the Americans supposed to stop the bombers if we don't have their names or their room numbers?"

"Tell your police to assign their people to the hotels I have given you. Have them look for two or three Arab men leaving the hotel together between 7:45 and 8:15. These men are trained to detonate the bombs if confronted, so they must not be given an opportunity to do so. I would strongly advise your people to fire stun guns immediately at any pair of people who look Arab and male. And they had better not miss. These bombs will kill any person within 60 feet. In a crowded train station, each bomb should be able to kill hundreds of people."

"What proof can I give the Israeli military that your tip is on the level?" Moses asked.

"The two of you are evidence; everyone knows who you are. You can tell them what happened these last several weeks and ask whether they want to have the deaths of thousands of people on their conscience. Plus, if they can access the floppy disks quickly enough, they will learn about our network of safe houses and the like. That would probably be most effective."

I couldn't process this information nearly as quickly as Moses—not given my state of anxiety. But I did have a question, one that Moses surely shared. "Why?" I asked. "Why are you doing this for us?"

"I should think that would be obvious," he said. "Your friend has convinced me that there is no future for my people in a perpetual war with the Jews and the Americans. Weapons grow more and more destructive, and the world grows smaller and smaller. We will all be dead at this rate. I have to do my best to stop it.

"In the process, I am going to make you both heroes—but especially Moses. You, Rabbi Gold, must tell the world what your friend did. And both of you must honor your promises to me from yesterday—about how the holy city of Jerusalem must be shared. When I go into the Negev this afternoon, can I rely on what you said?"

We both nodded. "Absolutely, you have our word," Moses said.

At that moment, we pulled over to the side of the road, less than 200 feet from the Israeli army building Hafeez directed us to enter. Moses held the envelope in his hand.

"I have one last thing to tell you," Hafeez said. "The Prophet Muhammad loved the Jews. He did not reject them, they rejected him—just as they rejected Jesus centuries before. Your people do not take kindly to hearing anyone who speaks outside of your tradition telling his followers that he is closer to God than other men. But you freely allow your Prophets that sort of status. You honor them, just as you reject Jesus and Muhammad.

"I decided to liberate you because I trust both of you. Moses, I trust that you in particular will not rest until you have done everything possible to teach the philosophy of Muhammad to the Western World. Only when they respect Islam as the equal of Judaism and Christianity will your people be able to make peace with mine.

"You must teach your people that each of the Abrahamic faiths has something unique to offer that the others do not. It is not enough to understand your own faith; *every* American, *every* Israeli, and yes, every Muslim, must understand the others as well. You must teach your people about Allah's transcendence, and the importance we place in our devotion to Allah. And you must teach your people that the deepest meaning of *jihad* is the struggle to overcome our own personal inadequacies—our greed, our ignorance, our selfishness. The Prophet made that clear, coming back from the Battle of Uhud, when he said that 'you have now returned from the lesser *jihad*; the greater *jihad* still remains as a duty for you.' Today, I am waging my final *jihad*. I am counting on you to continue that struggle.

"Go now, and accept my gift. Tomorrow, with your help, our peoples shall know peace."

"Hafeez, come with us," Moses said. "You can live in America. You'll get protection."

Hafeez simply shook his head and waved goodbye. "Go!" he said.

"Salaam aleichem, Hafeez Ali," Moses replied, as he left the car. I tried to speak, but before I could form a coherent word, Hafeez was gone.

PART II

CHAPTER VII

*"A word now to Professor George Mothersby. You've told your students that you've been out of college for 60 years and still haven't published a single article, let alone a book. You've told us that to become a tenured professor at one of the world's leading universities, all you had to do was walk into your classroom each day and rhapsodize your heroes. Well, sir, I can say that when I took 19ᵗʰ Century Philosophy from you, all I did was walk into your classroom each day and fall in love with the words and spirit of one philosopher after another. Those classes might have cost me a small fortune in terms of the path I've chosen, but you've taught me that regardless of whether or not it helps you make a profitable living, philosophy is the most practical discipline this university offers. For teaching me that lesson, Professor, you have become one of **my** heroes."*

Moses Levine, from his Valedictory Address
at Columbia University, 1978

New York City—September 1976. During the eighteen years in which Rachel Horowitz and I were married, she was never Moses' friend. And yet, by the time we divorced, it was not clear whose life Rachel had impacted more—mine or Moses'.

I can't speak for him, but when I enrolled in Columbia University in the fall of 1974, I expected to meet dozens of Rachels. Columbia, they say, is the "Jewish Ivy," the most prestigious college in the metropolitan area that dominates Jewish-American culture. So where else but Columbia would you anticipate meeting women, like Rachel, who were wealthy, intelligent, self-confident, feisty, opinionated, and proudly Semitic?

And yet, I didn't meet Rachel at Columbia. In fact, the woman who became my closest female friend there, Lisa Rhodes, was in many ways her opposite. I met Lisa at the same time I met Moses. It happened during a keg party.

In the fall of our nation's bicentennial year, Moses, Lisa and I were juniors. I lived with two roommates off-campus on the corner of 118th and Amsterdam. Moses and Lisa lived in Watt Hall. During meal times, my roommates and I always ate at their dorm, which was one of Columbia's nicest.

Watt's centerpiece was a large hall on the ground floor of the building. The hall was frequently the scene of official university events. For example, I once attended an address there given by the most popular person on campus—Bill Robertson, the Dean of Admissions. On the last Saturday evening in the September of 1976, this same hall was the venue for a big bash. It featured multiple kegs, a pretty nice sound system, and a wide variety of what are now known as "Classic Rock" albums. I'm sure I can speak for virtually everyone in attendance by saying that however many brain cells we had built up that week in the library, we destroyed at least as many on Saturday night.

I came to the party that evening with a friend who I'd met in a class on the history of ancient Rome. "Bud" Borenstein, as he was known, had one of the sharpest and most insightful minds I'd ever encountered. He was also, however, completely boorish when it came to women. That's why I was so surprised when I saw him sitting on a couch, carrying on what appeared to be a pleasant conversation with Lisa Rhodes. Prior to the party, Bud knew nothing about Lisa, but the same could not be said for me. Lisa was, by general consensus, the cutest girl in Watt. She was a natural, surfer-girl beauty, or at least she looked like one. (I doubt she surfed much where she grew up in Vermont.) Lisa "belonged" to Eric Morton, a big Iowa farm boy and the only Columbia Lion headed to the National Football League. I was well aware that as an outside linebacker, Eric could have swiftly mauled me had he caught me looking at his girlfriend for any length of time. That evening, though, I couldn't help but stare at Lisa as she sat back and conversed with Bud Borenstein as if they were old friends.

I must have been fifteen feet away from Lisa when Bud made his move. He lunged right at her and started kissing—or more precisely, *slobbering on*—her face. I froze for a second, and Lisa seemed to do the same. Then I moved my 5'5" 175 pound frame as quickly as possible toward the couch. She was trying to get up, and he was trying to stop her. I could hear her yelling, but I heard Robert Plant yelling even louder (the DJ was playing Led Zeppelin's *Black Dog* at the time). In order to get up, Lisa needed to use all her physical strength … and, as it turned out, mine. Bud was practically on top of her when I grabbed him by the shoulders and yanked until he finally let go of his prey, who sprinted away to the other side of the hall. Within seconds, I could see Eric Morton walking intently in our direction.

"You better get the hell out of here," I told Bud, but he didn't listen. He was quite plastered and couldn't exactly think as clearly as he did in history class. As I looked back toward Eric, I saw Lisa pull him by the arm and point directly to Bud and then to me. All the beer I had drunk that evening couldn't untie the knots in my stomach.

Just then, Moses stepped in front of Eric, and the two stood nose to nose. At 6' 5", Moses was every bit as tall as his friend, although barely half as wide. "*I'll* handle this," he told Eric.

"Get away from me," Eric said.

"Do you want to get expelled?" Moses replied. "Then cool

your jets." He was used to getting his way. At Watt Hall, Moses'
word was the single highest authority. (I do mean Moses Levine,
not his biblical namesake.) He intimidated virtually everyone
with his tall frame, razor-sharp mind and dark eyes. It also
didn't hurt his charisma among a group of East Coast book-
worms that he spoke with a relaxing southern accent.

"Fuck you, Moses," Eric said. "Do you know what that creep
did to Lisa?"

"Back off, man," Moses replied. "You touch him and you'll
never play football again. That's reality, brother. Just let me
deal with this. If I can't take care of this guy, I'll turn him over
to you."

Eric snarled in our direction. Then he made his right hand
into a fist and pounded it into his left. But he allowed Moses to
approach us alone.

"So who's the asshole?" Moses said to Bud and me in his
thickest Birmingham drawl.

I was waiting for Bud to speak. He didn't. "I'm sorry," was all
I could think to say. And it was sincere. I felt responsible for my
friend; it was my idea that he come to the party.

Moses checked me out a bit before responding. "I recognize
you from the dorm cafeteria. Tell me, you think it's cool to grab
a girl like that?"

"No, it wasn't him; it was the other one," Lisa said, agitated.
"This guy actually helped me get away."

"I see. Well then I owe you a debt of thanks," Moses said to
me, before turning to face Bud. "So you're the Don Juan. Are
you a student here?"

"Yes, and a good one, too," I interjected, wanting to say
something on my friend's behalf.

"Really," said Moses. "I bet your parents are very proud."

Bud still wasn't talking.

"Let me see your driver's license," Moses said.

That loosened Bud's tongue. "My *what*?" he said. "Why
should I give it to you? You're not the police."

"Not at all. In fact, I'm your defense lawyer. And the prosecutor's right over there," he said, pointing out Eric. "That's Lisa's boyfriend, you know. He wants to rip your skull open. So let me give you a choice. You can hand your license over to me. Or my friend Eric can come take it from you."

Bud was a bit bigger than I was, but he was no Eric Morton. Nobody on campus was as tough as Eric. Bud knew that, too. Eric's skills on the gridiron were no secret.

Bud thought for a moment and then gave his license to Moses, who took a pad of paper and jotted down some information before returning it. 'I think you'll be getting a call from the Dean of Students," Moses said. "We all want to make sure you don't pull anything like this again."

"Sorry," Bud groaned, as he faced Lisa.

"I think you better take off," Moses said. "Party time's over for the night." Bud began walking away. Before I could follow him, Moses reached his hand out to shake mine.

"I'm Moses Levine," he said.

"R...rich Gold," I stammered. "Good to meet you."

"Rich Gold. A tribesman, huh? Well, Shalom, Mr. Gold."

"Shalom, Moses," I said

"What kind of name is Rich?" he asked. "I bet they don't call you Rich at home."

"No, they don't," I said, smiling.

"Lisa," Moses said. "I want to introduce you to Richie Gold. It is *Richie*, correct?"

"That's what my parents have always called me," I replied.

"Thank you, Richie," she said, warmly. "It was nice of you to help me, especially if he's your friend." I realized then just how stunning she was, and how much intelligence and spirit were reflected through her eyes.

"Tomorrow at lunch," Moses said, "I'd love for you to eat at our table. Bring your friends too—not the groper, but the ones you usually eat with."

"We're a lot better company than that creep you brought tonight," Lisa said.

All my life, I've been attracted to unpretentious WASPy blondes, even more than to Semitic-looking women like the one I married. I've always attributed my taste in women to the fact that I grew up watching TV shows like "Bewitched" and "I Dream of Jeannie." I desperately wanted to marry someone like an Elizabeth Montgomery or a Barbara Eden, and even hoped I could get her to convert to Judaism. But I knew how ridiculous that all sounded. I was a short, stocky, melancholic boy who only had crushes on girls who were leggy, blonde and seemingly well-adjusted. It sounded like a formula for failure. So I kept my fantasies to myself and devoted most of my time to my studies.

When I came to Columbia, I continued to daydream about romancing Nordic goddesses, but they still seemed unapproachable. That changed once I met Lisa Rhodes and was able for the first time to get to know one of those girls as a real human being. I saw that she actually cared about me, and that did wonders for my self confidence.

It didn't take long after the keg party for Lisa, Eric and Moses to accept me into their group. Within a couple of months, the four of us were going off campus together to take advantage of all that New York had to offer.

As the only local of the four, I would sometimes schlep the gang to dinner with my dad and my baby sisters back in Teaneck, or to one of our antique stores in the City. But more often than that, I'd get tickets for the group to a night game at Yankee Stadium. That ball field was then and still is probably my favorite place in the world outside of Jerusalem.

Eric's preferred haunts were the downtown music clubs. He wasn't much into dancing, but he loved listening to rock, blues, folk, jazz, you name it. "Anything but country," he would say. Thank God he had his limits.

Lisa's day trips of choice were to the Midtown art museums. More than once at the Frick, I saw her stare at the same Rembrandt self-portrait for a solid fifteen minutes.

As for Moses, he invariably suggested that we head to Harlem. "It's the liveliest part of town if you know where to go," he'd say. Moses took us to a number of clubs there, but not all of them involved music or dancing. Three times a week, Moses either tutored or mentored at the Boys Club on 129th between 5th and Lenox. The first time the four of us went there, I had expected Eric to be treated like the big football star he was on campus. In fact, however, none of the boys paid him any more attention than they paid to me, whereas they stared at Lisa from the moment she walked into the building. That, at least, I had correctly predicted.

While some Columbia students wouldn't dare go to Harlem for fear of being mugged, that didn't become a concern of mine until the winter of my senior year. One night, Moses and I were walking back from the Boys Club when a short black man pulled out a gun and demanded our money.

"Hey man," Moses said to our assailant, just as I was reaching for my wallet. "We're not your enemy. We come here to help."

"You want to help? Then give me your God-damned money, honky!"

"I'm not a honky, I'm a person," Moses deadpanned. "I treat people with respect. You should too."

Our assailant laughed. "Respec'? Respec' this!" he said, waving his gun. "Now shut up and gimme your wallet!"

Before my friend could respond, I heard a voice from down the street.

"Moses, is that you?" the voice shouted.

Moses needed a second before he could identify it. But when he did, he smiled from ear to ear. "L.J.! L.J. Williams!" Moses called. "Help us out here!"

"What's happenin', my brother?" replied an older black man, approaching us with a smile of his own.

In a quick, smooth motion, our assailant hid his pistol under his jacket and began walking away. L.J. looked at our assailant and shook his head. "Freddie," he said, "where you going?" Freddie stopped walking. "You' a good-for-nothing criminal," L.J. told him. "You' damn right I saw what you're packing.

"And you, Moses. Why are you taking chances with him? He could have blown your brains out. When a bum with a gun asks for money, you give it to him."

"I was going to," Moses said. "But there's a right way and a wrong way –."

"Brother, you're crazier than he is," L.J. said. "A right way and a wrong way? Freddie only knows two ways—begging and mugging. They're both wrong."

"Mind your own business," Freddie said. "This ain't nothing to you."

L.J. smacked Freddie on the head with his open hand. "Like Hell it ain't," he said. "Moses helps out my nephew Jimmie at the Boys Club. He helps a lot of our boys. Sometimes, a few of us pick up Moses at the Club and go out for drinks. He teaches us about growing up in the South as a white man, and what it means to be a Jew."

"L.J., Freddie," Moses said, "this is my friend Richie Gold. In a few years, he's going to be a rabbi. Maybe you two can hear him preach someday."

L.J. smiled and nodded at me before turning back to our would-be mugger. "I don't think Freddie wants to hear anyone preachin'," L.J. said. "Not while he's still playin' with guns."

Freddie walked over to Moses and glared. "So you' a teacher. Why don't you teach me why white folks be preachin' about how everyone's equal in the eyes of the Lord, and then they hog everything for themselves? How's that?"

"If I were you, I wouldn't worry about skin color," Moses said. "I'd worry about finding a job that'll make you proud."

"He can't," L.J. said. "He's too full of hatred. He don't know the meaning of pride."

"I don't believe that," Moses said. Then he turned toward Freddie. "I tell you what. You wanted some of our money, and I'm willing to give you some." Moses reached into the same wallet that Freddie had demanded just a couple of minutes before. "Here's $50. How about you use it on something that'll make me proud I gave it to you."

"Put that money back!" L.J. said, shoving Freddie's outstretched hand away from Moses. "He don't need no handout. He can work."

"Of course he can. But I want him to have it just the same. Freddie, I help out at the Boys Club Monday, Tuesday and Thursday afternoons, starting at 4:30. Why don't you come see me in a few weeks and tell me what you did with my money? I also want to hear about your job."

Freddie took the money and put it in his pocket. "You' crazy," he replied, shaking his head as he walked away.

"Monday, Tuesday or Thursday at 4:30, don't forget," Moses hollered. "I'll be expecting you."

Unfortunately, Freddie never showed up.

After college, I enrolled in a New York rabbinical school, and Moses, Eric and Lisa left the area. That was when Moses went to Atlanta to work for the Southern League Against Poverty, or "SLAP." Atlanta is only a couple of hours drive from Birmingham, which allowed Moses to go home frequently to visit his father, who had never remarried after Miriam's death. SLAP hired Moses as a Policy Analyst and Organizer, and the job was as varied as the title sounds—he analyzed proposed legislation, conducted research, gave anti-poverty speeches, and helped organize regional anti-poverty organizations.

Eric also moved down the Atlantic Coast, but not nearly as far. He became a Washington Redskin. That was tough on me because I grew up loving the Giants, but I wasn't above sharing my loyalties. Besides, I never knew any of the Giants personally, and whenever the Skins came to Giants Stadium, Eric got me a ticket. What choice did I have but to root for his team?

Lisa enrolled in the psychology Ph.D. program at the University of Chicago. A pragmatist at heart, just like my mother, she decided to break up with Eric as soon as she chose her graduate school. She said she wanted the two of them to remain friends but wasn't comfortable being tied down to a man who lived halfway across the country and would be roaming from city to city with a pack of animals. As it turned out, she shouldn't have been concerned. Eric dated a bit, but he never met anyone he loved nearly as much as Lisa, so he kept telling her that after she finished grad school they'd get back together. And that's what happened—once she received her doctorate, she took a job as an Assistant Professor at the University of Maryland. It was the same year I was ordained and accepted a position as associate rabbi at Congregation Beth Hashem, a Conservative Synagogue in nearby Silver Spring. Eric, Lisa and I were reunited.

Eric Morton needed three years of pro ball before he could crack the Redskins starting lineup, but when finally given the chance, he came up huge. In his fourth year, Eric was second in the league in sacks at 14, and followed that up with a ten-sack campaign in which he also forced four fumbles and intercepted six passes. Off the field, Eric was active with a number of charitable organizations, including a group devoted to fighting poverty in the District of Columbia. As an anti-poverty activist, he was able to call on the help of his old friend, Moses Levine, who had been named vice president of SLAP. Local talk shows couldn't get enough of Eric Morton—maniac on Sundays, Mother Theresa during the week. Lisa, the professor, was kvelling with pride, as we Jews like to say.

On December 21, 1986, I was sitting with Lisa in the 20th row of RFK Stadium, right about the 50-yard line. It was cold that day, but she was in a terrific mood. Lisa had come to grips with the fact that she had found the man of her dreams despite what she may have thought when she started grad school, and that man was himself becoming one of the most popular personalities in the world's most powerful city.

Just before kickoff, I noticed a plane flying towards the stadium. It came closer and closer until finally, we could see it displaying a banner. "Lisa, will you marry me? Love, #57." My friend looked at me like she'd just seen a ghost. Then she broke down in tears.

"Go to him," I said.

"Now?"

"Yes, do it."

Lisa ran down to the field as fast as she could. As she made her way to the sidelines, I spotted Eric and saw them hug. The crowd went absolutely ballistic.

When Lisa returned to her seat, we didn't say a word about what happened down below. We simply watched the game, which the Skins won 17 to 14.

I had never been as happy for two people as I was that afternoon—or, should I say, early that afternoon. At 5:00, Eric was in an ambulance, about to enter the grounds of a hospital. He was pronounced dead on arrival.

Hypertropic cardiomyopathy. That's the term the doctors used for what took Eric's life. When he was in college, the sportswriters used to say that he had the heart of a Columbia Lion amidst a pack of house cats. His teams rarely won a game, but he was always in double digits in tackles. As a freshman, Eric showed signs of talent, though nothing earth-shattering. His career picked up dramatically in his sophomore year. He credited it to weight lifting, but as I learned only after he died, Eric's weight training was supplemented by chemicals. They provided the edge he thought he needed to compete at the highest level.

Eric's final game was especially hard-hitting. The Skins were playing the Eagles, a divisional rival that always brought a large contingent of raucous fans. Pumped up by the crowd and the pre-game festivities, Eric tallied three sacks that afternoon and looked fine at the end of the game.

Unbeknownst to Lisa, Eric had a genetic predisposition to cardiac disease. That, combined with the violent collisions of NFL football and the steroids that accompanied his rise to stardom, was a toxic mix. The result was that Eric's heart muscle thickened and his heartbeat became irregular. He saw none of this coming. A few minutes after the Eagles game ended, Eric opened his locker, sat on the bench, and collapsed, never to regain consciousness.

For the next several months, I watched Lisa try to cope with the stresses of being a first-year professor mourning the loss of her beneficent gladiator. It helped that she received plenty of sympathy. The entire D.C. area knew her as *the* Lisa who had received a marriage proposal at RFK stadium for all to see, only to learn that her fiancé had dropped dead a few hours later after taking performance-enhancing drugs. She especially couldn't handle seeing Eric referred to as a "cheater"—perhaps because she herself was wondering whether he had indeed received some sort of cosmic comeuppance. Lisa didn't subscribe to any organized form of worship, but she was religious in her own way, and the notion of karma was hardly foreign to her.

For a while after Eric's death, Lisa was the most important person in my life. I became her confidant, her closest friend, and, ultimately, her lover. We had come a long way from the time back in college when I saw her simply as a jock's appendage who would never think twice about dumpy little me.

As it turned out, I couldn't have been more wrong. Lisa was an extremely deep thinker, every bit as deep as the force of nature I came to know later as Rachel Horowitz. But while Rachel wore her depth on her sleeves—she spoke with authority about a range of disciplines — Lisa usually confined her oratory to the realm of psychology. She'd been that way as long as I'd known her.

More than anyone I've ever met, Lisa loved to analyze people. She was fascinated with how we were raised, how that's affected our development, and what tools we use to nurse ourselves into psychic health or torment ourselves into neurosis. Her obsession with all things psychological partially explained her love for Rembrandt: "the greatest revealer of the mind in the history of art," she would say. It also explained the extent of her devastation when she heard on TV that her fiancé had been doping himself to get a competitive edge. "If I couldn't figure that out about Eric," Lisa told me, "how am I worthy of teaching psychology?"

"Love is blind," I replied. "I loved the guy too. And I had no idea either."

I waited three full years after Eric died before finally asking Lisa the same question that he had asked her on his fateful day. I didn't do my talking with an airplane, but rather with my knees on the ground in her apartment. I told her I would never meet a soul as beautiful as hers for as long as I lived.

Lisa closed her eyes, and her face turned cold. "Aren't you forgetting something?" were the first words she could muster.

"Do you mean our religious differences?"

"Of course. They won't accept me at your synagogue as the rabbi's wife. I'm not a Jew."

"You can convert. Some of the most religious Jews around are converts."

"Richie, we've talked about this over and over again. Don't you understand? *I'm not Jewish.* You know I've thought about converting. I've thought about it a lot. But I can't do it, not if I want to keep my integrity. I can visit your synagogue; I can enjoy your sermons; I can even enjoy some of the prayers. But I'm not part of the Jewish people. How do you put it? I wasn't standing there at the foot of Sinai, watching Moses bring down the tablets and grimacing when he smashed them. I don't believe in any of that stuff, and the symbolism doesn't even speak to me. I'm not the kind of woman you need."

The better I knew Lisa, the more I understood that she was an intelligent, spiritual woman who took to heart Rabbi Akiva's words about loving thy neighbor. Yet despite all the time she spent at synagogue and the strength of our relationship, she still didn't want to be a Jew. I can't tell you how disheartened, even hopeless, that made me feel.

CHAPTER VIII

"People have become so apathetic about injustice and intolerance that whenever someone cries out against those evils, we blame the messenger. Well, I'm sorry to break the news, but if you can look at your society and be satisfied with what you see, you need to pick up the Torah and read. Read Jeremiah, Micah, Amos. Read any of the Prophets. That'll tell you what a Jew is—not some smug fat cat who's always getting his ego stroked, but an environmentalist with a picket sign or a whistleblower with a filed complaint.

"Once the Messiah comes, we can all shut up and relax. Until then, it's time to speak out."

Rabbi Moses Levine, addressing
Congregation Beth Hashem, 2005

Silver Spring, Maryland—February 1987. I've never been above pestering—or being a nudzh, as we say in Yiddish — but even nudzhes have their limits. After a few gut-wrenching weeks of prodding Lisa to accept my marriage proposal, I decided to let it go.

What choice did I have? A Jew should know better than to pressure someone to convert to a new religion. Historically, some of my people were told to convert to Christianity or meet our maker. More benign despots would allow us to leave the country. Others let us stay and keep our faith — if we were willing to be confined to a ghetto. Even in today's America, many of us have been told that if we hope to avoid spending eternal life in Hell, we had better accept Jesus as Lord. Under the circumstances, once my initial attempts to sing Judaism's praises didn't persuade Lisa, I couldn't bring myself to press the issue.

That didn't mean, however, that I could tolerate being alone. Lisa left a void in my heart that I was determined to fill. As a rabbi, I had a definite advantage over other 30ish singles in my ability to replenish the pond. I simply told a congregant who playfully referred to herself as a Beth Hashem *yentah* — meaning a gossip — that my old relationship had ended and I was looking to find a "nice Jewish girl" to marry. I knew that within minutes, several members of the congregation would be hard at work figuring out how to get their rabbi hitched.

The truth is that once Lisa and I called it quits, I felt rotten but had never *looked* better. Given my job title, in certain circles I could almost be considered a catch, which was a far cry from the situation when Lisa and I began dating. Back then, countless people would stare at us, no doubt singing the lines from the old Joe Jackson song: "Is she really going out with him? Is she really gonna take him home tonight?" While there was nothing I could do about my height—it would always be a few inches less than Lisa's—I was at least determined not to be the *butt* of any more jokes. Within a year, I added plenty of muscle and still had dropped 30 pounds. That was the shape I kept until the break-up. Only then did I slowly begin restocking my belly with pizzas and Snickers bars.

In total, I survived eight blind dates in four weeks. Rachel Horowitz was the seventh. Truth be told, I didn't care for her any more than the others, but she apparently saw something in me. She waited several days for a returned call and then, having heard nothing, took matters into her own hands. She came to my synagogue for a Shabbat service and heard me give a sermon on the Binding of Isaac — or the *Akedah*, as the story is known in Jewish circles.

I told my congregation that it had always bothered me to hear people interpret the Akedah as pointing out the importance of obeying God. "Because of this story," I told my congregation, "Abraham has gone down in history as the quintessential servant. His master says 'Kill your son.' And Abraham doesn't need to know why. He heard the command, and that's all he had to hear. "Frankly," I continued, "that Abraham sounds more like a Nazi executioner than a Jew. My Abraham is a little different. He isn't just any Jew, nor is he just any Patriarch. He is the very *first* Jew, a true pioneer. He is the one who saw for himself that only the one eternal source of all beings, living and dead, is worthy of the term 'God.' And Abraham had the will to commit himself to this philosophy when all around him worshiped idols.

"Does that man sound like someone who doesn't ask questions and just follows orders?

"If you want the Akedah to symbolize something meaningful, you don't have to rip apart your image of a great Patriarch. You only have to consider what finally happened, and why. At the end of the day, Abraham didn't kill his son. We learn, in fact, that such sacrifices are contrary to Judaism. The Akedah demonstrates in the most graphic way possible that some conduct is simply unacceptable no matter what the circumstances.

"A great story like the Akedah has many lessons. Perhaps the most powerful is that one generation has no right to sacrifice the next. Most people understand that we're not meant to be our children's executioners, but few appreciate their proper role as *trustees*. Think of the Akedah when businesses spoil the environment. Think of the Akedah when politicians run up the national debt. Think, too, of the Akedah when you contemplate a really good grade-school teacher you once had. That teacher could surely have made more money in another occupation, yet for some reason she chose instead to educate a future generation. She decided to enrich and nurture those who will follow her as adults. So did Abraham."

"Thomas Jefferson wasn't a Jew, but he often wrote like one. In a letter to Madison, he wrote that 'The earth belongs in usufruct to the living.' I'd never heard the term 'usufruct' before I read that letter, but it was the perfect choice. To possess property *in usufruct* means to have both the right to enjoy it for the present and the obligation to preserve it intact for the future. 'Usufruct' is a difficult word; it almost makes you grind your teeth to say it. But that's fitting, because holding the earth in usufruct isn't an easy thing to do. Consuming is fun, and serving as a steward can be frustrating. But Jews have no choice. We owe it to our descendants to let them inherit all the beauty we were given—every species of animal we can befriend, every rose we can smell. This earth, *God's* earth, belongs as much to our children as it does to us, just as Jewish traditions belong as much to us as to those who stood at Sinai with Moses.

"*That*, my friends, is what the Akedah means to me."

Rachel entered the sanctuary that evening about ten minutes after the service began. During my sermon, our eyes made contact on several occasions. Nobody else in the sanctuary listened with such palpable focus. She leaned forward in her seat as if she were witnessing an event, rather than hearing the latest schpiel from Beth Hashem's associate rabbi.

When I saw her during the Oneg Shabbat (the social gathering routinely held after Friday night services), I remarked on how engaged she looked during the sermon.

"I liked it," she said, without cracking a smile. "But I don't want to talk about your sermon. I want to talk about us."

"Us?" I said, thinking that there was no "us" and never would be.

"You weren't going to call me, were you?"

"Oh, I don't know, Rachel. It's not that we had a bad evening together —"

Rachel wouldn't let me finish my sentence. She often didn't.

"I want another shot—tomorrow tonight. I know a little jazz bar on 16th Street just across the D.C. line. The drinks are on me. C'mon, let's go."

I had never looked at myself before as dominatrix fodder. Had I thought hard about what I was getting myself into, I might have had the insight to say no. In any event, we went out the next evening, and she told me all about herself—much more than she had disclosed on our first date. Apparently, my sermon passed some sort of exam she was giving: she wanted to be with a rabbi, but not just *any* rabbi. She needed an inspired one — or so she told me.

I learned that weekend for the first time that Rachel was one of *the* Horowitz's. Everyone in Washington knew the name. Her father, Jerome, was the city's foremost real estate developer. He had built an empire of suburban malls that stretched from Manassas, Virginia up to Randallstown, Maryland, north of Baltimore. Rachel was the sole heir to the family fortune.

She claimed that she didn't talk to potential suitors about her family background for fear that she'd get trapped by a gold digger. "But I trust you," she said. "Besides, my parents are in good health, so I'm not likely to inherit the money any time soon." She told me she earned her MBA from Wharton and worked hard every day managing her family's philanthropic ventures.

"We're among the top ten private contributors to Jewish charities in the world," she said, with more than a trace of pride in her voice. "My parents have always looked down on affluent families who won't share their wealth."

Rachel and I stayed out that Saturday night until closing time. There was an aura of sexiness about her that I'd never felt before from another woman. As I have come to understand over the years, she could flip on that switch almost at will, and then just as quickly flip it off. Rachel has always seemed to know exactly what she wants and how to get it. No doubt, those were traits she learned from her father.

At 5'1", Ms. Horowitz was the first girl I had dated who was several inches shorter than me. She wasn't going to turn as many heads as Ms. Rhodes, but she was hardly unattractive. She had thick dark brown hair, which she wore down to her shoulders, an unmistakably Semitic nose, and beautifully full lips. She worked out regularly; to this day, her muscles haven't lost their tone.

The more time we spent together, the more I felt at ease in her presence and enjoyed her sharp, lively mind. Within a couple of months, Rachel and I had become an item. The following year, we were married. Had Moses and I been in close contact, he might have caused me to reconsider, but my old college friend and I had drifted apart and were essentially out of each other's lives—at least temporarily.

Sadly, that could also describe my relationship with Lisa. The two of us remained friends for a little while after our breakup but soon lost touch, thanks to Rachel. She wasn't comfortable that I had once proposed to Lisa and told me that, if I cared at all about her own psychic well being, I'd put that "Clairol Model" out of my mind. Reluctantly, I agreed.

In the fall of 1987, the Washington D.C. Jewish community, in conjunction with the Government of Israel, co-sponsored an "Israel Day" march and rally on the National Mall. Rachel and I were involved with the pre-event planning and led a group from Beth Hashem in the march itself.

I've always enjoyed marches and demonstrations. It's a shame when a Washingtonian doesn't. The sight of thousands coming together and showing their passion invigorates me, which may explain why I love sporting events so much. But those events celebrate a mere child's game. Marches, on the other hand, highlight some of the most profound issues of the day. Of course, when you're marching about a particular issue, no matter how complex, you convince yourself that anyone who'd disagree with you would have to be either mean-spirited or stupid. Let's face it: if spectator sports are designed for children, marches are for adolescents.

I was feeling especially energized when my congregants and I turned the corner of 14th and H Streets heading south down the hill toward Pennsylvania Avenue. Just then, my ever-vigilant Rachel pointed out some counter-demonstrators on the eastern side of the street further down the hill. We couldn't see them, but we could see the reaction they caused among our fellow marchers. "Nazis!" I heard one of the marchers yell. That started a chant: "Never again, never again, never again."

"C'mon," Rachel said to me. "Let's go mix it up with some anti-Semites. We'll teach the synagogue what it really means to be Jewish."

I told the Beth Hashemites within ear shot that we were taking a pit stop to check out the show off the side of the road. The commotion was centered on a large sign that hung from a maple tree. It read: "PALESTINIANS: THE NEW JEWS OF ISRAEL."

Rachel was livid. She pushed through a screaming crowd until she could get a piece of the action, leaving me in her wake. Then I heard her bellow: "You're a self-hating Jew, aren't you? You people are worse than Hitler."

The response was equally clear, though stated much more calmly and in a gentle southern accent. "I don't hate myself. I don't hate Judaism. What I hate is what our people are doing in its name. It's blasphemy."

I recognized the voice immediately, and I knew exactly where it came from. Just as Rachel had never before met Moses, I had never met his mother Miriam. But she was there in spirit that fall afternoon, questioning Israel's right to treat the Palestinians as somehow *less* than Jewish. Moses was the mouthpiece; his mother, the inspiration.

CHAPTER IX

"One of the things that fascinate me most about our 'War on Terror' is its impact on civil liberties. If we wanted to wage total war, we'd probably turn this nation into lockdown mode. We'd wiretap freely, shoot first and ask questions later, torture prisoners, you name it. Then again, if we did that, we'd have to change our country's name to 'Nazi America.'

"With that in mind, it's easy enough to defend civil liberties. But what about the times when the government gets a credible tip and traditional law-enforcement means won't prevent a terrorist attack? What then? Do we stand on principle, or do we allow law enforcement officials to do whatever it takes to get the job done?

"I'm not sure I'd always answer that question the same way, except to say this: what we can't have is a government that takes extraordinary measures to curtail traditional liberties and then, after the measures are taken, hides them from the media and the public. If we start doing that, I'll know we would have taken this 'War on Terror' way too far."

National Book Award-winning author Moses Levine, appearing on the *Eyes on America* program, 2001

Jerusalem—April 2002. After Hafeez left us at the back of the army building, Moses rang the buzzer and I banged at the door. "May I help you?" said a woman's voice, in Hebrew.

"Shalom," Moses said. "Ani Moses Levine."

"V'ani Richie Gold," I said.

Nothing happened for a few seconds. Then the door opened. We were met by a young female soldier who stared at us, dumbfounded. She obviously recognized our names, and despite our thick beards, she must have recognized our faces as well.

Quickly, our guide, Sgt. Major Esther Silverstein, ushered us inside. She then led us down a corridor, up a flight of stairs, and into a small windowless conference room. It was there that we summarized for the Sgt. Major and her base commander what Hafeez had told us about the bombs. Within minutes, a computer specialist was examining the floppies. By 1:20 p.m. (6:20 a.m. New York time), we had contacted the FBI headquarters in Washington D.C. and provided them the information Hafeez had given us. Unfortunately, they weren't so thrilled with the level of detail. Special Agent-in-Charge Wallace Smithson was particularly blunt.

"Let me get this straight. We don't know who the killers are, what exactly they look like, or where they'll be in the hotels. But you think you've given us enough information to justify shooting random people with stun guns? You've got to be kidding. I don't see a shred of evidence that the tip is on the level."

"I do!" said the Israeli computer specialist who had spent the last several minutes going through Hafeez's computer disks and who had walked in just before Smithson finished venting. "You wouldn't believe what's on these floppies—info on safe houses, info on weapons caches. And I mean *credible* information. I can tell you for a fact that we were about to raid two of the safe houses. I say the tip is legit."

"Interesting," Smithson said. "That might change things.

Give us a minute; we're going to put you on mute." For the next couple of minutes, we heard nothing from Washington.

"Alright," Smithson said, when he returned. "We have what, a little more than 80 minutes before we need people on the ground at those four hotels. I guess we'd better start lining up the teams. Is there anything else I need to know?"

"Just tell your agents how much we trust our source," Moses said. "We know what he went through to tip us off. He gave up his life."

"Or maybe he's just playing us for fools," Smithson said. "We'll find out soon enough."

Moses and I looked at each other and must have thought the same thing. Could it be that Hafeez was going to release us anyway, so he cooked up this idea to terrorize four American cities? No, I decided. He brought us floppy disks, and they apparently contained some decent intelligence. Besides, even granting that we couldn't be certain if he were on the level, there was so much to gain and so little to lose by following his advice.

That, at least, was my perspective. And that, apparently, was the way they looked at the situation in the Boston, New York and Washington offices of the FBI. In Boston, a total of four Arab men were stopped at the front and side doors of the Westin Boston Waterfront hotel, not far from South Station, and shot with stun guns. Two of those men were packing bombs under their shirts. The other two were headed to a convention for hospital administrators. At New York's Helmsley Hotel, less than a quarter mile from Grand Central Station, six men were shot with stun guns. Two were packing bombs. Four were heading for business meetings downtown. At the Washington Court Hotel, only a short walk from Union Station, two men were shot with stun guns and yes, they both were packing bombs.

At the Sheraton University Hotel in Philly, however, no stun guns were used. The Special Agent-In-Charge for the local FBI office, underwhelmed by the grounds for firing any kind of guns, disregarded orders from headquarters. As a result, after two tall Egyptian men walked out of the hotel and toward the 30th Street station, Special Agents directed them to freeze and lift up their hands. One did so, yelling accusations of racism against the agents and creating quite a scene. His partner capitalized on the commotion. He feigned shock and stumbled, but before he fell to the ground, he reached inside his shirt.

More than 100 people were injured on Ludlow Street, and 30, including the arresting agents, were killed.

But yes, it could have been worse — much worse.

The fortnight after we were released from the East Jerusalem dungeon was an absolute shock to my system. Moses and I became the most talked about people in the world—except, of course, for Hafeez Ali.

We spent most of the day of our release at the IDF facility where Hafeez had left us. From there, we were taken to meet the Prime Minister of Israel. He had heard about our part in foiling the terror plot in America, yet he was even more appreciative of the floppy disks we provided. IDF forces had already begun the process of raiding safe houses and capturing weapons caches.

Meanwhile, back in the States, the White House had informed the media that Moses and I had foiled a plan to set off eight bombs in four cities. So the next day, when we arrived at Dulles Airport, we were greeted with a hero's welcome. Dozens of reporters and cameramen were waiting for us, not to mention hundreds of well-wishers. We were escorted right past them and into the stretch limousine that President Forrest had arranged for us. Waiting in the limo were Rachel and the kids. I swear I'll never forget that moment when I climbed into the limo and they surprised me with their smiles.

The driver took us back to our houses so we could get a

good night's sleep and told us that he would pick us up the next morning and take us to see the President. That would have been fine with Moses, but it wasn't with me. I told the driver I needed to spend the first day back with my family.

Nobody likes telling the President of the United States to change his plans in order to accommodate their own. As it turned out, though, Forrest was happy to put off our meeting. While I spent the day with Rachel and our kids, Forrest was in Philadelphia surveying the one scene where American lives were lost and visiting the wounded at a local hospital. That night, every network showed the same clip from the President's brief address on Ludlow Street.

"The men and women whose lives were lost here did not die in vain," he said. "They died as a reminder of what will happen if we don't take seriously the depravity of terrorists. One day, they're flying planes into our nation's greatest landmarks. A few months later, they're trying to kill thousands at crowded train stations. And tomorrow, who knows? Perhaps they'll be trying to assemble weapons of mass destruction that can destroy entire American cities.

"Make no mistake—this is a war, and we'll continue to be at war until we destroy every terror network in the world. I hope the American people have the belly for a fight, because we're going to lose some lives. It's unavoidable. But you saw what happened yesterday — we took *aggressive* measures, we were proactive, and we saved thousands. That's what this war demands. We must take the fight to the terrorists, or they will bring it to us."

I watched that clip with my family, sitting in our living room. Rachel, who had been obsessed with Islamic terror for years, was ecstatic at the thought that our Government might finally have awakened to the consequences of inaction.

Never in my life had I felt so warmly about my wife as I did that night. She was being incredibly affectionate to me, and told me over and over again that it was a miracle I was still alive.

Once she had learned that the other hostages had been brutally murdered, she said, she was convinced she would never see me again. When Moses and I returned safely and were afforded hero status in the war against terror, Rachel didn't merely thank God that our family was reunited. She regained hope that the war against terror was still winnable.

On my first day back in Silver Spring, Rachel mostly wanted to know about the living conditions in the dungeon, and I described them in detail—the bars, the whips, the bedpans, all of it. We didn't, however, talk at any length about Moses' conversations with Hafeez, and I never once mentioned Moses' dreams.

Candidly, the day was spent primarily catching me up to speed on the lives of our children, everything from their school and their friends to their soccer seasons. Only a parent can understand that no matter the magnitude of the triumphs or tragedies in an adult's life, they seem to pale in comparison to even the smallest developments in the lives of one's children.

The next morning, Moses and I arrived at the White House by nine. There, waiting for us, were President Joseph Forrest, the Vice President, an Assistant Secretary of Defense, the Majority Whip of the Senate, and the Speaker of the House. Yes, these men pumped us for information, but mostly they wanted to express their appreciation for our part in averting what could have been a second 9/11. Forrest, especially, was brimming with affection. Near tears, he said to us, "I've never met anyone before who has saved so many lives or has been such a symbol of hope for all of us."

During our White House meeting, I couldn't have had a more receptive audience. My schpiel involved singing the praises of two men—Moses Levine and Hafeez Ali (whose body had by then been found in the Negev). I said that Hafeez respected Moses as both intelligent and open-minded, and wanted to persuade him to advocate repatriating the Jews from Israel back to Europe. Moses, for his part, simply wanted to talk

Hafeez into giving up the cause of violence. The result was that the two men spent countless hours discussing their views, until finally, Moses persuaded Hafeez that violence wasn't the way, and Hafeez became a soldier in the war against terror. I made sure my audience knew that my own role in our escape was basically non-existent. "Those men are heroes," I told them. "I did nothing. But at least I was paying attention, and now I can let the world know what I saw."

Rather than discussing the specifics of our stay in East Jerusalem, Moses turned his attention to broader issues. He wanted Forrest and Company to understand that he stood with them as a fighter against terror, but he was *not* against Islam.

"Terrorism is a cancer, and we have to fight it heart and soul, just like we fought the Nazis," Moses said. "But fighting terrorism doesn't mean we have to demonize terrorists, or that we shouldn't talk to them. Hafeez was a terrorist, and look at all the lives we saved by reaching out to him. I'm convinced we need to open a dialogue with any Muslim group that'll meet with us. We don't have to make concessions we're not comfortable making."

Over the next few weeks, Moses and I kept a low profile; we allowed our "lieutenants" to do the talking, and boy, did we have lieutenants. Every official who had been present at our White House meeting spoke on the air during the next few weeks about the "Heroes of East Jerusalem." Yes, I got some credit even though I neither asked for nor deserved any, and yet I don't doubt that they heard and accepted my central message: the one person to whom they owed the most gratitude was the Osama bin Laden look-alike, Moses Levine.

Never in my lifetime had I seen a living human being lionized more in the media than Moses after we returned from Israel. TV networks played back some of his earlier appearances on American television when he was speaking about *Exodus: Then and Now*. They also interviewed some of his former colleagues at SLAP, who hailed him as a man who hated poverty as much as terrorism. I especially enjoyed the interviews I saw of a couple of Moses' congregants who spoke about the awe inspiring spiritual environment he had created at Temple Akiva, the synagogue he had founded in Maryland after he published *Exodus*. All in all, Hafeez couldn't have asked for Moses to receive a better tribute.

Anyone who knows Moses well must have wondered how, for literally weeks, he could have stayed off the airwaves and allowed others to talk incessantly about him on TV. In fact, however, Moses was busy plotting his agenda for his own return to prominence as a talking head. Part of that agenda was to enlist me as a fellow spokesman for his causes.

Moses' initial public appearance was a two-hour spot on Barney Orloff's *Eyes on America* program, which aired on May 10, 2002, exactly one month to the day after we returned from Israel. He then spoke on six more national telecasts in the next ten days, and I was by his side for three of them.

Moses' agenda during that period was well-defined and consisted of several points. To those who had heard Moses speak at the Jerusalem conference on Moshe Rabbenu or who had grappled with the words of *Exodus: Then and Now*, much of what Moses had to say would have sounded familiar. But let's face it, in mid-2002, our nation had grown accustomed to seeing the mug of a certain tall, bearded, idealistic Semite and thinking of him simply as a fundamentalist war-monger. When Moses Levine, the "War Hero," returned from captivity to make his pitch, both the message and the messenger were jolting and powerful.

First, Moses argued, the President's War on Terror needed to be supported wholeheartedly by the American public and the Congress. Who could deny that there were many in the Muslim world who supported the killing of Americans by the thousands? Our President was a good man who was absolutely committed to protecting us and our allies, including Israel. We needed to trust in his judgment until he proved that he couldn't be trusted.

Second, if we wished to win a war on terror, we needed much more than a capable military. We needed to wage a battle for the hearts and minds of the Muslim world. We had to persuade them that terror wasn't the answer, and that America and Israel could be their friends. And "we" didn't just mean our government; it meant *all* Americans and Israelis. Each of us had a role to play.

Our President's job, Moses contended, was to make sure that he used military means appropriately. He couldn't use force unless it was necessary, and Heaven forbid he'd allow us to be seen as colonizers—Arabs despise nothing more than the image of Christians or Jews trying to take over their land.

The rest of us had a responsibility of our own—to embrace what was beautiful and holy in Islam. The expression "Judeo-Christian values" needed to be expunged from our collective vocabularies. The proper term was "Abrahamic," and it included Islam as much as Judaism and Christianity.

"We all understand Judaism and Christianity at a very basic level," Moses told a national audience, "but most of us don't know anything about Islam except that there was this guy Muhammad who spread the word of the Bible to another part of the world. That's not going to cut it. We need to understand the basic teachings of the Qur'an and the aspects of Islam that make it special—and I mean special in an *appealing* way. Once we show Muslims that we actually understand where they're coming from, more of them will reach out to us as friends."

Third, Moses said, though he was proud to call himself a Zionist, he considered himself a "zionist with a small z." Given the way the Jews came to control the land of Israel—conquering much of what the Arabs had settled and had never agreed to give away—Israel should be relatively small in size, even smaller than it is already. Specifically, Israel should give up all the Occupied Territories, once its security concerns could be adequately addressed, and the city of Jerusalem should eventually be ceded to the United Nations.

"Jerusalem belongs to all the peoples of Abraham," Moses said. "I can think of nothing more in keeping with the generous spirit of my religion than sharing our holiest land with our Christian and Muslim friends." Moses added that he wouldn't simply share the land; he'd proclaim that it should be devoted to promoting all three Abrahamic faiths, both in their uniqueness and in their ultimate harmony. *That* is what would make the land especially holy.

I'd be remiss if I didn't point out just how many people thought that last portion of Moses' agenda was absolute folly — and I'm not simply talking about staunch Zionists. Frequently, he would be chastised not only for giving away the store but for recommending a goal that was as unclear as it was irrational. "What do you mean by internationalizing a city?" he was asked during a televised debate. "Who'd control the schools? Who'd run the criminal justice system? It doesn't sound like you've thought this through."

Moses refused to take the bait. "I'm not going to specify all the details. This is a long-range goal. The Palestinians haven't shown they're ready to be partners for peace, and we haven't shown we're willing to help them get there. Right now, I'd commit myself to an ongoing dialogue with their representatives—whoever they happen to be at the time—and I'd give away large chunks of the Occupied Territories as a sign that the Jews oppose the occupation as much as the Arabs. But I wouldn't give up all the Territories until the Arab world has renounced violence and is prepared to live with the Jews and Christians in peace. And I wouldn't even think about giving away parts of Jerusalem until then. Trust me, we'll have plenty of time to work out the minutiae of who gets to run the city and how. Let's just agree now on the ultimate goal: to offer

Jerusalem as a gift to all the peoples of Abraham, not only the Jews."

Appearing on a show hosted by a Fundamentalist Christian minister, Moses was asked the question point blank: "How is it you have so much more love for the people who kidnapped you than for your own people? Isn't that what they call the Stockholm Syndrome?"

"I would think that if anyone appreciated what I stood for, it would be the disciples of Jesus," Moses began. "Think of First Corinthians, Chapter 13. 'Love is patient, love is kind. It does not envy, it does not boast, it is not proud. It is not rude, it is not self-seeking, it is not easily angered, it keeps no record of wrongs. Love does not delight in evil but rejoices with the truth. It always protects, always trusts, always hopes, always perseveres.'

"What that tells me is that the best way to fight a war is with love. It's certainly the best way to end a war. Jesus knew that loving your enemy isn't always easy. But what's the alternative? Pinning your enemy into submission? The Allied Powers thought they could do that to the Germans after World War I. Look what happened twenty years later."

Finally, as the crown jewel of his agenda for peace, Moses announced that he was starting an organization known as Peoples of Priests, or POP. The name was based on a statement in the Torah that the Jews shall be a "kingdom of priests and a holy nation." Moses took a little liberty in calling one billion Muslims a *people*, but it was necessary to get his point across.

"POP will honor two groups that have been misunderstood and underappreciated by the world: the Muslims and the Jews," Moses said. During each of his public appearances, he appealed for funding from anyone who shared his philosophy. On the last of our joint appearances, I announced that I would personally contribute $20 million of my own assets as seed money.

It was at that moment that my marriage effectively ended.

CHAPTER X

"I've always thought that in every generation, the perfect opportunity comes along for one person representing one movement to fight injustice. In the mid-1950s in the South, black people were treated like an inferior species, and then came Martin Luther King. In the early 1970s, women were looked at as the weaker sex. But then Billy Jean King beat Bobby Riggs at tennis, and now, only the Cro-Magnon men among us condescend to women.

"So what about today? Is there a man or woman whose time has come? I won't suggest a name—only a movement. We need a person representing Islam to show the world what that religion is all about. I'm talking about moderate, spiritual, peace-loving Islam, not the crazed, violent off-shoot we keep hearing about on the news. As president of POP, I'll do my best to explain the beauty that Islam has brought to my life. But I look forward even more to seeing one of my Muslim colleagues take over where I've left off. My goal is to ensure that POP produces an Islamic thinker who's more recognizable in the U.S. than any advocate of terrorism."

Moses Levine, president of Peoples of Priests,

kicking off POP's "Singing the Other Guy's Praises"
campaign, 2002

Silver Spring, Maryland—April 2002. Prior to my fateful trip to Israel with Moses, Rachel and I got along well. Sure, we fought sometimes, but our relationship seemed basically stable. In the dungeon, I missed her intensely, and during my first few days back in Silver Spring, I remember feeling incredibly lucky to have such a devoted wife.

Everything began to unravel when I revealed to Rachel some of the details of Moses' conversations with Hafeez. To me, those conversations were sacred; to Rachel, they were obscene—especially when Moses repeated his commitment to the idea that Jerusalem should become an international city.

"You know, at one point I actually wondered if I had sold that guy short," Rachel said, "but he's the same self-hating Jew he always was. So what if he managed to get a terrorist to back down? Look how he did it — by promising to go on TV and sell out the Jewish people. Some hero," she scoffed.

No, I didn't dare report to Rachel my own promises, but I did defend Moses'. "Honey," I said, "his position can be supported by Jewish law. You can't call him self-hating just because he understands Jewish values differently than you do."

"Are you kidding?" she replied. "Jerusalem's the heart and soul of Israel. Is he proposing to internationalize Mecca?"

"There's no dispute over Mecca. But there is a tug-of-war being fought over Israel, and Jerusalem's the prize. Without a compromise, they'll be fighting forever."

"And the compromise is to make sure that the Muslims have tons of holy land, the Christians have tons of holy land, and the Jews have next to nothing. Yeah, that works."

"When you think about it from his perspective, it does," I said. "I've been teaching for years about the Jewish philosophy on wealth. The key is that we only need so much wealth, and what we don't need, we should share. We don't *need* Jerusalem half as much as the world needs us to share it. "

"You're so stupid sometimes, Richie. Why should we be the ones to share? Both the Christians and Muslims have a whole lot more than we have. Let *them* share."

"We have to set an example."

"Of what? How to commit national hara-kiri?"

"Of how to practice what we preach!" I said, in a rare instance of raising my voice to Rachel during one of our debates. "Judaism is all about sharing. You learned that from your parents. Even the poor people who get charity are required to give alms. Plus, there are mitzvot in the Torah about sharing land. There's the requirement that the Jewish farmer leave the corner of his fields for the poor. And there's the *Yovel* [the jubilee year]."

In Biblical times, poor people often had to sell their land because they needed the money. The Yovel provides that every 50 years, all that land was returned to its original owners. Obviously, that helped to demonstrate that every piece of land ultimately belongs to God, but it was also a way of minimizing social tensions between those who have wealth and those who don't, which is exactly what Moses was trying to accomplish.

I pointed out to Rachel that the State of Israel had been around for more than 50 years, and yet there had never been a true jubilee year. The Palestinians who lived in Jerusalem before the Jews took over were never given their land back, and now you have a country where the Jews are well off and the Palestinians are mostly very poor. "That's not a Jewish state in the religious sense of the word," I said.

"You've lost touch with reality," Rachel replied. "It's like you've forgotten everything your mother taught you."

"Not at all. I've just learned a thing or two since she passed away."

Rachel rolled her eyes and ended the conversation, but she didn't threaten to leave me. That only happened when I brought up the issue of giving seed money to POP. Rachel may not have insisted on a prenuptial clause but that's not to say she felt I had an equal claim to the family fortune. I begged and pleaded with her to consent to a substantial donation, but she wouldn't. "I'm not a zionist with a small z," she said. "My Z is pretty damned large. I could give up parts of the West Bank and the entire Gaza Strip, but like hell if I'm going to give up on Jerusalem — ever!"

Despite Rachel's threats, I signed a check for $20 million. The donation stunned her, as I knew it would, but what choice did I have? I had pledged to Hafeez to support the cause that he and Moses agreed on in East Jerusalem. In return, Hafeez had given up his life and saved countless numbers of Israelis and Americans. Twenty million dollars was but a tiny fraction of my family's net worth. Paying that amount seemed the least I could do under the circumstances.

Before I turned over the check, I had told my wife that Moses had saved me from a horrible death, and I felt compelled to give him the money. She replied that if I did, our marriage was over. I don't think she really believed I'd go ahead with the gift, and I definitely didn't think she'd make good on her threat. But when she heard me announce my donation on the air, I returned that evening to find that she'd packed her bags and whisked away our children to a friend's apartment. We never again lived together as a family.

POP first opened its doors for business on July 1, 2002. During the first few months of its existence, my life could only be described as surreal. My wife of fourteen years had recently left me and taken our children with her. While I believe strongly enough in the privacy of children to leave my own kids out of this narrative as much as possible, suffice it to say that having them snatched from me overnight was as painful as anything I had to endure in East Jerusalem.

To make matters worse, Rachel was pressuring me to leave

our house and allow her and the children to move back. I was, after all, living in a mansion that had been paid for by the Horowitz fortune—it spanned 12,000 square feet and was built on a ten-acre lot. I seriously thought about playing the "gentleman" and leaving, but decided that the best way to get my family back was to plant myself in the family estate in the hope that Rachel would return. I should have known that the stubborn mule would refuse, and that I would end up living alone for years in what would soon feel like a mausoleum.

Back then, the strangest aspect of my life was that I was treated like a beloved celebrity whenever I left the mansion. Passersby on the street greeted me with thanks for helping to foil the Great Train-Bombing Plot. And my congregants were warmer to me than ever, especially after they found out about my marital problems. They must have thought of me both as a mensch and a family man, and blamed Rachel for our separation. This was easy enough to do because Rachel never publicized the reasons for our split. She simply took off, leaving me without kids but with a note. It told me to expect from her a written proposal on child custody and estate distribution issues, and requested that we not see each other for another eight weeks, "just like the last time we were separated; only this time, I won't miss you."

Looking back, I sometimes wonder why I didn't feel like a complete fraud. What kind of man spends millions of dollars that his wife brought to their marriage without her consent? And how can such a man be universally revered in his community? There's only one reason I was able to maintain my pride during that period in my life: I closely monitored the fruits of my $20 million donation and witnessed the blessings it bore.

"Peoples of Priests" was 100 percent Moses' brainchild. He founded the organization to foster bonding between Jews and Muslims in a manner that celebrated the highest principles of humankind. POP was devoted to the idea that the leaders of Jewish and Muslim communities have no monopoly over the

wisdom of their faiths. POP's charter cited the need to honor
the uniqueness and capabilities of every Jew and Muslim.
Laypeople must think openly and deeply about the great
issues of religion, Moses argued, and clerics must assume that
laypeople can grasp religious concepts at a relatively high level.
"Challenge them!" Moses liked to say.

Even now, it's difficult not to look back wistfully at POP's
early days. Moses quickly assembled a team of empathetic
intellectuals who shared a deep appreciation for their Jewish
or Muslim roots. They opened up offices in various American
cities. The three largest were in D.C., New York, and Los
Angeles. Moses wanted a major presence in those cities so that
he could lobby Congress and flood the national media outlets
with POP's ecumenical message.

I took an immense measure of pride in hearing about some
of POP's early initiatives. Each involved a tribute to a particular aspect of Jewish or Muslim culture. But here was the
key: in every case, Moses picked a Muslim representative to
lionize Jewish culture and a Jewish representative to lionize
Islamic culture. As it played out at conferences and on TV,
Moses' "Singing the Other Guy's Praises" strategy was a thing
of beauty.

Some examples of this strategy in action will remain forever
etched in my mind. Moses persuaded an Algerian-American
professor to take a sabbatical from his job at Emory University
and give talks on the endearing beauty of Jewish humor. Moses
also tapped an Egyptian who taught U.S. history in a Rockville,
Maryland high school to discuss the incredible accomplishments
of the Jewish people and the continuing dangers of anti-Semitism. To discuss such Jewish theological giants as Buber and
Heschel, Moses brought in a Lebanese-American woman who
had been a tenured philosophy professor at Columbia. She
didn't come cheaply, but she was well worth it.

On the other side of the ledger, I watched one rabbi after
another toast the magnificence of the Islamic religion and

attempt to sever from the American consciousness the association between Islam and violence. I personally contributed the name of a comparative religion scholar who had taught me at rabbinical school. He became POP's voice on Islamic values.

POP's most visible pro-Islamic spokesperson was none other than Moses Levine. It was through his warm, reassuring baritone and Osama-like face that millions of Americans came to appreciate Islam for the first time.

"I owe my belief in God to Islam," Moses acknowledged on the Harry Ripley show. "In rabbinical school, I was still shaky in my faith until I met a brilliant Muslim named Ismail. He taught me to revere God in a way that made God *real* to me, and not just a set of human ideals." Moses went on to explain that after meeting Ismail, he sought out other Muslim sages and found a philosophy of God that was less anthropomorphic than anything he'd heard about in mainstream Judaism or Christianity.

"Genesis talks about how God created man in God's likeness," Moses pointed out. "But the Qur'an says 'There is nothing whatever like unto Him.' I prefer what it says in the Qur'an.

"The Qur'an directs us not to limit Allah *in any way*, or to treat Allah as some sort of superman. It calls Allah the 'One and Only … the Eternal, Absolute. He begets not, nor is He begotten.'"

Moses then spoke about how Allah never takes human form. In fact, he said, no religion works harder than Islam to remove the human form from the holiest of places. The idea is to fight any tendency to associate Allah with our own image.

"Think about the word 'God,'" Moses said. "I adore this word above every other — and not the Hebrew words for God but the English word. I love it so much because it's flexible. It is subject to all sorts of modifications—godlike, godsend, gods, goddesses, you name it. That allows people to have different senses of divinity and still communicate our love for God to one another. As a pluralist, that appeals to me.

"But there's something really special and awe-inspiring about the word *Allah*. Whenever I hear the word, I'm reminded of why I love Islam so much. 'Allah' is a unique word—there's no masculine form, feminine form or plural form. You never hear people say "Allah the Father." You only hear the one word, *Allah*, which signifies uniqueness. Uniqueness and transcendence."

At that point, Moses became overcome with emotion and couldn't talk.

"You OK?" Ripley asked.

"I was just thinking about how beautiful … how peaceful it can be to remove all earthly concepts from our idea of God," Moses said. "When I take the time to contemplate pure divinity—limitless, eternal, ubiquitous, mysterious, grand-beyond-the-largest-scale—only then can I truly relax. Islam, if you really understand it, gives you that feeling. It directs us to worship the God that is — not our own ideals projected onto some man-made deity, but *Allah* — the one and only, the one who is both immanent *and* transcendent. Allah is here, Allah is everywhere, Allah is unbounded."

Moses went on to talk about what an amazing experience it was to join together with a group of Muslims and pray to the one God. "The first time I prayed in a mosque," he said, "I noticed the Muslims praying more intensely that I'd been accustomed to seeing from Jews or Christians. That made me wonder why that was. Well I'll tell you why — it's because they viscerally appreciate the greatness of God. Not the *likeness*, the *greatness*."

At that point, Moses let go of the look of awe and took on a tone of frustration. "God's essence," he said, "is so far above our comprehension that when we describe *God's will* we betray our principles. Yet that's exactly what people do whether they're Jews, Christians or Muslims. And yes, Muslims do it too. It's not like they're all sages, now is it?

"So many people of every faith can't seem to resist the temptation to turn God into a man. We succumb to the power that can be seized by taking God's name and manipulating it for our own purposes."

Moses' final statement on the topic to Ripley was perhaps his most emotional: "When I think about the golden ages of Jewish philosophy — it's no coincidence that many of our brightest minds lived among the people of Islam. Now look at us. Jews and Christians throughout the world have let terrorists hijack not only their understanding of Islam, but even the name of *Allah*. Who's being ignorant here? Tell me, *who*? Hafeez Ali came to understand the truth about Islam. Why can't the rest of us?"

CHAPTER XI

"You don't throw out the baby with the bathwater. You don't give up altogether on gainful employment just because you hate your job. You don't quit on marriage just because your spouse does something you dislike. So then why stop searching for God just because the old formulation is antiquated?

*"It's easy to justify giving up on the search by saying that we don't **need** God. But is it wise? The truth is that none of us need God. Then again, we don't need much. We don't need love. We don't even need to consume food through our mouths; we could survive simply by taking in fluids intravenously. The question is why would we **want** to?"*

Rabbi Moses Levine, addressing Temple Emanu-El, 1995

Washington, D.C.—October 1987. I'll never forget that moment in 1987 when I first recognized Moses' voice at the pro-Israel demonstration. I followed Rachel to where he was standing, flanked by two Semitic brunettes who had been yelling at some of my congregants as they walked down 14th Street. Then I waited until our eyes met and I noticed his own look of recognition.

"Moses? Are you out of your mind?"

"Rabbi Gold! Shalom!" he replied. "Ladies, I want you

to meet my old friend Richie Gold. He's now an illustrious Conservative rabbi."

"Good to meet you," said one of the women, reaching out to shake my hand. She was as civilized to me as she had been nasty to some of my congregants only moments before.

"I can see this is a sign from Hashem that we need to get back in touch," Moses said. "Give me your phone number."

I gave it to him. Then I asked if he could explain why he was standing on the side of a road with a provocative sign hailing the Palestinians as Jews.

"Think about it," Moses said. "They live like second-class citizens on their own land. They're treated like they're sub-human even though most of them are non-violent and hard-working. And they pray to the *one* God—a pure monotheistic God. They sure sound like Jews to me."

Rachel started arguing with Moses, but I pleaded with her to let me talk to him alone, and after giving Moses a glare from several circles deep in Hell, she walked away.

"Moses," I said, "you're complaining about Jewish injustice and oppression. But it's precisely because you're Jewish that you care so darned much about injustice and oppression. Don't you get that?"

He thought for a moment before responding. "Let's say I agree with what you just said. That doesn't excuse the Israeli Government."

"The Israelis are in a snake pit," I continued. "They're acting as humanely as possible under the circumstances."

"That's propaganda. You've been listening to too many Israeli apologists."

"We've got to talk," I said, shaking my head. "And I mean that on different levels. Call me."

I heard from him a week later. He managed to surprise me almost as much during the phone call as he had during the march.

"So Richie," Moses said, "guess what I'm doing with myself these days."

"You're not at SLAP any more?"

"No, I am. But I won't be for long. You've got to guess where I'm going."

"Hollywood?"

"Pretty close. I'm applying to rabbinical school."

"You're kidding."

"Seriously, I've got my heart set on Hebrew Union College. I'll do my first year in Jerusalem and the last four in New York."

I cross-examined Moses for at least a half-hour about his new ambition. How could I not? In college, he had always ridiculed me for wanting to be a rabbi at some "cathedral synagogue." That's a term used in American-Jewish literature to lampoon modern shuls as places where well-heeled narcissists pretend to practice the same faith as the poor Semitic peasants and peddlers who kept their communities together for thousands of years.

What's more, Moses had also argued with me about my theistic beliefs. "I don't get how you can worship God if most of your family died in the Holocaust," he would say. "Do you really believe He was punishing their souls—maybe for bad acts in their previous lives?"

Of course I didn't believe that, or that I was able to discern God's will in sending Hitler into our world. But I couldn't help but notice that soon after Hitler departed, we were given a country of our own. Maybe, I thought, God was behind all that. Who was I to say He wasn't?

"What made you want to be a rabbi?" I asked my friend, once it became clear he wasn't pulling my leg.

"It wasn't a *what*; it was a *who*. I met an old man in Atlanta named Charlie Willis. He begs on the street for most of the day. The rest of the time he writes philosophy. He calls himself a street-philosopher."

"I take it he's Jewish?" I asked.

"No, he's African-American."

"And he suggested that you become a rabbi?"

"I figured that out for myself, with his help. We talked about all the complacency in America—how people have become addicted to their comforts, and how little they seem to be bothered by all the suffering around them."

"And you're going to save their souls?" I asked, skeptically.

"Oh, nothing that grandiose. Charlie and I thought about how I could become an effective gadfly, that's all. What's the best way to shake people up who've stopped caring about anyone but themselves and their family? Why not grab myself a pulpit?"

Moses might have chosen his profession in order to become a gadfly, but I had very different goals in mind. I wanted to express my love for Jewish culture and spirituality, and minister to the needs of individuals. I hadn't thought much about being a scholar, but upon entering rabbinical school, I realized that if I wanted credibility as a rabbi, I had better soak up information like a sponge. I'd have to become an expert in the Torah and Talmud, be nearly as familiar with Jewish history and philosophy, and at least be conversant about the holy books of the other world religions.

As a result, I've always known more facts than Moses about most religious topics. It's not that he was ever ignorant about them; he simply had different priorities in life than digesting and imparting information. Moses never cared to inform as much as to *inspire*. And when he entered rabbinical school, he knew that before he could inspire anyone else, he needed to become inspired himself.

In typical fashion, he found that inspiration on the streets of Jerusalem.

When Moses met Ismail Safieh in 1988, Ismail operated a small falafel stand. Moses patronized the stand each day right before school. They didn't talk much at first, but gradually Moses would arrive earlier and earlier so that he and Ismail could converse about the Arab-Israeli conflict, American politics and other world affairs. Within a few weeks, Moses had built up Ismail's trust, which earned him an invitation to Ismail's home in the West Bank town of Bethlehem. That's where Moses learned that Ismail's greatest interest was not in the culinary arts, or even politics, but rather in mysticism. Ismail associated himself with an Islamic sect known as the Sufis.

Ismael, who had recently turned 70, explained that he had been studying with a Sufi teacher, or "murshid," for decades. He claimed to have learned many teachings from his murshid, but none more important than the idea that every existing being or thought is connected to every other as part of the same fabric or substance—the past as well as the future, the object as well as the subject, the "good" as well as the "bad." From this basic truth, he said, the essential teachings of all the great religions can be derived.

Despite his occupation, Ismail looked the part of a professor, sporting a long grey beard that Moses said was especially eye-catching on a man barely five feet tall. Ismail was not only extremely learned but also had quite a faculty for charming those around him. That was evident, Moses said, when he visited Bethlehem and witnessed one townsperson after another approach Ismail with hugs, questions or simply a warm word.

Moses shared with me the contents of his talk with Ismail in Bethlehem. "It was probably ..." he paused. "No, it was *definitely* the most critical day in my intellectual development," Moses said.

As soon as Ismail told Moses that he was a Sufi, Moses replied that his basic concern from the moment he arrived in Jerusalem was how to approach the concept of God. "I'd love to believe in God," Moses said to Ismail, "but just look around—all the poverty, the fear, the hatred. Does this look to be the product of a god?"

Ismail laughed when he heard those words. "Why do you let ignorant people define the great words for you?" he finally responded. "I do not pray to some sort of master architect who plans everything to maximize our happiness. I think of Allah simply as the *One*. Maybe I should say *the One and Only*."

Outside of Allah, Ismail continued, there exists nothing at all — no creation separate from the creator. That separate-creation idea is a teaching for children. The truth is that Allah is not separate from the world; the world is *in* Allah.

Ismail's words didn't confuse Moses, but his confidence in them did. Moses asked how Ismail could be so sure that there is complete unity in the cosmos.

"First of all, do not confuse faith with certainty," Ismail said. "Secondly, I am not proselytizing. I cannot give you faith in anything you do not want to have faith in. But I will tell you my secret: I am not hampered by tribal fever. This is the curse of the Jews. It explains why so many of you have forgotten Allah. You will not forgive Him for abandoning your tribe."

Moses, to his credit, asked Ismail if "tribal fever," to use his words, wasn't universal. "Don't your people have this notion of 'Manifest Success' — this idea that Muslims will triumph in this world because of God's will, and that this has been manifested through their success in great battles and their dominion over much of the globe?"

"Very good," Ismail replied. "You have looked a bit into our religion. Most American Jews know almost nothing about it. Neither do your Christians. They come on a pilgrimage to my town, expecting to soak in the spirit of Jesus, the 'Prince of Peace.' But they are not willing to work for peace. That requires sharing the wealth, and they do not want to share the wealth any more than the Jews do."

"Or the Muslims," Moses added.

"Perhaps the Sufis are different; at least I hope we are. In any event, we are only a small minority, and we have so little wealth to share."

Such type of banter would have interested Moses on any other day, but not then. He wanted to hear more about how Ismail came to embrace the idea of God. Ismail credited his Muslim upbringing.

According to Ismail, Muslims are taught that a human being is Allah's servant, not the other way around. The Christian God exists to save the souls of the faithful; the Jewish God to protect the Hebrews from the army of the Pharaoh. But Allah exists for Himself—and it's our job to honor Him regardless of the consequences. He alone is at the center of the world, not our leaders, and not even the Prophet.

Moses wondered if Ismail wasn't overly romanticizing Islam. But Moses kept his cynicism to himself and stayed focused on learning Ismail's philosophy.

When Muslims are young, Ismail continued, they learn two fundamental things about Allah. First, that He's absolutely unique and incomparable. And second, that He transcends our world. The rest they must figure out for themselves, any way they can.

Ismail told Moses that he came to his idea of divinity from the notion of humility. The more humble he became, the more he appreciated the power of all that transcends us—not only our bodies and minds, but every dimension of reality we're able to perceive. We are in no position, Ismail said, to characterize Allah—to assume, in other words, that He has human-like emotions or thoughts. We are certainly in no position to assume that we understand Allah's limitations.

Ismail decided that the only respectful approach, given our own minimal capacities in relation to the universe, is to conceive of Allah so as to maximize His greatness. We can imagine the existence of a being that is infinite, eternal, and ultimate in every way—one whose substance unifies and engulfs all that exists. The multiplicity we observe is surely transcended at some level that we can't understand, just as that level might itself be transcended by something else, and so on. So why not adopt a belief in cosmic unity? And, because that unity is surely worthy of our deepest veneration, why not attribute to that unity the name of *Allah*?

Ismail recognized that we can't relate as easily to his God as we could to the divine Superman a child worships. But this, he said, is a small price to pay to maintain our integrity.

"A man's integrity should be his most guarded asset," Ismail said. "He should always be a voice of truth, and he should never delude himself, no matter what the circumstances."

One day, when Ismail was still a teenager, he decided to stop thinking about animals, vegetables and minerals as isolated beings and concentrated instead on viewing everything he encountered simply as expressions of a single divine power. He went through this exercise continuously from sunrise to sunset. Whenever he felt his mind wander, he went back to meditating on the name of Allah, and was soon able once again to endow his world with divinity. A kitten became Allah's kitten, a tree became Allah's tree, and an idea—*any* idea — became Allah's idea.

Gradually, "Allah" stopped seeming like a remote concept, and by the end of the day, Allah had become the most relevant, compelling idea in Ismail's consciousness. But that was just the beginning of Ismail's spirituality.

The greatest gift in life, Ismail explained, is to be able to summon the idea of divinity to our *hearts*. It is one thing to view living beings intellectually as expressions of Allah; it is quite another to encounter them emotionally as divine beings.

When we perceive Allah's unity in all finite things and creatures, Ismail said, we experience them as part of the most beautiful, awe-inspiring being of all. And we also begin to recognize ourselves as divine vessels occupying a unique and cherished place in Allah.

You don't need to cultivate these emotions in order to experience love, Ismail added, but when you do cultivate them, you experience a type of love that can be summoned in more

places and at more times than any other. The love of Allah as
the foundation of life is true love. While it might toss about in
the wind, it will always stay afloat. Perhaps it is the only kind
of love that we can say that about—even the love of natural
beauty can be extinguished once the eyes and ears go bad and
the imagination dims. But the love of the divine shall last as
long as we revere the name of Allah. That one word—that one
symbol—when it becomes a strong enough object of our focus
is enough to fill our hearts with warmth and reverence about
the beauty of life.

Moses sat for hours in Bethlehem questioning Ismail about
his beliefs and spiritual practices. That was Moses' day to soak
up information like a sponge. In addition to hearing about God,
he was also told about Ismail's understanding, commonly held
among Sufis, that human beings are the product of thousands
of reincarnations.

"The soul," Ismail explained, "evolves to more and more
complex forms. Our next stage of evolution is to recognize our
own true nature and learn to live at peace with it. But that
requires learning first to live in peace with the world."

"You don't mean accepting the world as it is, do you?" Moses
asked.

"I am talking about accepting the world as a manifestation
of Allah's nature," Ismail replied. "But we must still work hard
to help it evolve over time into higher and higher states, just as
our own individual soul evolves from one body to the next."

Moses told me that by the time he got home that evening,
his mind was exhausted. "I didn't know which way was up," he
said. "I only knew that my destiny involved evaluating everything Ismail taught me."

I'm sure Moses was looking forward to many more meetings
in the town of Jesus' birth. But they were not to be. Two weeks
later, the falafel stand was closed forever. Ismail had suffered a
heart attack and died.

CHAPTER XII

"I can only imagine how it must have felt to serve in World War II. Our soldiers in that war represented a nation that had long stood for democracy, freedom of the press, religious liberty, and economic opportunity. And they took the power that comes from those principles and used it to stop genocide halfway across the world. What an honor it must have been to fight in that war, for that flag.

"But not all wars are like that one, are they? And just as there's nothing more beautiful than watching this nation use its power appropriately, there would be nothing uglier than watching us abuse the military might we've acquired. When you're the most powerful nation in the world, the one that others look to for leadership, you must never, ever come across as a schoolyard bully. Every time that happens, we all move a giant step closer to international anarchy, and I shouldn't have to remind you of the consequences of that."

Rabbi Moses Levine, speaking at a conference
of the Veterans of Foreign Wars, 2006

Silver Spring, Maryland—September 2001. On September 10, 2001, Americans thought they were as secure as the Swiss.

By 10 a.m. Eastern time the next morning, they finally understood a bit of what it was like to be an Israeli.

I began getting calls from my friends in Tel Aviv and Jerusalem almost immediately after the towers fell. They were commiserating, to be sure, but I could tell that there was more to their reaction than sorrow. They also sensed that America was about to become the loyal ally their country had long hoped we'd be. No longer would we complain when the Jewish state fought back against terrorism. No more would Middle East terrorism be seen as evidence that there was something wrong with *both* groups of Semites, Arab and Jew. Now, at last, America would recognize what Israelis had been talking about for years: that militant Islamic fundamentalism was a cancer and could only be destroyed by oncologists armed with powerful weapons.

Rachel was paralyzed at first, but she soon regained her fighting spirit. "We've got to declare war on those bastards," she said, referring to the enablers of the suicide bombers in Afghanistan and throughout the Muslim world. "If America and Israel work together, we can blow the whole lot of them back to the Middle Ages."

I reacted less with aggression than with fear. Nine-eleven seemed to me like the first stage in the realization of Moses' dire prophesy from *Exodus: Then and Now*, that the more we develop technologically, the more devastating our weapons will become.

Yes, 9/11 turned Moses into a bit of a prophet, but he didn't exactly feel like gloating about it. In fact, it depressed him on many levels, including the fact that it condemned him to having to listen to one smart-aleck after another remind him of how much he resembled the man of the moment, Osama Bin Laden. Personally, I would have shaved my beard in a flash. But not Moses. He didn't alter his appearance in the slightest. "I'm going to set an example for America," Moses preached from the pulpit. "I'm not going to run from that madman. I'm not going to change what I like about myself, and nobody else should either. It's fine to take some extra precautions, but we shouldn't give up our fundamental freedoms or our way of life—and we certainly shouldn't get facial makeovers."

In the months after 9/11, Moses came across as anything but the "stupid pacifist" that Rachel called him when she finished reading *Exodus*. He was once again a fixture on TV, in part because of everyone's fascination with his face. And on these appearances, his main thesis never varied: the nation must stand up to what he called "al-Qaeda's robbery of Islam's beauty."

"Violence should always be the last resort," Moses said, while appearing on the Harry Ripley show, "but sometimes we have to resort to it. Ecclesiastes said there is a time for every experience under heaven — a time for loving, for hating, for war, for peace. I don't agree that there's ever a time for hating. There are times for war, though, and this is one of them.

"We've got to stop al-Qaeda before it strikes again, and that means we have to break down its support system. The longer we wait, the more vulnerable we'll appear. Just remember that our war must be against al-Qaeda and the Taliban, *not* Islam. Our ability to empathize with Muslim moderates is the strongest weapon in our arsenal."

Moses could sound like a military man one moment and a peacenik the next. No sooner did he stop blasting the insanity of suicide bombing than he flew to the defense of a comedian who was fired from a network talk show for disputing the idea that the 9/11 bombers were "cowards."

"Call them misguided, treacherous, crazy … call them evil, if you'd like," Moses said, during a televised debate. "But don't distort who they are. That just makes us look stupid. Do we say the Nazis killed twelve million Jews when in fact they only killed six? So why do we call these bombers cowards when one of the most undeniable facts about them is their courage?"

Moses went on to credit the suicide bombers with a number of other qualities that people tend to respect; he called them organized, passionate, proud, and resolute. And, Moses added, they were able to tap into a large reservoir of anti-Western sentiment. "These people are formidable," Moses said. "We dare not underestimate them."

During the immediate aftermath of 9/11, Moses became friends with another recognizable person—perhaps the only man whose celebrity rivaled that of Osama Bin Laden. I'm referring, of course, to President Joseph Forrest.

Forrest and Moses were natural rivals, or so it would have appeared on the surface. Forrest was reliably conservative, a Republican, and anything but bookish. Moses was unpredictable but generally liberal, a Democrat, and a recipient of the National Book Award. Forrest was a traditional born-again Christian; Moses was a heretical Jew. Forrest promoted a tax cut package that would disproportionately help the wealthy; Moses argued for changes in the tax code to relieve many of the burdens on the poor.

Despite their differences, though, 9/11 joined these two men in the most symbiotic of relationships. Forrest recognized in 9/11 an opportunity to unify the nation, much as he once had unified a state from the Governor's mansion. Back then he had joined in a partnership with his state's Democratic Lieutenant Governor. Now, as President, having fed his base with the spoils of tax cuts, he sought out allies from across the political spectrum—allies who could communicate to America's liberals that the President's values were essentially their own. Moses, the intellectual rabbi with the fiery eyes, seemed an ideal candidate for the job.

While Forrest needed Moses, Moses needed Forrest even more. Moses realized that this was a pivotal time in history. He knew that by itself the power of his pen was no match for his look-alike's sword. Only the President of the United States possessed the authority to defeat al-Qaeda militarily and, through diplomacy, to marginalize Osama's support. While it's true that from Moses' perspective, Forrest was hardly the ideal person to captain our ship through stormy weather, Moses also knew that Forrest was the only captain we had.

The Levine-Forrest friendship was initiated by the President after watching Moses appear on *Meet the Reporters*. Forrest invited my friend to the White House, where the two spent the afternoon watching a football game. Forrest told Moses that he admired his integrity and respected his insights on Middle East affairs, but their substantive conversation lasted little more than ten minutes. Essentially, they filled their time by having a couple of beers, cracking some of their favorite tasteless jokes, and cheering on the tilt between Moses' Crimson Tide and Forrest's Texas Longhorns. Both men had gone to Ivy League schools, but each identified, at least athletically, with the state schools from their home states. In this case, the Tide won 27-24, and Forrest gracefully accepted defeat.

"We've got to do this more often," the President said. "Maybe next time we should see a game in style. What do you say we take Air Force One to a major bowl game, your choice?" Moses accepted and picked the Sugar Bowl. And it was there in the Big Easy, among Creole delicacies and soaring saxophones, that Moses Levine and Joseph Forrest came to see each other as allies.

Joseph Forrest was thus not exaggerating when, after Moses and I returned from our captivity in Israel, he referred to Moses as his "good friend." That friendship would become even stronger during the fall of 2002. It was a time when Moses' energies were spent growing POP into a national institution. But he would seize every opportunity to deepen his relationship with Joseph Forrest. By the year's end, I began to wonder if Forrest had filled the void in Moses' life left by the death of Eric Morton.

In this football-loving nation of ours, there are casual football fans, football fanatics, and people for whom football is a

religion. As strange as it may sound, Moses Levine belonged
in the last category. Watching a football game with him was
an unforgettable experience because, all of a sudden, he was
transformed into a different person. No longer a walking, talking
superego, he became a crazed, maniacal id. It's not that he
didn't appreciate the finesse side of the game; it's just that he
really loved the hitting. It enabled him to release the tensions
that he bottled up in his commitment to learning, praying and,
above all else, nurturing the planet.

The rumor was that when Moses was a freshman, he'd
complain constantly about having left the State of Alabama and
Crimson Tide football only to watch the "middle-school caliber"
play at Columbia. This was a man who grew up enjoying the
likes of Joe Namath, Kenny "the Snake" Stabler, Johnny Musso,
Ray Perkins and Mike Hall, the linebacker Moses said was his
favorite player of all. When Moses matriculated at Columbia,
the last person he was expecting to find was Eric Morton. Moses
said that watching Eric as a Columbia Lion was worth the price
of admission alone. "You shouldn't be here," Moses would tell
him. "You belong in Tuscaloosa, playing with the big studs, not
the mathletes."

Realizing that the pigskin changed him from a Jekyll to something of a Hyde, Moses evolved to the point where he preferred
watching Redskins' games on TV to being at a stadium, where
his emotions would be on public display. Usually he'd watch
the games alone in his apartment, but on Labor Day in 2002, he
received a call from the White House. It was Forrest's personal
secretary asking if Moses would like to join the President at the
White House and watch the Redskins open the season against
the Cardinals. It turned out to be the first of five football games
the two men saw together that season.

Sometimes, Forrest and Moses watched the games with a
couple of White House staffers. Other times, the two watched
alone. In either case, from kickoff to the final whistle, they
rarely spoke about matters of state. "We'd occasionally change

the subject to baseball," Moses told me. "Forrest is mostly a baseball guy, like you. But I've given him a finer appreciation for my sport. He loves corner play, just loves it. It was so cool to sit with the President of the United States and watch Darrell Green play his last season in the NFL."

I didn't begrudge Moses his Sunday afternoons at the White House. The problem was that while he was educating the President about zone blitzes and West Coast offenses, others were educating Forrest about the need to invade a country halfway across the world. I told Moses to warn Forrest that invading Iraq would be a huge mistake, but Moses refused. "The President calls me when he wants to take a break and watch a little football," he said. "I'm going to wait for him to bring up Iraq himself; I think I'll have more of an impact then. We'll have time, don't worry."

But I did worry. I worried when I heard Administration officials tell the media that the Iraqi people would line the streets of Baghdad, tossing flowers at the American troops and hailing them as "liberators." Knowing something about the Muslim people and their attitude towards Christian invaders, that sounded ridiculous. I worried when I heard that Forrest had so despised Saddam Hussein, Iraq's dictator, that he had been looking for evidence linking him to the 9/11 terrorists from the moment the planes struck the Towers. I worried when I read the columns by Paul Friedenthal of the New York Times, the self-styled expert on all things Middle Eastern. He argued for an invasion on the grounds that the liberal democracy we'd create would provide a shining example of the proverbial "City on the Hill" that other Muslim states would naturally try to emulate.

I worried that the real reasons for going to war had nothing to do with the official White House justification: that Iraq possessed weapons of mass destruction. It seemed that lots of people wanted to invade Iraq regardless of the existence of WMDs, so how was I to believe that the talk of WMDs wasn't a mere pretext?

Moses and I spoke at length about my concerns, which he fully shared. In fact, his passion on the topic was, if anything, greater than my own. Moses had hoped to bring up the topic with Forrest in early January 2003, once the Redskins' season was over, but Forrest was not as flush with spare time as he had been in the fall. On February 2nd, Moses met a Democratic Congressman who served on the House Permanent Select Committee on Intelligence and asked what kind of evidence we possessed that Iraq had WMDs. The Congressman responded that he wasn't sure. "I probably know as much about the evidence as anyone on Capitol Hill, and I'm not convinced," he said. That conversation only doubled Moses' resolve to speak to Forrest before it was too late.

Finally, on March 7, 2003, Moses was given a hearing at the White House. The President he saw that afternoon was hardly the same man he had come to know for the past year and a half. Forrest had lost his sense of humor and his amiable manner. He was now grim with determination, and his goals were clear: to remove Saddam from power and install, instead, a pro-American, democratic regime that would prove to the Muslim world the bankruptcy of dictatorships and terrorism. When Moses raised the issue of WMDs, Forrest replied that if they didn't exist, Hussein wouldn't have toyed with the inspection process. "Unless," Forrest said, "he's using us as a tool to fool Iran into thinkin' he's tougher than he is. Either way, the guy's been a menace for years, and we're gonna stop him once and for all."

Moses tried to argue, but it was no use—Forrest's top advisors were sitting in on the conversation and objected to every word Moses said. It didn't take my friend long to realize that this was hardly an opportunity for a legitimate dialogue. So he whispered in Forrest's ear: "Screw this. March Madness is coming up. Let's watch a tournament game in a couple of weeks without all these suits around. I'm out of here." And he left.

Moses was never a big fan of petitional prayer. "That's not praying to God," he told me. "That's praying to Santa Claus." Even in East Jerusalem during the day after Hafeez issued his threat to kill us, Moses didn't resort to beseeching God for divine intervention. He simply prayed for composure, insight and courage—in other words, he was petitioning his own psyche.

Nevertheless, during the week after the President launched the Iraq War on March 19, 2003, Moses voiced one petitional prayer after another. "I prayed for a phone call from the President's personal secretary," he said. "And, of course, I prayed for the ability to get the job done if I ever got that call."

Moses wasn't simply deflated by the coverage of the Iraq War on television; he was appalled. It seemed to him as if a good fraction of the country, not to mention the world, disagreed with the invasion, but not a single critic could be heard on television. "Who controls the media?" Moses asked. "Big Brother?" My friend wanted desperately to serve as the lone dissenting voice amidst what he called the "collective orgasm" of an American military victory. But he chose instead to wait for the phone call and a chance to talk to Forrest personally in the only way Forrest could respect: one loyal friend warning another so as to keep him out of trouble.

On March 28th, the call finally came. Moses was to go to the White House the next day to watch Kansas play Arizona in the Elite Eight. No, he couldn't have given a whit about the outcome. As a spectator of college basketball, Moses was somewhat north of "casual fan" but way south of "fanatic." As a peace advocate, however, his religious fervor was virtually unlimited. It meant the world to Moses to be given the chance to talk his friend out of the biggest mistake of his presidency.

This is how Moses described his visit to me soon after he returned from the White House:

"When I walked into his TV room, everyone had been telling him how well the war was going. Then the Secretary of Defense called to say that it looked like we found the WMDs—or at least we now knew where to look. I played dumb at first, saying things like 'That's nice. What do you think about the Jayhawks' back court?' My strategy was to make him comfortable until half-time and then get serious. I took the chance that we wouldn't get interrupted, or at least not more than a few minutes at a time, and it paid off. By halftime, he was in a good mood and open to whatever I had to say.

"I told him he was about to get his dick stuck in his zipper. Those were my exact words—I said them just the way he would have if the shoe were on the other foot. Then I lectured him about how Muslims feel about Christians taking over their land, especially when the Christians weren't even attacked first. It's not just a matter of pride to them; it's a matter of religion. I told him if he tried to take over their country and insert a friendly regime, it would cost us hundreds of billions of dollars and thousands of lives, and we'd end up leaving like a one-legged man in a butt-kicking contest. Oh, and Iraq would descend into a civil war and become a breeding ground for terrorism. I told him that too.

"Joe wasn't buying it. He assured me that his advisors had studied Iraq and promised that once we get rid of Saddam and his sons, the Republican Guard will give up, and the rest will be mop up duty. I had one simple question for him: 'How many of your advisers can speak Arabic? Give me a number, how many?' He thought about it for a minute and couldn't name a single one. Not one! So this is what I said: 'Get a couple of 20-somethings on your staff to call the Islamic Studies Department at the college they attended. Have them identify a handful of Islamic scholars who live in the Middle East and are friendly to the U.S. but can think for themselves. They'll bring you back to reality. But I can tell you right now how to close the deal. Send a message to Saddam through his friends. Tell him you're willing to talk terms. Tell him you're willing to leave him in power as long as he doesn't play any more games with WMDs and the United Nations. Tell him if he feels the need to play games, you'll finish the job."

And that's pretty much the way it played out after Forrest took Moses' advice. His staffers found some Muslim scholars, and they corroborated what Moses said about the Muslim attitude toward colonization and the likely outcome should the U.S. force a regime change in Iraq. At the same time, the WMDs we supposedly had found turned out to be a mirage. In truth, they never existed. Saddam simply fabricated the idea of having such an arsenal in order to intimidate his enemies, and the United States very nearly opened up Pandora's box because of it.

On April 22, 2003, the United States and the Republic of Iraq signed a peace treaty requiring Iraq to comply with all the terms that the United Nations had been demanding for years. It also created mechanisms to permit easy U.N. and U.S. access to Iraqi territory so as to ensure that the terms of the treaty were obeyed.

I can't overstate the abuse Forrest took from his core constituents about "leaving the fox in charge of the henhouse." Thankfully, our President had the guts to take that abuse. After his talk with Moses, enough experts had convinced him that following through on "regime change" would entail a near certain catastrophe for both Iraq and America.

During the days leading up to the treaty as well as the period after it was signed, Forrest had sent numerous lieutenants to hit the airwaves and educate the American public about the dangers of "adopting 22 million Iraqis." Forrest even co-opted Paul Friedenthal to write columns praising the treaty. Friedenthal wrote in the Times that:

> President Forrest should be credited for uncovering the mystery of the WMDs, bringing the dictator to his knees,

and establishing procedures that would prevent Iraq from ever again menacing the rest of the world. It's true that he left Saddam in power. Then again, I myself said before the war that Iraq is like the Pottery Barn—as the sign says, 'if you break it you own it' — and the President's intelligence told him that this is one place we don't want to own. I can't say that position is frivolous.

No, I don't suppose he could. The absurdity of America occupying Iraq should have been obvious to anyone with even a rudimentary understanding of Muslim history. I was as proud of Moses for educating Forrest about Iraq as for educating Hafeez about terrorism. Over the course of the next several months, Moses' role in turning the tide of the Iraq War was gradually revealed to the American public. That led up to a September 2003 press conference, in which Forrest finally acknowledged the full import of Moses' efforts. After explaining what my friend did to end the war, Forrest concluded by saying that "Rabbi Moses Levine saved my Presidency and I can't tell you how many taxpayer dollars. I could also say that he saved thousands of American lives. Then again, for him, that's old hat."

Indeed it was.

CHAPTER XIII

"People can say all they want about how science has undermined the existence of God. But I believe in the same God that was embraced by a skeptical, free-thinking scientist named Albert Einstein. He didn't like the old model, so he wrestled with the concept, read a little heretical philosophy, and came up with a God he could love. I call that the practice of liberal Judaism."

Rabbi Moses Levine, addressing
the World Spinoza Conference, 2003

Silver Spring, Maryland—September 1993. Moses was ordained as a Reform rabbi in 1993, a month after I was promoted to the position of senior rabbi at Beth Hashem. By then, I had already made a name for myself in the Washington Jewish community, in part because the retiring senior rabbi had little interest in doing anything outside of the synagogue and allowed me the opportunity to make a number of prominent public appearances. I was occasionally quoted in the Washington Post and often appeared on radio or TV whenever a representative of the Conservative-Jewish movement was needed to discuss public policy.

My views tended to be fairly mainstream for a non-Orthodox American rabbi, which was one reason I was such a sought-after guest. Like most Conservative Jews, I was a Democrat in my politics—liberal on social issues and moderate on matters of economics. (Yes, it may sound like an oxymoron, but "Conservative" Jews tend to be politically liberal. Our real political conservatives are mostly Orthodox.) I was also, as should be apparent by now, a staunch Zionist. I didn't support Israel's policy of building settlements in the West Bank and Gaza Strip, which clearly needed to be ceded to the Palestinians if we wanted a lasting peace, but neither did I blame Israel for failing to part with that land quite yet—not until the Palestinians demonstrated that they could live in harmony with a secure Zionist state. I had no doubt that the Israelis would give up plenty of land when a true opportunity for peace presented itself.

In short, in the positions I reached—and, for that matter, the manner in which I expressed them—I was no gadfly. During his first two years as a rabbi at Temple Emanu-El in Memphis, Tennessee, neither was Moses. I'm quite confident in that assessment, having attended his ordination ceremony as well as a service he led a year later, and having spoken to him on the phone at least once a month during that period.

Soon after he entered the Hebrew Union College, Moses decided to wait seven full years—five years of school plus two years as a rabbi — before he would use his voice in a way that would make his mother proud. "Seven years is the right amount of time," he said, after conducting the service to celebrate his first anniversary at Temple Emanu-El. "That's how long I set aside to learn my craft with an extra dose of humility. That's how long our patriarch Jacob had to wait before he could marry the woman he loved."

"Actually, it was fourteen years," I said, pedantically. "He thought he would have to wait seven, then Laban tricked him by giving him Leah, instead of Rachel, and he had to wait another seven before he could marry the real Rachel."

"I know," Moses said, "but you don't actually think I can

hold off for that long, do you? I'm pulling punches every time I give a sermon. I feel like a politician."

"Welcome to the job of rabbi."

"Please. That's not a rabbi. That's a master-of-ceremonies. A rabbi's a *leader*. An emcee tells the congregation what they want to hear, which is basically what I'm doing now. I preach a lot to the choir. It's innocuous drivel, but it makes them happy."

"So you think of yourself as copping out?" I asked.

"Absolutely. I use lyrical, poetic language to say a lot of nothing. I give them a tabula rasa; they write on it whatever they want to. Hopefully, it will make them comfortable enough with me that when I start *really* preaching, they'll be receptive."

Moses' "real" preaching began on a Sunday afternoon in the September of 1995. Temple Emanu-El held a special celebration to honor his second anniversary there. The congregation was told in advance that a big turnout was very important to Moses, as he would be giving a heartfelt statement about his philosophy as a Jew. Sure enough, the building was totally packed, with over 700 people in attendance. I saw it as a tribute to whatever "innocuous drivel" Moses had been dishing out during the previous two years.

I flew down from Washington for the occasion, accompanied by Rachel. She had met Moses a few times since their initial clash at the march to support Israel, but they had hardly become friends. I begged her to come to Memphis, and yet that did little good at first. It was only when I told her how much I was looking forward to seeing Lisa at the ceremony that Rachel decided to make the trip. During Moses' address to his congregation, Lisa sat on my left and Rachel on my right.

Moses wasn't at his most eloquent or provocative that afternoon in Memphis, but I've never heard him better introduce his guiding principles as a Jew. Even after he became one of the world's most famous—and then infamous — figures, these principles continued to ground his religious philosophy. I trust,

then, that you'll forgive me, my reader, if I reproduce Moses'
words in full:

"'The pursuit of knowledge for its own sake, an almost fanat-
ical love of justice, and the desire for personal independence
— these are the features of the Jewish tradition which make me
thank my lucky stars I belong to it.' So said Albert Einstein, a
man many claim was not a practicing Jew, but who has always
been one of my greatest heroes. In that one sentence, Einstein
points out some of our fundamental ideals as a people. Do we
measure up to them? Not entirely, but we haven't forgotten
them either. It is to those ideals that we owe many of our
accomplishments.

"The highest standards of our faith can easily be criticized
as unrealistic and unachievable. And yet, you have to recognize
the value these standards have played in all that our people have
done for the world. Look at the annals of history. Examine lists
of the great scientists, philosophers, spiritual leaders, political
activists and writers. Then ask yourselves to what extent Jews
are represented compared to their numbers in the population.
Here's a hint—the most recent 1995 figures I've seen estimate
that there are 5.7 billion people in the world and 13 million
Jews. That means that roughly 1 out of every 440 people in the
world is Jewish. So tell me, do you think 1 out of every 440 of
our planet's scientists is Jewish? Or our spiritual leaders? Or
our writers?

"And those of you in the public service professions—you
who earn a lot less money than you could elsewhere because
you want to serve the public interest—have you ever wondered
why you have so many Jewish colleagues? It's simple. *Jewish
ideals matter!* We violate them every day. And yet, just by
osmosis, they have an effect, a beautiful effect.

"Sitting in the audience today is an old friend of mine, Rabbi
Richie Gold. He saw me at a march carrying on against some
of the excesses of the Israeli Government in its dealings with
Arabs. And he pointed out that it was precisely because I am

steeped in Jewish ideals that it mattered so much to me that Israel be fair to its Arab population.

"Well, I could argue with Richie all day about Israeli politics. But I couldn't argue with what he said about the power of Jewish ideals. It's my Judaism that causes me to demand *more* from Jews than I'd demand from others. Maybe that's irrational; then again, don't most people demand more from themselves than from others? And when we criticize Israel, aren't we just criticizing ourselves?

"Now let's get back to Einstein. I look at what he said about the desire for personal independence, and I can't help but look at the Palestinians whose land we occupy. What kind of personal independence do they enjoy? What kind of virtue can we expect to take root in their environment?

"I don't doubt that in Palestinian schools, young children are taught to hate us and to deny our right to a share of the holy land. I don't doubt that many Palestinian adults would like to watch the Jewish people die a painful death. I'll grant you that. But the facts are the facts. The Palestinians are our neighbors. We *cannot* prosper unless they prosper. If we hope to live in peace, they must live autonomously.

"So partition the land, build a wall … do what you must do. But it's not enough for us to criticize the Arabs and look to the heavens for help. We're going to have to be generous with our land, and I'm not just talking about the Occupied Territories. Also, we're going to have to find Arab allies we can embrace. That's right, *Arab* allies. Quite a concept, isn't it? Ask yourselves how many Arab leaders we actually think of as friends. That number had better grow, and I mean quickly.

"If you took aliens from a distant galaxy, dropped them in Israel and told them that this was the holiest place on Earth, they would have to conclude that on our planet, holiness means perpetual war. It doesn't, you know. Holiness is all about respecting diversity and using that diversity to create an ever-evolving unity. When we respect Arab independence, when we give up some of our claims to disputed land, and when we reach out to them with love and not with rifles, then we might make Israel a holy land for the first time in a long, long while.

"Einstein also spoke about justice. And I have to agree with him that Jews have always hated injustice with a passion. Just consider all the biblical admonitions on the topic. Or the accepted doctrine that we were once slaves in Egypt—not just our ancestors, but we ourselves. To be a Jew is to never forget what that means.

"It says in the Book of Isaiah that the Jewish people should be *'a light unto the nations.'* In other words, we must become agents of justice in an often unjust world. And to be an agent of justice, each of us must be marked by our devotion to charity. The Hebrew root of the word 'justice' is *tzedek*, which is also the root of the Hebrew word for 'charity': *tzedakeh*. Not only our approach to ethics but our very language rests on the idea that to deny people charity is to deny them justice.

"Think of the implications of that statement. Think of how high it sets the bar. As long as there are needy people in the world—orphans, widows, sick, homeless—the Jew is compelled to help them, rather than live a life of luxury. When you head home tonight to your comfortable homes, remember that to ignore people's basic needs is to deny them *justice*. If this is the standard, who among us lives up to it? Certainly not the community in which I was raised.

"In Birmingham, Alabama, where I grew up, you couldn't help but witness the injustices heaped on our black brothers and sisters on a daily basis. The adults in my community wanted to see these horrors disappear but weren't willing to make waves with the Christian white majority. Ultimately, my community worked to take care of itself, even at the price of allowing others to suffer. And this is hardly surprising. The elimination of injustice may be a Jewish *desire*, but the peace that stems from one's own autonomy is a Jewish *need*. We wouldn't dare threaten the Christian whites who ran our city, lest we lose our homes and jobs and become a poor, nomadic people once again.

"Judaism is a religion of high ideals practiced by a people who want to help their fellow human beings but are also committed to protecting their own families. Sometimes a conflict develops and it gnaws at us—destroying our self-esteem regardless of which choice we make. To me, this conflict is precisely what makes us great as a people. We're never satisfied with our lot; there is always more we can do, either for ourselves, our families, or our world.

"Jews should know that we can't both achieve nirvana and work for justice. As for me, I'll take justice.

"That leaves me with the third of Einstein's principles—the pursuit of knowledge for its own sake. He wasn't talking about the power, riches or status that knowledge can bring us. He spoke about pursuing knowledge because the pursuit itself is irresistible. He meant that knowledge—or dare I say *wisdom*— should be as addicting for the Jew as heroin is for the junkie.

"Our people have had tremendous success academically. The Ivy League is full of Jews. So is the list of Nobel Laureates. Many of those scholars and researchers were surely learning addicts; otherwise they couldn't have achieved what they did. But again, we're *not* simply speaking about the love of learning truths. The goal should be to love truth so much that you're willing to stay with it wherever it leads, even to places our parents and teachers never wanted us to visit.

"Is that the traditional approach to Judaism? Einstein may have wished it were, but from what I can tell, it's not.

"I'll never forget hearing an Orthodox rabbi in Jerusalem teach that 'if you open your mind too much, your brains will fall out.' I took him to be speaking on behalf of our tradition. Jews are supposed to follow hundreds of dictates *as Commandments*. No secular philosophy, not even our own independent thought, should be allowed to shake our devotion to those Commandments or cause us to violate them.

"That rabbi's comment about the primacy of tradition over truth represents Judaism as it has been practiced for centuries. You can hear it in the words of Maimonides, who many consider the greatest of Jewish philosophers. Here's what he said in his *Guide to the Perplexed*:

> It is the object of the Torah to serve as a guide for the instruction of the young, of women, and of the common people; and as all of them are incapable to comprehend the true sense of the words, tradition was considered sufficient to convey all truths which were to be established ...

"Maimonides was saying that the idea of a coherent, intellectually satisfying religious framework is something few of us are able to grasp. *That* is one principle I'd like to see changed. As your rabbi, I pledge to tell you which Jewish teachings I believe and which I dispute, even at the risk of offending you from time to time. You may think my beliefs are misguided, but I hope you'll agree about the need to stop patronizing each other.

"Consider Exodus 19:5: 'Now then, if you will obey Me faithfully and keep My covenant, you shall be My treasured possession among all the peoples. Indeed, all the earth is Mine, but you shall be to Me a kingdom of priests and a holy nation.'

"You all heard it. The Jewish people shall become a *kingdom of priests* and a holy nation. We mustn't satisfy ourselves with giving the masses a bunch of nonsense, as long as the sages recognize the profound jewels that lie hidden beneath the nonsense. Priests must be able to think deeply, think for themselves, and have the courage to express their thoughts to others. Priests hardly respect the words of Exodus when they condemn another set of priests to ignorance and claim that such ignorance is for their neighbors' own good.

"During my next few sermons, I intend to present my ideas more concretely. You may think I'm wrong—and I may be wrong—but at least you'll know where I stand. In a week, I will address the congregation as to why I am now willing to officiate at marriages between Jews and Gentiles. This isn't the recommended Reform approach, but I say it's crucial if we hope to respect personal autonomy. After that, I will talk about the Jewish approach to charity. The net worth of American Jews today, I will argue, has made us complacent and threatens to defeat our commitment to justice. One of the things that used to make Jews so passionate about injustice is that we ourselves suffered from it; now that we're so damned well-to-do, maybe we don't care about it quite as much. We're consumed instead by the pride we take in our accomplishments and possessions, and the egotism that stems from this pride is gnawing at our spirituality. At a bare minimum, we are clearly obliged to dig a hell of lot deeper into our wallets than we have been doing.

"When I'm through speaking about charity, I'm going to make a series of addresses concerning the topic of God. You'll hear why, for example, I reject all attempts to portray God as having human-like emotions, including even *love*. You want to talk about the God of Love? I'll point out that this is the same God who has buried people alive after earthquakes. The devil didn't do that; it was God—and it wasn't done to teach us some kind of lesson either. Candidly, I think a lot of the traditional views on God are nonsense, and I hold these views responsible for turning off so many intelligent people to religion. We need to stop indulging our desire to rhapsodize God like 'He' is some sort of human ideal when we all know full well that if there is a God worthy of the name, that God would be nothing like us.

"Rest assured, though, that I do not simply intend to use this pulpit to preach my own personal beliefs. I will also cede some of my time at the pulpit to any of you who are willing to share your Jewish philosophies with the congregation. I'm quite serious about making sure that the words in Exodus Chapter 19 are respected in this building. This will be a congregation of priests, not a vehicle to showcase my talents.

"So there you have my introduction to the three values at the heart of Einstein's Judaism. But as important as those values are, I still see them as secondary to the true essence of the faith. I've touched on this point in different ways, but now let me make it directly. Do you want to know why *I* thank my lucky stars that I belong to this faith? Because of how we got the name Israel. It came from a man; the man known as Jacob. One night, he wrestled with the divine. It was brutal, and it left Jacob with a limp. But he survived. And for that, for living a life that involved grappling not merely with men but also with the divine, he earned the name Israel, which literally means 'the one who wrestles with God.'

"We Jews, as I've indicated, are a restless people. We can't deal too well with the gulf between our ideals and the practical realities of life. We live in a world where people and *peoples* compete for scarce resources. Where we are compelled to give to charity until it hurts but also to appreciate that charity begins at home. Where we are told about a God who is omnipotent and omnibenevolent and who can be such a source of joy and strength; then again, we are also told that somehow, this omnipotent, omnibenevolent God allowed six million sons and daughters of Jacob to go to the ovens.

"Even before the Holocaust, Jews in droves were abandoning their belief in God. Long before Hitler there was Marx. Today, we think of Marx as an enemy of religion and a self-hating Jew, and yet we all know how popular he became among our people. I'll tell you why — he was passionate about divine concepts, like justice, universal brotherhood, and fulfilling our potential as individuals.

"In the idea that Jews are wrestlers with the divine, you will find the concept that best harmonizes Jewish ideals and Jewish culture. Perhaps more than any other people, we question, dispute, lament, and pine for a better day—not in the Heavens but here on Earth. We don't so much whine as *kvetch*, and somehow our kvetching always has a moral tinge to it, as if we never forget the transcendent importance of morality, even when we complain about the slightest thing.

"As much as we love our world, who among us is satisfied with it? Who among us feels entitled to sit back and let it turn on its axis without our help, without our nurturing? Jews who believe in the divine recognize themselves as God's *partner*, not God's slave. Sure, that attitude takes chutzpah. But that's precisely what's necessary when you want to wrestle with the divine, day after day, and expect to survive.

"Once you recognize how we got our name, the values Einstein talked about become even clearer. Only with autonomy can we stage a fair fight with the Most High. And without it, we can barely even conceive of divinity, let alone wrestle with it. As for justice, we demand it for others because it has been denied for ourselves. In Egypt, we hadn't the room to wrestle. That's why we needed to bust out and actually resorted to *violence*. Finally, it is through our pursuit of truth that we are allowed to stage our struggles. We can't physically fight with angels. But we can challenge conventional wisdom. We can question the ideas of our parents or judges. And yes, we can even dispute the authenticity and veracity of our holy books.

"To be a Jew, a wrestler with the divine, means that no cow is sacred. Nothing, in fact, is more sacred than the love of wrestling, as long as what you're grappling with is worthy of the battle."

That was all Moses had to say on that September afternoon. By mid-November, Moses was spending most of his time dealing with complaints about his preaching lodged by many of the older and more established members of his congregation. By January of the following year, the Board of Trustees at Temple Emanu-El had formally requested his resignation.

CHAPTER XIV

"I've often wondered how different the world would be if religion weren't based on love and fear, but rather on honor: to honor God, to honor ourselves, and to honor one another.

"We can fear without loving. We can love without respecting. But in order truly to honor someone, you must treat them with both love and respect. Let's start with the way we treat each other here at Temple Akiva. I would like to ask each of you every day you walk into this building to treat everyone you meet with honor. I don't care how miserable you're feeling, how depressed, how sick ... never dishonor one of your fellow congregants. If we all fulfill this one principle, we'll be forever proud to be part of this spiritual community."

Rabbi Moses Levine addressing Temple Akiva, 2000

Washington, D.C.—January 1999. After his experience at Temple Emanu-El, Moses wasn't exactly a hot commodity as a rabbi. But that changed with his success as the author of *Exodus: Then and Now* and his frequent TV appearances as a talking-head. Once the political talk shows got hold of the guy, he started looking for a home in D.C. Lisa Rhodes and I were both living in Maryland, close to the line between Prince

Georges and Montgomery Counties, so Moses confined his search to that general area. He ended up renting an apartment in Northwest D.C. only blocks from the hip and largely Bohemian community of Takoma Park, Maryland.

In many ways, the community was well suited for Moses. It was educated, artsy and highly political. But my friend didn't find the Takoma Park culture sufficiently spiritual, so he took it upon himself to remedy that problem. With the money from his book sales and TV appearances—and frankly, from some seed funds that I gave him—Moses founded a Reform shul of his own, the first Reform synagogue in Takoma Park's history.

The groundbreaking of Temple Akiva took place on July 12, 1999. At the time, Rachel and I were still happily married. Our son, Seth, was eight, and our daughter, Esther, six. Rachel doted on them whenever she was not involved with her business, charitable or political activities. She worked diligently to fight anti-Semitism and support Zionism in the political sphere. In other words, we all had fun together, but we weren't together very often.

When I first entered Moses' new synagogue, I was struck by the quotation from Akiva prominently displayed in its foyer: "All my life I've been waiting to fulfill the concept 'You shall love Hashem, your G-d, with all your heart, with all your soul, and with all your might,' and now I finally have the chance." Jews are taught that the great rabbi serenely uttered these words shortly before he died, as his flesh was being ripped apart by the Romans. For Moses, Akiva's words became the signature statement in Jewish history: at once pious and rebellious, devoted to life yet unafraid of death. Akiva's gruesome sendoff was somewhat of his own choosing. The alternative—obeying the Roman edict prohibiting the public study of Torah—was simply not an option.

Perhaps even more famous than the quotation Moses displayed in his synagogue were Akiva's next words: "Shema Yisrael, Adonai Elohenu, Adonai Echad" (Hear O Israel, the

Lord our God, the Lord is One). The legend has it that Akiva drew out the word Echad (One) seemingly indefinitely, like a shofar blower who fights to continue his last note, until finally, as Akiva gave all the voice he could give to the concept of unity, he died.

I've heard Moses preach more than once about Akiva's sendoff. And each time, I was reminded that no matter how much pride I took in my sermons, I was no Moses Levine. My sermons spoke, whereas his sang, and it wasn't so much the words he chose as the spirit in which he delivered them — the warm voice, the intense eyes, and the sense that he was addressing God as much as man. Moses didn't simply talk to his audience, he *challenged* them. How, he would demand to know, are you personally fulfilling the Torah's goal of creating a people of priests and a holy nation? Are you—Mr. Attorney, Ms. Accountant, Mrs. Homemaker—worthy of the term *rabbi*? Are you worthy of the term *mensch*? And if you're not, how then can you call yourself an adult Jew?

Temple Akiva started out as a relatively small shul with fewer than a hundred families. It grew substantially but never attained over five hundred member families, even at its peak. The synagogue was simply too non-traditional to win any popularity contests. I loved it, but it wasn't exactly what most Reform Jews were looking for.

Some nights, Moses directed that not a single word be spoken in the sanctuary. Either he or his cantor would lead the congregation in the chanting of wordless melodies, or "nigguns," each of which could go on for five or ten minutes at a time, the idea being that the repetition would function much like the role of a mantra in a meditation ritual. The nigguns would be intermixed with similarly lengthy "moments" of silence in which the congregation would pray quietly, reminiscent of a Quaker meeting house. Moses realized his approach wasn't likely to attract many of the young Jewish couples in the D.C. area. Most didn't attach much value to spirituality. Instead, they wanted a synagogue where they could educate their children with a "sense of Jewish identity" and renew their own membership in the club by attending High Holiday services twice a year. That approach to Judaism depressed Moses, and the last thing he was looking to create was yet another Bar Mitzvah Mill.

"I'm not on the membership committee," he used to say, laughing.

Clearly not.

After Moses moved to Washington, he became a regular visitor at my house, in spite of his rather chilly relationship with my wife. Our home was located a quarter of a mile from New Hampshire Avenue in northern Silver Spring, not terribly far from my own synagogue. It had been built to Jerome Horowitz's specifications, back when the neighborhood was all farmland. The Horowitzes purchased ten acres and designed as its centerpiece a mammoth colonial, which was approached by a long tree-lined private road leading to a large circular driveway. Four marble columns graced the front of the mansion, as if to announce to all visitors that they were about to enter the presence of royalty—in this case, capitalist royalty.

Rachel had her favorite part of our estate, and I had mine. For Rachel, the hub of the house was its living room. Measuring over 30 feet square, with ceilings nearly 20 feet high, that was where we displayed our most exquisite paintings. The three masterpieces were originals by Seurat, Picasso and Chagall. In fact, the night Rachel left me, those paintings were among the few things she took with her from the house.

As for me, what I loved most about the mansion was its yard. Opening the back door, you walk out onto several acres of grass that gradually slope down towards a stream marking the edge of the property. Less than a hundred feet from the stream, I commissioned the building of a gazebo. It was there that I loved to sit and read, write, or simply look out toward the stream.

Something about that gazebo and the lawn nearby helped me feel both peaceful and invigorated. Perhaps it was the only part of the estate that seemed like it truly belonged to me, and not my in-laws.

Once the weather warmed up, Moses spent a lot of time in my back yard. I set up chairs there so that the two of us could discuss the holy books with other local rabbis. Whenever you're talking about ancient texts, it somehow seems more authentic to be outside in nature rather than inside a modern building adorned with televisions, CD players, computers and fax machines. In setting up shop outdoors, my hope was that we would be able to break free from the limitations of time and contemplate the past and future as well as the present.

One afternoon, Moses came up with an idea that had nothing to do with any rabbinic doctrine. He suggested that our yard would be a great venue to put on concerts for friends. When I mentioned that I was planning to throw a birthday party for Rachel in a few weeks, Moses decided to stage an event for the occasion. He went to work searching for bands who could entertain the roughly 75 people on the guest list. No, I didn't originally intend for him to be on that list, but I couldn't exactly exclude him under the circumstances.

After attending local music showcases, Moses selected two bands to play at the party. The opening act played for an hour. It was a pair of twin brothers—one played the electric-acoustic guitar, the other bass. They performed folk-rock tunes, most of which were originals. I liked the songs and loved the twins' vocal harmonies. As for Rachel, she spent the set mingling from guest to guest, talking about anything from real estate construction to Israeli politics to the Beth Hashem Board of Trustees. Fortunately, the Gold-Horowitz amphitheatre was large enough that Moses and the other guests who wanted to focus on the music could do so, and those who wanted to schmooze could do that too.

All the schmoozing stopped, however, when the feature band

started to play. They were a foursome, fronted by a dynamic female redhead with a raspy voice and a whole lot of attitude, and they mostly covered rock 'n roll classics. I don't think they performed more than a handful of originals during their entire two-hour gig.

My wife was their biggest fan. She spent their set dancing with one partner after another, each of whom received a big hug, and sometimes a kiss, when it was time to move on. Eventually, Rachel had relaxed to the point where she felt compelled to walk up to Moses and thank him, quite sincerely, for his role in planning the event. When Moses replied warmly that he was happy to help, Rachel blushed. She must have been thinking of all the nasty things she had said to me over the years about Moses. "I assure you, I don't deserve the honor," she said.

"Of course you do. You do so much for Richie."

"He's my husband, that's my job," she said, laughing. "So tell me, how does it feel to be a congregational rabbi? Do you like it more than being an author?"

"I like them both," Moses said. "A career should have variety."

"Yours certainly does," she replied. "Award-winning author, TV personality, congregational rabbi. What's next?"

Moses thought for a second. "Would you believe music talent scout?"

"Not from the sound of that first band, I wouldn't," she said soberly, before finally breaking into a laugh. "Just kidding. They were decent. I like this one more, though."

"I'm glad we put 'em in the right order for you," Moses said.

Just then, a couple of friends came over to Rachel and told her they were about to leave. That was her cue to end the conversation.

"I've got to run, but thanks again, Moses. When the music stops and the politics start, I'll go back to watching you like a hawk. But tonight, I appreciate what you did for my birthday."

To hear her say that was the high point of my evening. It was easily the high point of their relationship.

CHAPTER XV

"I applaud the free enterprise system. I applaud any baron of industry who produces socially responsible goods and services. What I don't applaud is the hoarding of wealth.

"Yes, I know. Some of my best friends are loaded. [Laughter] So were the Patriarchs of Israel. But ever since the time of Moses, a lot has been said about the virtues of sharing, and no matter who we are or where we're from, we'd better take it to heart.

"My Jewish heroes—the Prophets, the great rabbis, Spinoza, Einstein ... and may I add, Jesus—were brilliant men whose impact on our lives can't be measured. And yet they weren't fat cats. As we say in Yiddish, they weren't chazzas [pigs]. They lived humbly.

"Whenever you, as a businessperson, are able to make a lot of money, pat yourself on the back. Just be mindful about what you do with the money. And whatever you do, if you're Jewish, don't cite the Patriarchs in support of your own greed. That would only give my religion a bad name."

Rabbi Moses Levine, addressing
the U.S. Chamber of Commerce, 2004

Memphis, Tennessee—September 1995. Cleaning up after Rachel's birthday party, I recalled our flight back from Memphis years earlier, after Moses' second-anniversary "coming-out" sermon. She admitted to liking what he said about wrestling with the divine. That, you see, was Rachel's favorite concept in all of Judaism. She had always called it "God-wrestling," and yet she was clearly talking about the same thing he was: the Jewish disposition to focus our attention on what is truly great, not by accepting it blindly like children but by struggling with it. Rachel credited that attitude above all else for making the Jewish people both as productive and as exasperating as we've been over the years.

Rachel herself was a perfect illustration of what Moses was talking about. She was born an only child of affluent parents and easily could have centered her life on shopping malls and parties. But she had always had a hunger to better herself and make a contribution to the world. At a relatively early age, she decided to channel her restless energies through the dual prisms of commerce and Judaism.

At the same time that she studied economics in college and business in graduate school, Rachel was steeping herself in a variety of Jewish literature, both contemporary and ancient. At the age of 22, she spent an entire summer in Jerusalem, where she studied the Talmud at an Orthodox yeshiva and grappled with what she considered to be the inherent sexism of the Orthodox tradition. Jerome Horowitz once explained to me that he never feared for a moment that the Orthodox would "convert" his Rachel to their movement. "She's too much a product of women's lib," he told me. "There's no way she was going to cook and clean at home while the men were off praying and debating at shul."

While it's true that Jerome's daughter never became Orthodox, she emerged from the yeshiva with rather tradi- tional views about God and the state of Israel. Rachel clearly had no stomach for a preacher like Moses who loved to blast

conventional Jewish wisdom. As a result, though she appreciated his references in Memphis to the reasons why Israel got its
name, most of her comments about Moses' sermon were highly
critical.

For starters, Rachel detested what she called Moses' "clichéd
pablum about appeasing the Palestinians." As for the portion
of the sermon where Moses introduced some of his upcoming
talks, Rachel threw out one barb after another.

"I'd go crazy in that congregation," she said. "He's going to
tell everyone it's OK to marry gentiles, and if that means the
American Jewish community will assimilate and disappear
soon enough, I guess he's OK with that too. And then he's going
to tell everyone how rich and stingy Jews are? Give me a break.
The guy goes to Columbia, spends a little time at our estate,
and now he thinks we're all millionaires."

"Moses knows better than that," I said.

"Really? I bet that sermon's going to be nothing more than
a breeding ground for anti-Semitic stereotypes. Rich, cheap,
power-hungry, amoral … what did I leave out?"

"You've got him all wrong," I said. "Moses has never said
we're cheaper or less moral than anyone else. He's only trying
to make sure we live closer to our ideals."

"Is that right?" she said. "Well, what if my ideal is to be as
loving as possible to God and to think of Him as someone I can
relate to, someone who loves me right back. If I were in Moses'
congregation, I'd have to listen to him say that the God I believe
in doesn't exist. You heard the man: his God doesn't even *love*
us. And he's going to stand up there in front of hundreds of
people who just want a place where they can pray and tell them
they're praying to a figment of their imaginations. You don't see
that as pretty damned reckless?"

"If that's what he believes," I replied, "he has a right to say
it."

"But if *you* believed it, would you say it? I mean would you say it outright, so that your congregants would have no doubt that their rabbi thinks their God is B.S.?"

I didn't need long to answer her question. "Probably not," I said. "But maybe Moses is on to something. You know how many Jews are turned off to organized religion. Maybe by challenging tradition, Moses can engage more people and bring them back to the faith."

"Richie," Rachel said, "he's not a professor. He's a rabbi. Most of the people who show up to hear him speak are the ones who already *believe*. They don't need to hear a lecture about what's wrong with their views. They need him to mold those views into sources of inspiration. The ones who are alienated from the traditional God—the ones who might actually be open to what Moses is saying—*they're not at shul!* Don't you get it? He can't inspire them because they won't be around to hear."

I couldn't argue with her. I felt she was wrong in putting down Moses for his candor but couldn't figure out why. I only wished Moses had been on the plane to respond personally.

"Moses was probably the smartest person I knew at Columbia," I replied, "but he's as rebellious as he is smart. Like mother, like son."

"He's not just a rebel, he's a loose cannon. I'll never get over his act at the march in Washington. The Palestinians are the new Jews of Israel? Spare me."

"So he goes a little overboard sometimes," I said.

"*A little?* He should live in Jerusalem and watch his father get blown up on a bus. Then he can talk about how Jewish the Palestinians are. Sorry, but your Moses isn't fit to be a rabbi. He's just another self-hating Jew. They're a dime a dozen."

Less than three months after our trip to Memphis, that "self-hating Jew" got the word from his synagogue's president that he was going to be asked to leave. Moses called me immediately with the news, and I was hardly surprised. I had figured his days were numbered once he announced at his shul that he would be open about his beliefs. Mainstream Jewish congregations pride themselves in permitting heretics like Moses to speak out and challenge us to return to our ideals. Yet it is one thing for a congregant to serve as a Jeremiah with a bullhorn, and something else to preach as a community's *rabbi*. Moses wasn't satisfied with being a gadfly. He wanted to lead. I knew flying home from Memphis that he could be another Socrates, perhaps, but if he wanted to be a Pericles, or a David, he still had a lot to learn.

The synagogue president gave Moses the heads-up on December 22, 1995. As soon as Moses phoned me with the news, I ran upstairs to share it with my wife, who was in her study. I had just finished the story when we heard the chime of the doorbell. I returned to the ground floor and opened the door to two men in suits.

"We're looking for Rachel Horowitz," one of them said.

"She's upstairs," I answered. "Could I be of help? I'm her husband."

"I'm sorry. We have some bad news. We'll need to talk to Ms. Horowitz."

Rather than call to her, I walked, none too fast, up the stairs again. Standing in the door to her study, I said her name. Rachel looked up, her brows furrowed. She seemed to have been concentrating on a difficult problem. When she saw the look on my face, she stood up.

"What? Who is it? Are the kids OK?"

"Two men to talk to you. They said they have bad news."

Rachel took the stairs at a run. I remember worrying that she might trip, that she could fall down the stairs and hurt herself. She stopped at the bottom and, clinging to the banister, looked across the foyer to the men, who stood just inside the door.

"What is it? Tell me," she said. "What happened?"

"I'm Raymond Johnson," said one of the men. "My colleague is Peter Herman. What we have to say will not be easy. Is there someplace convenient where you could sit down?" Rachel just stood and stared. I led her into an adjoining sitting room and to the nearest chair. The men followed.

"We understand that your parents, Jerome and Esther Horowitz, were passengers on Small World Airways Flight 1227 flying from Crete to Tel Aviv earlier this morning." Rachel nodded, almost imperceptibly. "Peter and I both work for Small World, here in its Washington office. I am very sorry to inform you that your parents' plane lost power not long after take-off and went down into the Mediterranean. There were no survivors."

My wife was silent for a few seconds. Then she started keening. It was the sound I myself had made back in 1974 when I first came to grips with the fact that my mother was gone forever—the same sound that can be heard over and over again in jungles, prairies, mountains ... basically, in every spot where mammals lose their loved ones. A keen should never be confused with a cry. A cry comes from the heart. A keen comes from a place that is deeper still.

Over a thousand people attended the Horowitzes' joint funeral. Rachel delivered a beautiful eulogy. She praised her father as the most charitable person she had ever known and her mother as the bedrock of any success the family had enjoyed. Ten eulogies were delivered in all, three by U.S. Senators. As Chairman of the Board of Directors of the American Zionist Political Action Committee, commonly known as "AZPAC," Jerome Horowitz had worked closely with a number of Senators and Representatives on issues pertaining to Israel.

Among the attendees at the funeral was one Moses Levine. He knew Rachel wasn't his biggest fan but wanted to show his support nonetheless. I'll always remember sitting in our living room with Moses and a few of Rachel's cousins listening to her hold court about the cause of her parents' death. She was convinced they had been murdered by Arab terrorists. Investigators never confirmed that, but neither could they offer another explanation for the crash. Officially, its cause remains unknown to this day.

"I know what happened," Rachel told us. "Mom and Dad were big on convenience. Instead of flying El Al, they flew whatever airline had the best flight times. I'm sure some Arabs got on their plane and took it down.

"As long as I live," she continued, waving her finger at us as if we all had had something to do with the crash, "I'm going to fight those bastards with every drop of blood in my body. Watch me!"

As the Horowitzes' only heir and an already accomplished manager of the family charities, Rachel was considered a natural successor to Jerome's various ventures. Sure enough, she took them over, including his real estate business. Rachel spent the first two weeks after the funeral at home, supposedly to abstain from any kind of work altogether. But the truth is that within two days of her parents' death, her mind was beginning to focus on how she could run the family empire. She wanted to be every bit the executive her father had been. In fact, she wanted to *expand* the empire. Nothing less, she felt, would honor his legacy.

The significance of how wealthy I had become didn't hit me until Rachel went back to work. It was then that I questioned her sanity in not having demanded a prenuptial agreement. Make no mistake; that was *her* choice. Before we were married, I actually encouraged her to draft up a contract, as I didn't want her to resent me every time the issue of money was raised. But she would have none of it.

"A marriage is a lifelong commitment," she said. "I don't need a prenup. What kind of Jew comes before God, participates in a ceremony pledging herself to another person, and then breaks it off? I trust you, and I trust myself."

Rachel even went one step further and suggested that for

our wedding vows, we recite the passage from the Book of Ruth that says: "Where you go, I will go, where you stay, I will stay. Your people shall be my people, and your God, my God. Where you die, I will die, and there I will be buried. May God deal with me ever so severely, if anything but death shall come between us."

I heard that same set of vows recited at an earlier wedding and found the part about "dealing with me ... severely" to be kind of creepy. So I vetoed the idea. Then again, unlike Rachel and me, that other couple is still together.

It's impossible to deny the effect that money, *real* money, had on me. Like most Americans, rich and poor alike, I had previously seen myself as a member of the middle class—the hallowed middle class to which politicians love to pander. The fiction about my lack of extreme wealth survived the first few years of our marriage, but it couldn't survive my jaunt to Barbados when I accompanied the new President and CEO of Horowitz Enterprises on her private jet en route to a company retreat.

All the executives had known Rachel for years, but not as the top dog. It was an absolute hoot watching them operate. Some were shy and measured. Most, though, were far too ambitious not to display their feathers. Between the glad-handers and the brown-nosers, there was no shortage of entertainment. They seized every opportunity to treat Rachel as if she were either a childhood friend or the Pope himself. As for my wife, she was taking it all in with her characteristic intensity. By scrutinizing her staff in every way possible, she hoped to be able to identify a handful of people whom she could trust with the day-to-day management of her company.

Rachel had the luxury of taking over the Horowitzes' real estate business prior to the passage of the Sarbanes-Oxley law. CEOs could close their eyes with impunity as to what was going on beneath them. Many were little different from James Bond's arch nemesis, Ernst Staflo Blofeld, who once told his deputy: "Never mind the details. Just get me the diamonds."

Rachel didn't quite go that far. She was, by nature, a hands-on manager. But she saw managing the Horowitz's commercial ventures solely as a means to building the bottom line. She had faith that if she selected the right people to serve as officers and treated them with *honor*, not just respect, they would be loyal to the Horowitz name, and her companies would thrive. That way, she could be free to devote most of her time to what she truly loved: continuing to oversee the family's charitable foundation.

Soon, though, another activity would compete for my wife's attention. Only months after her parents' deaths, Rachel acquired her father's position as the head of AZPAC. With Rachel at the helm, AZPAC embarked on a new campaign. It would target any American politician who spoke loudly enough against the Israeli treatment of the Palestinian people. Believe me, AZPAC wasn't omnipotent, but it had enough power to destroy many a political career. Eventually, Rachel's work as head of AZPAC would become the activity that most defined her in my eyes.

While I fully shared Rachel's commitment to Israel, we expressed it in different ways. As a Zionist, I preferred the carrot to the stick. With Moses' encouragement, I sought out dialogues with Muslim clerics throughout America who truly loved peace, including some who opposed Israel's right to exist. If there is to be a Jewish state in the world, they argued, justice suggests it should be in Europe, the historical capital of anti-Semitic persecution. My public debates with those clerics were frustrating at times, but through these debates, I emerged wiser and better able to defend the Israeli position.

With respect to charities, I admired Rachel's decision to spread millions upon millions of dollars supporting Jewish organizations throughout the United States and around the world. But my instincts weren't nearly so magnanimous. To the extent I influenced the family's purse strings, I made sure the money would be spent right in our own backyard. In other words, I directed that we lavish money on Congregation Beth Hashem.

My goals were to create one of the most spiritual and fastest-growing Conservative synagogues in America, and I'd like to think we succeeded. It would be nice to credit our success to my good looks or oratorical skills. But this is America. So, naturally, I'd have to attribute our good fortune to greenbacks.

Our membership drive was jump-started from the first day that Rachel agreed to open the Horowitz family bank book. We immediately cut dues by 60%, which was quite enticing to the "two-day-a-year" Jews who'd been paying thousands of dollars annually to a shul they only attended on the High Holidays. We also expanded the seating capacity of our sanctuary, increased the salaries of our school teachers, and bought out the contract of the current cantor. To replace him, we hired two of the most renowned Jewish voices in America — a soprano and a tenor. When the two sang together for the first time, I knew they could do so much more for the hearts of my congregants than I could ever accomplish with my sermons. Yet that didn't bother me in the slightest, because sitting on the bimah I could benefit from the spiritual uplift as much as anybody. Often, I'd simply forget I was a rabbi and drift off in prayer.

On occasion, one of the older congregants would tell me that I was turning the place into a Christian church—or worse yet (in their minds) a Reform temple—but I didn't take their criticism seriously. I never took the next step of permitting choirs, guitars, or organs in the sanctuary services, as you'd commonly find in a Reform place of worship. I simply introduced the harmony of two superb voices in a building traditionally reserved for a single musical leader. How could that possibly violate the principles of my ancestors?

Many people have told me they'd rather listen to our cantors, a cappella, than any other Jewish musicians in America. I have to say, though, that those voices didn't come cheaply. Each of the cantors earned more, in fact, than our associate rabbi. As for me, I was able to work for $1 a year. The assets of Jerome and Esther Horowitz took care of any need for further compensation.

I was never embarrassed by the riches that the Horowitzes enabled me to lavish on my synagogue. Moses once told me that there was no better use of money than thoughtfully throwing it in a spiritual direction and then studying when the money made a difference and when it didn't. What I learned at Beth Hashem is that a rabbi—or at least *this* rabbi—should be as much of a General Manager as a quarterback. Our congregants knew it too: my roles as teacher and pastor were important, but no more so than ensuring that the classrooms were staffed with devoted teachers or that the sanctuary was filled with prayerful music. It's not easy to accomplish those goals on the cheap.

There was one respect in which my nouveau riche status bothered me. Part of me felt guilty every time I drove my 1983 Volvo up the driveway of the Horowitz estate, which upon my in-laws' deaths became the property—and residence — of Rachel and Richie Gold.

When the Horowitzes lived in the house, it had a very formal feel to it, both inside and out. They liked to entertain, and entertaining for them included impressing guests with all the trappings of affluence—a reminder that an evening with the Horowitzes should never be taken lightly. You can believe that the house changed dramatically once Rachel and I took it over; it took on a more comfortable, relaxed feel. But who am I kidding — at 12,000 square feet, it was still the home of aristocrats, and deep down I knew that Jews shouldn't live like aristocrats. Our only Lord should be the Holy One, blessed be His name.

After Rachel's parents died, she and I spoke briefly about selling the mansion and remaining in our "middle-class" home a few miles to the southwest. In theory, that made sense to her. In practice, she couldn't give up the big house—at least not until she needed to run away from yours truly—as it allowed her to feel that her parents remained a part of her life. I can't count the number of times she walked in the door and immediately began engaging them in a one-sided conversation.

"Do you think they can hear you?" I asked Rachel, interrupting her as she spoke to a picture of her father taken when he was a boy.

"I don't know," she said. "I guess I feel they can. You never talk to your mom?"

"Occasionally," I said. "I can't explain why, but I do it too."

CHAPTER XVI

"In setting our organization's goals, let's not aim too low. In fact, what do you say we shoot for the moon? Sure, we want to promote harmony between Muslims and Jews. Sure, we want to educate people about what makes our religions unique and beautiful. But those aims are modest and parochial. We also need some big, universal goals.

"If you're like me, you're sick and tired of living in a world where 'progressive' and 'religious' have become antonyms, and where everyone associates religion with fundamentalists. So why should we put up with it? We've got to show the folks in Middle America— Grant Wood's America — that their values and ours aren't all that different, and neither is our passion for God. We need people to understand that whether you're talking about Jesus, Moses or Muhammad, you're talking about a progressive thinker—not a rigid, right-wing conservative.

"Somehow, religion has lost its religiosity. We're going to bring it back."

Moses Levine, president of Peoples of Priests,
addressing his staff, 2002

Oslo, Norway—October 2004. Moses received his Nobel

Peace Prize in October 2004, a year and a half after he persuaded President Forrest to end the Iraq War. I flew out with Moses to the ceremony.

After he accepted his award, I was thinking about how reassuring it was that Moses hadn't mentioned his connection to his biblical namesake in well over a year. Then, in a moment of silliness, I turned to Moses and said "Well, look at you, a Nobel Prize laureate. You've now accomplished something even Moshe Rabbenu never accomplished."

"He has now," Moses deadpanned.

"You are kidding, aren't you?"

Moses stared at me, but he didn't say a word. He didn't have to.

"So you still think of yourself –."

"I've never stopped," he interrupted. "You thought that just because I don't talk about it any more, I no longer see myself as Moshe Rabbenu?"

My heart sank. "I assumed —" I began, but he interrupted again.

"To live like him, it's not about talking," Moses said. "It's about *doing*. I've been busy, Richie. I don't think anyone could deny that."

On the flight back from Oslo, Moses only wanted to talk about his co-Nobel honoree, Hafeez Ali, and his cause du jour, an idea for legislation designed to fight poverty and support public education. That's how Moses described the idea to me. When he began marketing it to the public a month later, he called it simply "Investing in Our Future."

Moses always had one of the most liberal minds I've ever known. To be sure, there were issues on which he sincerely sided with the conservatives. Yet his heart was invariably with the poor and the working class, and he despised governmental interference with civil liberties.

My friend was nothing if not shrewd, however, and he had realized for a long time that in American politics, "liberal" had become a dirty word. Moses taught me that if a progressive wants the public to agree with him, he has to remove any trappings of stereotypical interest-group liberalism from his rhetoric. Indeed, he has to frame his leftist thoughts in traditional, conservative values.

The bill that POP began to champion shortly after the 2004 elections was sponsored by two Congressmen from Wisconsin, a Republican (Paul Monk) and a Democrat (Edgar Parker). Privately, Moses credited Monk and Parker with being the bill's primary strategists and tacticians, but I never knew whether to believe him. He may simply have placed Monk and Parker in the same comfortable role that his dreams assigned to the brothers Isaac and Asher in their dealings with Moses' namesake. In any event, whatever Moses' role was behind the scenes, this much was clear: publicly, Moses was the bill's face, voice and benefactor. No, he didn't bankroll anything; in fact, his net worth had never approached anywhere near a million dollars. Still, by the end of 2004, most Americans had come to credit Moses with saving hundreds of billions of dollars that we were about to throw away in Iraq. If Moses was willing to propose a direction in which America should spend its money, the public was going to listen.

The proponents of the Investing in Our Future bill took care to ensure that it pushed the fewest number of right wing buttons possible. There would be no minimum wage hikes, no increases in traditional entitlements (such as AFDC or food stamps), and no additional bureaucracies. Yes, the bill would necessitate an increase in taxes needed to finance the measure, but the brunt of those tax hikes would not be borne by the poor or middle class. Instead, Moses simply persuaded Forrest to repeal some of the so-called "tax cuts for the rich" that were enacted early in his administration.

The bill had two components—one that required a non-recurring set of expenses and the other requiring expenses that, in theory, would continue forever. The first involved $100

billion in public works construction, centering on such areas as
mass transit development, sewer projects, and the rebuilding of
schools and hospitals. Most of the money would be earmarked
for the inner cities, but some would be spent on poor rural
areas. The result would be a massive investment in the infrastructure of the poorest areas in the country. And, as a bonus,
reasonably well-paying construction jobs would be provided to
tens of thousands of laborers in these areas, thereby removing
many of those workers and their families from poverty.

The bill's second component was cheaper in the short run
— $60 billion. The problem for the fiscally frugal, however,
was that this $60 billion amount would be a recurring budget
item; in fact, it would increase in future years in lockstep with
the Consumer Price Index. Moses' suggestion was simple to
explain. The money would be used to increase the salary of
every primary and secondary school teacher in the nation.
Administrators and resource specialists would get nothing
from the bill; nor would substitute teachers. The only recipi-
ents would be full-time classroom teachers—all 2.8 million of
them.

"We can't solve everybody's problems with just one bill,"
Moses liked to say. "What we can do is stop our schools from
being a national joke. Why should anyone go into teaching
today if they could double their money selling cars?"

The bill's education proposal represented a pay raise of
roughly 25 percent for the nation's teachers—or should I say
a *mere* 25 percent. "Twenty-five percent more than nothing
is still nothing," argued a Democratic Congressman from
Vermont. It was a perspective Moses might have shared himself
if he weren't so desperate to help out any way he could. He
simply refused to believe that prospective teachers would be
indifferent to the additional 25 percent in pay, and he knew
that nothing more would be politically feasible.

"To those who say we should reward the *best* teachers, not
all teachers equally," Moses declared, when testifying before

Congress, "you'll get no argument from me. If a teacher can't teach, he should be fired, and the unions should stop making it so hard on administrators to remove ineffective teachers from their jobs. By the same token, if a teacher is exceptional, he should be paid more for it. But the federal government has no business trying to determine which teachers are inspired, which are merely competent, and which have no business in the classroom. Decisions like that belong to the states and localities.

"Today, we're proposing that the federal government do its part to rebuild the excellence of our public schools, which used to be the envy of the world but no longer can compete internationally. What we're *not* proposing is to federalize our nation's classrooms. This bill is just a jump-start. Education begins and ends with the states and local school systems; they need to take primary responsibility for educational excellence. If you want that responsibility assigned to your federal government, move to Cuba or North Korea."

There you have it—red-baiting, states-loving, anti-union rhetoric. Moses might not have been as familiar with his inner Joseph McCarthy as his inner Eugene McCarthy, but he knew how to appeal to the heartland. He always enjoyed bringing conservative arguments to bear on an issue as long as his ultimate goal was egalitarian, peace loving and spiritual. In this case, he deeply wanted to honor the philosophy of his mother, the teacher of underprivileged black children, but he never mentioned her by name. Instead, he liked to invoke the name of Ronald Reagan.

"The great President Reagan spoke about a rising tide lifting all boats. That's what this bill is all about when it comes to investing in our children's future. If the schoolhouse is like a harbor, we need to raise the tide and lift every boat. Increase the salaries of public school teachers, and the private schools will follow suit. That means you'll have happier teachers and better educated students across the board. When this bill becomes law, it really will be Morning in America, just like President Reagan said."

The truth is that even though Moses rarely agreed with Reagan's positions on the issues, he loved the man's honesty and courage. To Moses, Reagan was a man of vision who didn't mind taking unpopular positions and stating them with conviction. Moses often pined for a day when this nation would elect a President who was just like Reagan except for two things: *she* would be a *liberal*.

The "Investing in Our Future" bill received plenty of conservative opposition. Talking about the idea of construction projects mandated by the federal government, Republican Representative Leonard Jackson said on the floor of the House, "We'd be better off building a giant toilet and flushing the money down. Then at least we could get on with our lives, instead of being caught up in a government nightmare that never ends."

Other political leaders focused their outrage at the rolling back of Forrest's tax cuts. They saw it as the beginning of a slippery slope that could usher in a new era of soaking the rich, and God knows how people in my tax bracket fight for every dollar.

Another large group of opponents to the bill, and the one that bothered Moses the most, was the school voucher crowd. For years, they had claimed that the problem with our public schools wasn't low teacher salaries but the fact that these schools are monopolies, and thus unaccountable to the marketplace. An alternative would be to provide vouchers to *all* American families, rich and poor alike, to use on the public or private school of their choice. That way, parent choices would supposedly weed out the bad schools and reward the good ones.

Moses and his colleagues at POP took pleasure in refuting these various arguments. The first was easy enough to dispose of. POP pointed out that we all had been waiting for years for the private sector to finance the necessary construction by itself, but that hadn't happened. So our economy obviously needed a little push from the government. "Why be afraid of creating high quality school buildings, or decent public transportation systems?" Moses said. "Private industry will oversee the work. The government will foot the bill, but it won't micromanage anything. Anyone who tells you otherwise is just fear-mongering. The next thing you know they'll be talking about 'Pool, right here in River City...'"

As for the argument against tax hikes, Moses was similarly dismissive. "Let me be very blunt," he said during a widely-watched debate. "*Nobody* will feel a difference in their taxes on account of this bill. The taxes of middle income and poor people will hardly change. And yes, the richest Americans might pay more, but they can afford to. You know it, and they know it.

"It irks me," he continued, "to hear people say that affluent Americans are going to leave this country in droves if they have to foot the bill for what I'm proposing. We're talking about patriotic Americans who often spend their weekends practicing religions that associate greed with the worst of vices. Do we really think they're such hypocrites that they'll kiss their country goodbye the minute there's a buck to be made elsewhere? Our business leaders deserve more respect than that!"

As the son of Miriam Levine, Moses reserved his greatest passion for the arguments against vouchers. "What's at stake is the creation of a caste system in America," Moses said on the Ripley show. "Let's say we keep teacher salaries low and give every kid a few thousand dollars to spend on the school of her choice. What'll happen? Rich families will take the money and spend it on the best private schools, which will still cost many times the value of their vouchers. Everyone else will choose among public schools and the poorer private schools— and they'll be taught by teachers who'll continue to get lousy wages.

"Whoever thought of vouchers is almost like Robin Hood in reverse. They want to take money that could be available to help middle class and poor Americans, and instead hand it to the rich to soften the blow when they shell out fifteen grand a year on Junior's education. So when Junior gets older, not only will the public school grads pump his gas, but on the weekends, their teachers can too. I'm sorry, but that just doesn't sound like America to me."

As the time approached for a vote on the bill, Moses was confident that his side had the better of the debates, and yet somehow they lacked a majority. The House wasn't a problem; it was the Senate. Many of Moses' allies wanted to force a vote and embarrass the naysayers, but Moses felt that this was too important an issue to achieve merely symbolic victories, so he brokered a compromise. Moses persuaded Monk and Parker to announce that they were withdrawing their bill and resubmitting an amended bill that cut a full $20 billion from the original proposal in public works construction costs. The Congressmen made the announcement on national television with Moses at their side. Moses then took the mike and singled out five Republican Senators who had challenged the inefficiencies in the original bill and forced him and his allies to reconsider whether they hadn't been cavalier about needlessly spending the taxpayers' money.

I'll never forget seeing Moses tell a national audience that he had taken on the personal challenge of providing virtually the same benefits to the American public at a significantly lower cost. "We're going to show the taxpayers what it means to treat federal moneys like our own," he said. "We have all sorts of cheapskates involved in this process—believe me, we know how to be frugal." The next day, with Monk and Parker back in their offices, Moses was interviewed on four different syndicated radio programs—liberal, conservative, he didn't discriminate. He praised Monk and Parker for their flexibility; he praised the five dissenting Senators for their resolve and their insight; and he personally assumed responsibility for any blame that was due.

Needless to say, at the time he was helping us "Invest in Our Future," Moses' public image was made of Teflon. Far from criticizing Moses for submitting an over-bloated bill, the talking heads and op-ed writers praised all concerned for handling the legislation in a manner befitting a democracy. As the New York Times reported in its editorial, "Moses Levine made no mistake here. You never call something a mistake when it's corrected before damage is done." Within three weeks of Moses' media blitz, each of the dissenting Senators that he had previously singled out had agreed to support the streamlined, but still massive bill. Soon thereafter, the modified Investing in Our Future proposal passed the Senate by the slimmest of margins.

Despite Forrest's support for vouchers before he came to Washington, once the bill garnered modest majorities in both houses, the President signed it. Call it loyalty, call it a change of philosophy, call it whatever you want—when the time came and his signature was needed to save the bill, Forrest was there when his friend needed him, at least at that point in his presidency. That, of course, was before Moses' name became associated with blasphemy and delusions of grandeur.

PART III

CHAPTER XVII

*"I can't believe it, Richie. I had another dream last night—another one of **those** dreams. I never thought I'd have another one again after we left Israel, and I hadn't until the Nobel Prize ceremony. But there was something about standing up there and accepting that award. I think it's a sign that I've got to work harder — you know, accomplish things that are more meaningful. Otherwise I'd be a big fraud, more like Arafat than Moses."*

Rabbi Moses Levine speaking at
his home to Rabbi Richie Gold, 2004

New York City—May 2006. Thousands of miles from Mount Sinai, Moses daydreamed about the Golden Calf. Sitting only four feet away, I could tell he was lost in reverie. What I couldn't understand was how he could pick such an inopportune time to ignore his surroundings. It's not like we were back in some dungeon in East Jerusalem. We were in the Big Apple being filmed in front of a studio audience and broadcast live to millions of Americans watching on television. The date was May 14, 2006, one that I will always associate with tragedy, no less than June 28, 1914, or September 11, 2001.

In his dream, Moses was walking down a mountain accom-

181

panied by the two brothers, Isaac and Asher. Not a soul spoke; they all were consumed by the gravity of the moment.

Isaac, the artist who had crafted the two large stone tablets, led the group, carrying Commandments 1-5. His brother Asher followed, carrying Commandments 6-10. The group's leader trailed the two brothers. He was thinking less about the Ten Commandments than about the hundreds of other laws he and his comrades had conceived during the weeks they had spent on the mountain top. He knew it was just a matter of time before all of these Commandments would become the law of his people.

They were less than a half-mile from the foot of the mountain when the leader told the brothers to put down the tablets. "I'll take them the rest of the way. Now go join the people." Tablets in hand, he continued to make his way down until he saw his own brother, Aaron, waiting beside the boulder they had designated as their meeting place.

"Moses, we have to talk," Aaron said, anguished. "You won't believe what I did."

Moses put down the tablets and gave his brother a bear hug. Aaron clung to him, as if for dear life.

"What is it, Aaron?" Moses asked. "What happened while I was gone?"

"You're going to think I acted like a traitor," Aaron said.

"Relax," Moses replied. "I know you're not a traitor."

"You don't understand," Aaron said. "You were gone for weeks. I was facing a rebellion. The people needed something concrete, something to remind them that God wouldn't leave them in the desert just to rot away. I didn't have a choice, I didn't —"

"Please!" Moses said. "Get a grip on yourself and listen to me. We did it, Aaron. We did it! We went up the mountain with nothing, and we're coming down with a set of laws that'll keep our people together for hundreds, even thousands of years.

As long as everyone's safe and sound below, it's OK. Whatever happened can be undone."

"You don't understand. What I helped build represents everything we stand against. It's a huge calf made of gold. I wanted it to give the people a sense of being blessed by God's Providence. But I didn't mean for them to worship it."

"No, I'm sure you didn't," Moses said.

"They see everything in that God-forsaken calf," Aaron continued. "Fertility, vitality, lordship, beauty —"

"I get the idea," Moses said.

"I'm telling you, the people were like children who'd just been orphaned. I didn't see any choice."

"Maybe there wasn't any," Moses said. "Look, we'll turn this into a way to teach them about the new law."

"What do you want me to do?" asked Aaron.

"Gather the people as if you're calling them to worship. Once they're all together, I'll speak to them about what they've done. You'll need to find Isaac and Asher and tell them to meet me on the mountain top with two new tablets. I'll head back up as soon as I finish my talk."

In Moses' dream, it seemed to be only a nanosecond later when he approached the calf with fire in his eyes. Hundreds of people surrounded the idol, all of them singing, most of them dancing. Moses paid them no mind. He simply walked past them so he could reach the icon as quickly as possible. As they realized who was approaching, the revelers froze in their tracks.

"I hold in these hands the Commandments of God," Moses thundered, as he stood next to the calf of gold. "I've spent weeks without human interaction of any kind so that I may keep the Divine Unity at the center of all my thoughts and feelings. The Holy One has inspired me to develop a new set of laws, the most critical of which have been inscribed in these two tablets. I intend these laws to form the basis of a permanent covenant between the Hebrew people and the infinite, transcendent One underlying all that exists, has existed or will exist throughout eternity.

"Let me be clear: these Commandments were written by me, a mortal man, not by the Holy Source of All Substance. And yet I consider them Commandments just the same. As your leader, I am duty bound to create for you a foundation that will ground our peace and prosperity for generations to come. In this task, I have been inspired by nothing more than the love of the One God. That love requires that God be honored every moment of every day. And so I have honored God during the weeks I spent crafting the laws of our people.

"In bringing you these laws, I came to honor you as well. To bestow upon you the greatest gift I can imagine—the prospect of a life lived cleanly, respectfully, reverently. But look at what you have done while I have been gone. You have created a god of your own, a competitor to the One and Only—a god made by man, not altogether different from a thousand other gods you could have chosen in its place. This is not *the* God. This is not my God. That God is unique—not one being among many, but Being Itself! We do not possess God for our own tribes. We recognize in God the light that shines on all tribes—and, for that matter, the darkness too. For everything that is, is in God. What we love, what we hate, all of it.

"I know how comfortable and natural it must feel to worship something magnificent and tangible like this calf of gold. Or if not that, to at least worship something we can relate to, a human-like god perhaps, some sort of ideal king or judge. But hear this: as long as we continue to worship gods that are not transcendent ... as long as we come to love our gods simply because they are so familiar to us ... we will not be worshipping God at all. We will simply be projecting our own ideals and hopes onto an imaginary deity that we create for our own purposes. To worship, to truly worship, is to honor God for God's sake, not ours.

"When I sculpted these stones, I thought they would

represent the strength of our community. But that is because I thought you would be ready for them. I can see now you are not. And in your idolatry, you have sapped these words of all their strength. Behold!"

With that, Moses smashed one of the tablets with all his force into the body of the calf, and yet the calf remained standing, whereas the tablet disintegrated. Moses then took the second tablet and smashed it into the ground, with the same result.

"Never again may you equate God to *any* form on this earth," Moses continued. "Associate God with everything. Equate God to nothing. Not to wind, nor water, nor even to the greatest among you. From this moment on, you must realize what it means to be a member of the Hebrew people. Hebrews are prepared to sacrifice everything they hold dear for the opportunity to proclaim their love for the Transcendent One. And Hebrews must live consistently with a body of law inspired by that love. My tablets were so inspired. And now, they are gone, and you have in their place a block of loveless, lifeless gold—magnificent, but ultimately worthless to our well being.

"So now I must go back up the mountain. I must pray that each of you will forsake what you have created during these past few weeks and ready yourselves for a life devoted to the only God that is truly unique. While I am away, meditate on these words:

"We cannot know what God wills, or even *if* God wills. We cannot know what God feels, or even *if* God feels. We cannot think of God in terms of any likeness or any characteristic of an earthly being. But we can love the life that reflects God's eternal presence. And armed with this love, we can come together one and all, in peace, justice, and humility."

With that, Moses left the calf, which stood intact, and headed back toward the mountain. His eyes remained as intense as before, but the intensity belied the doubt that was in his heart. "I know that Isaac and Asher expect me to be the figurehead, the personification of all things wise. But who am I to keep this up? Who am I to single-handedly shape the Hebrews into a 'people of priests and a holy nation'? I so wish that I could level with everyone—that I could explain to them who I am, and who I am *not*."

Moses later told me that his daydream about the Calf took only seconds. It began during a break in filming and ended after filming had resumed, when I was on the hot seat.

"Rabbi Gold, did you hear me?" boomed Harry Ripley's voice. "Should I rephrase the question?"

"Yes, please," I said slowly. Truthfully, I heard the question. I just needed more time to collect my thoughts.

"Fair enough," said Ripley. "I'd like to know if you've ever dreamt you were a biblical character."

It must have sounded to most people like an odd thing to ask — kind of like asking me if I'd ever wished I were a tree. But I didn't find the question strange as much as scary. It was OK for Ripley to ask it of me. I just didn't want him to ask it of Moses.

"I don't remember many of my dreams," I finally said. "When I do remember them, they're usually nightmares. And I'm not playing a role, I'm just myself, Richie Gold, having some horrible experience. That's sad for a rabbi to admit, isn't it? I should be more at peace."

"I've never thought of rabbis as being at peace," Ripley replied. "Aren't you all too troubled by the problems of the world?"

"You're probably right," I said, a little more relaxed. "Maybe I should just be blunt and say that I'm not very comfortable talking about my dreams. They're private."

"Nothing on this show is private," Ripley responded. "Otherwise no one would tune in. Am I right, everybody?" Ripley lifted up his hands asking for applause, and he earned more than enough to stay on the same track. "What about you,

Rabbi Levine?" he continued. "Have you ever dreamt that you're Job? Or Abraham?"

Gradually, a look of clarity returned to Moses' face. "I must have. I dream about many things. And the Torah is never far from my mind—it can't be far from my subconscious either."

At that, the look on Ripley's face changed. Until then, he had been acting his customary jovial self, but suddenly he became deadly serious. "Rabbi Levine, do you ever recall dreaming that *you*, Moses Levine, are *the* Biblical Moses?"

Moses Levine didn't immediately respond to Ripley. Instead, he lifted his right eyebrow in my direction. I had known my friend long enough to recognize that he was asking for help.

I laughed nervously. "Some things should be known only by a man and his God," I said, facing Ripley. "I include dreams in that category. You don't?"

"I'd say you can learn more about people from what they dream than what they think," Ripley said.

"How about we call your wife," Moses replied, "and tell her to listen while you share your dreams with the American public, *all* your dreams. I wonder how long you'd stay married."

"Wait a minute," said Ripley, a little miffed. "I wasn't asking you about *those* kinds of dreams. I was —"

"*Anything* we dream when we're asleep is personal," Moses interrupted. "I want your audience to know about my hopes and dreams for this world and for America. But I don't want to talk about what goes on inside my head when I'm sleeping. Guests on this show shouldn't have to share that. Maybe I'm being sensitive —"

"Just a little," Ripley replied.

"I don't think so," I said, interrupting their conversation. "Privacy is important. If a rabbi won't stand up for it, who will?"

"But Rabbi Levine has always preached about the importance of *sharing*," Ripley replied. "Sharing your money, sharing your land if it's in dispute, sharing your deepest thoughts about religion. I wanted to give him a chance to practice what he preached."

"Sorry," Moses said. "Once I turn off the lights and go to sleep, I sleep alone."

Ripley's studio was two blocks north of Times Square. Moses and I walked out of the building together and hailed a cab to get to Penn Station. The ride was spent in total silence—no sports, no politics, not even polite banter. When we arrived at the terminal, Moses told me that we needed to find a place where we could talk. But it was impossible. One person after another approached us to ask for our autographs. Mine too, not just Moses'. Finally, he threw up his hands and said, "We're going to have to wait until we get to Washington. Being a celebrity can be a nuisance, can't it?"

"I thought it was what you wanted," I told him.

"A means to an end," he replied, "as awful as it is necessary."

CHAPTER XVIII

"Is there anything more divisive than religion? You might say politics, but I don't think so. Here in America, members of one political party might get mad at the other, but at least we can all agree that we're demo-crats—democrats with a small 'd'—and that there's something beautiful about principles such as the rule of the majority and the rights of the minority.

"When it comes to religion, there has been no unifying force. And please don't tell me we're unified by a belief in God. Just because two people claim to believe in God doesn't mean it's the same God. Otherwise, after I finish lecturing about theology, people wouldn't keep walking up to me to say that I'm an atheist in rabbi's clothing. Believe me, I'm no atheist. I just don't buy into the traditional concept of divinity.

*"If you want religion to be unifying and not divisive, it's quite simple. Don't focus on the moral or theolog-ical wisdom you've found. Focus on the **search** for wisdom. A fellow traveler isn't someone who agrees with your beliefs; a fellow traveler is someone who shares your passion for the search. That's one thing all truly religious people have in common."*

Rabbi Moses Levine, addressing the
Washington, D.C. Islamic Center, 2004.

On the train tracks between New York City and Washington, D.C.—May 2006. The Ripley show airs at nine in the evening and is filmed three hours earlier. That gave Moses and me plenty of time to grab a bite and still catch the 8:15 Acela to Washington. I had hoped we could find a couple of seats together in the quiet car but found none. So we settled for a spot right behind the café car. There, we were treated to one cell-phone conversation after another by the passenger to our left—a bottle-blonde who apparently provided consulting services to nursing homes ranging from New York to Maryland. It's not like I cared a whit about what she was saying, but I would've had to be deaf to ignore it altogether.

Moses seemed to be engrossed in thought—or maybe another reverie—leaving me to my book, a recent tract about Jews living in 15th century Spain. Unfortunately, I couldn't concentrate. The Ripley show weighed too heavily on my mind.

Perhaps, I thought, I was exaggerating the threat Ripley posed. Then again, there was no denying the magnitude of what was at stake. Moses Levine wasn't just another rabbi. While he had his share of detractors, Moses was arguably the single most beloved figure in America. He was widely revered as an ambassador for world peace and interfaith dialogue. An accomplished anti-poverty fighter, he was as respected by the conservative White House as by the liberal establishment. And his name was commonly associated with a sweeping bill to attack global warming that was then being considered by the United States Congress.

Moses also happened to be my closest friend on the planet, as well as my hero. And yet I had no doubt that if the truth about his dreams were to emerge—the *whole* truth that is—the name of Moses Levine would become little more than a punch line.

How much of that truth, I wondered, did Ripley actually know? And how the heck did he find out? I hadn't a clue.

Our train pulled out of Wilmington, Delaware about 9:45. The nursing home consultant to our left was still chatting away, but the quiet couple who had been sitting in the row right in front of us had just left the train. They were replaced by a scruffy, red-haired man with a noticeable paunch, who appeared to be in his mid-50s. As soon as he saw Moses and me and proceeded to open his mouth, we could tell what he had been doing with himself.

"Well I'll be darned," he said, staring straight at Moses like he had seen a ghost. "I was just watching you on TV."

"Must have been the Ripley show," Moses said. "We filmed it this evening before it was aired."

"That's the one," the man said, his breath reeking of gin. "I wanted to keep watching, but I had to get home."

"Where's home?" Moses asked.

"Spotsylvania County," he replied. "The Commonwealth of Virginia."

"I know it well," Moses said. "You're halfway between DC and Richmond."

"That's right, Rab-bi Levine," he said, pronouncing Moses' title as if it were two different words. "I like to call it the gateway to the South."

"That's funny," Moses said. "That's kind of how I see myself. Not really northern; not really southern."

"I got no problem sayin' I'm plenty southern," the man said. "Allow me to introduce myself. My name's Jones. William Jones," he said, his tone suddenly more serious. "I've been following your career for many years—ever since you wrote that book."

"Oh, you read *Exodus: Then and Now*?" I asked.

"I did," Jones said. "It's got some wild ideas, if you ask me. Not that anyone's askin'."

"Please," Moses said. "I'm always interested in feedback."

"You want feedback, do you?" Jones said. "Real, honest-to-God feedback?" He was kneeling on his seat facing backwards toward our row and speaking at least as loudly as the nursing home consultant. I found myself feeling more and more confined and uncomfortable. "You're a godless man who calls himself a man of God, that's what I think."

"OK, Moses," I said. "Let's find some other seats."

"Wait a minute, Richie," Moses said. "You got that from reading my book?" he asked Jones.

"I got that from followin' your whole career," Jones replied. "I was a preacher too, you know. I had my own church, 'til they took it away from me."

"What happened?" Moses asked.

"I was married, but I had a little number on the side, one of my friends' adult daughters. Then the wife found out, and she hired a PI to take pictures. When she showed 'em to the folks at the church, I was hist'ry. Now I don't preach to nobody. I just drink."

"So let me get this straight," I said. "You're an adulterer and a drunk. But you're calling my friend here a fraud. Did I get that right?"

"Richie, c'mon," Moses said, before Jones answered. But answer he did.

"No, I'd say that's pretty accurate. I may be a drunk, and I may enjoy a nice young pair a' legs every now and then, but I know enough not to blaspheme the Lord."

"And how have I done that?" Moses asked matter-of-factly.

"You talk about the Bible like it's no more than a bunch of stories. You talk about Jesus like He's just another human being. You talk about God like He doesn't even love us—like your God is just a fancy word for nature."

"Well, that's not exactly what I teach," Moses began, but Jones interrupted him.

"You're an atheist who wants to use the name of God for your own purposes. So you invoke the name, and then you twist its meaning so that anyone who accepts the existence of the world can claim to be a believer."

"Moses has never said that," I chimed in, but Jones wasn't listening to either of us. He was back on the pulpit.

"The worst thing of all is that you have no faith that God'll look out for us. That's why you're always talking about how we're gonna blow ourselves up unless we fix our own problems. Those problems will be fixed, alright, but they'll be fixed by the Lord, once we put our faith in Him — once we stop worshiping ourselves, like you do." Any semblance of joviality was gone from Jones' face. And strangely, I had stopped smelling the gin too; I merely sensed the hostility. Moses must have felt it even more, for Jones was staring straight into his eyes.

"Do you know the difference between pantheism and panentheism?" Moses asked Jones.

"Sure do. One's a word real people understand—it's a type of atheism. The other's a word that godless intellectuals use to confuse people. That answer your question?"

"Moses," I said. "Seriously, let's go someplace else. Life's too short for this."

"No, no," he replied. "I'm fine. It's always useful to hear another perspective.

"Mr. Jones," he continued, turning to the inebriated ex-preacher. "I could call myself a panentheist, but I don't want to be accused of trying to confuse anyone. So I'll just say that you've misunderstood a lot of what I think. But in one respect, you've hit the nail on the head. I'm not waiting for God to save us. I'm not even waiting for prayer to save us. I do pray, but mostly, that just allows me to focus my own energies in a direction that I think is holy. I'm not looking for divine intervention. I'm looking for hard work—out of myself and out of everyone else who shares my goals. As long as you're drinking, by the way, you're not working."

"Don't cha worry about me, Mr. Rab-bi. I'll be getting off the sauce soon enough. Once my severance package ends, I'll need to find a new job. That'll straighten me up. Meanwhile, I'm gonna go get straight with Jesus. You wouldn't know much about Him, now would you?"

"Quite the contrary," Moses said, "I love to read the Gospels."

"Do you now?" Jones replied, sarcastically. "As literature, no doubt, just like the rest of the Scriptures. Well, it's not literature to me. It's the source of my spirituality."

I couldn't help myself. I started laughing. "Your spirituality?" I said. "What spirituality? From all appearances, you're just a nasty drunk."

Moses looked at me sternly and shook his head. Then he faced Jones. "So your reading of the Gospels tells you there's only one proper way to conceive of God, and that my perspective is blasphemous?"

"That it is, Mr. Rab-bi. The Bible said we were made in God's image. That tells you exactly what you need to know about the Lord. We all understand what it means to be godly, even I know. I've just strayed a bit, but I'll get myself back together— I'm already livin' without women; that's a heck of a start. Now I just have to learn to live without the juice, just like you've learned to live without God."

"Best of luck to you, sir," Moses said. If it were anyone else but Moses, I'd have thought he was being patronizing, but I knew my friend too well. "I'll be thinking about what you've said," Moses continued. "Maybe in the future I need to speak more clearly when I talk about my religious ideas."

"Oh, you speak plenty clearly," Jones replied. "That ain't the problem. You're bullheaded, like most of the godless people up north. Self-centered idol-worshippers, that's what y'all have become. There's a lot of ya' all over the world. That's why it's such a mess."

"I do wish you the best, Mr. Jones," Moses said. "But I think I'm going to get back to my book. I'm reading about panentheism. It's the idea that all of us are *in* God — we're all parts of

God — but God isn't just the sum total of things in the universe. God is transcendent."

"Man that's sad," Jones said. "They publish more and more books 'bout nonsense, don't they? Rab-bi, you enjoy your nonsense. I'll enjoy mine." He reached into his bag to grab another shot of gin just as the conductor was welcoming us all to Baltimore.

CHAPTER XIX

"There's no use in bullshitting, Richie. I know your wife doesn't like me. She disliked me even before I went into the rabbinate. Now she probably likes me even less.

"That's fine. I don't get my self-esteem from pleasing Israeli apologists. As long as she doesn't hire some modern-day Bugsy Siegel to whack open my skull, what harm could she ever do to me?"

Moses Levine, talking to Rabbi Richard Gold
soon after moving to the District of Columbia, 1999

Washington, D.C., May 2006: More than four hours had elapsed after the filming of the Harry Ripley Show before Moses and I could be alone. We were in my car heading to his apartment in Northwest D.C.

"So what's going on?" he asked. "I haven't mentioned those dreams to anyone."

"You've got to believe me, I haven't either. I swore I never would."

Moses closed his eyes. "Think about everyone you've talked to," he said. "Your father. Your sisters. Your *wife*." Having been married for eighteen years, fourteen of which were spent together, Rachel and I were expecting our divorce to be finalized within weeks of my appearance on the Ripley program.

196

"After you got back from Israel," Moses continued, "you must have said *something* to her."

"Nothing—not unless I talked in my sleep."

"If you were a sleep-talker, she probably stayed awake and listened," he said. "Or maybe she wired your bedroom." Moses wasn't generally snide, but when it came to a certain person, he made an exception.

"What about diaries or notes?" he asked. "I know you kept a journal."

"My God," I mumbled, before regaining my composure. "Could that have been what happened? Of course I took notes on your dreams. I analyzed them too. And you'll love this — I wrote that when you were awake, you saw yourself as the reincarnation of Moshe Rabbenu."

"Seriously?" he asked, obviously shaken.

"Yeah. What can I say? That was as interesting to me as the dreams. But I never shared the notes with anyone, not even Rachel."

"You had them in your house when you were living together," Moses said. "She could have found them."

"But those notes were in my private study. She wouldn't have gone in there. I didn't go into her study."

"You and she are very different people," Moses said. "Do me a favor. After you drop me off tonight, look for the notes. Maybe she got rid of them, or maybe she copied them and put them back in the wrong place. It wouldn't hurt to look."

"Rachel's got principles, Moses. I know you two weren't exactly friends —"

"I have a hunch she'd discredit me every way she could. I remember how single minded and passionate my mother could be about Jewish issues. Rachel's the same way. And I push all of her buttons, don't I?"

"She says you're the most dangerous man in America," I replied. "She calls you 'Goebbels-Lite.'"

"See what I mean? If Rachel took the notes and had them

publicized, I'd be just another in a long line of people she and her buddies have destroyed on behalf of Israel."

"Well, that's certainly true," I said. "But I still can't believe Rachel's the culprit."

"Just get the notes and show them to her," said Moses. "See how she reacts."

"She'll get indignant that I didn't trust her, that's how."

"Listen," Moses said, "maybe I'm worrying about Rachel because of a dream I had a few nights ago. It happened right after Ripley's people invited us on the show.

"Think about Numbers, Chapters 13 and 14. In my dream, I had gathered representatives of all twelve tribes and told them to go to the land of Canaan and spy on the people there. When they returned, it was just like in the Torah—one after another talked about how crazy it would be to attack because the Canaanites were so giant and powerful."

"I've always liked the image that we must have looked like grasshoppers by comparison," I said.

Moses laughed. "It's great literature, isn't it?" he said. "Anyway, do you remember that Caleb and Joshua were the only spies who thought God would let us conquer the land, and yet Moshe Rabbenu went against the opinion of the other ten and supported the invasion?"

"Of course," I said.

"That's not how it went down in my dream," Moses replied. "When I heard that ten of the twelve spies opposed an invasion, I decided to go with the majority. I said I would work up a plan to share the land with its inhabitants. So my solution wasn't military; it was diplomatic. I wanted to persuade the Canaanites to allot us a share of their land, and in return we would make them wealthy by stimulating their economy through trade.

"That's when Joshua and Caleb played their trump card. They stood in front of literally hundreds of my fellow Hebrews who supported them. And they said that if I weren't prepared to enter the Promised Land and attack with everything we had, I should step aside and let a new generation of leaders take over. They guaranteed a complete victory. 'That land has been promised to us, and we can seize as much of it as we want.' Those were Joshua's exact words."

"And what does this have to do with Rachel?" I asked.

"Who do you think was standing right between Caleb and Joshua when they took me on? She was dressed like a woman from ancient times, but her face was unmistakable. She stared at me the whole time, and I couldn't stop staring back. I was listening to the men, but I was looking at Rachel. It woke me with a jolt."

As soon as I got home that night, I made a beeline for my study. After minutes spent in a panic rustling around my files, I finally found the notes. It would be difficult to exaggerate what a relief that was—at first. But then I started ticking off in my mind all the mean comments about Moses that Rachel had made over the years. If only we knew how to dust for prints, I thought to myself, I bet we'd find my wife's all over those pages.

I decided to give Moses a few days to reflect on Ripley's questions before asking how he wanted me to proceed. In the meantime, I watched for signs that someone in the media had paid attention to what had so petrified us during Ripley's broadcast. From what I could tell, Moses' dreams were never discussed.

Our dodge was apparently successful. That time.

When I finally called Moses, he was planning a trip back to Harlem to attend a conference on the relationship between African and Jewish Americans. Even before he became known to the general public, Moses served as an unofficial ambassador between those two communities, thanks largely to the ties he established in college and as a representative of SLAP.

Moses and I had been talking for a while before I finally

brought up the purpose of my call. "So," I said, "have you given any more thought to the questions about your dreams?"

For seconds, he didn't respond. I had clearly struck a nerve. "All the time," he finally said. "And here's what I think: you've got to confront Rachel. Now!"

My wife and kids lived in a beautiful contemporary house in Chevy Chase, Maryland, a few miles southwest of my home in Silver Spring. Greeting me at her front door, Rachel didn't seem surprised to see me even though I almost never visited her unannounced. I invited myself in and sat down in the living room with an envelope in my hand containing some of my notes on Moses' dreams.

"Did you see the last Ripley show?" I asked.

"Of course, who didn't? The network promoted that show so much I was half expecting to see Moses part the Hudson River."

"Sorry, wrong Moses," I said.

"That's an understatement," she replied. "Actually I thought the show was a little disappointing. Moses lacked his usual Svengali charm. I wonder why."

"I think you know."

"You flatter me if you think I can read his mind," she said.

For about 20 seconds, I said nothing at all. I simply looked at her face, pretending that I was trying to come up with the right words, when all I wanted to do was transport myself back to the day when I knew Rachel so well I could tell instinctively whenever she was hiding the truth.

"Moses' dreams," I said, breaking the silence. "What do you know about them?"

"What dreams?" she asked, as if she hadn't a clue what I was talking about.

"Come on, think back to Ripley's questions. He asked if Moses had ever dreamt that he was *the* Moses—you know, Moshe Rabbenu. Have you heard anything about that?"

"From whom? From you? From Moses?"

"From anyone or any*thing*."

Now it was Rachel's turn to be silent. And I had at least part of my answer. "Why are you asking me these questions? What have I to do with *him*?" she said. "You're the one who's joined at his hip."

"You're being evasive," I said.

"So you're telling me the maniac thinks he's *Moses*?" she replied.

"I'm begging you," I replied. "Please. Just answer my question. What do you know about his dreams?"

Rachel got up from her chair and looked out the window, then paced around the room. "OK," she said grimly. "Let me say it this way. I only know what I've read in my own house. It is still my house, you know, until the papers are signed."

"Oi … gevalt." Those words came out of my mouth slowly, haltingly, as I realized how stupid I had been to assume she'd respect my privacy. Then again, that was the nature of our relationship—trusting each other at first, only to realize later how impractical that was.

"Do you have a copy?" I asked. Again, I was met with silence.

"Search my home all you want," she finally responded. "You won't find them."

"Come on, don't toy with me," I said. "Did you ever have a copy?"

"I've told you all you need to know. But I have my own question. This stuff about the dreams is another example of how crazy that guy is. Some of the things he's said and done—they range from dangerous to deranged. Yet you look up to him like he's divine. Why?"

"You've got it all wrong," I replied. "I don't see him as divine. Just the opposite."

"Now you're talking," she said.

"That didn't come out the way I meant it. Let me say it this way. I don't worship Moses. To me, he is very *human*. I've seen him make out with a woman, I've watched him throw food in a cafeteria, I've listened to him curse many times, I once saw him yell like a banshee, and yeah, I've even heard him adopt ideas about himself that sound certifiable. But as long as I've known him, he's personified Jewish values better than anyone else I've ever met."

"But Richie —" Rachel began. I wouldn't let her finish.

"A big reason why Christianity's so popular," I continued, "is that people need human role models for inspiration. The irony is that Christians can deify Jesus because they never knew the real man. I know the real Moses—I mean, the real Moses Levine. I know how pure his heart is and how hard he works for social justice. So what if he isn't perfect? That's the kind of role model Jews should have—not some mythical, heavenly figment of our imagination, but a flesh-and-blood reminder of the fact that we have only one God, and as Moses likes to say, He transcends the transcendent."

"Amazing," she said.

"What do you mean?"

"It's like he cast a spell on you back in college. You've already let him ruin our marriage. Now you're going to let him destroy what's left of your mind."

CHAPTER XX

"'What Hitler couldn't do to the Jews, intermar-
riage is doing.' I heard that mantra over and over
again when I was a kid. Now, rabbis don't dare talk
that way. We have a new mantra: 'We're welcoming
to interfaith families.' Of course, it's one thing to
welcome the families, and another to bless their
marriages. To most rabbis, that would send the wrong
message; it would suggest that a wedding between a
Jew and a Gentile could somehow be 'Jewish' when
in fact it can't. Well, I say that's not the issue. If any
man and any woman—or for that matter, two men or
two women—want me to come to their ceremony and
bless their union, I would be honored—both as a man
and as a rabbi."

Senior Rabbi Moses Levine, addressing Temple Akiva, 2000

Silver Spring, Maryland—May 2006. The phone rang as
soon as I came home after confronting Rachel about the notes.
It was Harry Ripley—not some toady, but Ripley himself. "Rabbi
Gold," he said, "you may remember the questions I asked you
about Rabbi Levine's dreams? I now have in my possession
what I'm told is a copy of the notes you took regarding those
dreams. I have a hundred pages in all."

"One hundred pages of *my* handwriting, is that what you're

saying?" I had already counted the pages of my notes earlier in the evening; sure enough, they added up to fifty, with handwriting on both the front and back.

"I'm told it's your handwriting," he said. "We're doing a story about Rabbi Levine for my show this week, but I wanted to give you a chance to look over the notes first and tell me whether they're authentic."

"I'm sorry, but what kind of journalist runs a story on a rabbi's private notes about another rabbi's dreams? That sounds like a tabloid."

"I hear you," Ripley said, "but when it comes to Moses Levine, the public's rights trump the rights of the individual. He's not just any rabbi."

Ripley said that his show was going to air in two days whether or not I took a look at the notes, but he agreed to send them via overnight delivery to my office and wait until air time for my response. Within an hour, I was knocking on Moses' apartment door, with the original notes in hand. He had been expecting me, and so, apparently, had someone else.

"Richie," she said, hugging me at the door. "I've missed you so much."

"My God ... Lisa," I said, surprised to see my old friend. I hadn't seen her in over a year, not since we both attended a White House party held in Moses' honor. The sad truth is that we had so fallen out of touch when Rachel and I were together that even after my separation, Lisa and I rarely spoke.

"I called her right after you called me," Moses said. "I think she might be able to help."

"What do you have in mind?" I asked.

"I'm not sure I want you to know," he said. "Not now. You might do best if you deal with the Ripleys of the world with some degree of innocence. People can tell when they're dealing with a cabal. It's hard to get the smoke to clear the room."

Moses asked us if he could have a few minutes alone to

look over the notes. He then said to Lisa, "Don't tell Richie anything."

No sooner had Moses left than Lisa gave me another hug. It felt so nice to be alone with her again. "I can't believe everything that's happened to my old college friends," she said. "Eric, Moses, *you*. I'm the only one whose life is the least bit normal. Of course, normal isn't necessarily good."

"What's the matter?"

"You could call it a mid-life crisis. Being a psychologist isn't as fun as it used to be. I think about you and Moses, you're talking to the Dalai Lama about God or discussing Israel with the President. And me? I'm teaching a pseudoscience.

"Then I come home to a husband who is bored silly practicing law. Or I drag my older son to temple to study for his Bar Mitzvah, and he complains the whole way there. What kind of life is this?"

"I've got to hand it to Don," I said. "I can't believe you ended up marrying a Jew. Now you even sound like one."

"Don's just a regular *Reform* Jew, Richie, not a Conservative rabbi. When I walk into a synagogue with him, I don't have to worry that anyone's whispering about me being a shikse. Half the couples in our temple are interfaith, and our kids are considered Jewish because they have a Jewish father, even though I never converted. You don't get the sense in our temple that interfaith families are second class citizens."

"Lisa, the facts are the facts. If you look at the numbers, intermarriage could lead to the death of the Jewish people."

"You're just reminding me of what I hate about organized religion," she said, laughing. "You honestly think that two people who fall in love shouldn't get married because they come from different ethnic groups? That's ridiculous. I could have been an atheist, I could have been totally apathetic about Judaism, my dad could have been in the Klan … and as long as my mom was born Jewish, your congregants would have accepted me as your Jewish wife. But if you had married me just as I was, they would have disapproved of both of us."

"Oh, c'mon," I said, "my congregation's not like that."

"That's what *you* think. Let's face it, any religious group that calls itself 'conservative' is not for me — I don't care what group or what religion. You could say I'm a disciple of Moses — *our* Moses. He's my prophet," Lisa said, smiling. I couldn't tell whether she was serious or simply mocking all the people who treated our friend like some sort of Messiah.

Just then, Moses called to me from the other room. I went into his study and answered a few questions about my penmanship. That's all he wanted to hear from me. "Richie, you can go home; I'm good," he said.

"But I want to help plan a strategy."

"I've got Lisa for that."

"You ... what?"

"You want to be helpful? Stay home tomorrow night. I'll call and let you know what you need to do."

"Please. I put you in this mess. I want to help you get out of it."

Moses laughed. "You didn't do anything wrong; you're a victim of circumstances, that's all. But I'm not going to worry about you right now. I've spent my whole life worrying about other people; it's time I looked out for myself. I'm going to frame this issue the way *I* want to."

"You and Lisa," I grumbled.

"She's my muse," Moses said. "Go look in the mirror. You don't exactly fit the bill."

I shook my head and walked toward the front door where Lisa was waiting. "We should see each other more often," she said.

"I'd love to," I said, smiling, "if it's OK with Don."

"Believe me, that's not a problem. He feels completely secure about our relationship. And he should. There's one thing about me that's very Jewish; I believe in honoring covenants."

I got my call the next evening at 7:30. Moses said nothing more than to watch ABC's *Eyes on America* program, which was airing in 90 minutes—or 24 hours before the Ripley show was scheduled for broadcast.

Eyes on America was a talk show like Ripley's, but much more serious. The host, Barney Orloff, considered himself a journalist first and foremost, not an entertainer like Ripley. Orloff rarely interviewed Hollywood celebrities, and only then when a celebrity took a stand on an issue of public policy.

"Tonight," Orloff said, "we have but one guest. I have no doubt you will find her story riveting. Ladies and gentlemen, please give a warm welcome to Professor Lisa Rhodes."

I stared at the screen in disbelief. Moses was incredibly charismatic and comfortable on TV, and yet he had chosen a neophyte as his mouthpiece. Sure, she looked great—almost like a professional actress—but so what? This wasn't a beauty pageant. Moses' reputation was at stake.

Moses later explained to me that he was taking a page out of the book of Bill Clinton, the scandal-magnet. "If a public figure's in trouble, it doesn't matter how articulate he is, he can't defend himself half as well as a strong, intelligent woman who speaks on his behalf. I'm not married like Bill was, so Lisa's the best I've got — an old, loyal friend. She's my Hillary."

Lisa began by thanking *Eyes on America* for giving her the chance to tell her story. Then she immediately turned to her prop. "I have in my hand a series of notes. They were taken by Rabbi Richard Gold and relate to his friend and mine, Rabbi Moses Levine."

"Have you spoken to Rabbi Gold about the notes?" Orloff asked.

"Not a word. I got them from Moses. But I can authenticate the handwriting. I've known Richie for 30 years. I went to college with him and Rabbi Levine."

"So what brings you to our show tonight?" asked Orloff.

"As you know, Rabbi Levine is beloved throughout the world. Some say he's done more for peace and against poverty than any other living person. But he also has his enemies. Moses preaches sharing, and many who have money or power — *or land* — consider him a threat."

"What does this have to do with Rabbi Gold's notes?"

"The notes provide ammunition to Moses' enemies. They discuss the dreams he had when he and Rabbi Gold were together in Israel those two horrible months. Moses' enemies got hold of the notes, and their contacts in the media were about to turn this into a big story. So I came this evening to make sure people hear the truth and not some spin fueled by hatred."

"We're honored you chose to tell your story on this show," Orloff replied.

"My pleasure," Lisa said, smiling for a moment, before continuing with the task at hand. "If anyone wants to demonize Moses, I'd ask you first to consider who we're talking about. All Moses has done with his life is help the needy of the world and build bridges between communities at war. And for that, he has enemies. It says a lot about the human condition."

"Tell me about the dreams, Professor Rhodes."

"Over and over again, beginning when he and Rabbi Gold were in Israel, Moses has had visions of himself as being in the position of the Biblical Moses."

"Let me get this right. Rabbi Levine, in his dreams, thought he was *the* Moses?"

"Yes," Lisa said, before pausing, "and not just in his dreams."

Orloff wasn't prepared for that response, and I wasn't prepared for his dumbfounded reaction. I knew that the producer of *Eyes on America* was a major contributor to Moses' charities. I naturally assumed that Moses had closely choreographed the interview with Orloff's boss, and that Orloff would simply be an actor playing a role. But that wasn't the case. The deal, I later learned, was that while Orloff wouldn't badger or humiliate Lisa, he was otherwise free to be himself. He was also given very little information about the notes prior to the interview.

"Are you saying that when Rabbi Levine was in Israel, whether he was awake or asleep, he came to believe he was the reincarnation of the Biblical Moses?"

"Yes. Even today, he sees himself in that way." Listening to those words, I literally cursed myself for having written things like "Moses' dreams have become his obsession. He actually believes when awake that he, Moses Levine, is Moshe Rabbenu reincarnated." Lisa could have said that Moses had since changed his mind about that. I'm sure she would have said whatever Moses told her to. But, for better or worse, my friend directed her to speak the truth.

"And you're also saying that Moses Levine has continued to dream that he is the Biblical Moses, even after returning from Israel?" Orloff asked.

"Yes, that's true," Lisa said.

"Correct me if I'm wrong, but he's never admitted any of this publicly."

"Would *you*?" Lisa said. "He knows some of his religious views are out of the mainstream. But his values aren't, and his achievements speak for themselves. He'd rather focus on those."

"What is it about Rabbi Levine's theology that is so, if I may say, *radical*, that would permit him to think of himself as *the* Moses?"

"To begin with, he doesn't worship Moses. He thinks of Moses as a man, *just* a man, and he'd say the same about Jesus, Buddha and Muhammad. Rabbi Levine says he has but one God, and that God has never taken human form. My friend also accepts the possibility of reincarnation. I understand that plenty of rabbis over the centuries have taught that people are reincarnated or resurrected."

"Wait a minute," Orloff said. "Do you know of other rabbis who claim to be incarnations of a biblical character?"

"No, but that's missing my point. People talk about the Biblical Moses with such reverence. And yet my friend sees Moses simply as human. That's how he could let his dreams affect his beliefs. It's not that he thinks of himself as a god. He's iconoclastic, that's all. For him to worship Moses would be like you or me worshiping a golden calf."

Orloff wiped the sweat from his forehead. He was starting to look like Nixon during his debates with Kennedy. "Folks, I really hate to say this, but I must: we'll be back after this message from our sponsor."

ABC ran commercials for two full minutes. I spent most of the time shaking my head, wondering why Moses was coming clean to all of America. After the break, Orloff asked Lisa to talk about herself. She spoke about her research at the University of Maryland. Then she attempted to bring her psychological insights to bear on the topic at hand.

"I realize that many of your viewers will think that Moses Levine is delusional. Tell me, Barney, that hasn't crossed your own mind."

Orloff smiled for the first time in minutes. "I have to admit that it is a very ... unusual claim."

"Look at it this way," Lisa resumed. "He found himself in an impossible position through no fault of his own. The most he could have asked of himself was somehow to stay sane. Then, night after night, he had these *powerful* dreams in which he found himself in the position of the Biblical Moses."

"I'm trying to picture myself in his shoes," said Orloff. "I'd probably have gone mad."

"You and a whole lot of people," Lisa said. "I say he was coping as best he could. I don't think that's crazy at all. Psychologically, it's actually pretty healthy."

Lisa went on to recount a conversation that Moses and I had during one of our bleakest moments in East Jerusalem. "So,

Rabbi Levine says to his friend: 'Richie, you've read rabbinic essays on reincarnation. You know that a number of rabbis have believed in it. Is it *irreligious* to say that Moses could have been reincarnated in the body of someone alive today?"

"What did Rabbi Gold say?" Orloff asked.

"It was a typical modern rabbinic answer — he said he believed in an afterlife but had no idea what it might be like. Rabbi Levine thought about what Rabbi Gold said and promised that he'd keep an open mind. But then he went on to say that his new beliefs *felt* right to him, and he was going to hold on to them, at least for the present."

"How do you explain the fact that he has continued to dream that he's Moses, even after returning to the States?"

"He still might need those dreams to stay sane," Lisa said. "Maybe he wasn't prepared for all the adulation he received when he got back to America."

"What about Rabbi Levine's enemies? What do you see them doing with this information?"

"They're as fascinating to me as Rabbi Levine," Lisa replied. "Really, they're more so, because Rabbi Levine's just a man who was put in a tough position and is coping the best he can. He's not harboring ill-will; he's thinking about his world, his *God*. He only wants to lend a hand.

"But his enemies, they're troglodytes. I swear to you— they fill their minds with fear, as if seeing the sunlight would somehow blind them. Ever since Moses came back from Israel to a hero's welcome, they've been in that cave, trying to figure out a way to bring him down."

It was a Hillaryesque performance—one moment Lisa praised her friend, the next moment she demonized her own version of the "vast right-wing conspiracy." In this case, it was a vast "ultra-Zionist" conspiracy. But Lisa dared not use those words. They would even have offended me.

CHAPTER XXI

"I've received some incredible honors over the years, but nothing ever like this one. I've always thought of the Nobel Peace Prize as the penultimate award a man or woman could ever obtain. Of course, there's a greater prize out there that continues to elude me, and it's starting to make me frustrated.

"Someday, I hope to be named one of People Magazine's 50 Most Beautiful People. And if that happens, I'll know I will have lived a full life."

Moses Levine, in his address
accepting the Nobel Peace Prize, 2004

Silver Spring, Maryland—May 2006. As soon as Lisa finished spilling the beans during the *Eyes on America* program, my phone started ringing off the hook. The first call was from Harry Ripley, who was upset that Orloff had scooped him.

"Believe me," I told Ripley. "I didn't know Lisa was going on Orloff until I saw her on TV."

"So I'm supposed to think this is some sort of coincidence?" asked Ripley.

"I wouldn't exactly call —" I began, but Ripley wouldn't let me finish my sentence.

"One day I tell you I have the notes, and I show you the courtesy of letting you authenticate them. The next day, with no advance notice, I hear about the notes on someone else's show. You never even called me back. You just *screwed* me!"

"I screwed *you*? You're the one who's doing the screwing. Someone steals my notes about my friend's personal business, and you were going to tell the whole world about it? What kind of trash journalism is that?"

"It's the kind you and your wacko friend deserve," he said. Then he hung up.

The next caller after Ripley was Moses. He was in a good mood; Lisa came across on TV just the way he would have wanted.

"What do you need from me now?" I asked him. "Do you want me to go on TV?"

"I want you to put on an old Stones CD—say *Let it Bleed* or *Sticky Fingers*—have a few drinks, and stop taking everything so damned seriously."

"Moses," I said, "let me help."

"You want to help? Stop feeling so stressed and guilty. Just be like Captain Kirk. When he has the fate of the galaxy on the line, what does he do? He finds an alien and makes out with her."

"Hmmm," I said. "Maybe I should get me one of those green slave girls from Orion."

"Now you're talking," Moses said, laughing. "Honestly, I need you to be yourself. As long as you're stressed out, you're useless to both of us."

My way of doing Moses' bidding was to step back, forget about taking dramatic action, and study how the public was reacting to Lisa's revelations. It didn't take me long to get started. On the night of the *Eyes on America* show, I was inundated with phone calls from congregants. They wanted to know if Lisa's story was true. When I admitted that it was, they all said the same thing: Moses was nuts.

I pleaded with them to appreciate Lisa's remarks about the hell Moses went through back in Israel, and how hard it was for him to cope, especially when he was having those dreams. But no one wanted to hear about the reasons for his beliefs. To my congregants, Moses Levine was delusional, narcissistic and hypocritical; in short, he was a fraud. By equating himself with *the* Moses, my friend had fueled the dislike that so many people feel for religious leaders.

It's a widely held view, causing all sorts of resentment, that clergymen see themselves as especially close to God. In Moses' case, that attitude had apparently been exposed in the clearest way possible.

I wanted to fight back on my friend's behalf. I wanted to convince my congregants of certain things I knew to be true, like the fact that Moses Levine was one of the least narcissistic people I've ever known. But how could I prove that after what they'd just heard? If Lisa couldn't make the sale, I certainly couldn't. Moses would have to be his own spokesman.

Soon, he realized that for himself. Moses decided to make an appearance on the Orloff show, but he put it off for a full week after Lisa took her shot. He, too, needed to spend a few days taking in the public's reaction, and that reaction can be summarized in a single word: *brutal*.

One radio caller after another suggested that the Nobel Committee strip Moses of his prize. "They should have done it with Arafat, they should do it with Levine," echoed the refrain. A couple of shows invited callers to comment on who was more evil—Moses or Arafat. When I was listening, the calls were pretty evenly split.

For the most part, I was able to retain my composure when listening to these shows, but I almost lost it when I heard a familiar voice call in to the Dave Hudson radio program. The voice suggested to Hudson that we put Moses through some sort of ordeal to determine if he was who he says he was. "Maybe tie him up and put him in a tank of water. See if he can escape. Houdini was Jewish, and he could escape. It shouldn't be any trouble for Moses Levine, right?" It wasn't until he was finished that I could identify the voice. It belonged to that crazy drunk on the train, William Jones.

Moses appeared on the Orloff show eight days to the minute after Lisa. I had expected to watch the show alone, but much to my surprise, Rachel came by a half-hour before the telecast and didn't leave until it was over.

She was in a better mood than I'd seen her in a long while. Credit the new man in her life. His name was Elliot Fineman, and he was a Senior Partner at Hawkes Greenbaum, one of Washington's most prestigious law firms. Fineman headed up its real estate department.

Fineman was also on the Board of Trustees of the Capital Jewish Congregation, the oldest, wealthiest and largest Reform temple in D.C. I knew the place well, including the senior rabbi. According to Rachel, Elliot was fluent in Hebrew, knew the liturgy cold, was schooled in the Talmud, and was active with Jewish charities. "I think you'd have a lot of respect for him," she said.

Maybe so, I thought to myself, but would I *like* him? I've met my share of Jewishly-active suits over the years who were dominated more by their egos than their Judaism. As Moses might say, Fineman's involvement in the city's leading fur-wearing, limousine-liberal Jewish cathedral couldn't help but make me skeptical. Then again, his character was of little concern to me. If he made Rachel happy enough to take the edge off her demeanor, I'd be in his corner.

As the telecast was about to begin, I asked Rachel why she wanted to watch the show with me and not Elliot.

"What, are you kidding?" she asked. "Moses made our marriage crash and burn, so I wanted to be with you while we watch the same thing happen to him. It's only fair."

"You're so sure he's toast?"

"Absolutely," she replied. "I've rendered him toothless and

clawless. Look at how desperate he got last week, putting up your old girlfriend to shill for him."

"Rachel, you're a real sweetheart, you know that?" I said.

"Shhh. The fraud is about to start talking."

"Let's get right to what everyone wants to know," Orloff said, beginning the show. "Did Lisa Rhodes tell the truth about your dreams?"

"Yes, she told the truth about everything," Moses said, calmly. If the previous eight days had been harrowing to Moses, he sure didn't show it.

"So you really had a series of dreams in which you thought you were Moses—*the* Biblical Moses?"

"Yes."

"And the dreams have you convinced that *you* are Moses reincarnated?"

"Oh, I don't know if I'd say they 'convinced' me. I'm not positive about it."

"But you go through life from day to day believing that Moses' soul is in your body?"

"I do, and I'm not comfortable denying it. Maybe I'm crazy … but at least I'm not a liar."

"You continue to go through life thinking you are Moses? This isn't just an idea that you had when you were in Israel?"

"No," Moses replied. "I still see myself that way."

Watching the telecast live at my home, I was amazed at how matter-of-fact Moses appeared. He looked almost at peace. Obviously, Orloff had the same thought.

"Rabbi Levine, I have to say, you seem like none of this has fazed you. Have you been paying attention to all the controversy your dreams have caused?"

"Of course, and I've found the reaction fascinating."

"Yeah right," Rachel scoffed. "He's freaking out. I just know it."

"*Fascinating?*" Orloff said. "Is that what you call listening to one person after another insult you and everything you stand for?"

Moses laughed. "That's not the part that's so interesting. It's no secret that people enjoy tearing celebrities down. It makes them feel better about themselves."

"Not exactly a newsflash, is it?" Orloff said.

"What's fascinating," my friend continued, "are the debates I've heard in the past couple of days about whether people's souls are reincarnated, and the discussions about what Moses was really like. Jews aren't supposed to think about Moses as divine, yet it's pretty obvious that many Jews see him as something more than human."

"You seem to be able to distance yourself from the whole controversy. How?"

"It's simple. No matter what anyone says about me, I don't question what I've been able to accomplish. Maybe that sounds immodest, but it's the truth. I've saved a lot of lives. I've called attention to the scourge of poverty and the dangers of global warming. I've preached peace when others were preaching war. Over time, hopefully, people will realize that my public record is more important than my private thoughts and dreams."

"You mentioned immodesty," Orloff replied. "Isn't it your ego that's at the heart of all this controversy?"

"Ya think?" Rachel interjected. But Orloff wasn't finished making his point.

"It seems that people are questioning whether you've become too full of yourself. I have the impression that the more famous the person is, the more we demand humility."

"People *should* demand humility from their celebrities," Moses replied. "But you've set up a dichotomy between pride and humility. It's a false dichotomy. You can have both."

"How's that?" Orloff asked.

"We need pride to accomplish anything. It's central to building a strong character. Pride is what causes kids to go to school when they don't feel like it and pushes adults to work hard when we could get by with less. With pride comes self-esteem, and who doesn't deserve that? Imagine seeing a dog or cat that was capable of doing all the things we do. Imagine how amazed we'd be by that animal and how wonderful we'd think it was."

"What about humility, Rabbi?"

"That means different things to different people. For me, it means realizing how tiny you are in relationship to God." Moses paused for a moment. He told me later that he was actually fighting off tears. "I'll tell you what hurts me, Barney. When people accuse me of putting myself and Moshe Rabbenu at the top of some evolutionary scale, and placing everyone else — Jesus, Muhammad, *everyone* — beneath us.

"I've never said that, and I've never thought that. To me, a human being is a human being. Some of us are smarter than others, some are kinder, some run faster, but from a cosmic standpoint, we're all basically the same animal. And we *are* animals, make no mistake. Compared to God, we're microscopic specks. I'd say that we have more in common with the flatworm than we do with God."

"And by *we*," Orloff said, "you're including Moses and Jesus."

"I'm including anyone who has appeared on Earth in a human form."

"This is as good a time as any," Orloff said. "We're going to take a break and be right back after these messages."

"Does he really think people are going to buy his act any more?" Rachel asked.

"I'm sure he doesn't know," I replied.

Rachel was nonplussed. "I mean ... here's this guy ... he says he's Moses—not Abraham or Isaac, but *Moses*—and then he goes on the air and spouts off his theology. Who wants to listen to this clown sermonize?"

"I do," I said, without cracking a smile. "He makes a lot more sense than Elliot's rabbi. I know that guy. I know the kind of church he runs. Isn't it considered Episcopalian-Jewish?"

"Cute, Richie," she replied. "Very cute."

What can I say? She was getting on my nerves.

Immediately after the commercials, Orloff allowed Moses to make a statement rather than respond to any questions. He spoke directly to the camera and not Orloff.

"I realize I sound sacrilegious to many of you. I realize you might think I'm insulting your religious beliefs. The truth is I'm not trying to act sacrilegiously, and I'm not trying to insult anyone. Mr. Orloff asked me about my beliefs when it comes to God and man. I could have dodged the issue, but I felt like I owed you candor, and I certainly wouldn't lie. If this means I've said things that offend you, I'm sorry."

Orloff's first question after Moses' statement was how Moses came to think that his namesake was more like a flatworm than he was like God.

"Do you have a few hours?"

"How 'bout you give me the short version?" Orloff replied.

"Alright, start with this: I didn't come to God through the Torah."

"The *what*?" Orloff asked.

"The Torah, the Bible."

"Sorry, I couldn't understand you," Orloff said, laughing. And I could hardly blame him. Moses had lost most of his Southern accent over the years, but every now and then it presented itself, and it took you aback when it did.

"When I was growing up," Moses continued, "I loved the stories in the Torah, and I learned a lot of my values from them. But I thought of them as stories. I didn't take them literally. And I wasn't satisfied about what they said about God.

"The Torah makes God out to have a very human personality. It didn't ring true to me. So for a long time, I didn't believe in God at all. By the time I enrolled in rabbinical school, I had become a little more open about the issue, but I was still basically an agnostic."

"That sounds pretty strange for a rabbinical student," Orloff said.

"Definitely. I didn't tell anyone at my school. Richie Gold knew; I confided in him. He asked if I understood what I was doing. I told him that anyone who struggles with the question of God is qualified to be a rabbi. Even now, I don't think people *need* to believe in God to be spiritual — certainly not to be ethical. But for me, once I came to look at life as a unified whole, and once I came to address this infinite unity as 'God,' my life became more meaningful."

"If you didn't come to God through the Bible, how did you?" Orloff asked.

"From reading, from thinking, from talking to people. I asked myself: what do we all mean by 'God' when we're not just creating the human ideal? That's how I realized that God stands, above all else, for the 'ultimate.'"

"Is your God a *concept* or a *being*?"

"My God is Being itself. God is a *Thou*, not an *It*. An 'it' you try to comprehend. A 'Thou' you try to address. To glorify.

"Now, it's true that at first I thought of God as a concept. I studied the issue intellectually. I decided the world was unified at the highest possible level by a single substance, a single combination of mind and body. The entire universe became for me a living, interrelated whole. Whatever mortal forms I saw in nature—animals, plants, you name it—I thought about them as if they were merely parts of a greater unity, like cells inside our body. And I conceived of this unity as an infinite, *ultimate* Being who's responsible for all that is or ever will be."

"That's your God."

"That's my philosophy. But remember, I've tried to move beyond philosophizing. When I contemplate living beings as expressions of God, I'm not so much analyzing them as *communing* with them. The thought that they're unified in

God inspires love for everything that exists. And that, to me, is the essence of monotheism.

"Hopefully, you can see now why stories about human beings, even Biblical stories, don't have much to do with the God I'm talking about. I try not to limit God by using human terms to describe divine attributes. I imagine God without limitations. My God is present everywhere around us and in us, but also present in dimensions we can't even imagine."

"So you never think of God in human terms?" Orloff asked.

"Well, I wouldn't say '*never*.' There is this idea I play with occasionally to remind myself how great God is.

"Traditionally, Jewish people think of God as the Creator and Lord of the universe. They assume God shapes the universe with one loving, complex thought after another, and those thoughts are supposed to epitomize what we mean by God's wisdom. To me, that picture is too limiting. It makes us think that everything that happens is something God *wills*, and I don't buy into that. I like to think of this entire universe, not just this planet but the whole universe, as a single, instantaneous, supra-conscious 'dream' of God. And then I think of God as eternally 'dreaming' an infinite number of universes."

"What is it with you and dreams?" Orloff said.

"I don't really mean the word literally."

"But you *do* believe you are literally the reincarnation of Moses."

"Asked and answered, counselor," Moses replied, smiling.

"He's actually enjoying this, isn't he?" said Rachel. I didn't respond. The answer was obvious.

"Do you think of God as the foundation of values?" Orloff asked.

"Ultimately, my God is the foundation of all that exists. But when I think about values, I'm struck by how much they reflect the prism of our cultures. Of course, I won't deny that the idea of God can inspire our values. It doesn't have to, but it can. It has with me."

"This is making my head ache," Orloff said, laughing. "I could be interviewing Angelina Jolie, and instead I get you? I'm going to have to talk to my producer."

"Sorry," Moses said, half-smiling. "If I were you I'd rather be talking to her, too."

"I can't believe your friend," Rachel said. "People are ready to tar and feather him, and he's giving them a philosophy lesson."

"If you don't mind," Orloff said, "I'd like to bring up something you may find distressing. It has to do with the anti-global warming bill your group has been spearheading."

"Alright," Moses said, with a look of concern I hadn't seen since the show began.

"I hear that after the dream story broke, many Congressmen who had said they'd support the bill have announced they're reconsidering their positions."

Moses didn't respond at first, at least not audibly. But his eyes did the talking for him. He looked like Jeremiah about to erupt.

"Do you want to make a comment about that development?" Orloff asked.

Moses closed his eyes. He clearly intended to respond, but for once his quick wit failed him. Whatever he *wanted* to say he instinctively knew should never be spoken in public.

"How can I dignify any threats to destroy the environment?" Moses said, finally. "Seriously, how do my thoughts about Moshe Rabbenu have anything to do with whether our government needs to protect our climate before it's too late? Are we getting close to the tipping point on global warming, or aren't we? If we are, why the hell are we doing nothing about it?" Moses was now resorting to his best Birmingham English. "Ask the churchgoers on Sunday who are so damned mad at me — ask *them* if their religion commands us to respect God's green earth. Don't ask me. Ask them!"

After another commercial break, Moses took questions from

the audience. It was clear from the hostility in some of those questions that my friend was simply rolling a boulder up a hill.

"I think the Fat Lady just sang," Rachel said, as she was leaving the house. "If you want to help your buddy, go buy him a home in a retirement community, maybe near Boca. He might like that."

"Bitch," I replied under my breath. But by that time she had already gone.

My mind flashed back to the spring of 2002, when Rachel bid me adieu. A year later, we decided on an informal distribution of the estate, a distribution we later confirmed in writing once the divorce was final. My share was $60 million plus half of the value of the family mansion.

I realize $60 million-plus sounds like a lot of money, especially for a rabbi, but relative to her slice of the pie it was nothing. Rachel walked off with assets valued at more than a billion dollars, much of which was earned during our marriage. Maybe I could have done better had we litigated the matter, but I felt morally obliged to accept a relatively small share. After all, she and her family earned virtually all of the money, and my feelings for her, when Moses was out of the equation, had remained generally positive. Still, when Rachel watched Moses' reputation implode on the Orloff show and then had the chutzpah to gloat about it, I found myself wishing I had taken the woman to the cleaners.

CHAPTER XXII

"Many Jews obsess over how few of us there are in the world. They worry that Judaism will soon be extinct, and that worry consumes them every bit as much as their love of Jewish learning or commitment to prayer. Personally, I have no fear that Jews will disappear. We've survived for thousands of years; we'll survive thousands more—assuming our planet can do the same.

"My fear is different. I'm worried about the extinction of Unitarian Universalists. You all don't have the track record we do as survivors. And you preach a message that doesn't work so well during times like this one, when people need promises of immortality and don't deal well with ambiguity and shades of gray. But this world needs you to survive ... and to thrive. My God, do we ever need that. Religion has divided people for so long, and the effects have been devastating. I know of no spiritual community better equipped than you are to bring warring peoples together in the name of universal dignity, open-mindedness and love."

Rabbi Moses Levine, addressing the Southeastern
Unitarian Universalist Summer Institute, 2005

Port Antonio, Jamaica—June 2006. I've spent a lot of money over the years. Never, though, has my money been better spent than when I rented a villa in Jamaica a few weeks after Moses appeared on *Eyes on America* to discuss the controversy about his dreams. Actually, my insight wasn't so much the renting of the villa as the willingness to purchase plane tickets for my friends to get there. I purchased six tickets in all—one for myself, one for Moses, and four for Moses' guests. Yes, four.

As soon as we came into her parents' money, Rachel and I began taking two or three expensive trips a year. Frequently, we'd invite our friends to accompany us, but we never thought of paying for their plane tickets. Then, one day when I was flying to Auckland, I met a man who was kvetching about having to spend the money to go halfway around the globe just to attend a wedding.

"I hate having rich friends," he told me. "I know this guy from my temple in Buffalo. He's got more money than he knows what to do with. So when it's time to get married, where does he have the wedding? Why not New Zealand? Beautiful place, perfect weather ... of course he'd never stop to think it'll eat up my budget just to get there.

"Funny thing is, when you first make friends with someone who's got money, you figure you'll get some benefits out of it, right? Maybe they'll take you on their yacht or buy you *really* nice presents. Instead, what do I get? A hole in my wallet the size of the Pacific."

I sat stone-faced, not letting on that he could have been speaking about me. But from that point forward, I was reluctant to invite my friends anywhere luxurious (other than my home) unless I was willing to pay for their trips.

The idea to go to Jamaica came from my father. He called to congratulate me on my divorce, which became final less than a week after Moses struck out on *Eyes on America*. "You really need to celebrate your freedom," he said. "Go to the islands and relax. And take Moses; he needs the rest even more than you do. I've heard about this town in Jamaica—not very touristy, and it's supposed to be gorgeous."

He was referring to Port Antonio, which is well east of Jamaica's three major tourist destinations: Negril, Montego Bay and Ocho Rios. It's a pain to get to Port Antonio, but once you've arrived, you appreciate the more pristine environment and the dearth of natives auditioning to be your drug dealer, prostitute or all-purpose servant. I know for a fact that Moses couldn't have dealt with the three Jamaican tourist traps without turning the vacation into a week-long discourse on class, status and power—not exactly what I had in mind.

When I asked Moses if he were up for the trip, he seemed hesitant. Then I told him that the ticket was on me. That was met by another pause on the telephone.

"Ticket?" he finally said. "Or tickets?"

"I was thinking just the two of us would go."

"Think again, and you've got a deal," he said. Moses was never one to shy away from an opportunity. "How about you give me 24 hours to see if I can put together an all-star lineup? You might have to buy a total of . . . let's say . . . six tickets—two for us, and four for ... well, four for our sanity. Can you handle that, Richie Rich?"

He knew I couldn't refuse — not after I had written down his most intimate thoughts and left them to be pilfered by his worst enemy. My only decision was whether to ask who I'd be subsidizing. But I decided against it. Moses was planning a surprise party. I chose to consider him the host and me the honored guest.

As it turned out, I was prescient.

Aside from books and clothing, Moses brought only two things to the island—snorkeling gear and table tennis equipment. As soon as I told him there'd be a table at the villa, I knew he'd make sure we'd resume our epic ping pong battles from college.

Whenever I played ping pong against Moses, I'd be hit with the same realization: the guy put a spin on every shot. *Every* shot! And that wasn't just his approach to table tennis; it was his approach to life. He was always thinking, always scheming, and the result was never what you'd expect. There was inevitably an idiosyncratic flavor to it, as if each of his actions was a painting, and the "spin" was his means of affixing his signature.

In planning our trip to Jamaica, Moses' signature steps were in choreographing the cast of characters and the times of their arrival. He knew I was landing at the Kingston airport early on a Sunday afternoon, so he made sure that he and his four guests would already be at the villa halfway across the island by the time my plane landed. After a typical harrowing Jamaican cab ride, I walked into the villa to the sound of applause and saw three familiar faces.

The first person to greet me was Lisa's husband Don, a frustrated lawyer if ever there were one (and I have the impression that there are zillions). He was followed by Lisa and Moses, who had his arm around Lisa's shoulder. Don didn't seem to mind in the slightest. "I'd almost rather have an alcoholic husband than a jealous one," Lisa once told me.

"Richie," Moses called out. "I want to introduce you to a couple of my good friends. Let's go outside."

I barely had a chance to drop my bags, let alone say hello to Don and Lisa, when I found myself accompanying Moses to the back terrace and down a lengthy flight of stairs that led to the villa's prime attraction, an inlet of the Caribbean Sea. From the steps, I could see that two women were swimming a fair distance from the shoreline.

"Ayelet? Carrie?" Moses hollered. "Can you hear me?"

"Coming," one of the women called back. The two raced to

the dock, with the woman named Ayelet barely out-touching her friend for the victory.

Ayelet Gefen was unusually tall—6' 1" as I later learned—and positively stunning. Her hair and skin were as dark as Moses', which was hardly surprising given her name. Her family had immigrated to America from Israel twenty years earlier, when she was sixteen.

"You must be Rabbi Richie," Ayelet said. "Thank you so much for inviting us to Jamaica. That was so generous of you."

"Thank my ex-wife. Her family made all the money."

"Well then ... thank you, Mrs. Gold, wherever you are," she said, laughing.

Just then, the woman next to Ayelet gave her a nudge and cleared her throat. "Oh, what am I doing?" Ayelet said. "Allow me to introduce you to my friend Carrie."

"Ayelet and I actually just met a few hours ago," said the other swimmer, after greeting me and shaking my hand. "But we kind of hit it off, didn't we?" The two women smiled at each other, and then turned to Moses. He was extremely close to both of them and had been for years. To Ayalet, he was an intimate friend. To Carrie, he was the boss at work. She ran POP's Salt Lake City office.

"The ladies' chemistry with one another was pre-ordained," Moses said, in a pseudo-prophetic voice. It was the same voice he'd often assume in ridiculing people for treating him as the voice of God on Earth. Moses thought that was nonsense—"all human conduct comes from God," he liked to say — "mine, yours, Hitler's, everybody's."

As we walked back toward the villa, Moses' arm now around Ayelet's shoulder, I laughed to myself about my friend's obvious intentions. Carrie wasn't quite as tall or as blonde as Lisa, but she was still, quite clearly, "my type." Her soft Nordic features were framed by long flowing hair, which was every bit as thick as Lisa's. Here I had been divorced for two weeks, I thought to myself, and Moses was already trying to set me up, and with a shikse, no less. It was so like him to look after my love life; whenever Moses saw a glaring need, he would always take it upon himself to meet it.

I was reminded of the word *dayenu*, which a Jew always says on Passover. *Dayenu* means "enough!" But it's not like it sounds. We say the word as an expression of joy and appreciation. It would have been *dayenu* had God simply led us out of Egypt, but he didn't stop at that; He gave us the Torah. It would have been *dayenu* had he given us the Torah, but he didn't stop at that; He led us to the Promised Land. And so forth.

In my case, it would have been more than *dayenu* had the good Lord led me to Port Antonio, sat my fanny on a bench overlooking the sea, and allowed me simply to smell the Caribbean air. And yet He did so much more. My first evening at the villa was supposed to be relaxing, but it turned out to be exhilarating. We played some games, took a late-night dip, and engaged each other on topics ranging from Einstein's theory of relativity, to the relative merits of Kubrick and Spielberg, to the increasing workaholism in American culture. But mostly we simply enjoyed each other's company. That turned out to be the real treat, even more than the locale or the activities.

The villa had four bedrooms, each of which contained a queen-sized bed. Lisa and Don occupied one of the rooms, Carrie and I took up two others, and the fourth was shared between Moses and Ayalet.

I'd never thought of Moses as a particularly private person, but there had always been certain things he kept close to the vest, and his love life was one of them. I knew he had been intimate with two or three girls over the course of his years at Columbia. I wouldn't call any of them steady girlfriends, though, nor would I describe his feelings for them as infatuation, at least not in the overpowering sense of that term. Those girls were his friends before they were his lovers, and the friendship always seemed more important to him than the romance. From what little he told me, I assumed that this pattern of sporadic intimate relationships with friends continued for Moses throughout his years at SLAP and rabbinical school.

Once Moses became a rabbi, I had heard many a woman talk about him, just not as a single, available man. It was almost assumed that he would never be hitched, as he would be too busy saving the world to devote the attention a woman required from a monogamous relationship.

I had first heard Moses speak of Ayalet Geffen when we were in East Jerusalem. She was one of the few women for whom he ever confessed to having romantic feelings. Ayalet met Moses at a Palestinian rights march in Dearborn, Michigan, back in 1992, before Moses became *Moses*. She was a student at the University of Michigan Law School looking to pursue a career as a public defender. At the march, she rushed to Moses' aid when he was besieged by Arab-Americans who thought of him as a garden-variety Zionist who had been trying to infiltrate their rally. The irony is that Moses came to the march to defend Palestinian rights and interests, but some of the rhetoric he heard went way too far for his sensibilities, so he started arguing with other marchers. Ayalet, it turned out, agreed with virtually everything Moses said and lent her voice to his. They spent the rest of the march together (two Jews among thousands of Muslims), exchanged phone numbers, and struck up a friendship, one that became even more powerful after Moses became a celebrity and had begun to question who he could trust and who he couldn't.

I enjoyed watching the two of them interact in Port Antonio. Ayalet clearly venerated the man. She asked him for his opinions on many things, and while she felt free to argue with him at times—as you'd only expect from the head of the Lansing Public Defender's Office—even her arguments proved that she had listened carefully to Moses' points and tried to give them their due.

From time to time, Ayalet asked Moses for advice on personal matters—such as whether she was making the most out of her career, should move to the East Coast, or should have children. Moses did his best to answer — he was, after all, a rabbi, and rabbis have to dispense advice—but he never seemed comfortable playing the role of life coach.

"How can I act like a guru?" he said. "I'm a Jew! No matter how much I achieve, I'll never be satisfied with my life. I'll always remind myself that I should be more learned or productive. And I'll always feel guilty about not being happier. Gurus aren't nearly so restless."

Several days after coming to Port Antonio, I finally got a full night's sleep. Everyone hit the sack by eleven, and I didn't wake up the next morning until ten.

As the benefactor of our week in paradise, I was given one of the bedrooms facing the Caribbean. Pulling open the drapes that morning, I expected to see my friends lying on the beach below. Instead, all I saw was sand and water. When I put on my swim trunks and headed down to the kitchen, I was met by Carrie at the foot of the stairs.

"We're alone," she said, smiling; "just you, me, and these two notes."

"Gang," the first note said, "Lisa and I are headed to the Port Antonio golf club to play 36 holes. We've been talking about doing this for years—36 holes to decide the family's best golfer. If she wins, she gets breakfast in bed every Saturday and Sunday for a month. If I win, she has to watch five hours of Ultimate Fighting with me and my buddies. We'll be back early in the evening. Wish me luck. Don."

"So who are you rooting for?" asked Carrie.

"Definitely Don," I said, laughing. "I'd like Lisa to have to watch the UFC."

"The second note is from Moses," Carrie said. "'Ayalet and I are going to Ocho Rios to retrace the life of James Bond. We're going to see the waterfall from *Dr. No*, the cave from *Live and Let Die*, and Ian Fleming's estate. I'm totally psyched. See you tonight. M.'"

"He's always loved Bond movies," I said. "He has this annoying habit of saying the lines before the characters do to show off that he's memorized them."

Carrie smiled. "Whenever I see Moses at work, he's so intense. It's nice to see a more playful side of him."

"Are you jealous of Ayalet?" I asked, with uncharacteristic frankness. My question was meant to be innocuous; I only wanted to know whether Carrie would have liked to have spent the day hanging out alone with Moses. But Carrie assumed the question was intended more broadly.

"Oh gosh no," Carrie said. "He's not my type, not in the sense that he and Ayalet ... you know. Moses is my friend and my mentor. But he looks like —"

"Osama?"

"Well, yeah. Doesn't he?"

"Sure," I said, with a sigh. "You know, people say I look like George Castanza from *Seinfeld*. How do you think that makes me feel?"

"George is cute," she replied. "Teddy bear cute. It's just his character that's so pathetic."

"Don't worry; I've never been caught in the office sleeping with the cleaning lady."

Carrie didn't miss a beat. "Of course not, you're too smart to have been caught."

Carrie and I had breakfast and walked down to the beach. It was then that I realized what had been puzzling me so much about her. From the first evening we all spent together, she seemed to feel unworthy of the invitation to the villa, as if she were a mere commoner surrounded by royalty. And yet, when it came to expressing her opinions or explaining her perspectives on life, she was one of the most self-confident women I had ever met. She could also be very direct.

"So I'm curious," she said, as we spread out our blankets on the Caribbean sand. "What did Moses say about me before you agreed to fly me down to Jamaica?"

"Nothing. Not a word," I said.

"Really?"

"He wanted to surprise me," I said. "He knew it would be a pleasant surprise."

Carrie blushed. And that endeared her to me even more than before. My thoughts then turned to Moses and to the fact that the man who knew me as well as anyone in the world, a man whose wisdom I had always admired, had selected *this* woman for me to spend time with in paradise. It made me feel twice as humbled in her presence as she could possibly have felt in mine.

"Do you know what else I've been thinking?" Carrie began. "How great it would be if time could just stop, and instead of having one week to spend at this villa, we all had six months. You, me, Moses, Lisa, Don and Ayelet—six months away from our responsibilities, without any risk that we'd mess up our lives back home. But there'd be one rule: we wouldn't be able to do a single thing that people would view as productive. We couldn't write any books, legal briefs, or even letters. We couldn't create any works of art. We couldn't even work hard to get ourselves in better physical shape. All we could do is hang out together, relax, and commune with the source of life. How does that sound?"

I didn't want to tell her what I was thinking—that it would sound a lot better without Moses, Lisa, Don and Ayelet. "I'd probably get too fat," I finally replied.

"But you wouldn't," she said. "Our sabbatical wouldn't be about hedonism; it would be too spiritual for that."

"In that case," I said, "I'd rather it last six years than six months."

Carrie and I lay out that morning on the beach by the villa for at least an hour. From the very first day we met, I had loved being around her, whether we were talking or just taking in the scenery. She was both easy-going and engaging, which is not something I can say about too many people.

Earlier in the vacation, Carrie had learned that I liked to swim and that I loved a challenge. So she proposed that for "our first date"—her words, not mine — we swim to the other end of the inlet. The trip was nearly a third of a mile.

For a moment, I wondered if she were suggesting some kind of swim competition—an aquatic equivalent to the Don/Lisa battle that was taking place at the golf course nearby, only without prizes for the winner. But Carrie had to know that a race was out of the question—this Castanza would have been as likely to experience heart failure as "shrinkage." Clearly, the competition Carrie had in mind would be purely between me and the sea, with my "date" cheering me on and helping me out, if necessary.

I took up the challenge and, wouldn't you know it, finished the entire journey with only a moderate amount of dog paddling and floating. Being near Carrie gave me such a rush of adrenaline that I probably could have swum twice as far if I had to. The simple fact is that I was in no position to fend off her charms. I was like a prisoner released from jail, only in my case the jail was a mansion and the warden was the memory of a failed marriage to a woman who had once loved me, but had long since decided that I was not the man, and certainly not the rabbi, she had married. That experience had convinced me that there were worse things in life than being alone. After meeting Carrie, though, I was convinced there were better ones as well.

Once I made my way across the inlet and onto the beach, I found myself attempting to recall every biographical fact that

I had heard about Carrie Larson. There weren't many. I knew she was raised in Provo, Utah by two school teachers. Her father was of Norwegian extraction, her mother German. I knew also that she went to college at the U. of U., as I like to call her state university, where she did a double major in comparative religion and elementary education.

After graduating from college, Carrie taught for seven years in the Salt Lake City public schools. At the same time, she continued to develop her interest in religion. In the summer of 2003, Carrie flew out to Washington, D.C. to serve as a volunteer for POP. She was neither Jewish nor Muslim; she simply adored the goals of the organization and the express manner in which it hoped to bring together two warring, misunderstood peoples. Carrie said that POP's ecumenical spirit was akin to that of her own religion—Unitarian Universalism, or "UU," as it is known by its adherents. So yes, Carrie was a UU who went to the U of U.

Lying on the Jamaican beach next to this beautiful soul, I couldn't help but laugh when Carrie referred to herself as a "militant Unitarian." Before I had met her, I would have thought that was an oxymoron. My understanding was that UU wasn't an "ism" at all, let alone one that could inspire militant devotion. I had seen the UU's simply as liberal-minded people who lacked the muscle tone to define what they stood for. This point was made over and over in familiar Unitarian jokes, like "What do you get when you cross a Unitarian with a Jehovah's Witness? Someone who rings your doorbell but doesn't know why."

No doubt it was Carrie's passion about religion that enabled her to persuade Moses to expand POP's charter to include UU as one of not two, but now *three* Peoples of Priests. She convinced Moses that just as Judaism and Islam were majestic communities that have suffered from a widespread lack of respect, the same could be said about Unitarianism. Besides, Moses liked to support any group of spiritual progressives who wished to come together in weekly meetings, and he had a special place in his heart for the UUs because of their relationship with God. "In their own way, they're God wrestlers," Moses told me. "No religious group is better able to engage theists, atheists, pantheists and panentheists *as equals* under the same tent."

When Moses included Carrie's faith under his group's umbrella, she quit her job as a school teacher to open up a chapter of POP in Salt Lake City. She was charged with explaining to the public the vital role that UU's could play in healing and unifying our planet.

After we finished swimming, Carrie insisted on treating me to lunch at Port Antonio's most expensive restaurant, which overlooked an inlet not terribly different from our own. "It's the least I can do to repay you for the plane tickets," she said, and I gladly accepted her offer. While we ate, I regained enough of my strength to question Carrie for the first time about her religious community.

"I heard that there are only a quarter-million UU's in the country. Is that right?" I asked.

My question brought on a big grin. "Your data's out of date," she replied. "Before we were included in POP, all of our congregations combined had only a quarter of a million members. But in the last three years, we've *tripled* our membership."

"You're kidding."

"I'm dead serious," she said, still grinning. "Do you remember Moses hitting the TV circuit and telling everyone to check out the UU's if they hadn't found a religious community that worked for them? Back then, he was probably the most popular man in America."

"I'd say so," I replied.

"We've always known there was a huge, untapped pool out there waiting for us. We just needed someone to publicize that we weren't just a bunch of wishy-washy liberals—that we actually had a reason to exist other than to host interfaith marriages."

I couldn't help but laugh. I had been to a Unitarian church maybe five times in my life, and four of them were to attend weddings between Jews and Christians.

"See what I'm talking about?" Carrie said. "Even you laugh at us. We were a joke."

"Oh, come on," I replied. "All religions are punch lines these days."

"But UU wasn't even considered a legitimate religion—not until the last couple of years. Now that Moses' reputation is shot, maybe we'll go back to where we were."

I felt like she had just slugged me in the face.

"Look, I blame myself for taking the notes. I never should have —"

"I wasn't getting down on you, Richie," she said, visibly concerned that she had embarrassed me. "I was only explaining the situation. Nobody knows what'll happen with POP any more. I just know what *was* going to happen. The UU's in the organization were preparing to lead a delegation to the Middle East and broker a lasting peace between Israel and its neighbors. I don't mean we were going to try; we were going to succeed!"

I had to raise my eyebrows at that comment. She sounded like a wild-eyed teenager. "That's a little easier said than done," I finally replied.

"It wouldn't be quick and it wouldn't be simple, but we could pull it off."

I played along. "How?"

"UU's are natural mediators. One of our basic reasons for existing is to create a world community where everyone can live in peace. We're Universalists, right? We want more than anything else to figure out what's best for the world as a whole, not just our own people."

"The Jews could say the same thing," I replied. "So could the Christians."

"I don't agree," she said. "You're both saddled by your histories. Jews have been looking out for themselves; you've had to.

You're fighting a war with the Arabs over land that used to be theirs and that they never agreed to give up. And the Christians, they've tried to take over the whole world—converting people at the point of a sword. Even now, their missionaries want to persuade people that everyone on the planet should be Christian. Do you think they have credibility with the Muslims?"

"The UU's are different. We haven't done anything to undermine our objectivity. Think about it: one of our key principles is that we're free to follow the truth wherever it leads. We don't have a holy book and a long line of priests to tell us what to think, or how.

"Plus, we're devoted to the inherent worth and dignity of every human being. When we talk about war, we don't act like some lives matter more than others. We care as much about the Muslims in Palestine as the Hebrews in Israel. Can you say that about American Jews—or even American Christians?"

"I suppose not," I acknowledged. "But I still don't see peace coming to the Middle East anytime soon. And when it does, it will be because the Jews and the Muslims put their own houses in order, not because of Unitarians from America."

"I guess time will tell," she replied. "I won't make any predictions, not with all this stuff going on about Moses." Carrie excused herself from the table and allowed me a moment alone with my thoughts. I found myself wondering why I was so incredibly drawn to passionate, opinionated women.

No sooner did she get back to the table than she threw out another gem: "You know what I think? Your friend Moses is a closet UU."

This time I just shook my head and smiled.

"You don't agree?" she asked.

"Do you believe what you're saying, or are you just trying to egg me on?" I asked.

"I don't just believe it. I'm convinced of it."

"Not only is Moses Jewish," I replied, "he's the most Jewish person I know."

"Come on. He's constantly butting heads with Jewish tradition."

"Precisely. And that's what Jews do."

"OK, fine. So Jews are taught to question the tradition," Carrie said. "But you're always supposed to side with it in the end. Moses is as likely to side against it as with it. He's different when he's dealing with Unitarianism. He's like a fish in water. He buys into *all* of our principles. He's not tied to any one Bible; he associates himself more with his planet than his tribe; he believes in compassion, truth and justice above everything … except for peace. That's totally a UU attitude. He's a fighter, but what he really fights for is peace, not for domination by some ideology. I'm telling you; he's a UU through and through."

"I'm afraid your rhyming is better than your judgment," I said. I didn't want to be so blunt, but what else was there to say? Carrie was feisty and quite the ambassador for Unitarianism, but she had a lot to learn about my faith. And her boss.

Carrie and I walked all over the town that afternoon. By the time we returned to the villa, so had everyone else. The first question on my mind was answered by simply looking at the faces of Don and Lisa—clearly, she had won the golf match. "She beat me 4 and 3," he said. "We were playing match play rules. If it had been stroke play, I might have won."

Lisa laughed. "I was going to do whatever it took. I wasn't about to lose that bet."

"Hey, Moses," I said, while my friend was mixing a martini. "Do you know what you were called today? A Unitarian."

"What, are you kidding? I've probably been called everything under the sun today—certainly every four-letter word."

"I don't mean stateside, I mean here in Jamaica—by that lady." As I pointed to Carrie, she waved back to Moses.

"She knows better," Moses answered.

"No, I really don't," Carrie said. "Deep down, I think you're a UU who can't bring yourself to renounce your old religion."

"Sit down, my dear," Moses said. "Here, take my drink; you need one. You've heard me complain a lot about my religion, but that doesn't mean I'd think for a second about switching teams. Rabbi," he went on, facing me, "tell this shikse why I'm not a Unitarian."

Did I ever. First of all, I said, he's a Jew because it connects him to his family, especially his mother. He's a Jew because he loves the aesthetics—the chanting of the old melodies, the Seder plate and the bricks of Jerusalem. He's a Jew because it's so holistic—it doesn't just connect people across space, it connects people through time.

He's a Jew, I went on to say, because he loves the Hebrew language—he adores listening to music sung in Hebrew; those aren't songs to him; those are *prayers*. He's a Jew because he loves God, and our religion permits him to worship the God that he himself has chosen, not one he was required to worship as part of some official dogma.

He's a Jew, I continued, because he loves Jewish ethics. The same universalistic spirit that Carrie appreciates so much in Unitarianism, I pointed out, came from Jewish roots. He's a Jew because he's totally committed to *tikkun olam* (a Kabbalistic term that literally means "repairing the world" and connotes social action and the pursuit of justice). He feels personal responsibility for making sure that the Jewish community becomes a "light unto the nations," and especially a beacon of peace. I've never seen anyone so devoted to that goal as Moses.

He's a Jew, I added, because Hillel was a Jew, and so were Jesus, Akiva, Spinoza, the Baal Shem Tov, Freud, Einstein, Buber and Heschel.

He's a Jew, I went on, because our culture venerates education. Why do you think the Ivy League needed quotas to keep us out so soon after our families emigrated here from Europe?

Finally, I said, he's a Jew because he likes the jokes. He likes to laugh at himself, and that's what Jewish humor is all about.

"Hey, Don," Moses interrupted. "What happens when a Jew with an erection runs into a brick wall?"

"He breaks his nose," Don replied, without missing a beat.

When I finished, everyone sat in silence while we awaited a response from Carrie. "Maybe Moses is a *Jewish* UU," she said.

Moses didn't even crack a smile. "That's what I love about you," he replied. "You're relentless."

Indeed she was, especially once she started talking about her religion. We spoke some more about it that evening, but mostly the gang commiserated about how sad it was that we would have to split up the next day and, in the case of some of us, face the music that had resulted from my service as a scribe.

I had arranged for a van to take us all back to the airport at Kingston, where we caught the flight to Miami. From there, Carrie would fly to Utah, Moses to New York, Don and Lisa to D.C., and I to Boston, where I was giving a speech at the Harvard Divinity School on, of all topics, "Life after Death in Judaism." The speech had been planned before the flap over my notes became public, and the Divinity School didn't have the heart to tell me to stay home. (As it turned out, I ended up speaking to a packed house—no doubt because of the controversy.)

At the Miami airport, Carrie and I were scheduled to fly out of adjacent gates, and we waited together for about an hour at the terminal. My flight was the first to be called. While it was boarding, the gate area was jammed, and I noticed several people staring at me—the price of celebrity. I would so much have preferred privacy at that moment, which is ironic considering that whenever Carrie and I were alone together in Port Antonio, we did nothing I wouldn't have been comfortable doing in a crowded airport.

"Last call for Flight 279 to Boston," the flight attendant announced.

"Are we going to see each other again?" she asked.

"Absolutely," I said. "I just don't know when." I gave her a hug, but it didn't feel right. She was the first person who had made me feel like a man in years, and yet I was hugging her like I would have hugged my father. So I pulled her head back and gave her a kiss—a kiss that must have lasted twenty seconds.

When it was over, we held each other's hand for a moment and then, just as Carrie was beginning to cry, I reluctantly let go. "Goodbye, Carrie," I said, before turning my back on her to walk toward the plane. People were looking at me, but I didn't care. I wasn't thinking about myself. I was thinking only about Carrie the Gentile and the idea of forbidden fruit.

CHAPTER XXIII

"Because I tend to be politically liberal, a lot of people ask me why I identify myself more with the South than the North. It has less to do with the fact that I was born and raised in Alabama than with the importance to me of civility. Southerners are raised to treat people with respect. They listen to what you have to say, and it seems like they actually care about what they're hearing. Plus, they're taught not to be arrogant or aloof. When I'm down south, I feel more valued, even if I'm talking to someone with a totally different world view.

"I know a lot of Northerners who think I'm being taken in by phoniness. They tell me that a Southerner can be nice to your face, and then, when you turn around, they'll badmouth half the things you've said. Well, maybe so, but I'll tell you this: I live for the chance to meet people, share ideas, and build bridges. Anyone who makes that experience pleasant helps me feel at home."

Moses Levine, addressing a conference
sponsored by the Southern League
Against Poverty, 1985

New York City—July 2006. I'm tempted to say that no one benefited as much from our vacation in Port Antonio as I did, but that might not be true. That trip may have saved Moses' sanity. He was holding up pretty well before the vacation, but I'm not sure he could have withstood the next couple of months without the week we spent in paradise.

Back when he was planning our jaunt to Jamaica, Moses was also putting together a whistle-stop tour of the East Coast to promote POP's proposed bill to combat global warming. The tour was scheduled to begin shortly after we came back from Jamaica and would involve traveling by train from New York to Miami with eight other stops in between. In each city, Moses would give a public address about climate change. According to his plan, when the trip was finally over, he would rest for a couple of days in Birmingham, and then spend the next month in D.C. lobbying members of Congress about the bill. Several POP staffers had already begun that job, but none had Moses' personal connections with lawmakers. Then again, none carried Moses' recent baggage either.

Suffice it to say, the tour didn't exactly go as planned. The first change was to jettison the train travel. One of Moses' assistants pointed out that in many circles, Moses was as loathed as he was once loved. She went ballistic at the idea of Moses traveling in a manner that would allow anyone to track him down and shoot him at will. After a battle, Moses relented and agreed to charter a private bus for the trip. But that's not all. As soon as the specter of assassination was raised, Moses' staff began planning one security measure after another. They hired bodyguards and arranged for bulletproof glass at each podium. Fearing that the Bible Belt would be especially dangerous, one of POP's vice presidents even proposed that Moses go no further south than Baltimore, but at that point my friend put his foot down. "I might as well be dead already, the way you all want me to live. I'm not avoiding the South. That's where I'm from, and I can think of no nicer place to die. Shema Yisrael,

Adonai Elohenu, Adonai Echad." He didn't spend much time on the "Echad" but he didn't have to—his staff understood the allusion.

I didn't see Moses' speech in New York, but from what others have told me, it was jubilant. Thousands showed up to honor him and pledge their support for his latest political battle. Whenever Moses took on a cause, whether it was fighting poverty, promoting peace, or protecting the environment, he focused on the topic like a laser beam. In his speeches on climate change, Moses honored me by borrowing the word "usufruct" from the sermon I gave soon after I met Rachel. I had later given Moses a transcript of my talk, and he liked the concept, so it had become one of the cornerstones of his diatribes against global warming.

"We hold this planet in usufruct for our children's generations, and our grandchildren's, and our great-grandchildren's," he liked to argue. "We're the trustees. If we want to pave some roads, or build some tall buildings, that's fine. But we don't dare melt the glaciers, or flood the coasts, or kill species after species of animal. We don't dare treat this planet like our own personal play toy. It belongs to God, and we have a covenant with God to act as its caretakers — not its owners, its *caretakers*! When we guzzle energy like swine, we abuse that covenant."

The Trenton stop also went over well, as did the stop in Philly. But Moses reported to me that the further he went down the coast, the more he detected that things had changed with the audience. "I'm not picking up the same level of enthusiasm," he said. "I'm almost wondering if a lot of these people show up just to gawk at the weirdo who thinks he's Moses."

I had long since returned from Harvard by the time Moses' entourage approached the D.C. area. At his request, I agreed to join them the rest of the way. They picked me up in Silver Spring, and we headed down together to Richmond. This would be the first Red State stop on the tour. The POPers, as I called them, were bracing for a different kind of reception, but they didn't quite know what to expect—not even Moses.

In Richmond, Moses' people had rented space at the Virginia Commonwealth University, not far from where Jefferson Davis lived when he was the president of the Confederacy. Moses once took me on a tour of Davis' home, as well as a number of other old Civil War landmarks in the area. He was a student of the period, like so many southerners you meet. The difference between him and most of his fellow white Alabamans, though, is that his sympathies lay with the men in blue.

Moses planned to talk in Richmond for a little over half an hour, which was the standard length of his speeches on that trip. The crowd numbered about 1000, fewer than we had seen at any point up north. After a few minutes, we could hear chanting from the back right of the audience. Then another group closer to the center joined them, followed by still another group in the back left, and then a fourth group further toward the front. Right in the middle of that last group was one William Jones—the drunk who had confronted Moses on the train from New York to D.C.

In all, there must have been a good 200 people chanting, and their words were unmistakable. "Hyp-o-crite, blas-phem-er, re-pent now. Hyp-o-crite, blas-phe-mer, re-pent now." They occasionally changed the tempo, but never the message, and every syllable was distinctly pronounced. They were creating their own version of a niggun, using a repetitive melody to generate a certain mood. In Moses' case, however, nigguns involve wordless sounds intended to foster a sense of love, whereas in Richmond, the chanters were using emotionally charged language to demonstrate their defiance.

Those of us who came to listen and not to heckle still outnumbered the hecklers four to one. We tried many ways to shut them up. We shushed them, yelled at them and even tried reasoning with them. Nothing worked. They had come to make a non-violent but confrontational statement, and they were baiting us to see if we were willing to use violence to stop them. Fortunately, no one did—this was, after all, a crowd of Moses' disciples. The result is that the protesters chanted for ten more minutes until, finally, Moses announced that he was canceling the rest of the speech, and his crowd of supporters disbanded.

That evening at the Richmond Hyatt, Moses and I sat together and watched the aftermath of our little nightmare on TV. The whole episode had been captured on film, and you could hardly turn on a national news show without seeing at least a 30-second clip from Richmond. The cable news producers, bless their hearts, quickly dredged up talking heads on both sides of the issue, and they went at it with gusto, much to the glee of their sponsors.

Moses' defenders lamented the lack of respect for free speech in our society, where a man who has done so much good for so many can't even give a talk on behalf of the environment. But the hecklers had their backers as well, including a couple of overstuffed preachers who spoke about the "irony" of the situation.

"Don't 'cha just love these liberals," said the Reverend Samuel Beecham, with the obligatory Southern accent, even though he was from Wisconsin. "They don't have any problem with protesters disrupting World Trade conferences or undermining support for a war. But as soon as people of faith express themselves against the forces of Satan, they blow a gasket."

The Reverend Paul Alsmere, appearing on the Christian Channel News Hour, pointed out an even greater irony. "What kind of Moses is this?" he bellowed. "No boils? No frogs? No darkness? The real Moses could have at least given those hecklers laryngitis. But I could hear them chanting, loud and clear. They were having a good old time, and he couldn't do anything about it. He must have left his rod at home by mistake."

It was the most fun they've had in the Bible Belt since *Hee Haw* went off the air.

Whereas Moses was frazzled when I said goodnight to him at the Richmond Hyatt, he looked like a different person the next day. There was a gleam in his eyes and a sense of serenity on his face that I hadn't seen in quite a while, not even in Port Antonio.

"I hope you didn't dream last night that you were Akiva about to be martyred," I said to Moses.

"Actually, I dreamt I was in bed with Ayelet. Thanks for the reminder," he said, grinning.

Whatever it was, something worked, for Moses was ready to do battle. On the bus to Charlotte, he told me to relax and let him take care of everything, and spent the whole trip alone drafting and editing a document.

The following afternoon, we were at the Hayes Recreational Field Complex on the campus of the University of North Carolina at Charlotte. When Moses came to the podium, he looked out on a crowd that was a fair bit larger than the one in Richmond and had many familiar faces. They weren't hard to recognize; we had had plenty of opportunity a couple of days back to watch them chant.

Moses brought two documents to the stage and carried one in each hand. After quickly surveying the crowd, he made his decision; we were about to hear the talk that he drafted during the bus trip from Richmond.

"Friends," he began, "all of us here today share something in common: we care deeply about making this a better world. We might disagree about how that's done, but you wouldn't be here if you were apathetic. I don't have an answer to apathy. I don't even know where to start. But with you, I can open a dialogue, and once there's a dialogue, there's hope."

That's as far as he got while he owned the floor. In Richmond, they let him talk for a little while; in Charlotte, they obviously preferred the cut of their own jib.

"Hyp-o-crite, blas-phem-er, re-pent now. Hyp-o-crite, blas-phem-er, re-pent now. Hyp-o-crite, blas-phem-er, re-pent now." It was louder by half than at our previous stop. The talk shows had broadcast Moses' impending arrival in Charlotte, and even more members of the not-so-silent majority wanted to be in on the fun.

What they would find was a different Moses this time around. In Virginia, he had been tongue-tied. In fact, he reminded me of President Forrest right after the Towers were bombed, continuing to sit in a classroom, practically motionless, for seven minutes. Forrest had no clue how to respond that day, and neither did Moses in Richmond. He was in shock, trying to process the new world in which he found himself. "It pisses me off to see the progressives dump on Forrest for freezing up in that school room," Moses once told me. "Let *them* be President and show how poised they'd be under the circumstances. Then they can dump on the man."

Well, Forrest rebounded quickly, and so did his friend Moses, once he was given time to collect his thoughts on the way down to Charlotte. "Hyp-o-crite, blas-phem-er, re-pent now," he said into the microphone, in unison with his hecklers. "Hyp-o-crite, blas-phem-er, re-pent now." They kept chanting, and Moses joined them for more than a dozen refrains. He even played along by emphasizing the word "now." Finally, be broke off the chant and said: "Very well. I shall do as I'm told. So should we all."

"HYPOCRITE?" he exclaimed into the microphone. Moses had created quite a scene — his voice projected by a microphone, his eyes ablaze, while an un-miked rabble of hundreds chanted their mantra. "You bet I'm a hypocrite!" Moses boomed into the crowd. "Everyone who speaks out in favor of values and dares to challenge others to do good is a hypocrite. We can never measure up to our ideals. Such is not the human way.

"Ours is the path of imperfection. We can be lazy, mean, selfish, ignorant. We can fall off the proverbial horse, and some of us never get back on. But others do—wiser for the experience. And therein lies the path of virtue.

"BLASPHEMER?" he went on, continuing to shout over the chanting. "What mortal can speak of God without blaspheming? God is immanent in this world, yes. God is ubiquitous—just open your eyes, and you will see manifestations of the divine. But God is also transcendent, with an essence that's unknowable. 'His face,' as we Jews like to say, shall never be revealed to human kind.

"When we speak of God and use human language, we do so crudely. We limit God when we characterize the divine. We restrict God's greatness, and who are we to do that? We claim to be inspired by God, but where do our paths lead? Often to vice, to error, to ugliness.

"So to you who call me a blasphemer, I plead guilty. It's nothing to be proud of. But what choice is there? The only way to stop blaspheming altogether is to completely give up talking of God, and this I am unwilling to do."

I was hoping the chanters would eventually give up and let Moses speak his piece. But they just kept on going, and so did he.

"We agree that I should minimize my blasphemy. We agree that I should minimize my hypocrisy. And yes, we agree that I should repent for my mistakes. REPENTANCE—*teshuvah* — is the beginning of enlightenment. Only through genuine teshuvah can we understand where to draw the line between virtue and vice.

"How important is teshuvah? Consider the words of Jeremiah, the Prophet. 'Turn back, O Rebel Israel—declares the Lord. I will not look on you in anger, for I am compassionate ... I do not bear a grudge for all time. Only recognize your sin; for you have transgressed against the Lord your God.'

"Wait a minute. Did you hear that? Jeremiah *blasphemed*! He spoke of God in terms of possessing a human emotion — compassion. Who is Jeremiah to characterize the mental state of God? Who is *any* person to describe God in terms of a human emotion?

"But I do love Jeremiah's message. We must turn back, we must *repent*, for we all have transgressed and rebelled. Once we repent, then we will locate virtue and happiness ... then we will stop being so consumed by our guilt, our anxiety, and all the other products of our sins.

"To you who heckle me, *I thank you for reminding me of this lesson*! I hope what I am saying is audible on film, because I want everyone to know how I feel. In the past, I have repented every year on Yom Kippur, the Day of Atonement. But today, July 13th, shall be for me a second Day of Repentance. For as long as I live, on this date, I shall repent of all my sins against God. These voices I hear shall be forever in my mind as a reminder of the value of teshuvah."

Moses didn't stop at that. He went on to talk about global warming, but just a bit. He could tell that the audience was having a difficult time understanding him, and he didn't want his latest talk about the environment to interfere with what he had to say about teshuvah.

No sooner did he go backstage than I managed to reach him. He had a simple question: "Do you think the TV people were able to record my speech?"

I was about to respond when I heard a shot ring out. Then another. And then a third. The last two shots were fired by Moses' bodyguards. They killed the man who fired the first one, but not before he had plunged a .38 caliber bullet into Moses' chest.

PART IV

CHAPTER XXIV

"I don't oppose the right to bear arms any more than the right to bear legs. Now I wouldn't let people own assault weapons, and I'm big on laws that impose waiting periods or that keep guns away from ex-convicts or the mentally ill, but I wouldn't prohibit most Americans from owning simple handguns or rifles. You might as well try to ban alcohol. Firearms are as embedded in our culture as cold beer.

"So yes, in some respects I side with the NRA. And yet, I'm thoroughly alienated by their romance with guns. In fact, I'm disgusted. Why do so many Americans actually like guns? What's the joy in aiming a rifle at some defenseless animal, blasting the life out of its body, and putting its remains on your wall? And why would you want one of those weapons lying around so that one of your children could find it and begin the romance for a whole new generation?

"Frankly, one of the things I love most about Jewish culture is that so few of us hunt."

Rabbi Moses Levine, addressing
Temple Emanu-El, 1995

Charlotte, North Carolina — July 2006. I sat at Moses' bedside for more than an hour before he regained consciousness.

When he woke up and glanced around the room, he must have assumed we were alone. In fact, at least twenty of his friends who had attended the speech on global warming were lining the hospital's halls and cafeteria.

"It was so different up north, wasn't it?" he said, fighting off the pain from his wound. "I've always thought of myself as a southerner, but now it's pretty clear they don't want me around any more."

"What makes you say that?" I asked. Moses managed a smile, but I imagine it would have hurt too much to laugh.

"Richie, it's beginning to look like my fifteen minutes are just about up," he said.

"Are you kidding? You're all over the news."

"Did they film the shooting?"

"I don't think so."

"Bet you didn't know I looked into Jones' eyes before he fired the shot." Moses said.

"Really. Could you tell he had a gun?"

"Not at all," Moses said. "I had no idea what he was up to—other than to heckle me. I saw him in Richmond; I pretty much expected him to follow us to Charlotte."

"When we saw that schmuck on the train back in May, I told you we should have gotten up and left as soon as he started insulting you. I could tell he was crazy."

"But not a killer," Moses replied. "Who could have known that? Anyway, I'm sure there are a million others just like him who'd love to have taken that shot. I've offended quite a few sensibilities." He smiled again.

We sat in silence for a minute or so. Then Moses spoke again. "One question, Richie. Can you promise to answer it honestly?"

"Depends on the question."

"It *depends*?" he said, visibly upset. "Look at me. You're not going to grant me one honest answer?"

"Alright, I'm sorry. Ask away."

"How do you feel about Carrie?"

"I like her. I like her a lot."

"You just *like* her, or is there something more?"

"This is what you want to talk about — me and Carrie?"

"Can you answer my question?"

"Fine," I said. "Yeah, I think she's great. But she's not Jewish, and she's not going to convert. She *shouldn't* convert. She already has a religion."

Moses shook his head in disgust. "After all we've lived through, you still think religious differences should get in the way of love? Amazing. Don't you get it? You can have your religion, and she can have hers."

I could feel my stomach contracting. This was not a conversation I wanted to have. "I'm a Conservative rabbi; I've got to set a good example. You know the effects of intermarriage. Even if the kids were raised Jewish, it's not the same. When the mother is from a different culture and she doesn't convert, in a generation or two, the family won't be Jewish. We can't afford to lose any more families, not after the Holocaust."

"Oh … the demographics," Moses said. "How I love to hear about the stinkin' demographics. Listen, aside from the religious differences, you met a woman you're compatible with, right?"

"Maybe."

"Maybe?" he asked.

"OK, *probably*."

"And how often can you say that?"

"You want the truth?" I asked.

"Just this once."

"She may be the first woman I've been compatible with since Lisa." For a moment, I wanted to leave it at that; then I realized that Moses deserved a bit more candor. "I don't know what it is about Carrie, but she disarms me. When I was with her, and especially that day when the rest of you took off and left us alone, I just felt warmly about everything—about her, about what we were doing ... even about me. That was probably the most amazing thing of all. And as beautiful as I thought she was, inside and out, she treated dumpy little me like a prince—I can't explain that either."

Moses smiled. "Then screw all this demographic B.S.," he said. "If you want to be happy, take care of your love life. If you want to help the Jewish people, tell your congregation it's not the demographics that's killing American Judaism, it's the *obsession* with demographics."

"Look, I know your viewpoint: what makes Judaism great are its ideals, not its statistics."

"Correct," he said. "And romantic love needs to be an ideal we affirm, however it springs up — gay or straight, within the faith or interfaith. Maybe if people thought of Judaism as more open to intermarriage, it would seem more progressive and we could pick up more converts."

"Let's be real, OK?" I replied. "Converts are great, and I love to hear intermarried couples tell me they're raising their kids Jewish. But they're not the meat and potatoes of Judaism. It is now what it always has been: families with two parents who were born Jewish."

"You're hopeless, aren't you?" Moses said. At least he knew better than to argue that Jews can increase their overall numbers by being open to intermarriage. I had the better part of that debate. His real argument was: demographics, schme-mographics; love is more important!

"Here's what I want you to do," Moses continued. "Call Carrie. Tell her POP is consolidating operations. She'll have to close her office in Utah. Tell her to come to D.C., and we'll have a job waiting for her when she arrives."

"You want *me* to tell her?"

"I think she knows I'm, uh, kind of preoccupied at the moment. Now go and leave me alone with my pain."

So I did — as did the others who had followed Moses' ambulance from the stage where he had tried to out-heckle the hecklers. Moses was hospitalized for two full weeks and very nearly died. The bullet had narrowly missed his heart, but he suffered a collapsed lung and, more importantly, a near-fatal wound to his spirit. Moses didn't seem suicidal—he loved life, he loved *God*, too much for that—but he acted as if, in an important respect, that bullet had found its mark.

"When hope goes," Moses once told me, "so does our joy. When joy goes, so does our humanity." For that reason alone, Moses was determined to stay optimistic about our planet's future. Charlotte never shook that optimism, but it did make Moses question whether he personally would ever make a difference again.

It took me a few days, but I finally did Moses' bidding. I called Carrie and delivered the message about needing to close her office. At Moses' request, I also relayed the offer that she could move to Washington and work out of POP's headquarters, if that's what she'd like.

"I'll think about it," she replied. "Tell me this. Why didn't Moses call me directly, or at least have someone from the office call me? Why did he have you do it?"

Of course I couldn't admit the truth. "Do I have to remind you of everything he's going through these days? He was just delegating a task, that's all. I told him I'd take care of it. Listen," I added, "you should at least come out for a few weeks. And please, stay at my place. I have plenty of room."

More than 11,000 spare square feet, to be exact.

Carrie arrived at my Silver Spring home two weeks to the day after Moses was shot in Charlotte. When I answered the knock on my door, I was delighted with what I saw. I'd been worried that she'd greet me with some phony "I've missed you" look, as if she hadn't had anything else to think about since our goodbye kiss in Miami. But she kept it real, as people like to say these days. She didn't crack a smile and said simply, "Thank

God I'm finally here. Let me put my stuff down and then you can fill me in on the whole nightmare."

We must have spoken for five hours that night. The next day, she left early to go to POP's offices downtown. I didn't see her until the evening when she walked into my synagogue, just in time for Shabbat services. It made me nervous to see her there; I assumed she would be evaluating my sermon much as Rachel did during her first trip to Beth Hashem. But Carrie's visit to the synagogue only confirmed that she and Rachel were two very different women.

Carrie didn't come to the shul to check out a potential mate, nor to be mesmerized by the wit and wisdom of a rabbi. She came to pray. And pray she did, with the same fervor that I would have expected from an Orthodox man in Mea Shearim. No, she wasn't moving her head up and down like a yeshiva bucher. But her ability to feel the spirit was palpable from the swaying of her body and the serenity in her face.

I had heard long ago that Unitarians weren't especially spiritual — that they were basically political people who wanted to join a community devoted to intellectual inquiry and social service. It wasn't until I spoke to Carrie in Jamaica that I learned what nonsense that was. "Some of us are died-in-the-wool atheists," she said. "Others are devout believers in God. And we define God in all sorts of ways. It's always fun to compare notes."

It became increasingly evident to me how seriously Carrie took the idea of a "people of priests." She, in fact, was one herself, which only stood to reason. She wouldn't have inspired Moses to alter the mission statement of his organization had he not seen her, in essence, as a peer, instead of a member of his "flock."

That night, back at the house, Carrie and I mulled over her future. Moses had convinced her that POP should close down most of its offices, and that if circumstances didn't change, POP might have to disband altogether. For the moment, Carrie worked on POP's global warming campaign and would continue to do so as long as the bill was under consideration by Congress. "But then what?" she asked me.

"Simple. A new UU seminary opened up just south of Baltimore. You can live here and commute up there. And I'll tell you what. If you get your degree, I'll build you a church."

"Stop it, Richie; this isn't funny."

"My God, I've never been more serious in my life!" I replied, with the intensity I normally associate with my more famous friend.

While I couldn't help my visceral reaction, it was more dramatic than I had thought was appropriate. When Carrie had first agreed to stay with me, I decided to avoid the drama and keep things Platonic. She was a guest in my house who was under a lot of stress about losing her job. To make a move on her under those circumstances would have seemed like an act of abuse.

Still, after she arrived and we began spending time together, I couldn't deny what was happening. I was falling in love — with her smile, her voice, her laugh, her intelligence, her openness, her passion, her spirituality … and her chutzpah. It was that last trait that made me especially confident that she'd be a successful minister.

After I convinced her that I was on the level, Carrie told me she'd think about my offer. Then she kissed me, and suddenly, all the lectures I had ever heard about the evils of intermarriage sounded like pure, unadulterated gibberish.

CHAPTER XXV

"Here's one thing I don't understand about global warming: if it scares the daylights out of me, and I don't even have any kids, how is it possible that so many people who do have children don't seem to care? My generation isn't going to have to suffer much because of this issue. We're not going to starve in the African desert. We're not going to lose our homes here in Manhattan or down the Eastern seaboard. It's the next generation or two who will pay the price for our addiction to fossil fuels, not us.

"Somehow, though, that doesn't make me feel any better. I'd like to be able to walk outside on a warm December afternoon and not feel fear. I'd like to know that the sea will always be filled with fish, the Arctic with polar bears, and the mountains with snow. That would make me feel better than knowing that my SUV is filled with gas. Of course, maybe if I had a kid, I wouldn't be so concerned about the environment she'd live in when she grew old. Maybe I'd think instead about the fun she could have today, when I take her on a nice, warm December drive in my new Ford Explorer. Maybe I'm just missing out on the joys of energy consumption.

*"So you can call me old fashioned, or say I'm a
stick in the mud, but when it comes to our burning up
the planet, I still have to ask the question: **why?**"*

Moses Levine, addressing an assemblage
of thousands in New York's Central Park, 2006

Atlanta, Georgia—February 2006. The genesis of the
global warming bill that was consuming so much of Moses' and
Carrie's time was a week-long conference POP had convened
the previous winter in Atlanta. The invitees included prominent scientists, businesspeople, clerics and politicians—almost
400 in all. Virtually everyone who was invited showed up.

I attended the conference from start to finish. It was inspiring
to see the politicians and theologians defer to the scientists,
and to see the businesspeople put aside their biases. Most
importantly, the scientists made their explanations as simple
and clear as possible.

I give myself a ton of credit for learning so much that week.
My secret was to enroll in all the breakout sessions subtitled
"Designed for Those Who Failed Physics for Poets." At least I
knew my limitations.

When the week was over, nearly all the attendees reached
the same conclusion: the global warming problem is real and
will be devastating if we don't attack it soon. Yes, the speed and
horrors of its effects had been exaggerated by some, but that
was no excuse for living in denial.

The conference gave Moses a new raison d'etre. He knew,
however, that nothing he did would matter unless he was
willing to suggest a price tag. People were waiting for one to
be proposed at the end of the conference, but Moses wasn't
ready—not even close.

First, he reached out to those luminaries who might have
expected to be invited to the conference but weren't. Moses
told them that POP needed allies who nobody could accuse of

being brainwashed in Atlanta. They'd likely be the most effective advocates for the plan.

Next, Moses hit the TV talk show circuit. His task was to scare the daylights out of the American public without being specific about how to solve the problem. "People smarter than you and I have devoted a lot of their brain cells to this stuff," he told Ripley. "If you don't mind, POP's not going to form any conclusions until we've read every word they've submitted. This has to be done carefully, because it's all about going to war. We've already decided to fight. Now, we've got to figure out *how*."

Moses saw the conference attendees as his foot soldiers in a battle royal against the interests of inertia—both the corporations that market fossil fuels and the bloated consumers who burn them up at record rates. At the front lines were the business execs who agreed to splash television and radio outlets with advertisements. Their ad campaigns blanketed the coverage of the Final Four. That year, you couldn't think about college basketball without hearing the words "fossil fuels" and "carbon footprint."

More than two months after the close of the conference, Moses finally announced the price tag: $60 billion, and I mean $60 billion *per year*. Nothing less, POP concluded, would put the problem of climate change in the rear-view mirror.

POP's proposed legislation provided that, in the first year, federal funds would be spent in five areas: $10 billion on research to design the energy-efficient automobile of the future; $10 billion on research involving wave-energy facilities designed to capture the untapped power of our oceans; $10 billion on solar energy research; $10 billion to support the construction of mass transit systems; and, last but not least, $20 billion to build nuclear power plants.

No, that wasn't all — not hardly. The bill also proposed a $3 per gallon tax hike on gasoline. And because this tax increase would be regressive, it would be funded through reductions on another regressive tax: that on social security. The plan was to protect poor and middle-class Americans as much as possible, but not to the point where they were allowed to continue their present love affair with the automobile.

"So much for the NASCAR generation," Moses told me right after the bill was proposed, confident it would pass. Back then, if Moses fought for a bill, you wouldn't want to bet against it.

During the days before my notes became public, all signs looked great that climate change legislation would pass. More Senators and Representatives had announced their support than their opposition, and the support was bipartisan. The only real questions were what type of bill they'd send up and whether Forrest would sign it. Officially, our President was staying non-committal until he saw the final language. Unofficially, Moses heard from his friend that if the gas tax idea didn't cause an uproar around the country, POP could count on Forrest's signature.

"I can't believe he'd say that," I told Moses. "When this guy took office he acted like global warming was an illusion."

"You don't understand him like I do," Moses replied. "He's the most loyal non-Semite I've ever met, and he knows I saved his Presidency."

"So he'll sign this based on loyalty alone?"

"Pretty much," Moses said.

"That's scary," I replied.

Moses simply shrugged and smiled.

Sadly, though, erosion in the bill's support began almost immediately after Lisa's appearance on the Orloff show. During the next few weeks, as Moses' reputation deteriorated, so too did the chance that the bill would pass. There was no denying its association with Moses and POP. In fact, that partially explains why the bill was so popular when originally proposed.

Soon after Carrie came to stay with me in Silver Spring, she suggested that Moses' shooting might actually save the measure. "Never underestimate the power of sympathy," she said. "Now that a lot of people feel sorry for him, they might not torch the bill out of spite. Maybe they'll consider it on its merits."

And so they did. During the next week or two, the tone of the debate changed on the TV talk shows. The ad hominem attacks against Moses stopped. Instead, viewers were treated with reasoned debate about the reality of the global warming problem and whether POP had proposed sensible measures to solve it. Obviously, the gas tax received most of the attention. Some talking heads praised the tax not only for the impact it would have on climate change but also as a way to stop financing Muslim governments. Others argued that it would have unacceptable and disastrous effects on major sectors of the American economy.

Even Moses acknowledged that a $3 per gallon increase on gas prices would take a bite out of many family incomes. He added, however, that if we didn't curb consumption, the long term shock to the economy would be greater still. "The gas tax is crucial," he said. "If you address supply but not demand, you're not fighting a *war* against global warming; you're just waging a losing battle."

By mid-August, 2006, the debate over the bill had reached its saturation point. It was clearly time for our representatives to cast their votes. Believing that the bill would die unless Forrest used his bully pulpit to rally the troops, Moses requested a meeting with his old friend, and one was set for the morning of the 17th. Moses decided to bring a few colleagues with him to the White House, including Carrie.

Carrie picked Moses up at his apartment at close to 6:00 that morning. She didn't return home to Silver Spring until nine in the evening. When she walked in the door, she ran right into my arms and gave me a kiss that lifted me higher than I'd been in weeks.

I misunderstood what it meant.

"He's going to support the bill?" I asked, when our lips were finally separated.

Carrie kissed me again. This one was shorter and less dramatic, but it felt just as warm.

"Richie," she said. "I want you to know that I love you."

"I love you too, sweetheart."

"I really just discovered that after I flew here," she continued. "When we started hanging out, I felt we could talk all night and day and never get bored. And you've been so supportive of me—even with all the hell you're going through about Moses. I'll never forget that."

It was all I could do to avoid rolling my eyes. This woman was saving me from a clinical depression—why shouldn't I have been supportive? "I couldn't possibly have done as much for you as you're doing for me," I finally replied. Then we hugged again.

"I don't want to leave," she said. "I don't want to convert to Judaism, but I don't want to leave. I want to be wherever you are for as long as I live. You can be you, and I'll be me. OK?"

I didn't answer. I couldn't speak. I just kissed her.

For a minute, maybe two, we both ignored the question I had asked when she arrived at the house. Then she reminded me — I had wanted to know about the President.

"A couple of years back, I met a guy who went to college with Forrest," she began. "He said that if there's one thing to keep in mind about the President it is this: he goes through life failing to understand about twenty percent of everything he hears. He's so used to people talking over his head that he probably doesn't care any more. He doesn't think he needs to comprehend everything. He's like a dog, just trying to sniff where to go — only in his case, he's trying to sniff the best way to run the world. Sometimes, he gets it right. Other times ..."

"This is one of the other times?" I asked.

"He told Moses that if not for the whole mess about the dreams, he was going to support the bill. But that's because he had trusted Moses' judgment. 'If you had told me the scientific community is asking us to change our lifestyle to fight global warming, that would have been good enough for me.' Those were his exact words."

"Then came the notes," I said.

"Yup," she replied. "Forrest said he can't trust the judgment of anyone who's suffering from delusions—especially someone who's trying to make gas unaffordable."

"That's the term he used, 'delusions'?"

"You got it."

"What did Moses say?"

"He said, 'Even if I am off my rocker, don't punish the whole damned planet for it.'"

"Good point," I replied.

"It didn't shake Forrest," Carrie continued. "He goes, 'I wasn't the valedictorian at an Ivy League college. I didn't win a National Book Award or a Nobel. I got elected President because I'm a regular guy living in a democracy where the average voter's got an IQ of 100.'"

"Actually, it's probably higher than that," I interrupted.

Carrie laughed. "I was thinking the same thing. I'm sure Moses was too. But we didn't say anything. Forrest was just proving his own point.

"So Forrest says, 'I don't understand anything about global warming. I hear people arguing all sides of this issue. I trusted you and your group to figure this out for me. Now I can't trust you any more. If I thought I was Napoleon, would you trust me?'

"We argued with him, but it was pointless. Forrest's mind was closed from the minute we walked in the door. How did he put it? Oh yeah: 'this dog won't hunt.'"

"You know what's going on," I said. "He was elected because of the Christian Conservatives, and they all think Moses is the devil's spawn."

Carrie thought for a moment. "I take Forrest at his word.

The debate about global warming was way over his head. He basically told Moses that since he didn't know who to trust on the topic and didn't have any independent thoughts about it, he won't shake up the economy over it."

"It kind of makes sense," I said, "except for the part about a guy like this running for President in the first place. So how did Moses react?"

Carrie paused for a moment. "Well, he wasn't happy. But he didn't really want to talk about it, at least not to me. He kept asking how you and I were doing."

"That sounds like Moses," I replied.

Carrie and I spoke a little about how everyone at POP had agreed there was nothing left to do to save the bill. Then I looked her in the eyes and made the request that I'd been thinking about for quite a while. No, not *that* request—I had something more pressing in mind.

"Go ahead and say it," I said. "Just say it. Get it over with."

Carrie looked at me and gave me a kiss, or to be more specific, a peck. Then she grabbed my shoulders and shook me over and over again.

"You damned, fucking, note-taking idiot," she said, tears flowing from her eyes. "Why did you do it? Why, damn it, why?"

I had never heard her speak that way before, or since.

CHAPTER XXVI

"I've always been proud that there are so many Jewish social workers. Social workers aren't terribly well paid. Nobody kisses their tuchus, or addresses them by some highfalutin' title. Their parents don't brag about them to their yenta friends. Their working conditions are often difficult. Even the people they help aren't always appreciative. And yet, year after year, bright, highly-educated Jewish adults decide to join the field. Why is that?

"If you can answer that question, you'll have learned most of what there is to learn about Judaism."

Moses Levine, addressing the Conference
of Jewish American Social Workers, 2002

Washington, D.C.—August 2006. The House vote on the global warming bill was taken on August 21, 2006, only four days after Moses and Carrie were rebuffed at the White House. Not surprisingly, the nay's had it, and the margin was just about what everyone expected: 227-198, with ten abstentions.

Carrie and I spent the day of the vote with Moses at POP's Capitol Hill headquarters. I expected the mood to be somber, but really it wasn't; there was even a sense of relief in the air that everyone's collective ordeal was over. A couple of the younger staffers went out and bought some liquor for the occasion, and we all partook. One person after another toasted what Moses and POP had accomplished since the organization was formed. And I'm quite sure that nobody thought for a second that the global warming issue was dead.

"It'll take some time, but we'll have to resurrect it," Carrie said. "What choice is there?"

After we self-medicated for a couple of hours, someone suggested getting some air. So the group took to the streets—about twenty of us in all. POP's offices were on Pennsylvania Avenue, S.E., between 3rd and 4th. We headed up Pennsylvania toward the Capitol, passing by one Library of Congress building after another—first the Adams, then the Madison, and finally the Jefferson. The walk relaxed Moses, because he had such fond memories of the Library from his *Exodus* days when he was still an unknown rabbi who couldn't hold a job.

We were heading north to the Supreme Court Building when one of the staffers pointed out the gathering that had assembled on the Capitol steps. There must have been 200 suits in all, maybe more. At the top, standing with a microphone in his hand and a pair of cameras pointed at his face, was Representative Billy Beamon.

Beamon was a classic bully. A Texas Republican like his pal Forrest, when around the President he would turn on the charm like an embassy hostess. But back on Capitol Hill, he was all about exerting power through fear. You either deferred to him or readied yourself for a scorched earth struggle, because he'd take aim at you with every weapon he had — gossip, slander, and especially, ridicule.

Yes, Billy Beamon was renowned for his biting sense of humor. Many bullies are.

"Look at the slug on the top of the steps," Carrie said, taking note of the Congressman. "Shouldn't he be at home gerrymandering?"

"You know what he's doing," Moses replied. "He's come to brag about ruining the environment. I recognize that crowd—oilmen, car barons, Congressmen. My God—Carrie, I can see both Utah senators up there."

"This is making me ill," she said. "Let's get out of here."

"No way," Moses said. "Where's your sense of adventure? I want to go up and eat some crow. It should be fun."

Carrie and I could only shake our heads. By the time we were ready to argue with him, he was already walking toward the assemblage at a decent clip. Moses was so clearly recognizable that Beamon couldn't help but notice him as he approached the steps.

"Oh, lookie here," Beamon said, interrupting his planned comments. "Guess who's coming to pay his respects. It's Moses Levine! Let's give him a round of applause." Beamon clapped, and the audience did the same, though the applause was soon followed by laughter, which was obviously what Beamon was looking for.

"Now, now, everyone. Please, be gracious. Rabbi Levine's had a difficult time lately. He worked hard for the bill that went down in flames today, and yet he has the class to congratulate us on our victory. Maybe he really is Moses! What do you all think?"

More laughter.

"I've always had an incredible amount of respect for Rabbi Levine. I think the whole country does. You can hardly blame him for thinking that he is a 'Prophet like none other—the only man whom the Lord singled out, face to face.'

"Do you like my scholarship, Moses? I got that phrase right out of the Old Testament! Ever since you proclaimed yourself God's Number One man, I've been reading about you. I hope Jesus isn't jealous. I don't want him to think I've switched teams." He seemed to have expected laughter, but this time he heard none. Maybe his fans had begun to realize what a boor Beamon could be.

"*I have to say*, though," Beamon continued, "your bill ... well, that didn't impress me. It would have crippled our way of life, Moses. That's just not — how do you say it?—that's just not kosher! If you want to tax gas so much that only your rich friends like Rabbi Gold can hit the road, I'm sorry, but that idea is *road kill*.

"Look," Beamon continued, "I shouldn't be so harsh. Moses has suffered a lot of pain, and he's done a lot of good. Every now and then even friends have to disagree. Sometimes, I have to eat some humble pie; today, maybe it's Moses' turn. But tomorrow, I hope we can work together and take on a common enemy. If there's something real to all this global warming hysteria, well then, I'll be right there to fight it. Of course, there'd be a good way to fight it and a bad way to fight it. We need to understand the difference.

"In America, if you want something done right, invest in a company or form one of your own. Then go out there and compete with other companies to make exactly what the people demand. If you want something done wrong, walk over to that Rayburn Building down the street, knock on the Democrats' doors, and ask one of them to spend billions of dollars of *your* money to solve the problem. Oh, they'll spend it alright. They won't know what the heck they're doing, but they're good at spending your money. Nobody's going to make them accountable to you; no market's going to punish them if they screw up. But if all you want is to feel pride that you've identified a problem and made an effort to solve it, then sure—get the Government involved. Tax, tax, tax, and let the bureaucrats give it a shot."

While Beamon was talking, Moses had climbed the steps to the top. The rest of us had no idea what Moses was thinking about doing—or even *if* he were thinking. He had, after all, tossed down a few drinks. Then again, Moses could handle his liquor.

Finally, as if to remind us that even Job's patience was limited, Moses walked up to the Congressman and whispered into his ear. Beamon looked at one of his friends and shrugged his shoulders. Then he addressed the crowd once again. "Rabbi Levine would like to say a few words. Everybody, I give you the legend himself, Moses Levine."

Just then, I flashed back to the countless hours I had spent in the dungeon with my eyes closed listening to Moses and Hafeez talk. I felt complete trust back then in Moses' competence. When I remembered that trust, I decided to show him the same respect on the Capitol steps.

"First off, let me congratulate each and every one of you," Moses began. "I know what it's like to be on the winning end of a Washington fight. It's pretty darned sweet. It must be especially sweet when the butt you're kicking belongs to someone you think is full of it," Moses said, laughing. "Am I right?"

The group was silent for a moment, but then as Moses' laughter continued, his reaction was met with a hearty round of applause, seemingly sincere.

"When you get the chance to taste victory like this, for heavens sake, relish it!" Moses continued. "God knows you'll have days like the one I'm having. If you remember what it's like to be on the winning end, that'll get you through the losses.

"I'd like to think you folks who killed this bill didn't fight us out of greed. If you truly believed in the morality of your cause, I have no quarrel with you. The great thing about living in a democracy is that all of us are free to get together and reason things out. Sometimes when we do that, we'll just have to agree to disagree. This is one of those times.

"As for Congressman Beamon's remarks, I concur in some of them. Maybe not all" — again, Moses started laughing — "alright, maybe not even most of them, but leaving that aside, I need to add to his comments about the private sector. To all the businesspeople here today, I personally challenge you to support research to discover new ways of generating energy without destroying the environment. That must become the central goal of American industry.

"The businessmen and women who take on my challenge

should be considered national heroes, just as much as any traditional soldier. You might not be risking your lives, but you'd sure be defending your country. In fact, you'd be defending your entire *planet*. To me, and I'm sure I speak for Congressman Beamon, that would make you heroic … not to mention, holy."

Carrie and I arrived home that evening at ten. I was exhausted, but she didn't seem the slightest bit tired.

"I still don't get how Moses could have walked over to that snake," Carrie said, "especially after Beamon was laughing at him in front of hundreds of people. And then Moses gives a speech congratulating them and treating Beamon like he's a public servant and not a public enemy? That's crazy. Moses knows exactly what kind of menace he is."

"True, but when Moses met Hafeez, I'm sure he didn't look at him as a choir boy."

"You can't possibly be comparing Beamon to Hafeez," Carrie said. She had obviously heard many a story over the years about our warden in East Jerusalem. Hafeez's name had become beloved to most Americans despite his involvement in terrorism before he met Moses.

I went on to tell Carrie that there were a couple of things she had to understand about Moses. "First, no matter who you are, or how much you've insulted Moses or worked against him, if you invite him to enter into a dialogue with you, he'll accept. I've never known him to make an exception. Second, if Moses sees a chance to get something accomplished that he really cares about, it doesn't matter how depressed or angry he is; he'll get back to work. Put him in a big crowd of multimillion-aires and politicians, and he can't help but start lobbying.

"Honestly, Moses didn't look at this bill in terms of winning a competition; he just wanted to get work done. Tomorrow there'll be some other cause. And he'll fight for that one tooth and nail. That's the way he is."

"I can't argue with you," Carrie said, shaking her head.

"It comes from his philosophy of Judaism," I said. "When you think of the ideal of some religions, you think of a monk who spends his time mostly in prayer or in contemplation. Now, Moses loves to pray and learn, but the most important thing to him is the work he does to repair the world. That's his religion. He considers *tikkun olam* the clearest way to honor God."

"It's a lot like how I see Unitarian Universalism," Carrie replied, "only I've never met a UU who's as committed as Moses."

"Well," I replied, "I've never met another Jew who's as committed as Moses. But he's only doing what we're all taught to do.

"There's a Talmudic passage Moses likes to cite that's attributed to Rabbi Elazar. 'One whose wisdom exceeds his deeds, to what is he like? To a tree that has many branches and few roots, so that when the wind comes, it plucks it up and turns it over … But one whose deeds exceed his wisdom, to what is he like? To a tree that has few branches and many roots, so that even if all the winds in the world come and blow upon it, they cannot move it out of its place.'"

Carrie sat for a moment with a puzzled look on her face. "That's odd," she said. "I'd think the writer of that passage had it backwards. I'd think we'd need wisdom to know what deeds are truly good."

"And I'd say we all have a moral sense that tells us in our hearts the difference between good and bad," I replied. "Once we start doing good, we know it, and it becomes a habit. But just because you're wise doesn't mean you'll get off your tush and help the world. You can easily get caught up in your own thoughts and never really make a difference for anyone else. I think that's what Elazar was saying."

We talked a while longer until finally, Carrie let me in on

what she had been wrestling with all day in the back of her mind.

"As of ten minutes ago—literally ten minutes—I am officially unemployed."

It struck me as an odd comment—not exactly funny, but how could it be serious? "Ten minutes ago you were in the bathroom, here."

"No, that was eleven minutes ago. Then I picked up the phone and left a message for Moses at the office that I wasn't going to work for POP any more. I thought about the positions that were available, and none of them excited me. So I quit. And you know what? It feels good, *really* good."

"Wow. I can't imagine you not working for POP."

"I'll be fine. I'll go back to Utah to see my folks ... maybe travel for a while. Then I'll probably try to get my old teaching job back."

That comment hit me like a right cross. "Wait a minute," I said. "The other night you were saying that you and I should never be apart, that you wanted to stay with me. You did say that, right? Was I hallucinating?"

"No, I said it," Carrie began, but then her words came out haltingly. "I've said ... I've said a lot of things that made sense at the time, but ... you've been divorced, what, a couple of months? And that's about as long as you and I have known each other. What kind of person could come here and date you on the rebound, take advantage of your hospitality, and then ask you to build a brand new church so she can preach? It's not even your religion."

"On the rebound? Oh please," I said. "Rachel and I haven't been together for a while. That ball bounced off the rim years ago."

I also pointed out that I had more stinking money than I knew what to do with and would love to spend some of it developing a promising career and supporting a religion that was, in many ways, harmonious with my own. But my main argument, the one that came from the heart, was that I didn't want our relationship to end—not then, not *ever*—and I was hoping she felt the same way.

No, I wasn't in denial. I hadn't forgotten that I was a Conservative Jewish rabbi and that Carrie was a self-proclaimed "militant Unitarian." I also hadn't forgotten Jewish demographics, or all the times I've argued that our people needed to marry within the faith. For better or worse, I just couldn't fight the fight any longer. Having fallen for Carrie, I saw only one path to happiness, and the only thing standing in its way was an abstract argument, and a debatable one at that.

"Here's my advice," I told her. "Go back to Utah. See your parents. Don't neurose about what you should be doing in two months or two years. Just clear your head. I'll still be here waiting if you want to come back. And if you do, I'll never ask you to leave. I promise."

"Let me think about it," she said. "But ..." It was clear she wanted to add something. She simply couldn't get it out.

"What is it?" I asked. "What do you want to tell me?"

"Alright," she replied. "This is going to sound so ungracious. I don't mean it to ... look, I'm just going to say it. I can't be involved in a big war against global warming and then live in a mansion. I don't need to live in a little apartment like Moses does, but this place is too much. What I preach, I practice—at least I try to."

Well, I thought, looking at the gentile I'd fallen in love with, so do I — most of the time.

CHAPTER XXVII

"I feel so sorry for clergymen who have to take a vow of celibacy. What's the point — to support some artificial distinction between the body and the spirit? Spare me.

"Judaism's a bit more enlightened, but we make our silly distinctions too. We're supposed to think that God is incorporeal, right? Not me. I agree with Spinoza — the mind and the body are two attributes of the same universal substance. That's jargon for saying that God is flesh, every bit as much as spirit. Everything you touch and smell is in God, just like every thought and emotion. If you look at it that way, there's no reason not to celebrate finding a woman whose touch and smell makes you feel ... well, you know ... amazing."

Moses Levine, talking to Rabbi Richard Gold
in Port Antonio, Jamaica, 2006

Silver Spring, Maryland—August 2006. One week after the global warming bill was killed, I drove Carrie to Reagan National Airport. She left for Utah without promising to return, but I felt confident that she'd soon be back in Washington for good.

Carrie was a strong motivating force in my life. For starters, after she said that she couldn't live in a mansion, I was determined to sell the house without further delay. I had been thinking about doing it from the time the divorce was finalized, but it is one thing to entertain an idea, and another to be committed to action. I told myself that whether or not Carrie came back to live with me, I'd be out of that house within four months. I even had in mind a replacement: *any one* of the thousands of mid-sized split levels that were built in the 60s or 70s and were always hitting the market in or around Silver Spring.

Carrie also motivated me to take some pounds off ... and some years. In fact, she made me feel at least ten years younger. The morning after POP lost the global warming vote, Carrie made reservations for us at a spa in West Virginia, and the next day, we were on the road. At Meadowbrook Spa, we either hiked or swam for most of the day. Had I been with anyone else, I probably would have confined myself to hot tubs and back rubs. To be honest, we enjoyed that too, but at least we earned the right to enjoy it.

At the spa's Olympic-sized swimming pool, I spent quite a while watching Carrie do laps and wondering what in blazes she wanted with a slug like me. But in the back of my mind, I was beginning to learn the answer. I could sense it whenever we had a conversation. Our life was lived through the same prism—a prism that interprets everything according to the values it either affirms or opposes. In both our cases, our values were steeped in a passionate commitment to religion, and while superficially our religions were quite different, at bottom they were extremely compatible. That's why we'd so often complete each other's sentences. That's why when one of us raised a topic, the other would be at least as interested in discussing it.

Oddly, though, at the same time I was smiling at the thought of finally finding my soul mate, I couldn't erase my first marriage's failure from my mind. It made me wonder how I was entitled to enjoy such a wonderful relationship after having screwed up that marriage so miserably. More to the point, I had previously blamed Rachel for our breakup, but somehow, falling in love with Carrie made me realize that I may have been more of the culprit than Rachel.

Feeling lonely after Carrie returned to Utah, I arranged to see Moses at a local café. As soon as we sat down, he peppered me with questions about Carrie. I said that I planned to propose to her but not until a year after my divorce was official.

"Why wait if you're certain she's the one?" he asked.

"It seems like the right thing to do," I said. "I have to convince myself that I have the right attitude about marriage. Maybe I didn't treat the first one with enough respect."

"Maybe you were married to a controlling … what is the word I'm looking for?"

"Does it rhyme with 'witch'?" I asked.

"You're a mind reader," he said, smiling.

We talked about Moses' plans for the future, given that POP had become a shell of what it once was. It was closing all its offices outside of New York, Washington and Los Angeles, and running the remaining operation would hardly require all of Moses' limitless energies. Moses said that he was toying with the idea of writing another book — perhaps a complete exposition of his philosophy — but he wasn't quite ready. "When I write that book, I'd need to be a recluse for a year or two."

"Moses," I said, "you don't need to write a book. You need a woman. I know just the person, too."

"Ayelet?"

"Who else? She and Carrie get along great. If things work out, maybe we can have a double wedding."

"You're crazier than I am," he said, laughing. "You really think I'm going to get married? What's next, the house in the burbs with the white picket fence? I can see it now, Ayelet and I, a couple of rugrats and a dog living out in Olney. I'll build my own deck, perhaps I'll take up gardening. Yeah, that's me alright."

"Forget the gardening," I said, "but definitely get the dog. You know the old joke, if you want a friend in Washington —"

"Get a dog," Moses said, laughing. "Richie, I thought you knew me pretty well by now. I've always had way too much going on in my life to be in a stable relationship."

"Oh, stop taking yourself so seriously. You've got the same needs as the rest of us. It's about time you took care of them. The world will be fine."

"I suppose," he sighed.

"I think you owe it to everyone to give Ayelet a call and see what happens. You should hear yourself — you talk like Yenta the Matchmaker when it comes to Carrie and me. It's time to listen to your own counsel."

He did. Moses always listens, and he always reflects on what he hears. But he decided against calling Ayelet—that would have been too pedestrian. Instead, he showed up unannounced at her door in Lansing.

With Carrie having flown back home to Utah, and Moses having flown out to see Ayelet in Lansing, I thought about taking a day trip of my own—maybe down to Monticello. But then I realized that it would be more fun simply to drive to Blockbuster and pick up a few DVDs. I planned to spend the day relaxing with my best friend in the world—myself.

Halfway through the first *Kill Bill* movie, Rachel called. She was supposed to drop off our kids the next morning but asked if she could bring them over right away so that she and Elliot could leave town for a few days. I could hardly say no. At the moment, we were on relatively civil terms, and I wasn't going to do anything to disturb the peace.

I had expected Rachel to take off as soon as she came, but she felt like chatting. After speaking a bit about the kids, we made small talk about the movie I'd been watching. Rachel wanted to know if I thought Uma Thurman was sexy, and I had to say yes, being neither gay nor blind. Then I brought up the subject of Carrie. Rachel took me aback; she actually sounded like she wished us the best.

"I hate how jealous I was of Lisa," she said. "Why did I feel so threatened?"

"I really don't know," I replied. "I was always loyal to you."

"*Loyal*?" she said. "You call spending —"

I wouldn't let her finish. "Look, it wasn't disloyalty. Maybe it wasn't fair what I did; maybe it wasn't what a husband should have done —"

"I call that disloyalty," she said.

"I never left you. I never cheated on you. I never stopped respecting you. I just felt an obligation to spend some of the money I thought was mine to spend."

"Anyway, it's all water under the bridge now," she said. "You did what you had to do, and so did I. I don't regret what I did."

"Me neither, but it's still sad when a marriage ends. By the way, how are things with you and Elliot?"

"Great," she said. "We have a lot of fun together."

"What do you guys like to do?"

"It's crazy how much time we spend at the synagogue. Thank God Reform is becoming more like Conservative. Would you believe a couple members of the clergy over there are shomer Shabbos [observant of all the Sabbath rules] and keep kosher?"

"Kosher or *kosher-style*?" I asked. "I bet they eat un-kosher chicken."

"Well, alright, kosher-style. But still, no shellfish, no pork, no ham, no cheeseburgers. This isn't the Reform I remember from when I was a kid; back then, most of the men didn't even wear yarmulkes in the sanctuary."

"It has changed, you're right," I said. "People demand more authenticity from their religions these days."

"Unless you're Unitarian," she said, smiling. "Sorry, I couldn't resist."

That was the old Rachel peeking out again. I had told her earlier that Carrie was thinking of becoming a UU minister.

"Richie," she said, "I brought a couple of books for you to give to your friend Moses." She handed me John McGraw's *Brain & Belief* and Antonio Damasio's *Looking for Spinoza*. "Tell him I feel bad that Congress didn't pass his global warming bill, and that I'd like to talk to him about these books."

"You want to talk to *Moses*? Since when?"

"Since the vote on the global warming bill. I'm not very happy about it."

"What, are you kidding? You're responsible for that vote—100 percent responsible."

"Don't get me wrong. I'm thrilled the world doesn't worship at the guy's feet any more. But that doesn't mean I want to mess up the environment. The more they talk about global warming on TV, the more I realize how crazy we're being, guzzling oil like this. I guess every silver lining has its cloud."

I didn't quite know what to make of Rachel's request, but I did promise to give the books to Moses. Believe it or not, I actually thought she wanted to make peace.

My hope was not to see Moses for a while after Rachel dropped off the books. He had called me the day before from the Lansing airport and told me to wish him luck. Admittedly, his visit was unannounced, but Ayelet almost never travels, he said, so he had every reason to expect her to be in town.

Well, Ayelet was in town, alright, but Moses didn't stay for long. Just as Rachel was pulling out of my driveway, Moses was pulling in.

"Don't tell me," I said, greeting him at the door, "she's in trial and she couldn't see you?"

"Oh, we saw each other," Moses replied. "I saw Rachel

too—just a minute ago when she was driving away. She waved at me and smiled as if we were friends. What's up with that?"

"She was dropping off the kids. She wanted me to tell you she's sorry about the global warming bill."

"Yeah, right," he said, laughing. "If she's sorry, I'm a fundamentalist."

"Honestly, Moses, I think she feels badly. Politically, she's pretty progressive on a number of issues. She just doesn't agree with you on Israel."

"So I've gathered."

"She also brought a couple of books for me to give you. She said she wants to talk with you about them."

Moses raised his eyebrows at first—just like I did when Rachel gave me the books—but then he took a look at them.

"I've been meaning to read this Damasio book. I try to read everything about Spinoza sooner or later. What's this other one, *Brain & Belief: An Exploration of the Human Soul*?"

"Got me."

"So it's a book about the soul, huh? Mine's sure taking a few hits. Do you want to hear the latest?"

"I'm all ears," I said.

"I see two cars in Ayelet's driveway, so I figure she's home. But when I knock at her door, no one answers."

"What time was it?"

"About nine in the evening. I didn't want to have to call her on her cell phone. I wanted to surprise her in person. But since nobody answered, I started dialing. Just before I hit the send button, I heard someone coming to the door."

"Ayelet?" I asked.

"Yup. She was in her bathrobe. She looked great. But when she saw who it was she just about fainted."

"Guess if you had it to do over again —"

"I might not have picked a night when she was having sex," Moses said, laughing.

"Seriously," I said.

Moses didn't say a word. The look on his face said plenty.

"Wow," I said. "You've become quite the schlimazel. So who was the lucky guy?"

"A criminal prosecutor. She said they haven't faced off in court for a while, but he handles a lot of cases against her office. It's like that old movie, *Adam's Rib*."

"I'm really your lucky charm, aren't I?" I said, shaking my head. "First, my notes. Then my matchmaking advice. You're probably wondering what I'll think of next."

"You didn't tell me to drop by her house without warning. This one was on me."

"So what happened? Did the guy come out of the bedroom?"

"You know it. We had a nice little chat—once he put on his friggen PJs. It sounds like they're quite the lovebirds. They started dating about ten days after we got back from Jamaica, and now they spend every other night together."

"I'm sorry."

"Nothing like this has happened to me since college," he said.

"You mean that freshman from Carolina."

"That's the one. I'll never forget walking in on her and another girl making out on the top bunk."

"What was it you said: 'I'll take the winner'?"

"Nice memory," Moses said. "Anyway, I guess I'll just go home and read your ex's books."

"Do you want to take the DVD's I rented? I got the *Kill Bill* movies and *Reservoir Dogs*. The kids are here so I can't see myself watching them today."

"High-brow stuff; I'm impressed."

"Well, you know," I said, "I go for the intellectual themes. Blood … guts … more blood."

"I think I'll pass," Moses said. "I'm going to read about Spinoza and the soul."

"Enjoy."

"I'm sure I will," he said, smiling. "Rachel's always had my best interests at heart."

CHAPTER XXVIII

"There'll be times in your life when you think you're invincible. There'll also be times when you feel like a loser, and you won't be alone—others will tell you that, too. Maybe your wife will take off, or you'll get fired from work, or some DA will decide you broke the law.

*"The temptation whenever things go wrong is to blame everyone else. It's never our own fault, is it? We're too precious to merit blame, our hearts are too innocent. They, the accusers, **they're** the troublemakers.*

*"Well, in my experience, when things fall apart, it's usually a little bit of **their** doing and a little bit of mine too. If you're equipped to face that fact and deal with your own responsibility for every crisis you face, you'll be able to handle anything life has to throw at you."*

Moses Levine, giving the Keynote Speech at Columbia University's Commencement ceremony, 2004

Silver Spring, Maryland—September 2006. I had the kids for exactly one week after Carrie flew back to Utah. By the time I dropped them off with their mother, who had returned from her mini-vacation with Elliot, I had hoped to hear from Carrie that she was coming back to Maryland. She called, but only to say that she was spending a lot of time with her family and avoiding "heavy" thoughts as much as possible. It made sense; I was just being impatient.

As I was leaving Rachel's house, the cell phone rang. It was Moses—or should I say the voice identified itself as Moses and had the same tone as his voice, but the Moses I knew had never sounded so desperate.

"I've got to see you … right away," he said. "Are you doing anything?"

"Nope," I said, "come on over." I would have preferred a breather from drama of any kind, but that wasn't meant to be.

Moses arrived dressed in a faded Crimson Tide T-Shirt and a ripped pair of jeans. He looked like he hadn't slept in a week; all his color was gone, and his eyes were bloodshot. As soon as he saw me, he gave me a hug that must have lasted ten seconds. Then he started to cry. I'd seen him cry before—like whenever we were together near the end of Yom Kippur, for example—but this time he looked different. These weren't tears from being spiritually moved. These were tears of shame. I could see that even before he started talking.

"I'm going to tell you the whole story," he began. "You're not going to want to hear it."

"Sure I will, Moses," I said.

"NO YOU WON'T!" he yelled. It was the voice of hostility— yet another side of his personality I didn't recognize.

"A few days ago," he began, "I got a call from your ex-wife. She wanted to know when I'd finish the two books she bought me. I told her I was already done with the Damasio and I'd call her as soon as I'd read the McGraw. When I finished it yesterday morning, I let her know. She said she'd be over in the evening with a bottle of wine, and we could talk about it then."

I had to interrupt: "A bottle of wine — Rachel?"

"I'm not making any of this up, I swear."

"But didn't you think that was strange, her coming to see you with a bottle of wine?"

"Let me tell you the story. I don't want to talk about it, I want to *unload* it."

"Alright, fine," I said.

"She came over in a red sleeveless dress. She looked great. I'd never been a huge fan; you know what I'm saying? But last night was different. She looked *really* good, she was tanned, her hair looked nice —"

"I get the picture," I interrupted. Why would I want to hear him talk about my ex-wife like that?

"Are you going to keep doing this?" Moses replied. "Richie, pretend you're back in East Jerusalem. Do whatever you have to do. Sheket!

"Anyway, she poured us some wine and asked me about the books. I told her it was pretty clear why she'd given them to me: they both argued against the belief in an immortal soul. That was McGraw's central point. And while Damasio's book was largely a tribute to Spinoza, he also explained scientifically how closely the mind and body work together—the idea being that when the one goes, so does the other. Rachel was telling me that because Moshe Rabbenu's body died in the wilderness, his soul couldn't possibly inhabit my body.

"She asked me point-blank whether after reading those books, I still believed that I was the Biblical Moses reincarnated. I told her I hadn't really altered my sense of self, but I do try to listen to reason, so I was giving the issue some more thought.

"Then we spoke about Rachel's life—the guy she's dating, her charitable activities, even her real estate business. The whole time she's talking, she's pouring more wine. I was still pretty sober, but she's starting to get lit. I'm sure you've seen her like that before." (I had, but I didn't reply—the reference to East Jerusalem effectively shut my mouth.)

"After we talked for a while, Rachel got up and walked right over to me. She asked if I held her responsible for ruining my life. I answered her honestly.

"'Darn right I do. If not for you, nobody but Richie would know about my dreams. People wouldn't think I'm crazy. Nobody would have tried to kill me in Charlotte. The country would have passed the global warming bill. Who knows what else I could have accomplished?'

"At that point she started laughing. 'Accomplished? You could have sliced up more and more of Israel, that's what you could have accomplished.' Those were her exact words. Then she went into a ten-minute diatribe against my views on the Middle East. She accused me of being one of those Jews who won't be happy until our people are getting stepped on, so then we could wax eloquent about how moral and selfless we are, and how pure our religion is.

"She really worked herself up. And I have to hand it to her—she never made those tired arguments against Islam that Americans love to make. She never called it a violent religion or said that there was something wrong with any religion whose founder was a military commander with a lust for land. She knew that would have rolled off my back. All she talked about were Israel's security needs—for a buffer of land surrounding its holy places and its cities. Her point was that the idea of Zionism needing a smaller z is absurd, since even if Israel were to keep all the disputed territory it would still be barely a speck on the globe. She said that if the Arabs would only take care of their own like we take care of ours, the Palestinians would be just fine.

"Then she started with her mantra: 'Be a man, Moses.' At first, she'd follow it with words like 'Don't sell out your people. Don't treat them like schmoes. Be a man.' But then she left off the philosophizing. She just stated the mantra, once, twice, three times. It was creepy.

"I was sitting on that wooden chair in my living room when she went to the kitchen to get some more wine. Before she sat back down, she walked over to me and started rubbing my back. It felt good. I don't know why, but it did. And she didn't stop. She was silent now—no more mantra, just two strong hands. She unbuttoned my shirt, but she didn't do anything other than rub my back, over and over again. I began to relax. The creepiness was gone—or at least I had forgotten it. Then she walked over to me and unbuttoned her own shirt. She sat on my lap and placed my hands on her breasts, and she said the mantra again.

"I'll spare you the details. I know you'd appreciate that. Let's just say I couldn't resist her. We started kissing, we undressed. I asked her if she were using protection. 'Of course I am,' she said. 'What do you take me for?' We went into the bedroom and … I won't say we made love. There was no love there—certainly not from her. At one point, she was on top of me, she had just bitten my ear, and I wanted to see her eyes. When I looked up at her, she looked back at me like a demon. I didn't see a soul in those eyes—none at all. The real Rachel, the one who fell in love with you and had your children … she was somewhere else. The body on top of me was simply doing a job. But boy, what a job. It didn't take me very long to finish—not after I saw her eyes. I knew something was terribly wrong, but I finished. I *god-damned finished!*"

I thought for a moment that Moses had nothing more to say. He walked to the kitchen and left me alone for a few moments. When he returned, he had a glass of water for each of us.

"After it was over," he continued, "we lay in silence for five, maybe ten minutes. I can't be sure how long it was because I actually passed out and started to dream. Once again, I saw myself as Moses coming down from Mount Sinai. I had the two tablets in my hands. But this wasn't the first time I carried them; this was the second, after I had smashed them into the Golden Calf. I had just said goodbye to the brothers, so I was alone, preparing to meet the people down below. That's when I saw her.

"She was standing directly in my path with her arms crossed in front of her body. And she asked a simple question: 'Who are you?'

"I told her I was Moses. And I asked her who she was.

"'As far as you're concerned, I'm the goddess of reason.' That's what she said. But she didn't look like any goddess. She looked exactly like Rachel.

"'So,' she said, 'if you're Moses, *really* Moses, go ahead and perform a miracle for me. Just one will do.'

"I said that I wasn't a miracle worker, and that the transcendent God works *through* nature, not apart from it. I told her that the miracles in the Torah are only myths.

"She shook her head with disbelief. Then she started laughing. '*Only myths*? You call yourself Moses, and yet you think of the stories in the Torah simply as myths?' She went on to lecture me about the importance in scriptural writing of *symbols*. She said that at the deepest levels, everything in the Torah is symbolic. Stories about miracles have a symbolic meaning that's very profound. So what if they're not literally true? She told me that if I'm so hung up on biblical literalism, I've got no right to call myself Moses; I don't even have a right to call myself a rabbi.

"I started arguing with her. I told her that most people take the Torah at close to face value, whether she likes it or not. They believe that God emotes and acts like a human being because it says so over and over again in the Torah. They think homosexuality is a sin because it says so very clearly in the Torah. Or perhaps they've rejected those beliefs, and call themselves atheists and opponents of religion, and they become spiritually dead.

"She interrupted me to say that she didn't ask me what most people believe. She simply asked to see a miracle, and yet I couldn't produce a single one.

"I told her it was my passion to fight human ignorance and especially religious ignorance. It's the source of so much hatred, so many wars. But she wouldn't let me get on my soap box. 'Just show me a miracle,' she said. 'Last chance.'

"Right then, the only miracle I could think of was to try to convince Rachel that I was truly Moses. But I couldn't conceive of how. That's when it came to me. I had to stop thinking of miracles as fictional events that alter the laws of nature as we know them. Miracles take place within the framework of natural laws, and yet they're still sources of profound *amazement* to those who are living in harmony with their world. They're inexplicable, they grip your heart as well as your mind, they make you say 'wow,' and they make you ask 'why?' Anything that fits that description is a miracle.

"And that's not all I realized. I had to stop seeing Moses as a flesh-and-blood person, but rather as a symbol. The same applies to the other biblical personalities. The Symbol-of-Moses parted the Red Sea just as the Symbol-of-Muhammad ascended to heaven from Jerusalem and the Symbol-of-Jesus walked on water.

"As I focused on the idea of Moses in particular, I stopped thinking of him as a man who led the people of Israel out of Egypt and more as the symbol of a vessel. Through him, Jews can come to appreciate the meaning of ethical monotheism to the best of our own abilities. He can inspire us to obey the laws of morality, lead lives of holiness, and cleave to the One who is worthy of worship. And if that means taking the Torah as literal truth because that's all someone is capable of doing, so be it. But if it means comprehending Jewish teachings well enough to be able to perform miracles on demand—*true* miracles, not the stuff we teach to kids—that's even better. As a guy who's been so hung up on religious fundamentalism that I haven't appreciated what 'miracles' really meant, to equate myself with this incredible vessel was pure folly.

"At that point, I opened my eyes, and the mountain was nowhere to be found. I was lying on the bed, and Rachel—your ex-wife, not the goddess of reason — was sitting up, gazing at me. She was the first to speak. 'Had enough?' That's all she asked. When I didn't respond, she continued. 'Because if you haven't, we can do this again next week and the week after. We can do this as many times as it takes for you to come to your senses.'

"'No, that won't be necessary,' I finally told her. 'I get it. I'm no Moses. For starters, Moses wouldn't have done what I did tonight. If that's the point you were trying to make, consider it made.'

"Those were the words she needed to hear. She nodded and began getting dressed. I looked over, and it was like seeing a witch who had just given you a lust potion. You know she did it, you know it's not right, but you can't help yourself either. Even after we had sex, I still craved her body—and I mean in the worst, worst way — but at least I knew not to touch it. There'd been enough of that.

"She was fully dressed when I was still naked in bed, practically in the fetal position. I was scared shitless, and my whole self-concept had been shattered. She looked at me, and for the first time, I actually saw warmth in those eyes—or maybe it was just pity.

"'You might not believe this,' she said, 'but what happened tonight I did for you. You'd been dreaming too long. I thought you'd want to snap back into reality. I figured I owed you that much. It's not like you can do much damage any more, whether you've come to your senses or not. You've been exposed, Moses. You're not the prophet you thought you were. At the end of the day, you're just a man who's doomed to dust like every other human animal.'

"'Alright,' I said, 'so I'm not Moses, but does that have to mean there's no afterlife? Is that what you think?'

"'Face the facts,' she replied. 'We have no clue what happens after we die. To be Jewish is to think about that stuff as little as possible and spend our time perfecting the only lives we really know about. If you want my opinion, I'd say that if there is a life after death for us, it would be nothing like this one. The idea of one earthly soul being reincarnated in another sounds silly—an illusion that helps people cope when they're facing death, like when they've been kidnapped. Get my drift?'

"I got it alright. As much as I've ever understood anything, I got it."

When Moses finished his story, it was as if a veil had been lifted. He still wasn't himself, but at least a little color returned to his face.

"Do you know what I'm going to do?" he said.

"What's that?"

"I'm going back on the Orloff show, and I'm going to apologize to the country for equating myself with Moses."

"You don't owe an apology to *anyone!*" I said, defiantly. "You never made any of that an issue. All you did was tell the truth when you were accused."

"But I've made a fool of myself," he said.

"Bull. You've done more for this planet than just about anyone alive today. You were put in an impossible position, and you found a way to deal with it. That's not being a fool. That's being a survivor."

"You know what makes me most furious with myself?" he replied. "For years I've prided myself on always following the voice of reason. Why do you think I love Spinoza so much? He was one of philosophy's greatest disciples of reason. But remember what I told you in East Jerusalem — he also taught that an even greater form of knowledge than reason is intuition. I took that as license to follow my gut even when my mind would have led me elsewhere. I can see now that I totally misinterpreted what Spinoza was saying. Intuition is supposed to build on reason; it's not supposed to undermine it. I've been an idiot, Richie, an absolute idiot!"

I couldn't help myself. "My mom used to tell me that a little learning is a dangerous thing."

"No kidding," Moses replied. "I can just imagine the number of times in the course of history that a true genius has inspired people to believe something really stupid, or even dangerous, just because they've misinterpreted his meaning."

"I think that's called the history of religion, my friend."

Moses nodded. Who could argue the point?

"I'm still going on Orloff," Moses said. "I still have to come clean."

"Fine, just promise me this—you'll do it with your head held high."

"OK, that much I can promise."

When the time came to speak his piece, Moses handled himself with incredible dignity. Of course, that's just my opinion; I'm sure each of you has your own. By now, just about everyone in America has seen Moses' "announcement" on the Orloff show.

Prior to the telecast, the network hyped it for days. Even if you missed the telecast, you could easily watch the reruns—the cable news shows analyzed Moses' statement relentlessly. That was made easier by the fact that Moses limited his address to roughly five minutes. He took no questions from the audience. He didn't even allow Orloff to interview him. He simply came on the air shortly before the telecast ended, read a prepared statement, waved to the crowd, and walked off the set.

For those of you who've been living on Mars (where global warming isn't yet a problem), here's what he said:

"Good evening. My name is Moses Levine. I came on this show to speak directly to the American people and clear up a problem for which I'm responsible. As most of you know, from the time I was held captive in an East Jerusalem dungeon, I had allowed myself to believe that the soul of the Biblical Moses had made its way into my body. I am here to dispel that idea once and for all.

"It was not my intent to raise with the public any comparison between me and the prophet who led the ancient Hebrews out of Egypt. It was only when others threatened to publicize my beliefs that I acknowledged holding them. Recently, something happened that led me to understand that I've been suffering under delusions. I was hit over the head by a dose of reality, and it felt like a forearm from a linebacker. It stung, no question about it, but the pain was a small price to pay for regaining my rationality.

"Please allow me to state categorically and permanently that I am not Moses. I'm not even a prophet. I'm just a man—with the same appetites, the same passions, and the same capacity for ignorance as any other person. I fooled myself into adopting a self-image that wasn't valid. You must have already known that. Now, I do as well.

"I've been thinking a lot lately about the extent to which an apology is in order. People generally don't apologize to the public simply because they've privately held an opinion that turned out to be wrong. Nor should they have to apologize. My case is different, though. I've held myself out as a leader — a leader of a local Jewish congregation, a leader of an ecumenical religious organization with chapters all over the country, and a leader of political causes that helped to shape the federal budget. I've also received various awards, most notably the Nobel Peace Prize. The result of all this is that for many people, I became a role model. To any of you who looked at me in that way, I deeply apologize for my lapse of reason.

"To the rest of you, I offer no apologies—only a lesson. It has to do with the corrupting influences of power. I'm but the latest in a series of human beings who have allowed themselves to become drunk with their own importance simply because they've managed to make a contribution or two to the events of their day. The irony is that the man whose soul I thought I shared, Moshe Rabbenu, is considered to have been the greatest of Jews precisely because he was supreme in his *humility*. The rabbis teach that others surpassed him in learning, but *no one* was more humble. For that reason alone, I don't merit comparisons to him. While I don't view myself as having been pompous or even self-centered, I can hardly credit myself with humility. Well, maybe I can take that credit now that I realize how ridiculous I've been … but not before, when I dared to compare myself to one of the fathers of my people.

"Do you know what's funny? I've always been such a non-traditional thinker. I've especially had problems with religious myths, and how literally we're taught to take them. But of all the myths I've heard, few seem as far fetched as the idea that I, Moses Levine, should inhabit the soul of any biblical prophet, let alone Moshe Rabbenu. Then again, I guess that's no crazier than the idea of thousands, if not millions, celebrating when a group of men willingly flew airplanes into two of the world's largest buildings. As someone who's lost his mind, I've had plenty of company.

"Let me close this evening with a demonstration that I've taken to heart the magnitude of my mistake. Effective immediately, I am withdrawing from my position as rabbi at Temple Akiva. Effective immediately, I am withdrawing from my position as president of Peoples of Priests. Effective immediately, I am pledging to abstain for at least two years from any political activity. I intend to use that time for introspection. I might do some traveling, maybe even some writing. But the first order of business is to take myself seriously again — not as a prophet, just as a man."

CHAPTER XXIX

*"Jewish tradition speaks of hundreds of mitzvot, or 'commandments.' But as far as I'm concerned, every promise we make creates another mitzvah — every business transaction, every marriage vow. When you think about it, every time we make an assertion of fact we're commanded to tell the truth; we're implicitly promising that we're **not** telling a lie.*

"Reasonable people can disagree about whether the notion of promise keeping is the single most important component of Jewish ethics. But this much I can say with confidence — to honor your promises, more than anything else, is what it takes to have a good name in the Jewish community."

Rabbi Moses Levine, addressing Temple Akiva, 2000

Silver Spring, Maryland—September 2006. During the first week after Moses' mea culpa, I glued myself to the radio and TV. For the most part, I'm happy to say, the talking heads dealt with Moses rather kindly. Even the right-wing commentators seemed satisfied that he had both accepted responsibility for his "delusions," to use Moses' own term, and paid the ultimate sacrifice of withdrawing from his positions of power. Time after time, Moses was praised for handling the matter with class.

But let's not kid ourselves — much of the public continued to believe that he had one too many toys in the attic.

Over the next few months, Moses was a fixture at Temple Akiva, yet he never once set foot on the bimah. While he'd show up for Torah discussions and adult-education seminars, he refused to open his mouth, not even to ask a question. He explained his conduct to me by saying that he didn't want to affect public discourse in any way for a two-year period. When that man gave his word, it was as good as gold.

Plenty of politicians and other public figures would call on Moses and seek his advice. They were turned away empty-handed—except for Forrest. He knew not to ask Moses to talk about public policy. Instead, he'd invite Moses to the White House, and they'd spend a couple of hours watching ball games. When it came to sports, Moses was as opinionated as ever. Even if the topic had some relationship to the world outside of sports—such as how to deal with baseball players who used steroids—Moses would permit himself the right to speak his mind. "It helps keep me sane," he told me. "Sports are my refuge."

While Moses was visiting the White House, Forrest also liked to raise the topic of women. One night, when Moses took me with him to watch a Redskins game, Forrest couldn't stop pleading with him to settle down. "It's time you found yourself a Mrs. Levine," the President said. "You've aged a lot over the past few years, maybe as much as I have."

"Oh more, for sure," Moses replied. "You don't let things get to you. I get more neurotic every year. If I make it to 80, I'm going to be one crazy old man. 'Hello noice? I know I've called you in here four times in the last fifteen minutes, but my head's hoiting.'"

"That's what I plan to be like," I chimed in. "It's the only way to grow old."

"What if you're not Jewish?" Forrest asked.

"Then you convert," Moses replied. "You can always convert back after you get home from the hospital."

Forrest wasn't the only one of Moses' friends who wanted to see him hooked up. He seemed a bit lonely when I went to visit him at his apartment, where he was always reading books about religion or philosophy. Sadly, there were no women in his life he could be intimate with. Ayelet had taken herself off the market for good. She wrote to Moses in a friendly letter that she and her lawyer friend flew to Vegas and got married "at the smallest chapel we could find."

As for me, I was having considerably more success in the companionship department than Mr. Levine. After about six weeks in Utah, Carrie decided to come back. As soon as I saw her at the airport, she planted a kiss on me that must have rivaled in intensity (if not in sorcery) anything Moses received from my ex-wife. When it was over, Carrie grabbed me by my cheeks and said "From this day forward, Richie Gold, I promise never again to leave you, no matter what happens."

I pledged the same to her. And I meant it. It was a great thrill when I was able to escort her on November 29, 2006, to our new home—a four-bedroom split level in Kensington, Maryland.

On the morning of Wednesday, February 7, 2007, five members of the Port Antonio Six—everyone but Ayelet—boarded an El Al jet from New York's JFK International Airport to Tel Aviv. We were all paid guests of the Israeli Government.

Despite the controversy surrounding Moses' dreams, the Government of Israel continued to view Moses and me as international heroes for presenting them with Hafeez's floppy disks, a source of countless leads against Middle Eastern terrorists. The Israelis were turning our East Jerusalem dungeon into a national monument and invited the two of us to attend the opening ceremonies, which would be held precisely five years to the day after we were captured. Much to my embarrassment, Moses finagled from the Israeli Government a free trip for our closest friends. Ayelet was asked to come, but she declined, having missed a lot of work due to her recent honeymoon.

On the flight to the Promised Land, Moses explained to us that as soon as he returned to the States, he would begin writing a book entitled *The Philosophy of Moses Levine*. "It's going to be pretty complete. I'll talk about ethics, metaphysics, episte-mology, politics, my interpretation of Scripture ... I'm sure it'll be too long for publication."

We all laughed. There were millions of people throughout the world—foes as well as fans—who would buy anything Moses wrote, long or short.

Moses and I have a pretty dark sense of humor, so we chose to spend the night at the same hotel we stayed at just before our capture five years earlier. We didn't, however, have the oppor-tunity to hail a cab the next day. The Israel Defense Forces had arranged for our party to be shuttled around and guarded by a four man security detail. Two of the guards were brothers named Asher and Isaac. Moses and I couldn't believe our ears. I'm sure the names were just a coincidence, but they spooked us both.

The Levine/Gold Dungeon Museum—its English translation — was set to open at noon on February 8th, the day after we arrived in Israel. We were scheduled to preview the facility that morning at 9:30. Needless to say, the museum was anything but grand in size. It was intended to resemble the dungeon just as it appeared when Moses and I lived there, except that the stench had been removed. I wasn't going to complain about that change. I never wanted to smell that dreck again.

We spent the better part of a half-hour examining our old home. Don, Lisa and Carrie walked around in obvious amaze-ment. They'd occasionally ask a question, but for the most part gazed in silence, clearly awed by what they were finding. Moses and I, though, shared a number of our observations with each other. I was especially fascinated by going through the guards' desk and by looking at the pictures of the dead captives on the wall. When we were in the cell, we only had one opportunity to examine the pictures up close before they were taken away from us and posted on the opposite side of the dungeon. They were much more horrible when viewed at close range.

When the museum curator finally suggested that we should leave and let them get ready for the grand opening, Moses asked to lie down on his cot one more time, and the curator obliged. So we all waited for five or ten minutes, while Moses communed with the place of his now famous dreams. I had no interest in climbing back in my old bed. It would have reminded me of all the hours spent essentially straitjacketed while Moses and Hafeez went at it. I wanted to remember Hafeez as a liberator, not as a jailor.

Once it was time to leave, the curator walked up the stairs first, followed by two of our guards and then by Carrie, Lisa and Don. Moses and I remained with the brothers Asher and Isaac in the dungeon, taking our last looks at the cage. That's when I heard that dreadful sound again.

You all know what it was — the sound of a gunshot. And it was followed by another. The first was fired by Isaac Jacoby into the chest of Moses Levine. The second was also fired by Isaac, but into his own temple. Precisely why Isaac shot Moses I couldn't tell you. Isaac never regained consciousness after he was shot. Moses did, but only briefly.

While Asher sobbed over his brother's body, the rest of us attended to Moses. "Donald," Moses whispered, tears falling from his eyes. "You know I love your wife. Don't let anything happen to her."

"You're going to make it, Moses," Lisa said, fighting off tears of her own. "Be strong for us."

"This time I think my number's up," he replied. "It feels different. Richie? Give me your hand. I'm sorry I won't be there when you and Carrie get married."

"Don't talk that way," I said. "You'll be at the wedding."

"Listen, my friend," he continued, coughing as much as talking. "I want you to tell the world my story—all of it, the good, the bad ... even the ugly. Don't let anyone else hijack the truth. Will you promise to do that for me?" More coughs.

"If that's what you want," I told him.

"I guess I'm not going to write my philosophy after all," he said.

"You don't have to," I replied, still holding his hands, though I wasn't as skilled as Lisa at fighting off tears. "You've written it through your actions. They say more than any words."

"Not these words," he replied. "Shema, Yisrael ... [more coughing] Adonai, elohenu, Adonai E...chad."

And with that, Moses was gone.

POSTSCRIPT

On September 15, 2007, Congregation Beth Hashem will play host to many of the nation's most prominent politicians and business leaders. They will be in attendance as we officially name our sanctuary the Moses Levine Memorial Hall of Prayer. Our keynote speaker will be President Joseph Forrest.

Undoubtedly, many who attend the event will bring a healthy dose of skepticism about the person we are honoring. But no matter what you think of Moses as a prophet, you can't help but view him in the same way that the Emperor Napoleon viewed the great Goethe. Upon seeing for the first time the brilliant German novelist, poet, playwright, scientist and statesman, Napoleon said simply "Voila un homme."

That was Moses—he was a man among men. And a Jew among Jews. Even Rachel has finally come to that conclusion.

THE END

ACKNOWLEDGMENTS

I wish to thank every person I've encountered over the years who has made me proud to be associated with the Jewish people. At the top of this list are my parents, Evelyn and Julius Spiro, who taught me that Judaism is two parts pragmatism and three parts idealism. Or is it the other way around? I'm still trying to answer that question for myself.

I also wish to thank my wife Kathleen, who has read this book over and over again, and never ceased to improve it. Every time she hands me a marked up draft, I am reminded of the old saw that a manuscript is never finished, it is merely abandoned.

Next, I am obliged to thank my daughter Rebecca, who has aspired to become a rabbi since well before her Bat Mitzvah. Even as a middle school student, Rebecca was one of this book's editors. She remains the only member of this family who has received a national award for writing about religious philosophy, heady stuff for a fifteen year old.

In addition, I'd like to express appreciation to those who have deepened my exposure to non-Jewish religious traditions. Allow me to single out Bonnie Dixon, who encouraged me to present my ideas about Spinoza to the Southeastern Unitarian Universalist Summer Institute, thereby enabling me to write at some length here about the UU movement. I also wish to thank Alexandra Halpern, who confirmed my respect for Sufi Islam. I consider both Sufism and Unitarian Universalism to be kindred in spirit to my own personal approach to Judaism.

Allow me further to acknowledge the contributions of my friends who took the time to read this manuscript and share their comments. To name just a few, Suzanne Barry, Ken Feigenbaum, Judy Jarrell, Tom Pitman, Kim Reinken and Pete Winn have not only contributed to this book but also increased my self-confidence as a writer. I owe them a tremendous debt of thanks.

Finally, I wish to thank two Jewish clergymen who have meant so much to my development as a Son of Jacob. Ramon Tasat is, quite simply, the most gifted cantor I have ever heard. Hearing Hazzan Tasat sing prompted my late father to say that "the cantor is the most important person in a synagogue, even more important than the rabbi." I can't disagree with him. Hazzan Tasat doesn't merely lead a congregation in song, he leads a congregation in *prayer*. It is difficult to imagine a rabbinic sermon that could lift my spirit more than the sound of his voice. As for Rabbi Gerry Serotta, I must begin by saying that much of the confidence I have in this book stems from the fact that Rabbi Serotta has read the manuscript and offered his comments. But Rabbi Serotta isn't merely a scholar. In fact, he isn't primarily a scholar. Like Moses Levine, he is first and foremost a vehicle of *tikkun olam*. To quote a friend, if everyone in the world were like Gerry Serotta, the Messianic Age would be upon us.